...BREATHTAKING...
JOHN LE C...

—Quincy Patriot Ledger

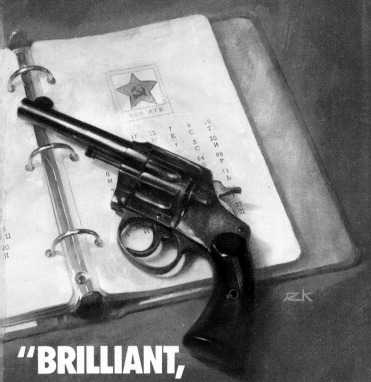

"BRILLIANT, GRIPPING, HARROWING!"
—Boston Herald

(For more extraordinary acclaim, please turn page . . .)

FIREBIRD

James Carroll

A SIGNET BOOK

NEW AMERICAN LIBRARY

PUBLISHED BY
PENGUIN BOOKS CANADA LIMITED

NAL BOOKS ARE AVAILABLE AT QUANTITY DISCOUNTS WHEN USED TO PROMOTE
PRODUCTS OR SERVICES. FOR INFORMATION PLEASE WRITE TO PREMIUM MARKET-
ING DIVISION, NEW AMERICAN LIBRARY, 1633 BROADWAY, NEW YORK, NEW
YORK 10019.

Published by arrangement with E. P. Dutton. The hardcover edition was published
simultaneously in Canada by Fitzhenry and Whiteside, Limited, Toronto.

First Signet Printing, March, 1990

2 3 4 5 6 7 8 9

SIGNET TRADEMARK REG. U.S. PAT. OFF. AND FOREIGN COUNTRIES
REGISTERED TRADEMARK — MARCA REGISTRADA
HECHO EN WINNIPEG, CANADA

SIGNET, SIGNET CLASSIC, MENTOR, ONYX, PLUME,
MERIDIAN and NAL BOOKS are published in Canada by Penguin
Books Canada Limited, 2801 John Street, Markham, Ontario,
L3R 1B4
PRINTED IN CANADA
COVER PRINTED IN U.S.A.

For Lexa

Author's Note

My brother, Brian Carroll, and my old friend Gerald Galbreath read early versions of this book, responded generously and made useful suggestions. My friends Richard and Doris Goodwin, Dan Wakefield, Don Cutler, and my wife, Alexandra Marshall, gave me important advice throughout my work on this book. Deborah Olson was an invaluable help in the preparation of the manuscript. I gratefully acknowledge my debt to all of you.

PART
ONE

PART
ONE

1

Every city should be so beautiful, every hill should have such a gleaming pinnacle.

As the train clacked across the Potomac River railroad bridge, he had his first glimpse of the U.S. Capitol. And he felt suddenly that things would be all right.

Washington had always been a dream city to him, and even now he had images of its monuments, plazas and statues vividly in mind. As if to see the real things he leaned closer to the window. A rush of warm air from the line of transoms hanging open on their hinges streamed across his face, making him aware of the stubble of his whiskers. He put his hand to his cheek. He'd taken the long train trip as a rare excuse not to shave. The unfamiliar feel of his bristly skin amused him; who'd have thought it—careful Chris Malone looking like a bum!

"Union Station!" The conductor came into the car crying, "Union Station, seven minutes!"

The depot in Kansas City was called Union Station too, and Malone once more pictured the scene that had taken place there two days before. Even from the distance, as his train left her behind, he had seen Beth's shoulders shaking, and for an awful moment, as he waved back at her, he had had a shocking urge after all to do what she had asked, to leap from the train, despite his orders, and stay. But it was impossible. He'd have had to quit. He'd have had to abandon an idea of himself that he'd had since he was twelve. It was impossible. That was what they'd both seen in the end, even if neither had admitted it. Between them, finally, it was all impossible.

"Union Station!" The conductor drew abreast of Malone, snagged the ticket stub from its clip on the baggage rail and leaned down across the vacant aisle seat to peer out Malone's window. Pointing, the white-haired trainman said, "There it is, son. Greatest city in the world. Look at the Washington Monument. 'The Big Pencil,' my boy used to call it. Nothing like it in Kansas City."

"I noticed." Malone smiled. The conductor had told him earlier that he himself was from Baltimore. "Kansas City is a cow town," Malone said, "and I hate cows. I grew up near the Chicago stockyards."

"Oh God, what a stench! How'd you stand it?"

"Vicks Vapo-Rub on your upper lip." Malone laughed. "You can't smell a thing."

"Well, you won't find stockyards in Washington, thank God. Washington was designed by the same guy that did Paris." He beamed with that announcement, then added earnestly, "Paris, France."

Once more Malone found him irresistible, and he felt grateful for the way in which the conductor's easy affability had brightened the trip. At first, heading across Missouri, he'd thought the trainman was treating him so warmly because he'd witnessed the farewell scene with Beth and was just trying to cheer up a dejected man. But then Malone decided that the conductor was always friendly. He was largehearted with everyone.

Now he was displaying his affection for a city. "And lookit there, see that black spire? That's your Post Office Building, right downtown on Pennsylvania Avenue, a bull's-eye inside the Federal Triangle. Didn't you say you worked for the Post Office?"

Malone averted his eyes, unable to repeat the lie. Not lie, he told himself. But he had misled the man. Well, it was half true. His assignment was to the Washington Field Office, which was housed on the top three floors of the Old Post Office Building. The conductor had drawn a wrong conclusion, was all. Malone nodded, aware that the train was slowing down. "Yes. I'm reporting in tomorrow."

"That gives you all day today to see the sights."

Malone laughed, indicating his rough clothes, his rumpled white shirt, sleeves rolled past his elbows, and khaki pants. "To get my suit pressed, you mean. And find a room." Another lie. He already had a room, prearranged in one of the boardinghouses on East Capitol Street that incoming agents used. For two days now, despite his attraction to the conductor, Malone had deflected the man's harmless queries. Agents, like the people they tracked, treated their true identities as something to hide. But Malone demurred, for he misled without a veteran's nonchalance, and now he realized that his uneasiness had accumulated. The conductor leaned closer toward the window, the aroma of pipe tobacco pouring off him. Malone looked up at him and was startled by the affection in the trainman's eyes. Affection for the city, yes. But affection, also, for the people on his train. And, Malone saw, for him.

"I haven't quite leveled with you, actually," Malone said. The impulse to be himself with the man surprised Malone and relieved him. "I'm an FBI agent."

The conductor straightened up, impressed. "A G-man! But, golly, you look so young."

Malone laughed. He was twenty-nine. "I used to be older," he said.

The conductor pointedly looked Malone over. "I thought G-men wore suits and ties."

Malone opened his hands. "I'm in mufti. It's like the army. Between posts you're on your own, which is the only time you are."

"And your new job is D.C.?"

"Right. The office is in the Post Office Building, which is what I meant to say. Not that I'm a postal worker."

"You know J. Edgar Hoover?"

Malone shook his head no. "He used to swear agents in, but not anymore. He works down the street at headquarters—Seat of Government, they call it. SOG. In the boonies we call it 'Soggy Ass' because bureaucrat agents wet themselves if they run into Hoover." Malone laughed at his own outrageous indiscretion. It surprised him that he trusted the conductor enough to talk this way, but he did. "The field office is the assignment a knuckle dragger like me wants, not headquarters."

"Still it's Washington. You must be a hotshot, eh?"

"Just a gumshoe." Malone shook his head, and added with an air of self-mockery, "My specialty in Kansas City was the National Train Wreck Statute."

"Well, hell, what's more important than train sabotage?"

Malone put his hand on the conductor's sleeve. "I hate to tell you this, but every train derailment I investigated was caused by boys putting boulders on the tracks to see them crushed. I arrested one kid at a soda fountain. He was fourteen years old."

"It's serious business though, if you've ever seen—"

"I know." Malone realized he'd made light of the wrong thing. "I didn't mean it wasn't serious." He just meant that after a year of prowling the modest streets and arrow-straight roads of Missouri and Kansas, investigating small-town bank jobs, leftover deserter cases and, yes, minor train derailments in towns named Diamond, Abilene and Fort Larned, it was hard to recall the sharp idealism with which he'd joined the Bureau after finishing night school in Chicago. Washington, in its bronze and marble grandeur, enshrined that initial vision, didn't it? Malone wanted to embrace it again. Order against anarchy, integrity against deceit, the Bureau against hoodlums and thieves, not young pranksters. To Malone the FBI was a fraternity of high-minded, brave but modest men, and he still felt a measure of awe to be part of it. And hadn't awe like that in other men—but for *America*—built this city? This city to which he—no "hotshot," by any means—had now been summoned for reasons beyond his grasp and, for that matter, beyond the grasp of his slightly resentful colleagues in Kansas City. Malone didn't have any letters of censure in his folder, but he didn't have any letters of commendation, either. Why *had* they singled him out? Every agent claimed to dread assignment to Washington but secretly he longed for it, because Washington defined the borders of the noble realm—

He checked himself. Next he'd be humming "America the Beautiful." Next he'd be thinking it didn't matter that he'd just lost Beth.

"There it is," the conductor said. He pointed at the vaulted roof of the mammoth railroad terminal just coming into sight as the train turned a last bend into the southwest switching yards. The white marble building glistened in the morning sun.

"Union Station!" he called, straightening up. He offered Malone his hand. "Good luck." And then he faced the rear of the car—"Union Station!"—and began to head off.

But another thought stopped him, and he turned back to Malone. "It's the most beautiful train station in America," he said. "It's modeled after the Baths of Diocletian. . . ." He winked. "Whatever the hell that is."

"It was a building in ancient Rome. It's ruins now, but they say it was magnificent."

The conductor was impressed again. "How does a rube like you know that?"

Malone laughed. It was true. He *was* a rube. "I wouldn't know it," he said, "but I was in Rome as a GI during the war."

The conductor stared at him with a sudden, obvious sadness. When he spoke then his voice carried a weight he had kept at bay before. "My boy was with Mark Clark's Fifth Army."

"So was I."

"My boy never got to Rome. They killed him in Salerno." The conductor hesitated, then said quietly, "I knew there was something about you I liked." He smiled with a fresh dose of the old affability, but Malone saw it differently now, saw what it cost him. "You *are* older than you look." Then he grinned. "And probably smarter. Good luck." He turned abruptly. "Union Station, next!" he called, heading down the aisle. "Washington, D.C."

Malone hoisted his duffel bag onto his shoulder, picked up his suitcase and began working his way along the aisle. He was the last passenger to leave the car, having waited for the conductor to come back, so he could say that, if his son was buried in Arlington, he would visit his grave. But the conductor hadn't returned.

When he stepped from the train to the platform, the

late summer heat clamped down on him. Other passengers jostled him and a redcap pushing a luggage-laden dolly nearly ran him down. "Coming through!" the porter called, and Malone had to move quickly to get out of the way. Already perspiration was running inside his shirt. He was still looking for the conductor, and so when two men stepped out of the bustling crowd he didn't notice them until they were on either side of him, pressing.

"Are you Christopher Malone?" one of them said.

Now when Malone looked he saw that they were wearing suits and hats, even in that heat. Instinctively he recognized the way they had fallen into step with him. One was a half pace ahead, the other a half pace behind, angled in such a way that each could pin an arm. All three of them kept walking.

Malone shifted the weight of the duffel bag on his shoulder, to balance it. "Who's asking?"

The duffel blocked his view of the man to his right, but the one on his left, with an acne-scarred face, seemed vaguely familiar.

When neither replied, Malone picked up his pace a bit. To his knowledge incoming agents were not met at train stations. But was policy different in Washington? Why weren't they explaining themselves? He wanted to slap his coat pocket for the reassuring lump of his credentials or press his right wrist into his hip for the familiar bulk of his gun. But he was in shirt sleeves. His gun and credentials were in his suitcase. He hadn't shaved. He wasn't ready to deal with the Bureau.

At the head of the train platform, just shy of the entrance to the terminal proper, Malone saw the conductor and stopped. He lowered his duffel bag and put his suitcase down. The conductor was checking over a clipboard with another trainman.

Malone looked from one of his fellow agents to the other. "Are you guys here for me, really?"

The one who seemed familiar nodded.

"I appreciate it, but I was looking forward to being on my own today. I have a rooming house. I don't need the help, but thanks."

"We're glad to help, Malone. We're giving you a lift."

"I don't go on duty until tomorrow."

"You're coming in with us."

Coming in? It was a phrase cops used in B movies, but still it set off a visceral alarm in Malone. He had made his share of arrests, and he knew about the steely impersonality the act required. These agents had it now. "What gives, guys?"

The man reached into his coat for his credentials folder and he held it open for Malone to read.

John Kershaw. He'd never heard of him.

Malone glanced toward the conductor, who was now staring back at him with a confused expression. To the conductor, did this look like an arrest?

The other agent picked up Malone's duffel bag. Kershaw said, "Let's go."

Malone looked back toward the conductor, who was still staring at him. Now it wasn't the trainman's son Malone thought of, but his own father. His father had been a man without affection.

When the conductor raised his hand and waved, Malone nodded, and turned away, but he felt a rush of emotion that frightened him. What was happening?

They walked through the bustling crowded terminal. The Baths of Diocletian? Malone tried to calm himself by remembering what the trainman had said. The vast room had a high, ornately decorated vaulted ceiling, but otherwise it seemed like any big-city train station. The noise of track announcements and overloud talk and passengers being greeted had accumulated in the air to form a permanent din. A huge clock hung like a chandelier and below it men and women thronged row upon row of staid wooden benches, newsstands and ticket windows.

Baths? Did that mean, in Rome, crowds like this went naked?

At the doorway leading to the street and the bright morning, Malone and his escorts had to fall into single file—Malone in the middle—because of the press of travelers, redcaps and cabbies looking for fares. The tense bustle heightened Malone's uneasiness. What the *hell* was happening?

At the nearest curb, below a sign that said No Stopping, but still under the terminal's overarching canopy and still, therefore, in the shade, sat what Malone recognized at once as a Bureau car. The uniformed cop who'd been standing by it waved when he saw Kershaw and moved off.

The second agent hefted the duffel bag and suitcase into the trunk and slammed the lid shut, then got behind the wheel of the car. Malone and Kershaw slid into the backseat.

In the privacy of the car Malone expected that they would explain. But as the driver headed into the avenue that ran at an angle along the base of Capitol Hill, no one spoke. Malone decided, then, that neither would he. Wait your subject out, went one rule. He would wait Kershaw out. He stared across the plaza and up the terraces at the graceful white dome that crowned the hill. From that hill with its balustrades and stone benches the view would sweep along the green mall past the Potomac to the hills of Arlington.

Yes, buddies of his were buried there. He would pay *them* a visit. Beneath the confusion he felt at Kershaw's brusque reception was a layer of the old sadness. A soldier's sadness. Now he felt a rush of resentment that Kershaw had stopped him from having one last word with the conductor.

"I wanted to ask that conductor if his son was buried at Arlington."

The driver found Malone's eyes in the rearview mirror. "That seems a little personal."

"He was killed in Italy. I was in Italy. I would have visited his grave. What's the harm in that?" Malone turned to face Kershaw and waited until Kershaw looked at him. "Will you tell me what's going on?"

"Relax, Malone. You'll know soon enough."

When the driver turned down Pennsylvania Avenue Malone glimpsed the clock tower of the Old Post Office Building, the site of the WFO. "Hey," he said with sudden alarm, "my rooming house is on East Capitol Street. That's the other way, isn't it? Where are you taking me?" Malone recognized the Mellon Art Gallery.

"We're headed toward the field office. You can't take me to the field office without letting me go to my place first. Good Lord, how can I report looking like this?"

"We're not taking you to the field office. We're taking you to headquarters."

"Headquarters!"

The car slowed as it approached Ninth Street. Malone's alarm redoubled when he saw the driver's arm go out, indicating a turn. At Ninth and Pennsylvania, a full two blocks shy of the Old Post Office, loomed the huge eight-story Justice Department Building. Soggy Ass!

"Christ, Kershaw, I haven't even shaved!"

Kershaw faced him. "That's a point." The agent took his hat off and looked out the window. The car, having made the turn onto Ninth, was slowing down. Kershaw looked out at the sidewalk, scanning the street quickly and carefully, but for what? Numerous people strolled past the massive Justice Building, some with cameras, the ubiquitous tourists. A hot-dog man under his bright umbrella was opening a soda pop for a child.

"Lean into the corner," Kershaw said quietly, "away from the window. Cover your face with this." He handed Malone the hat.

Malone did as he was told, but now his blind obedience, like that of agents on a raid, served to keep his anxiety at bay. He forced himself to think, to pay attention, even if he couldn't understand. He was aware of it when, half a block down Ninth Street, the car turned into the cut-through, stopped at the enormous grilled gate for the guard's once-over and then pulled into the building's inner courtyard.

When the car jolted to a halt, Malone lowered the hat from his face and looked around. A fountain dominated a terraced platform in the center of the landscaped courtyard. Malone remembered that in his one brief visit to this building the year before, he and his classmates, having just been sworn in, were photographed around that fountain.

Kershaw got out of the car and stood waiting for him.

When Malone got out Kershaw gestured toward the steps that led into the building, but Malone shook his head. "If I'm reporting in, even here, I have to have my credentials. You know that."

After a hesitation Kershaw nodded at the driver, who went to the trunk and opened it.

Malone stepped around Kershaw to bend into the trunk, where he efficiently unsnapped his suitcase. From under a pair of shirts he withdrew his leather "creds" folder and his holstered revolver. Then he took one of the shirts and his shaving kit and closed the suitcase. From the duffel bag he took the rumpled blue jacket of his good suit. Then he straightened and faced his escort. "Okay, Mr. Kershaw, lead the way. But show me to the men's room first, would you?" He grinned with a patently forced joviality. "Hell of a long way from Kansas City."

It reassured him that they let him go into the lavatory alone. He was *not* under arrest. He was one of *them*. As quickly as he could, he shaved and put on his fresh shirt. He slipped his holster and gun through his belt, adjusted his suitcoat over it and then placed his credentials in his inside pocket. When he looked at himself in the mirror he laughed. FBI agents, with their vests and drooping gold watch fobs and collar pins and cuff links and snap-brim hats or, in summer, their straw fedoras, were the most fastidious dressers in law enforcement. Police and criminals alike mocked them for their foppish uniformity, and Malone had never felt at ease. Now, for once, with his shirt open at his throat and with his wrinkled khakis and hopeless jacket, he looked like the man he knew himself to be. His dull brown hair was freshly slicked back, his part sharp enough to focus on, and his face glistened from the shave. But still he hadn't relaxed. What the *hell* was going on? He slapped his hip for the familiar bulk of his gun. He forced a laugh now, shrugged once and winked at himself in the mirror. "You're under orders, bud," he said aloud.

Someone behind him coughed. Automatically, Malone tensed. For the first time he realized that a pair of legs was showing from under the door of a toilet stall. A cloud of cigarette smoke hovered above it. The legs made no move to get up. There was the sound, now, of a magazine page turning. The man would not know that

Malone was alone in there, that he was—had it come to this already?—talking to himself. So he responded, in a different voice, as he left. "I sure am, Joe. Sure as hell am."

Kershaw was waiting in the corridor, alone now, his hat in his hand. When Malone appeared, Kershaw turned without a word and led the way to a bank of elevators. Malone bunched his soiled shirt and shaving kit under his arm and followed.

Kershaw and Malone were by themselves in the elevator, a last chance. "What do you say, can't you give me a hint? What's going on, Mr. Kershaw?"

Kershaw faced him slowly. "Don't you read the papers?"

"Not today I didn't, no. I was on the train, as you recall. Why? What's in the papers?"

But the elevator stopped. The fifth floor. The doors opened and Kershaw led the way out.

Malone had to walk briskly to keep up. The uniformly dressed men passing in the corridor eyed him openly, though the secretaries in their summer dresses, clicking along in heels, pointedly not chewing gum—Hoover hated gum—kept their eyes on the polished terrazzo floor. What were his rumpled khakis and lack of necktie to them? The doors they passed, dark wood with frosted glass window panels, were marked only with numbers that told him nothing. Finally, after a turn in the long hallway, Kershaw opened a door. This one was marked 555, and below that the name and title: John Brigham, Assistant Director.

Brigham! He was the head of one of the Bureau's six divisions, and now Malone remembered when he'd seen Kershaw before. Brigham had given a routine lecture to Malone's intake class at Quantico the year before, and Kershaw, his assistant, had turned the flip pages of a chart board. Malone remembered that Brigham was head of Division Four, or DI, for Domestic Intelligence. Brigham had come across as a laconic, inarticulate man, though a natty dresser. He had been in charge of the Bureau's case against Alger Hiss, then just under way. He'd predicted that it would be seen as the Bureau's finest hour.

But that was a year ago and Malone was acutely aware that since Brigham's prediction, the Bureau's star witness, a slovenly repentant traitor named Whittaker Chambers, had tried to kill himself, and the long-awaited trial of Hiss had ended inconclusively only weeks before with half the jury unconvinced that the gentleman had ever been a spy. But it wasn't the failure to convict Hiss that made gumshoe agents like Malone look askance at the Domestic Intelligence Division. DI handled the massive campaign to weed out security risks, and its requests for background—the ticklers were marked with red tabs—were greeted in field offices with groans. Malone had appropriated the attitude of most agents in the hinterlands, and they knew better than anybody that those checks of thousands of government officials, and even stenographers and janitors, were turning up nothing.

Kershaw opened the door and held it for Malone. To his surprise it led into yet another corridor, narrower and darker. The doors along the corridor were solid wood and unnumbered. It was impossible to guess what was behind them. This corridor was so narrow that Kershaw had to walk a step behind Malone. He pointed the way, and they walked its length. At the last door they stopped. Kershaw opened it. A small windowless room with a dark wooden table and two chairs, nothing else. If this had been a field office and not headquarters, Malone would have called it an interrogation room. He faced Kershaw.

Kershaw had his hand out.

Malone dutifully gave him his soiled shirt and shaving kit. Kershaw said, "I'll have your credentials too, please. And your gun."

Malone was more mystified than ever, but he was also trained; he handed his folder and weapon over.

Kershaw seemed suddenly relieved, perhaps by Malone's automatic compliance, and now his standing there in silence had the character almost of lingering. Neither man dropped his eyes. Finally Kershaw nodded, turned and left. Something in the way he did so made Malone realize that Kershaw's job was finished.

A few minutes passed. Malone's mind floated; what
could he do but wait?

He had just rested his haunch upon the edge of the
table when the door opened again. A man about Malone's size entered. His hair was silver but he didn't seem
that old otherwise; in his forties, Malone guessed. Something about him made Malone wonder if the man was
FBI. He had one hand behind his back.

Malone stood up.

The man said, "May I have your hands, please." He
spoke with a forced gruffness, as if, usually, he was far
more amiable with strangers.

"Sir?"

"Put your hands out."

Malone did as he was told, and before he could react
the man whipped a pair of handcuffs from behind his
back and clamped them on Malone's wrists, an expert
move.

"I don't understand," Malone said. "What have I—?"

The man started to turn, but Malone, even with his
hands manacled, grabbed him. Without meaning to he
crushed the arm until the man winced. "You have to tell
me—"

"Get your hands off me."

Malone released his grip and dropped his eyes to the
cuffs on his wrists, his fingers extended. For a moment he
felt nothing but the outrage of this violation. Cuffs on his
hands? Who was this fucker? When Malone raised his
eyes, the man had turned away. Only by the fiercest act
of will was Malone able to check the impulse to grab him
again as he crossed to the door.

The man left the room.

Silence filled the place where he had stood.

Calm yourself, Malone said. And think. But he couldn't
think past the outrage that he, an FBI agent, should be
subjected to this, here, in the heart of the FBI itself. His
trust in the Bureau was absolute.

But handcuffs were absolute too. That clash made
Malone feel crazy.

The door opened abruptly.

The man who'd cuffed him stood there. Malone stared

through the extended fingers he still held in front of his face. He took in details he'd missed before. The man was wearing a sharply pressed brown summer suit. He had a newspaper folded under his arm. Despite the heat he seemed cool. His self-possession, what enabled him to remain in that threshold, studying Malone, explaining nothing, was a quality Kershaw had lacked. His eyes, once they'd met Malone's, had not moved.

Malone lowered his hands from his face and took a step back.

"I apologize for this," the man said. His abrupt kindliness was as shocking to Malone now as the violence of his cuffing had been before. His voice was calm and Malone could feel himself backing off from his own anger, easing slightly toward calmness himself, alert for reasons to trust this man, to trust the Bureau again. Yes, the Bureau. This was the Bureau, he told himself, and what could he trust if not that?

"My name is Webb Minot. You're Christopher Malone. And you are here because of me."

The man spoke with an accent. Was it New England? There was a precision in his articulation that Chicagoans and Kansans lacked. It was the difference in speech between Roosevelt and Truman, and Malone focused on it as a way of getting distance from his anger. He tried to keep his voice free of feeling—anger, but also hurt—when he said, "Can you explain what's happening?"

"Yes. Why don't we sit down." Minot reached past Malone to pull out the chair for him. Then he circled the table to sit opposite. He put the newspaper, still folded, to one side. "First things first," Minot said. And he reached into his breast pocket and pulled out a thin stainless-steel rod, three inches in length, and tipped with a small glistening hook, a tool that Malone recognized immediately as a lockpick. Minot dropped it on the table between them. "Take the cuffs off, Chris," he said quietly.

A lockpick, not a key. Malone realized at once that he was being tested. He raised his eyebrows, staring at the pick, feeling the calmness spread through him fully, at last, as his mind clutched at the recognition: not a crime, a test. Relief washed through him. Later, perhaps, it would infuriate him again, that the Bureau was still playing chicken-shit, hazing tricks on him, but at that moment, the fact that he was being tested—not being arrested—filled him with gratitude. Oh for Christ's sake, he said to himself, eyeing the pick, a test! I can do a test! Pass or fail, at least I'm not crazy. At least the Bureau hasn't betrayed me!

It took agility and deftness to unlock handcuffs on one's own wrists even with a key. To pick such a lock, even such a simple one, involved working past only three notched traps, and still required a delicacy of touch and a steadiness that the contortion of wrists bent back upon themselves would surely make impossible. Houdini had done it all the time, of course. Malone never had.

When he took the pick into his hands he had the strange sensation that he was watching someone else. A brimming glass of water would have been safe in those hands, he realized to his amazement.

Immediately he applied the tiny hook to the lock and, as his father used to say, he threw his mind out the window. He found the first notch easily, felt the minute click, raising the lever gate, and moved past it. But also he felt the barest numbness in his fingers, for the angle at which he had to bend them down to the lock cut off the circulation.

He felt the second notch and pushed through it: click.

Then, not in his mind or memory, but in his hands, he was in his father's presence, his father leaning over him while he, on his knees, worked the lock of the door of freezer chest number 37 at the Swift packing plant behind the stockyards. He was fourteen. The odor of the slaughterhouse, the most familiar odor there was, filled his nostrils, revolting him, but also reassuring him, soothing him, taking him home. It was the first time his father ever let him take a crack at a lock on a job. A disgruntled meatcutter had thrown the freezer keys away; it was a pin-tumbler lock, he remembered. He could feel the cylinder bars opening to him, snapping into alignment as he slid by each tiny gate. What had astonished him at the time was the sure knowledge, once he'd begun, that he would find his way through the axis of the plug on his very first try. And he had. His father heard the last click when Malone did and as his father pushed down on the stainless-steel handle, pulling the door open, he slapped his son's back, the only sign of his approval, then or later.

Whenever Malone picked a lock, even a simple one, his satisfaction took the form of a blast of cold freezer air full in the face. He felt it now. The cuffs popped open.

Instead of reacting, Minot lit a cigarette. He offered one to Malone, who declined.

Malone rubbed his wrists as he'd seen bailed felons do. "Now will you explain what's going on?"

Minot nodded. "First, to say that if you hadn't been able to do that, this project, as far as you're concerned, would have ended right here. You'd get your gun and your badge back, we'd put you in a nice room at the Harrington, where you could rest up before going into the field office tomorrow to work bank cases and fugitives."

Malone pushed the cuffs away. "But as it happens, I did it."

"As neat a job as I've seen. Your file has it right about you."

"What's my file say?"

"The locks course last year at Quantico—Peter Hubbard, remember him? He made a particular notation about your . . . he called what you have a gift."

"My father was a locksmith, that's all."

"I gathered that." Minot took a deep drag and watched the smoke as he exhaled. "He was known as 'Smith' Malone."

"Is that in my file?"

Minot nodded. "Your father's deceased, I understand."

"He died while I was in the army."

"I'm sorry," Minot said, but somewhat automatically, an acknowledgment that this was no fresh loss. Or did he know Malone's secret, that his father's death had been no loss at all, but a great relief?

A silence fell between them. Malone realized that he had no prior experience of an agent like Minot. Agents were not given to brooding silences and penetrating stares. Introspection was not a mode of theirs. Minot seemed to welcome the gaps in talk that other agents compulsively plugged. Or was this just a continuation of Malone's being treated like a felon?

The features of Minot's face were flattened somewhat and his complexion was sallow, as if he hadn't seen the sun all summer. He lacked what Malone thought of as the essential masculine ruddiness of an FBI man. Or was this a pallor that went with a long assignment to head-quarters? Malone had an impulse to reach across the table and loosen the knot in Minot's printed tie.

"You were in Italy," Minot said.

Malone nodded.

"Conducted yourself well."

"Not particularly. I was overseas and back in six months. Took a piece of shrapnel in my shoulder, just bad enough to get me back to Chicago."

"Where you finished school at night while running your father's business in the daytime, supporting your mother and your sister."

"That's right."

"And half your paycheck is still deposited in her account in Chicago."

"I still help out, yes. What's the relevance of this?"

"Why the Bureau, Chris?"

Malone was mystified by this overly personal line of questions. Instinctively, he played it light and forced a grin. "The usual reason for guys my age. 'Gangbusters.'" Minot arched an eyebrow, and Malone caught the hint of condescension. He knew better than to say he was serious, that the radio show glamorizing the Bureau had stimulated the only dream he'd ever had of the man he wanted to be. From the time his father built them a crystal radio set, he and his siblings couldn't get close enough to it. Tuesdays and Thursdays, seven o'clock. . . . The door opened on Malone's memory. It was a memory of sounds—tommy guns, sirens, cries of "Come and get me, G-man!"

He looked up at Minot. "Do you remember how they used to give clues at the end of those shows?"

Minot nodded, but vaguely. The radio was not a realm of his.

"Nationwide clues, they called them." He had been twelve years old. He used to sit with his back against the curved oak leg of the parlor table. He could still feel it pressing his spine. "What I remember about those clues is that the thugs they described always had moles, scars and tattoos." Malone laughed. "How many tattoos have you arrested? Who the hell has moles?"

Malone was aware suddenly of Minot's eyes, which were yellow; not really yellow, but a lustrous film had fallen across them, like the gelatin shutter across a kleig, signifying he did not know what. Indifference? Disapproval? It was as if Minot had hidden himself behind his stare. Malone had known men to do that in the army—in the war. In their eyes Malone had seen such pearly sadness as he saw in Minot's now. A drinker's eyes, that's what they were, and the recognition shocked him. Minot had an agent's sharpness but below it lay this hint of collapse. A drinker's collapse Malone knew about, and now his memory made him shudder. He closed it down.

Minot said, "Do you know what 'Gangbusters' was?"

Malone watched Minot apply the cigarette to his mouth, squinting through the smoke, waiting. He, who had listened for years to that program, shaping a dream of himself from its voices, a dream he had begun to live, realized suddenly that the answer to Minot's question was no. He did not know what "Gangbusters" was. As a boy going to bed, his mind was always full not of angels or saints but of the dark-suited men, the men without names or only one name. "Hold it, FBI!"

Minot said, " 'Gangbusters' was part of FDR's campaign to make Americans think the government—G-men or the New Deal—would save them."

Malone stared at Minot, trying to get his mind around this new thought. Minot was looking at him like a know-it-all Ivy League professor. "You make it sound sort of . . . calculated."

Minot shrugged. "FDR knew what he needed. He wanted Americans to look to Washington and by God, after Pretty Boy Floyd and the Barkers and Dillinger, they did. J. Edgar helped give Roosevelt his good name in the small towns that should have hated him. Hoover made Americans feel part of something virtuous and manly."

Manly? It seemed a strangely self-conscious word for an FBI agent to use. Malone did not know what to make of Minot. But perhaps *manliness* was it, the essence of what had drawn boys like him. Malone remembered the night of his decision. He was in his bed listening to the sound of his brother's breathing. The loneliness he felt—an adolescent loneliness—was the precondition of his longing. It wasn't only the virtue he wanted or the manliness or the glamor of the arsenal. There was something else, but he couldn't name it. He remembered propping himself on his elbow and with the hard edge of his rosary's silver-plated crucifix scratching letters in the maple headboard of his bed. The darkness made him blind but he gouged away; two rough letters, *C.M.* In his mind the "Gangbusters" announcer intoned the ritual refrain, "Theirs is the brotherhood of sworn allegiance." Chris swore too, carving the additional letters, *FBI:* "I will be one of them."

Minot was watching Malone, waiting for him to speak. Why the Bureau? Did Minot really expect him to answer? Agents made their judgments about each other without requiring intimate expression on personal questions. Yet Minot sat calmly there across the table, a benign, inquiring look in his eyes, his rheumy eyes. It was like sitting on adjoining barstools with a spur-of-the-moment buddy. Malone leaned back. "I grew up in a small, crowded house back of the yards. The stockyards. There were narrow limits to our world. All of my brothers and sisters still live on the South Side of Chicago. But, I don't know, I was different. Those radio shows made me feel there was a place for a fellow like me in the world out there—that's how I thought of it: the world out there. Where something serious was happening, something important. Something bigger than grinding keys for Swift or Armour. That was my brothers' idea of heaven, a lock job with the packers." Malone laughed. "But not me. No, I bust my tail for something else. I graduate law school and I get my telegram signed 'Hoover,' which my

mother still has framed on the wall by the front door, and
I wind up what?" He laughed again, and now Minot did
too; a pair of agents who had penetrated the myth by
embracing it. "A glorified flatfoot in Kansas City knocking on people's doors to ask them if their neighbor reads
The New Republic."

Minot's laugh trailed off. He carefully snuffed his cigarette, saying, "But now you're in Washington."

"Yes." Malone's eyes snagged on Minot's. "And are
you going to give me a tour, sir?" Malone felt a rush of
the anger he'd first felt toward Kershaw.

"No, Chris, I'm not."

"Then maybe you'll explain what the hell is happening
to me." Malone picked up the handcuffs and dropped
them again, displaying the insult he felt.

"Do you know where you are?"

"Of course."

"I mean what office?"

"Brigham. Domestic Intelligence. Democracy's fight
against the Communist Party of America."

Minot shook his head. "The CPA is nowhere, never
has been, Gus Hall and a ragtag bunch of misfit garment
workers. Hoover is insane on the subject, of course, has
been since he worked for Palmer. Jews and Reds—he's
nuts on those two subjects and when they come together,
it's dynamite. But his intensity serves a purpose, Chris.
The man is a fox. We go from Dillinger to the Nazi
saboteurs to the Jew anarchists. We may not need the
New Deal anymore, but by God we need the FBI! The
more Reds under the bed, the more agents we need to
pull the covers back. Mr. Hoover is great at what he
does."

"I didn't say he wasn't. I happen to think well of the
director."

"Good. Glad to hear it. Around here it pays to do
that." Minot smiled and began to fish another cigarette
from his pack. "Anyway, as you were saying, you *do*
know where you are."

"Domestic Intelligence. That's what you are?"

"A piece of it. I run a little shoe-box operation in the

back room." Minot grinned. "A dead-letter box, I should say. My office is known in these parts as Siberia."

"What is it?"

"SE."

Malone shrugged. "Never heard of it."

Minot smiled, his point. "Soviet Espionage, SE. If only all things were so simple. A subdivision of Foreign Counterintelligence, which is a subdivision of Domestic Intelligence."

"I'd think Soviet Espionage would be pretty important, given—"

"Hoover's obsessed with *Americans,* don't you see? The Gus Halls, the Dalton Trumbos and Lizzy Bentleys. All those liberal Jews on the attorney general's list."

"So what do you do?"

"The most meaningless and impossible job in the Bureau."

"That's quite a claim, given some of the jobs I've heard about."

"I keep track of actual, identified Russian agents—MGB and GRU both; two hundred and fifty of them operating out of here, a hundred and seventy-five out of New York and another thirty out of San Francisco. And I've had a total of twenty-two men to do it with."

"Identified Russian agents? I don't believe it. Why haven't I heard about it? A secret like that."

"It's not secret. The Soviet intelligence network, the *real* one, is completely open. It's the diplomats, Malone. The embassy. The UN Mission and the Consulate in San Francisco. Nothing secret about it. Nothing glamorous about tracking these guys. Not like going after Alger Hiss. That's why Brigham and Hoover ignore it—which is what it meant when they gave it to me."

Malone didn't answer for a moment. If Hoover *really* ignored the Soviets, that meant they couldn't be all that dangerous, didn't it? Minot's impatience with his superiors wasn't unprecedented in the Bureau, but it was making Malone uncomfortable and he was in no hurry to endorse it. Maybe *this* was a test too. Even Malone heard the uncertainty in his voice when he asked, "But what can the diplomats do?"

"They're the key. Nothing goes to Moscow from this country except through them. They have complete freedom of communication—radio, cable, diplomatic pouch. They have freedom of movement and they have freedom to contact whoever the hell they want."

"I thought they were restricted, like our people in Russia are." Malone had to rein his impulse to defend Hoover. The restrictions on the diplomats neutralized them, no?

Minot shrugged. "I have a dozen agents for surveillance. You can imagine how effective they are with five hundred subjects to track. I don't even get support from the local office, which is busy, like everybody else, looking for Reds in the U.S. government. There's a bootblack who has his stand in the Pentagon Concourse. He's been hard-interviewed a dozen times by Brigham's people and by the field office both. Why? Because twenty years ago he gave five bucks to the Scottsboro Boys defense fund and because he admits to owning Paul Robeson records. That bootblack is why Brigham's agents have the best-shined shoes in this building." Minot stopped abruptly and snapped the ash off his cigarette.

Malone waited, apparently indifferent. But inside he felt himself being drawn into currents he wanted no part of. Was Minot describing anything more, finally, than a Bureau turf fight? Malone hadn't asked to be part of this, and he reminded himself that to mistrust Minot was not the same thing as mistrusting the FBI.

Minot said, more calmly, "There are MGB men posted downstairs, for example, photographing *us* as we come and go from this building. Same at the field office. They have a file on every agent in D.C.; same in New York and same in San Francisco. That way they know what we look like when we tail them. They're better at it than we are and this is *our* territory."

Malone nodded slowly. "That's why Kershaw made me cover my face when they brought me in." It soothed him to think there had been reasons for the insults he'd been dealt.

"That's right. If we work out the deal I have in mind, it all hinges on their not having made you. You will have never been here. You will have never been in the FBI. You have two main qualifications: locks and Kansas City. Anybody that's worked for me is on their bulletin board."

"What deal?"

"One other question, first."

"What?"

"You're not married, I gather."

"No."

"There was a woman in Kansas City."

"That's not in my file."

"What's the story?"

Malone shrugged. "She'd never left Kansas. She was very close to her family. She couldn't see coming with me."

"You asked her to?"

"Yes. I asked her to marry me. She said no."

"It's over?"

The question seemed unbearably cruel to Malone, and it panicked him to think of answering it. Over? His relationship with Beth Fraser over? Is that what her refusal meant? But it was his refusal too. He had refused to quit the Bureau. He shook his head. "I don't know. I told her I'd write her."

Minot studied him, considering how to put his next statement. Finally, he said flatly, "There will be a woman involved in this assignment. Is that a problem?"

Malone abruptly picked up the handcuffs and shook them at Minot. "You've got to tell me what the hell is going on!"

"First, you have to tell me if you're in. I can't lay it out for you and have you walk away from it. I also can't order you to do it, because there is a very good chance it will turn out badly for you."

"How badly?"

"For starters, you could die. Or worse, you could foul it up and get a letter of censure from the boss." Minot grinned.

Malone refused to treat what he was feeling lightly, but he knew by now that his anger was irrelevant, and so apparently was his confusion. Only the clear urgency of Minot's will mattered, that and the decision whether to

submit to it or not. He said coldly, "Those were the risks
I took when I joined the Bureau." He made the statement without underscoring it, but also without stuttering
through it, the implicit melodrama of their profession.

Minot made a show of sizing Malone up. Then he
displayed his own decision in a small brisk nod.

"You wanted important work. You wanted something
serious. I promise you, this is the most serious thing you
will ever do."

For a moment Malone said nothing. He heard no clicks
in that silence, no gates lifting or locks snapping open.
But he and Minot had just said yes to each other and both
knew it. To Malone it was as if now, after an intermina-
ble stretch of time—it had begun, in fact, when those
agents met him at the train—he was free to breathe
again. The pain left his chest. "So tell me," he said.

Minot sat forward, leaning across the table. "We're
not in the back office anymore, Chris. This is what's
happened: a secret's been stolen." He pulled the newspaper
between them and opened it with the print facing
Malone."And it's our job to find out how."

Malone stared at the paper. The *Washington Times-
Herald,* September 24, 1949. And the headline bold across
the top: ATOM BLAST IN RUSSIA DISCLOSED and under it,
the line "HST Says US Dominance in A-Weapons Has
Ended."

2

"Is he in?" John Brigham stood opposite Hoover's secretary. On either side of him stood Minot and Malone.

Miss Gandy's eyes snagged on Malone's rumpled khakis, his open shirt. Even though the windowless anteroom was stifling, the fan on the table beside her desk was not turning, as if her comfort in that heat counted for nothing. So how else but with unconcealed disapproval could she greet the sight of a man at her desk in a rumpled jacket, an open collar and no tie?

When she looked at Webb Minot, he smiled too broadly, and Malone sensed that as his way of goading her. Malone picked up instantly that her disdain extended to Minot, but Minot was perfectly groomed. No, her attitude confirmed Malone's own intuition that Minot was some kind of misfit.

But why would a misfit be a supervisor, even in "Siberia"? In her regard for agents Miss Gandy functioned, famously, as the director's echo. She quite openly conveyed her disapproval of Minot—of course he would sponsor this derelict—by looking abruptly away, at Brigham.

The sight of the assistant director seemed to reassure her. He was the tallest of the three, and the creases of his suit were blade-sharp, even in that weather. There was a flamboyance about him that went beyond what even Malone sensed was the more tasteful discretion of Minot's appearance. Brigham's wavy hair was a perfect blond flow. His shoes, obviously a summer trademark, were black-and-white wing tips. This was a man who was not reluctant to draw attention to himself and in the curious definitions of Bureau hierarchy, that security marked him as a member of the director's inner circle.

But why would Brigham be one of Hoover's favorites now? Hadn't he been in charge of the Bureau's end of the Alger Hiss trial? Even in Kansas City they knew that Brigham had been the one to insist on building the court case not on Whittaker Chambers, who'd performed so dubiously before HUAC, but on the Woodstock typewriter. The much-touted FBI laboratory analysis—scientific method applied to crime—was supposed to overwhelm the jury. But it hadn't. Hiss undercut Brigham's strategy simply by claiming to have given the crucial typewriter away before the notorious Pumpkin Papers were typed, and half the jurors had believed him, refusing to convict.

By what trick had Brigham survived that failure? Malone could guess: some combination of the abject submission and the stoic resolve that Hoover required of his subordinates—that and the fact, reports of which had swept through every field office in a week, that Brigham and his wife had just named their infant son John Edgar.

"Just a moment, Mr. Brigham," Miss Gandy said. She stood, smoothing her dress primly, and crossed to the door behind her. She opened the door discreetly and slipped in.

Brigham took the handkerchief from his coat pocket and patted his right hand with it. He offered the handkerchief to Minot, who took it and likewise wiped his hand. He held the cloth for Malone.

"What's that?"

Minot and Brigham exchanged a look.

Minot said, "He doesn't like damp palms."

Malone felt that his eyes, fixed on the handkerchief, were fixed on the emblem of a surrender he was not prepared to make. "My palms are fine," he said.

Minot shrugged and returned the handkerchief to the indifferent Brigham, who pocketed it now, since it was soiled, on his hip.

Miss Gandy reappeared, holding the door wide. "The

director will see you, Mr. Brigham," she said, as if the other two weren't there.

As Malone followed Brigham and Minot into J. Edgar Hoover's office he felt a rush of panic—he wasn't even wearing a tie!—and the mystery into which he felt himself being drawn seemed suddenly ominous. Most street agents would have preferred storming an armed fugitive's hideout to a strained meeting with Hoover. Malone's attitude was more complicated than that, however, for Hoover had functioned in his mind since boyhood as a figure of everything he believed in and trusted. So how could he not feel thrilled, despite the circumstances, to be ushered into Hoover's presence? Still, as he entered the office his right hand fell involuntarily to his trousers, on which he discreetly wiped his palm.

Hoover's office on the fifth floor of the Justice Building was on the northeast corner overlooking Pennsylvania Avenue and Ninth Street. Its walls were curved. Its windows ran from floor to ceiling. And in the center of the blue carpet was a floating Bureau seal—Fidelity, Bravery, Integrity. The windows were open and the sheer curtains wafted in the light summer breeze. At his over-sized mahogany desk Hoover sat watching them enter. Malone's first impression was that the director was smaller than he'd seemed in Bureau training films, but wasn't that because his office was so big—Malone was still defending him—his desk so imposing? For a man whom Malone had never actually laid eyes on before, Hoover's face was remarkably familiar. But then he remembered that he'd seen it on every fourth wall in the Bureau. Malone was aware of it when Hoover's eyes locked on him. It was an effort not to look too quickly away.

Standing to Hoover's left, behind him slightly, was Tolson, the alter ego. Like Hoover he was wearing a white summer suit but Tolson's was double-breasted. Hoover wore a vest. Both men displayed colorful silk handkerchiefs in their breast pockets and each one's necktie was set off by a gold collar pin. It was as if their clothes had been laid out by the same valet. If Mr. Hoover's inner circle dressed like dandies, Malone realized with a shock, it was because they took their cues from him. To

Malone, suddenly, the three men looked like Kansas City hoodlums, and, in comparison, Minot's more subdued appearance evoked, once more, the image of a professor.

But immediately Malone felt guilty for disapproving of Hoover's appearance, and it disoriented him to find himself tilting toward Minot. Hoover was the one he had to trust, not Minot. He was still off-balance. He wished suddenly that he could go out and come in again, but now alone. Now wearing a tie. Now reporting on Klan activities, say; something he knew about. He would tell Mr. Hoover that the Ku Klux Klan in Missouri and Kansas is based in courthouses and sheriffs' offices and *that* was why they hadn't stamped it out.

Hoover stood up as Brigham approached his desk. "Hello, John," he said.

"Mr. Hoover." Brigham reached over the desk for Hoover's hand and he held it firmly.

Hoover indicated Tolson. Brigham shook with him, then swept an arm back at his companions. "You know Inspector Minot, Mr. Hoover."

Hoover and Minot shook hands without speaking. When Tolson made no move toward him Minot only nodded in his direction and stepped back.

Brigham said, "And this is Special Agent Christopher Malone, just arrived from Kansas City."

Malone was surprised at Hoover's grip, the strength of it, and for as long as he held him by the hand Hoover stared at Malone, openly sizing him up.

To his own surprise, Malone did not shrivel. His anxiety receded, as if the very act of being measured by Hoover reinforced those things in a man that made him worthy of it. Malone wanted to say, Thank you, sir. He didn't, but a powerful sense of simple gratitude choked him nonetheless. After a moment Hoover let go of Malone, introduced him to Tolson and then sat. In front of him on his desk was an open folder, a file, on the tab of which Malone read his own name. Hoover peered at the topmost page while saying, absently, "You're from Chicago. . . ."

"Yes, sir." Malone was relieved to hear the confidence

in his own voice. No one would guess how moved he was.

"What parish?"

It was not a Catholic's question, but a Chicagoan's, and Malone was disarmed. "Saint Gabriel's, sir. South Side, back of the yards."

Hoover nodded, still bent over the file. "Some of my best men are from Chicago." He fell silent for a moment, idly turned a page, then said, "And Kansas City. How did you like Kansas City?"

"Fine, sir. Though I'm happy to be in Washington."

"Good, Mr. Tolson here is from Missouri. He seems to have made a nice adjustment to Washington." Hoover looked up suddenly and smiled. It was a warm smile, genuinely friendly. "I'm sure you will too."

"Yes, sir."

Hoover leaned back in his chair then, away from the file, eyeing Malone now. "Mr. Brigham tells me you're quite the locksmith."

"My father was a locksmith. I learned a few things from him."

"What's the difference, Malone, between an ordinary tumbler lock and a combination lock?"

"A tumbler lock, sir, is held shut with small pins, three or four of them typically. A key opens it by pushing all the pins up at once. To pick a lock like that you just feel your way through each gate pushing the pins up one at a time. A combination lock, like that one"—he pointed to the safe behind Hoover's desk—"is held shut with a bolt. But the bolt depends on disks, not pins. Each disk is notched, and when you line all the notches up by turning the wheel to the right numbers, it makes a slot into which the bolt falls, opening the lock."

With a slight toss of his head Hoover indicated the safe behind him. "Could you open this lock?"

Malone noticed that on top of the safe sat a small potted plant and a framed copy of Kipling's "If." If, he thought, his eyes falling to the combination dial. He looked quickly at Minot; this wasn't the simple cylinder lock on a pair of handcuffs. The tests weren't over yet. If he failed to pass them he was back on the street, an agent like all the others, as, until moments ago, *he* had been. Wasn't that all he wanted to be? For an instant he felt an urge to say, No, sir, I can't do it.

But, really, such a thing was unthinkable by then. His responses to the Bureau were automatic not first because they'd trained him, but because their training had given form to the fact that the Bureau was the bolt that held his own parts in place. And here he was, the focus point of the Bureau's own gaze. Hoover's. Malone was suddenly different, for what he wanted now was nothing less than to be an agent whom J. Edgar Hoover thought of as his own.

He studied the gray steel door of the safe, the combination wheel and, next to it, the chrome handle, knobbed at the end. The handle told him what he needed to know; freezer doors at Swift had had that handle. It was a Mosler safe. "I could take a crack at it, sir." He forced a smile when he heard his own pun. "With your permission, of course."

Hoover made a steeple of his hands, studying Malone. But Malone was reading Hoover too. What the director did supremely well was judge his men. His ability to see into them was the secret of his success. The harsh standards and arbitrary pronouncements and personal aloofness, all in combination with carefully doled words of praise, letters of commendation and incentive awards, added up to a method of administration before which even the most hard-shelled agent laid himself bare. It was no surprise to Malone that, under Hoover's gaze, he felt completely known. What surprised him was his own simultaneous sense that he saw into Hoover in return. Was it a kind of sacrilege, to feel like Hoover's equal? Or was it a kind of, in the Catholic sense, grace?

The director pushed himself back in his chair toward the side of his desk, toward Tolson, opening up a space in front of the safe.

Malone looked at Minot, aware that Hoover had barely acknowledged him, yet Malone felt that Minot was the man in charge of tests. Minot's was the permission he needed. Minot's eyes flickered, the barest nod.

Malone crossed in front of Brigham and circled behind

Hoover's desk. "Ideally I would have a stethoscope. When the disk slips into place, the bolt drops just that fraction of an inch into the notch and you can hear it." Malone hitched his trousers and stooped to the safe. He pressed the chrome handle as far as it would go. "It's the handle that gives me pressure on the bolt while I turn the wheel. That pressure is what gives me the click. When I hear the click I know that I've found one of the combination numbers."

"But you don't have a stethoscope," Hoover said.

"The other way to tell is by feeling the friction in your fingers. The friction decreases when the bolt presses into the notch."

"Sandpaper, you need sandpaper," Tolson said.

"No, sir. It's not that subtle. Not with this handle to give me pressure." He craned around to look at Brigham. "But I could use that handkerchief, Mr. Brigham." When Brigham handed it to him Malone smiled. "Have to keep my hands dry."

Malone began to work the wheel, touching his cheek to the cold steel of the door. The room fell absolutely silent while the others watched him.

Malone, in his mind, stood hunched over his own shoulder, watching too; he was hunched over his father's shoulder, another scene in the packing plant, a more dangerous one. A dozen people were crowded around, including the manager of the plant as well as the doctor who'd come with the ambulance. It was the doctor's stethoscope that "Smith" Malone was holding against the door with the same hand he used to slowly turn the wheel, first this way, then that, constantly pressing down with his other hand on the chrome handle with the small knob at the end.

"Hurry up," the plant manager had said. "There's a man freezing to death in there!" The supervisor, the only man who knew the combination, had inadvertently shut himself in.

"Smith" Malone took his face away from the freezer door long enough to give the manager a look, a simple look that said, Don't hurry *me,* mister. And the manager stepped back. Malone went back to his work.

And a few moments later he straightened up and jerked the handle. The door opened.

That blast of cold air.

The doctor rushed into the freezer. A long silence, the cry muffled by the frozen carcasses of beef: "He's alive! He's still alive!"

Now Chris Malone straightened his back. He kept his grip firm on the safe handle while looking up at Hoover. Hoover was still staring at him over his folded hands. It unsettled Malone to see Hoover's glare as a version of his father's. But compared with his father's Hoover's expression was benign.

Malone pushed the handle down.

The bolt popped free and he pulled the door of the director's safe open. Inwardly he felt exhilarated: I did it! The thrill startled him, and instinctively he stifled it. He opened the door just far enough to let them see his achievement, far enough to feel the air, but also far enough that for a moment Hoover's secrets were lying there in easy reach. An open safe usurps attention absolutely. Malone couldn't keep himself from peering into it, and his eyes went immediately to a manila envelope on the largest shelf. It was marked with a red letter *V*, which Malone read at once as "Victory." Automatically he assumed the envelope held papers to do with the end of the war.

But the V-marked envelope and whatever else the safe held were none of Malone's business, as Hoover made clear by leaning forward to swing the door of his safe shut again.

When Malone faced Hoover, the director seemed far from pleased. But Malone only shook his head. "If you want a safe that can't be opened so easily, sir, you don't want a Mosler. You don't want this handle here. Without the handle I'd have no way of keeping pressure on the bolt and pressure is what gives me the clicks. You want a safe with just the wheel. No handle. A Mifflin. Or a Nicholas. To crack those you have to drill or use dynamite."

Hoover, instead of speaking, swiveled slowly to face

Brigham. "Tell me what you have in mind," he said quietly.

"Yes, sir," Brigham replied. He looked quickly at Minot as if unsure which of them should conduct this briefing. But Minot was staring at his hands. Brigham looked back at Hoover and cleared his throat. "The key, sir, is the cable traffic. Under Operation Shamrock, as you know, we have been delaying and copying all of the Soviet transmissions from the embassy here in Washington to Moscow. The commercial cable companies cooperate with us, and the Army Security Agency intercepts their radio transmissions out of the airwaves. So we have a complete set of everything the MGB has sent home, going back more than five years."

"Except what they take out in the diplomatic pouch."

"Yes, sir."

"And all this material is in code."

"That's correct, sir."

"Just pages and pages of numbers." Hoover looked at Webb Minot, with an old irritation. It was a useless exercise, one he had opposed from the beginning. He'd only approved it when Minot had said that if the Bureau didn't collect the traffic the army would, and then, when it was established a year ago, the CIA. It had galled Hoover every time he thought of it, which wasn't often, that agents of his were carting boxes of microfilmed messages out of Western Union offices every morning before dawn, and taking them— "Where is all this material now anyway?"

Though Hoover was still looking meanly at Minot, Brigham answered. "In the subbasement at Ident, sir. The first thing we did two weeks ago when you gave us your order was to do a complete review and analysis of that traffic—"

"But you can't read it because it's in code, a code we've never broken, which is why Shamrock is useless and has been from the start. ASA code breakers can't read it and neither can you. Am I right?"

"Yes, sir, you are."

"I don't like to waste my men on wild-goose chases, Brigham, and you know it. Or you should. What in

blazes are you starting with that stuff for? The president
is on my back about this. He called me again this morning. He asked me if we're going to be able to crack this
thing. I told him, of course, we could. He said nothing
the Bureau has ever done compares with the urgency of
this, and I told him I understood that. And I told him my
men understood it too."

"Yes, sir."

Hoover checked himself. His staccato outburst had had
the effect of derailing Brigham utterly. When he glanced
at Malone, Malone felt embarrassed for the director. The
idea of someone else—even the president—pressuring
Hoover was unthinkable. Malone wanted to take his side
again. But how could he? Hoover pressed Brigham. "I
wanted you to develop leads from Bentley and Chambers."

"I am, sir. I have thirty men reviewing everything they've
given us. I have—"

Minot looked up at last to interrupt. "Mr. Hoover,
we're here to talk about only one small part of the larger
effort. You're probably right. It's the least promising
part, and as it happens it falls under the purview of my
office. But we are all working double-time on this because we do understand how urgent it is. The Reds are
inside and we have to do everything we can to learn how
they got there and get them out. No stone unturned, Mr.
Hoover. Isn't that what you want?"

Hoover stared at Minot, reading him for insolence.

Malone sensed the tension between them, and he
thought that Hoover would surely dismiss Minot.

But he didn't. He said nothing, and his glare softened
not a bit, but there was a perceptible physical sagging as
he exhaled, an implicit surrender. And Malone sensed
the enormity of this crisis more in Hoover's body than he
had in Hoover's words.

Minot continued. "So we did an analysis of the traffic
going back to 'forty-four. You're right, of course. We
can't read it. They use a code book. And then they use a
one-time cipher pad, encoding everything twice. ASA
cryptanalysts have been attacking the system all this time
with no luck. The double encoding is what makes it
unbreakable. But we can learn some things from the

cipher texts themselves, even without breaking them. For example, Mr. Hoover, when my men looked back over five years' worth of traffic last week they discovered that the Soviets send a regular number of message groups every day, with a variation of plus or minus five percent. Obviously, they meet a transmission quota even if it means, on slow days, filling out the message groups with nonsense numbers. This regularity of signals quantity is totally consistent going back to 1944." Minot paused. Malone sensed that it had been a long time since he'd had Hoover's attention like this. "Totally consistent," he said carefully, "with one exception."

Minot stopped and after several beats it was apparent that he was waiting for some reaction.

Hoover only stared at him.

Tolson, with the air of an underling opening the door, said, "And what would that be?"

Minot did not drop his eyes from Hoover's. "For a single period of six weeks, traffic from the embassy to Moscow increased by factors of from five to, at peak levels, fifteen."

"When?" Hoover asked.

"The summer of 1945. Just before and after Hiroshima."

Brigham said, "The theoretical problems of atomic fission had all been solved; it was the engineering breakthroughs at the end that enabled us to make a bomb that worked. The Manhattan Project climaxed in those weeks. The Russian cipher traffic almost surely represents summaries of the concluding data from Los Alamos. If we could read it, it could tell us who we're looking for."

"But we can't read it." Hoover, ignoring Brigham, was addressing Minot. "You just said we can't."

"Up to now we haven't. That's right. But I've brought in a new cryptanalyst, an old man named Abetz—"

Tolson said, "I know Abetz. He's some kind of a priest."

"That's right," Minot said. "He's a German Jesuit, a Bible scholar at Catholic University. He spent most of his life in the Middle East, deciphering ancient Mesopotamian hieroglyphics. The man is a cryptanalysis Einstein. He came here during the war. He did some work for me, but only for as long as it took to beat the Nazis. He's not given to government work, and he's only agreed to come on again because of the connection with the bomb."

Tolson leaned to Hoover's ear and whispered, but audibly, "He ran the German ciphers out of Amagansett."

Malone remembered that Amagansett was the Long Island town in which Nazi agents had set up a radio station. FBI agents had captured it, arrested the Germans, then manned the radio station through the war, sending transmissions that the U.S. wanted Germany to hear.

Minot said, "Father Abetz reproduced the entire German cipher system building on the few scraps of a code book the Nazis had all but destroyed."

The Amagansett bait-signal operation had been one of the FBI coups during the war, and Brigham had highlighted it during his presentation to Malone's intake class. If Amagansett had been Minot's show, that might explain why Hoover, despite his disdain, deferred to him now.

"After the war," Minot went on, "Abetz went back to Catholic University. He's retired there. ASA would have given anything to recruit him but he wouldn't think of it."

"But you spoke to him."

"Yes. I showed him what we found in the Soviet traffic, that jump in volume just before Hiroshima. He understands the urgency of what we're dealing with. He's the one who told me what we need."

"Which is . . .?"

"What makes the cipher unbreakable, as I said, is the double encoding. The one-time pad is a series of number groups that are added in the second stage to the numbers already encrypted, in the first stage. The one-time pad is destroyed as soon as it's used. We can never get ahold of that. But the first stage depends on a permanent code book and copies of the code book are maintained. Father Abetz says that if he could get inside the first stage of the cipher he would have a shot at cracking the second, piece by piece."

"What do you mean?"

"We have to get the code book."

Hoover abruptly swiveled away from Minot to look out his window. The parched leaves of the tops of the avenue's elm trees were visible, swaying gently in the same breeze that wafted the curtain. "And how do we do that?"

"Christopher Malone does it, Mr. Hoover." Minot paused to look at Malone, who was staring back at him, aghast. It was like having handcuffs slapped on again, but now they snapped shut on his lungs, choking him. Coming after so many shocks, this one seemed for a moment to shut him down. Did it signal, after all, the onset of his craziness? That Minot was speaking as if he believed what he was saying made Malone want to cry out, Stop! He forced himself instead, when Minot turned back to Hoover, to stare mutely and listen. "Malone enters the code room of the Russian embassy on Sixteenth Street. He opens the safe. He copies the code book, then returns it to the safe and leaves everything as it was. They never know."

In the silence that followed Minot's statement, Malone looked at the other agents, waiting for them to dispose of Minot.

Tolson snorted but said nothing. It was up to the boss to deal with this.

Brigham too seemed to be waiting for Hoover to react. Hoover would speak for all of them, saying, This is insane and irresponsible fantasy. He would yell at them, Get out! Get out! He would turn to Malone and say, This isn't your fault.

Hoover was still looking out his window. Without facing back to them he said, "Does Malone understand what would be involved if he got caught?"

Minot looked at Malone. The son of a bitch, Malone thought. He expects *me* to answer. Of course I know. The Russians will simply bury me underneath the whale shit. No one will ever hear of me again.

But Minot's eyes never wavered, and it was his merciless resolve, finally, that steadied Malone, forcing him to do what, at bottom, he *wanted* desperately to do.

"Yes, sir," Malone said, though holding Minot's eyes, not Hoover's. "I understand."

"No other agents would be involved in the entry," Hoover said.

"That's right, sir," Minot said.

Tolson made a show of his skepticism by saying dismissively, "Surely the Russians would have changed their 1945 code book by now."

Minot shook his head. "Igor Gouzenko, the defector in Ottawa, was a cipher clerk. He has outlined their entire routine for us. Because of the breakproof one-time pad, the Russians feel no need to change the code book. Every residency has a different version. In Canada they hadn't changed it in seven years. Now that Gouzenko has come over they've probably changed it in Ottawa. But I'd say it's worth the gamble that they haven't changed it here."

Hoover continued staring out the window in silence. Finally he nodded once, then swung back to them. He leaned toward Malone and raised a finger at him. Malone noticed Hoover's red college ring, a ruby? Hoover, like Malone and like many agents, had gone to a local night school while working days. In Hoover's case, George Washington University near the White House. It would never have occurred to Malone to wear a college ring. To his knowledge, Loyola didn't even have them. Jeweled and dated rings, like girls in rumble seats and football weekends, were what real colleges offered. Malone hadn't pined for such trappings, the paraphernalia of a communion that simply did not exist in his life. Besides, he wasn't a man to wear jewelry on his fingers. It surprised him that Hoover was.

Hoover was staring at him for effect. "Do you think you can do it?"

Malone imagined himself shrugging cockily: You bet. But he had no capacity for counterfeit nonchalance. The gravity of the moment for Malone was not a matter of the danger or the difficulty of what Minot proposed, but of the way in which it realized his absolute ambition. Mr. Hoover was prepared to believe in him, but only if he believed in himself. He chose his words very carefully. "A lock is only a lock, sir. Once I'm inside the code room, I'd have a chance. If it was a safe like yours—" He

smiled. Hoover only glared at him, and Malone suddenly
felt a stab of panic that he had made a mistake in opening the director's safe, as if he'd laid bare one of Hoover's character flaws.

"Mr. Hoover?" Despite himself Malone could hear the
jokers in the squad room, their wide-eyed parody. *"A
character flaw?"*

He looked uneasily at Minot. "How I get into the code
room is another question."

Minot touched Malone's elbow, to silence him, but
Minot's touch also reassured him. Minot is calling the
shots and for some reason, Malone understood, he believes I can make them.

Minot had taken over the briefing. "We're working the
entry out now, sir. Obviously, B and E is impossible. The
Russians aren't the Poles. The embassy on Sixteenth
Street is the most heavily guarded building in the city.
You recall their 'renovation' of two years ago. Fortifica-
tion is more like it. Steel shutters barricade the windows
at night. All the door locks were made in Russia and
installed by their own crews." He said, aside, to Malone,
"A lock is not 'only a lock' in this case. You're going to
have to teach yourself from scratch on these." He turned
back to Hoover. "Every possible entry point is bugged.
We have the layout down cold. We know where the
guardposts are, and we know how the wires run. And
that's why we know the usual black-bag job is out."

"How do you have the layout?"

"We've been dusting the place from across the street
for months, from the National Geographic Building. You
authorized the watch when they began the reconstruction."

Hoover glanced at Tolson.

What the hell is "dusting"? Malone thought.

But the director knew, and Tolson, having picked up
on his glance, said, "Dusting was authorized on a single-
use basis. There is no standing order permitting it because of the potential for contamination."

Contamination! Malone felt suddenly as if he were
back on the quick-target range at Quantico. With every
step he took a new enemy popped into view. Something
else to fear. He remembered hearing about a new sur-

veillance technique that used invisible radioactive particles. "Dust," no doubt. No wonder Hoover was suddenly so sensitive. But Malone understood that if Minot had really violated policy, Hoover himself would have rebuked him. Tolson was just getting the director's distance from the technique on record.

After a respectful pause—time for the rebuke to settle but also time for Minot to say with his silence that it meant nothing to him—Minot continued his briefing. "What we propose to do, Mr. Hoover, is send Malone in through the front door. The Russians will open it for him and treat him like a guest. What I need from you, sir, is authorization to place Malone in the Protocol Office of the State Department."

What is this shit? Malone stared at Minot with fresh incredulity, aware of yet another surge of blood in his ears. How many times was this going to happen? One minute a safecracker and the next contaminated, and now a table setter? What *is* this shit? But he forced himself to listen, just listen, as if Minot were talking about someone else.

"As far as anyone at State would know—apart from Mr. Acheson or whomever you had to brief—Malone would be an auxiliary Foreign Service officer just returned from assignment abroad. His assignment in Protocol would be on the embassy services staff and Sixteenth Street would be on his desk. It would take us a period of time to establish him and then—"

"I'll leave that to you, Minot." Hoover shifted his gaze to Brigham. "No paper, John," he said. His voice was firm, sure. He knew exactly how this was played. "You talk to Acheson. Tell him you're speaking for me. Get Malone his job. Even if Acheson asks for it, no paper. Nothing in writing anywhere."

And that order of Hoover's sealed the magnitude of what they had just decided, and, as far as Malone was concerned, the reality. "No paper!" The authority with which Hoover, the King of Paper, had said those two words, violating his own rules, was absolute to Malone, and it was enough. Hoover's authority, now displayed, eliminated Malone's ambivalence.

He saw for the first time what it was that had made Hoover so durable. Agents in the field regarded Hoover with a combination of worship and disdain, but both were off the mark. Malone sensed that Hoover's power lay in his simple ability to push through obstacles toward what he wanted. Always, of course, the obstacles were other men like Acheson. It was smart to be afraid of Hoover because his will was the wringer through which everything passed. Malone knew that he himself, having just been squeezed through Hoover's rollers—not Minot's, he reminded himself—was nothing special. When it came to accomplishing the purposes of the Bureau every agent and clerk, and for that matter, many congressmen, cabinet secretaries and, some said, even presidents, were just so many bed sheets to be wrung and hung out to dry in the bleaching sun.

Hoover went on in the same affectless voice. Determination, Malone thought, reduced to a solid state. "Tell Acheson nothing about Malone's true mission. Don't mention that our target is the embassy."

Brigham began to object. "Mr. Hoover, I can't imagine that the secretary—"

Hoover waved impatiently. "The secretary of state believes in niceties. He would tell us that every nation in the world will protest our violation of the diplomatic sanctuary. He'll say Russia should get the same treatment other nations get. If not better." Hoover snorted. "Hell, Acheson would call a press conference on us. Get all those news jackals in the same room and quote the Bible at them and say J. Edgar Hoover just wants to bring down Harvard."

Harvard? Malone thought he'd missed a connection. What did Harvard have to do with anything?

Hoover had leaned forward and was sighting along his finger at Brigham. "If we break into the Russian embassy, Acheson will say we have to let them break into ours once just to keep it fair. Acheson will be all over us. But not if we don't tell him what we're after. If we just say we want to plant our man in the State Department on an urgent national security case ordered by the White House, do you know what he'll think? He'll think we're

investigating *him!* And that's perfect! Let him think it!
He knows what we had on that rat Hiss. He knows what
we could get on him. He'll bend over backwards to give
us what we want."

He fell back against his chair to say more quietly, "If
he doesn't . . ."

The meat hook, Malone thought, and what he saw was
a roomful of misshapen carcasses hanging from pipes, drying
in the freezing air. He saw sides of beef, whole pigs,
security cases, the vapor rising off ice.

" . . . we *will* investigate him. We'll find out why our
distinguished secretary of state is so protective of these
Communists." He pronounced the word as if it were
spelled *Cominists.* "He's a man with a guilty conscience.
He just hopes I don't ask why. If he bucks me on this, I
will."

Hoover pulled decisively up to his desk again; he had
spoken. Malone guessed that at some point in every
interview he gave a speech like that. He closed the folder
over the file on the center of his desk.

It was not Acheson's file; with a start, Malone remembered that it was his own.

The FBI derived originally from a Justice Department
force that was established in the first decade of the century by an attorney general named Charles J. Bonaparte,
the grandson of Napoleon's brother. The Bureau seemed
to want an emperor from the start and in 1924 it got one.
From the beginning everything the FBI did was done in
Hoover's name, as if he *personally* searched through
those files for each felon's fingerprints, *personally* compiled those reports on crime, *personally* arrested Baby
Face Nelson and shot it out with Dillinger. It was more
than bureaucratic genius at work—making himself the
embodiment of virtue, the darling of Congress, the only
indispensable figure in government. Malone saw that it
was that determination of his, but magnified. The FBI
was the institutionalization of one man's fierce will and
its success or failure depended on what informed that will
and what became its object, and, eventually, its fixation.

Webb Minot said, "Mr. Hoover, what we've outlined

is only the first step. If Malone succeeds in getting us a copy of the code book, that will just be the beginning. I'd like to bring the cryptanalysis process under my own control—removing it from the army. Father Abetz won't work for the ASA anyway. I'll need space and support. I'll need an IBM tabulator and I'll need a team of translators. I need it all now."

Hoover nodded impatiently and said to Brigham, "Give him what he needs, but keep it outside the Bureau. Nothing in the field office. Nothing in the SOG." Hoover faced Minot. "No files, do you hear me?"

"Yes, sir."

"We don't go into other nations' embassies. We do not do that. Do you understand?"

"Yes, sir."

Hoover swung in his chair to look at Malone. "Do you?"

"Yes, sir."

Hoover stared at him in silence for a long time, not moving, as if holding his flattened face against a window. Then he said, having apparently decided that in Malone it was strength he should appeal to, not weakness, "You have already served your country well. You're the kind of man that's made the Bureau what it is. I can see that. I want you to carry the ball for me this time. I won't forget it. I hate to send a man on a job without backup. Sometimes I have to. I wouldn't do it, though, unless he was one of my best. I appreciate it, Chris."

Malone felt like a warrior standing on the threshold of a room from which his father-king had just dispatched him. Hoover had not imposed hs hands upon him, nor had he anointed him with chrism. Why then did he feel ordained? Malone could more easily have reached for a mote-filled shaft of the sun than explained Hoover's power over him at that moment. It made Malone believe for the first time that he could do whatever it was that Minot wanted. He could handle what was coming, and if he had to—this feeling was usually regarded in an FBI man as subversive—he could handle it alone. Even if he couldn't explain it, he would never again be mystified by this eccentric figure's power over his men. His power, now that he felt it, over Malone.

Malone wanted to acknowledge it, and he said to his own and everyone's surprise, "Mr. Hoover, I hesitated to come in here because I didn't have a tie on. I felt naked without my credentials." He stopped, aware that the others had shifted awkwardly. He could feel Tolson's eyes burning into the side of his face. What he meant to say was, Sir, I don't feel naked now.

Minot intervened. "Thank you, Mr. Hoover." The meeting was over.

Hoover stood and shook hands with each of them across his desk. Firm handshakes. And dry.

Brigham turned and led the way toward the door.

But suddenly, from behind them, Hoover asked, "What are you calling it?"

"Sir?" Brigham froze with his hand on the knob, his head craned across his shoulder.

Minot stood motionless with his back to Hoover.

Malone wanted to face both ways: toward Minot, whose alliance felt powerful and trustworthy, but also toward the director, from whom he'd just received such a jolt of authority. But when he looked, the director, who had resumed his seat, seemed diminished from across the width of his office. He was hunched over his huge desk, his eyes disproportionately small, his hands clutching at each other. Malone was reminded of a caricature drawing he'd seen in a left-wing journal. It showed Hoover as a weasellike creature, a ferret, in fact, the shrewd animal that drives quarry out of its lurking corners by relentless poking and pursuit. "America's Ferret," the caption had read. And Malone had thought, Well, perhaps he is, but maybe America needs one. Yet now the memory of that drawing made him shudder.

"The operation, Minot," Hoover said. "What are you calling it?"

Minot looked at Brigham: This is yours to deal with.

But a veil of helplessness had fallen over Brigham's face. Despite the fact that Hoover had explicitly demanded a wall of separation between the operation and the Bureau proper, this was a question Brigham should have anticipated. The wall would be there if the operation was a disaster—the diplomatic furor following exposure. But if it was a triumph, Hoover would announce it. Special operations were always named. It was important when Hoover eventually made them public—usually in his testimony before appropriations committees—that they have that certain ring.

John Brigham had not become assistant director for Domestic Intelligence by giving in to panic. Malone sensed that he was acting on instinct when he said firmly, "SES, sir. We're calling it SES. Soviet Espionage Special."

Hoover shook his head no.

So much for SES.

He glanced up at Tolson for the bond of his disapproval. Tolson was shaking his head too.

Webb Minot turned around. "I'm glad you mentioned it, Mr. Hoover. We need a designation, and I have one to propose to you, sir. For your approval." He paused. The mask of his perfect neutrality was firmly in place.

Malone sensed the depth of tension between them. Wasn't Minot's superior sense of himself implicit, and wasn't it somehow justified? Minot was doubtless one of those agents who regarded Hoover with disdain. But Minot would also appreciate Hoover's gift for manipulation. For a moment it was as if Malone were seeing the director through Minot's eyes, seeing him not as an ordaining father figure—Malone saw how masterfully he himself had just been handled—but as a bent old washerwoman, her finger crooked and shaking. Like an old woman Hoover saw everything through the lens of his naîveté; good versus evil had become the Bureau versus everything else. But that narrowness gave him his focus—the lens, Malone realized, through which he started his fires.

Minot said simply, "Firebird."

No one reacted.

Finally Hoover repeated the word. "Firebird."

Was there a tentative approval in the director's voice?

Tolson read it that way and joined in. "Something red. That's good."

Hoover swiveled slightly to look at Brigham, who said quickly, "That's the thing that rises out of ashes, right?"

Hoover nodded. He could see his speech already—the resurrection of national security. "Firebird," he said again, and he faced Minot. "Like fireball, referring mostly to the A-bomb itself, I guess."

Minot shrugged. "Actually, sir, I was thinking of Stravinsky."

Stravinsky?

Malone was immediately aware that Minot's reference meant as little to Hoover and the others as it meant to him. Stravinsky was a composer, no? But Firebird as music—what was that?

Minot was not explaining. After a moment he said, "It would behoove us to keep in mind an example of Russian genius."

3

Dupont Circle was the hub of three of the city's most important avenues: New Hampshire, which ran down to Foggy Bottom and the State Department; Connecticut, which was anchored eight blocks away at the White House; and Massachusetts, along the northwest leg of which were sited the embassies of more than sixty countries. Inside the circle itself was a tidy park, a grassy enclave transected by walkways with benches and trash bins. At its center was an elegant white marble fountain that consisted of an overflowing saucer held aloft by gracefully draped Roman maidens. The flowing water cooled the air with its tranquil cascade.

One of those seated on the marble lip of the fountain, to all appearances, like the others, idling away the late afternoon, was Chris Malone. He was still dressed in his rumpled khakis, though now his suitcoat lay folded beside him. It had been an hour and a half since he'd left Justice. In the darkened basement firing range he'd joined a throng of tourists who were just finishing the famous tour. The tour agent shredded a paper target with his tommy gun, stunning the crowd with his weapon but reminding Malone that from now on he himself would be unarmed. He'd left the building as one of the tourists, though he had his own reasons for being awed. And now, still the sightseer, he was bent over a dimestore map of the District of Columbia. He was not merely perusing the grid and spokes of the famous streets, however, but memorizing them. Dupont Circle, Scott Circle, Washington Circle, Longfellow's Statue, Saint Matthew's Cathedral, The National Geographic Society, Farragut Square, McPherson Square, the Scottish Rite Temple—all landmarks of his new terrain. But his eye flicked regularly back to a particular stretch of Sixteenth Street, between L and M, a bare five blocks from the White House, and even less than that from where he was now sitting. Though it was unmarked on the map, one of the stately, turn-of-the-century mansions on that block served as the chancery, embassy and ambassadorial residence of the only other nation, as of today, that had the bomb.

Malone had just read the newspaper accounts of Truman's announcement; American scientists were staggered not because the Russians had mastered the theoretical physics of atomic fission—Soviet physicists had helped lay it out in the thirties—but because a war-ravaged nation whose industrial economy was in ruins could mount the huge technical and engineering effort required to solve the practical problems associated with fission. The United States, at a cost of two billion dollars and only under the impetus of defeating Hitler, had mobilized the best minds in the West and the core of American industry itself, operating at full capacity over three years, to solve the near infinite number of such problems—how to fabricate pure uranium, for example, and then how to fabricate tons of it. With the Russians' atomic explosion, the American scientists were chastened. They had regarded their own government's obsession with secrecy as absurd, even as they submitted to it. And they were outspoken in dismissing as paranoid the steps taken to prevent "Communist" infiltration of the Manhattan Project. As a group, they could never forget, for example, that Oppenheimer had been forced to sever ties with his fiancée because she had been a Communist, and when he did, she killed herself. To the scientists, as to most academics and intellectuals, the fear of the Reds, which was culminating in ubiquitous FBI security checks and insulting loyalty oaths and wildly undisciplined congressional investigations and the heinous blacklists, was like the alarmist boy's fear of the invisible wolf. But now, it turned out, the wolf had come. The wolf had eaten the boy and was preparing to eat the very elders who had ignored him.

Malone looked up from the city map to let his eye drift around Dupont Circle. A young mother in a white dress and a loosely knitted shawl was bent over her baby's buggy, sliding it to and fro. A pair of high school boys were playing a lackadaisical game of catch; they tossed the baseball with an end-of-the-season nonchalance. He noticed the colored women crossing the circle toward their buses, maids coming from Massachusetts Avenue mansions. A postman was resting on a bench under the shade of one of the larger elms, his elbow cushioned on his worn leather bag, which, since the day's letters were all delivered, had collapsed in on itself. So had the postman, for that matter.

On the gently curving street that formed the perimeter of the circle, the traffic had thickened with Washington's end-of-the-day retreat. The rush north and west, toward Cleveland Park, Kalorama, Georgetown and Chevy Chase had begun, but the commuters drove quietly by, as if they too were soothed by the tidy green park and the fountain's nubile figures and their veil of gently splashing water. Malone tried to put the tranquillity of the late summer scene together with the new sense of urgency all those people were surely feeling: The Russians had the bomb!

Or was the urgency only his? The Soviet atomic explosion was no mere event of the century for him, no mere blinding flash of light, mushroom cloud, a thousand suns in the sky, shatterer of worlds, killer of cities, ender of America's time of dominance. Far more simply and immediately, without his having known it, the Russian bomb was what had brought him, Christopher Malone, to Washington from Kansas City, to a solo assignment, as yet undefined, under orders from J. Edgar Hoover himself. He found it hard to believe that the meeting in Hoover's office had actually taken place. The Russians had the bomb? The real surprise in Malone's life that day was that Hoover had called him Chris.

He stared down at the map again, the grid and spokes,

the circles and squares, the monuments and great buildings
—what had any of it to do with him? He fixed his stare
on the block of Sixteenth Street between L and M, but
he saw nothing. He was like a man lying on a hill to look
at the stars, yet seeing only the black spaces between
them, the emptiness between the brilliant lights. The
lights did not exist for him. As, apparently—he glanced
around the park again—the bomb did not exist for the
dozing postman, the beatific young mother, the boys at
their play. As if by a trick of his eyes, even these figures
seemed suddenly like shadows to him. The famous ball of
fire had made him blind. He might as well have been
crossing into that busy avenue there behind a white cane.
Blind, yes. As if that were his exact condition, he felt a
sudden rush in his other senses, the feel of cool marble
against the skin of his left palm, the sound of squirrels
clacking up the bark of trees, a whiff of autumn in the air
despite the clammy heat. He felt the mystery of what was
coming, sucking at the edges of his calm.

He was not blind, and what told him so was the sight of a
woman crossing into the circle from P Street, from the
direction of Rock Creek Park and Georgetown. She wore
a loosely fitting brown dress that rippled around her as
she walked, like a filament, an aura. Even from this
distance, her grace registered, how her woman's body
moved, stirring the air, giving off its own freshness, a
breeze of it, to quicken the stale afternoon. As he watched
her, he thought of women he'd seen on the great avenues
of Rome during his one R-and-R in Italy, and he felt a
pang of boyish awe, as if he were still an inexperienced
GI, gawking at the most sophisticated women in the
world. Their ancestors' statues graced fountains like the
one behind him everywhere, but he hadn't known that
yet. All he had known then was they didn't have women
like that on the South Side of Chicago. A like thought
struck him now, but about Kansas City, not Chicago.
How poised she was. He watched her unashamedly, as if
he were a Roman gigolo hanging around the piazza until
such a woman stopped under his stare and asked him to
live with her. He remembered what a slick lieutenant

told him once about their dresses: Their dresses become
like wind if they are made of silk. Women love silk for
the way it flows around their limbs when they are walking,
clinging to their bodies. If their bodies were made only to
wear such dresses it would be enough, the lieutenant
said, and then added slyly, but their bodies are made for
other things too, and laughed.

She walked purposefully into the park, maintaining a
rapid clip. Malone wondered if the impression she was
making on him—he had no thought now of the Russian
bomb, of being blind—was indeed an effect of the dress
she was wearing. He tried without success to distinguish
among the aspects of her appearance. Her limbs were
long, the curves of her hips and breasts pronounced. She
moved like those Roman women, sexy but not vulgar.
Was it the walk itself, the way she placed her feet, swung
her bag, kept her head steady above the rhythmic flow of
her body? It was impossible on seeing such a woman, so
cool, so secure, so decisive, to imagine her in the throes
of passion, moaning with love. But it was impossible also
not to want to.

As she drew closer, Malone averted his eyes so as not
to stare openly, but still he watched her, as if looking for
traces of the man she'd been with. The brown material of
her dress—yes, silk—contrasted with the pale white of
her legs and arms, the delta of her throat, her face. Her
skin was white like the marble maidens'. But unlike them
there was no ambiguity in her expression. Her thin lips
were pressed together, her brow firm, her gaze fixed on
something far away. Wasn't that a dancer's trick, he
wondered, a way of centering? Didn't they stare at a
single point in space, even while twirling? Silk is a woman's trick, he thought. Is her gaze, as well? Malone
recognized the questions of a greenhorn Yankee hick.

Her eyes were dark, that was all. There were no tricks.
If her eyes dominated her face, perhaps it was because
her black hair was pulled severely back and pinned behind. Once Malone actually saw her eyes, he clung to
them. After a moment he understood that her fierce gaze
was fixed not on a point on some indeterminate horizon
toward which she strode. She moved steadily toward the

center of the park, toward the very fountain on the lip of
which he sat.

Inspector Minot had ordered him to wait there. His
bags were to be delivered to an apartment Minot had
already arranged for him. When everything was ready,
Minot had said, someone would come for him.

With a surge of panic that he had so far kept at
bay—the panic of a boy sent too young to Italy, too
young for such women and too young for war—Malone
realized as this woman approached that what her stunning dark eyes were fixed upon was him.

If she could look so directly, so could he. He faced her
and waited.

"Hello. You are Christopher Malone."

"That's right," he said.

"My name is Anna."

He was aware of her accent at once. German, he
thought. She stood before him with both hands fixed
upon her bag. Ordinarily he'd have come to his feet and
offered his hand, but he understood that the moves, so
far, were hers to make. He remained where he was,
though it meant looking up at her awkwardly. She was
taller than Beth, the farm girl who had refused to think
of leaving Kansas.

Beth Fraser. He remembered in particular how, when
she was in his arms, he could kiss the top of her head.
Still he had never thought of her as short. When he'd
said good-bye to her at the Kansas City train station, she
had hid her face against his chest. When he forced her
away from him so that he could see her eyes one last
time, they were so filled with despair it had frightened
him.

"You are to come with me," Anna said.

It was a straightforward statement, uttered without
inflection, but to Malone it seemed absurdly melodramatic, a line out of a wartime movie. The woman's exotic
accent destroyed any chance he had of seeing her as real.

"I beg your pardon." He smiled at her coolly. "You've
made a mistake."

"Mr. Minot is waiting for us. I am to take you to him."

"He could have come himself." Even as he said that

Malone knew it was wrong. Minot, who as head of SE was well known to the Russians, could not be seen with him, especially here only blocks from the embassy. But surely Minot would have sent another agent, not this woman. Suddenly Malone realized that the other agents would keep their distance too. The pair who met him at the train that morning, for example; he had not seen them again.

She did not answer, as if she knew he had just refuted himself.

"Am I to follow you? From a distance, I mean?"

She shook her head. "I suppose we should go as if we are together." She turned slightly, and waited.

He stood gathering his jacket and folding the map. They set off together, in step. Malone hooked his jacket over his shoulder and gave her a side look as they left the fountain behind. She was not much shorter than he was. Now that he saw her close he realized that, despite the impression she'd made on him, she was not a beautiful woman in any conventional sense, not pretty at all in the midwestern way Beth had been. Her nose was finely shaped but large and her eyes were sliced thin like almonds, as if an ancestor had been Chinese. Malone sensed that she was younger than he was, but in her body, its large bones, a certain gravity as she strode along, he sensed something maternal that might have undercut the magnetism she possessed, but didn't. It was as if one of the fountain statues had come alive, such was her hold on him. Perhaps it was simply that she knew more about what was happening right now than he did. She knew more, it struck him suddenly, about everything, and to his surprise that made him feel not inexperienced and therefore awkward, embarrassed, but drawn to her and able, for the moment, to follow where she was leading.

Connecticut Avenue, running north in a steady but gradual incline, was a street of fancy shops. The woman walked it as if she owned one. Malone eyed her intermittently in the reflections of the store windows and several times it surprised him to see himself at her side. He noticed that she was wearing a wedding band and a diamond on her ring finger. He wanted to ask about her husband, but they walked without speaking to each other. At the curbstone of R Street, waiting for the light to change, their eyes met for a moment. Malone had an urge to look away from her, but didn't. He said, "You're German."

She shook her head. "French," she said coldly, and he assumed that he'd insulted her. The light changed and she stepped into the street, apparently indifferent to whether he stayed with her.

But he joined her and once more they fell into step in silence. Altogether they walked three long blocks before she led them away from Connecticut on S Street, a narrow residential street that sloped downhill a short distance ahead to Massachusetts Avenue. The buildings were less grand than on either avenue, row houses and, on one corner, an apartment building. At that corner Anna turned again, separating herself from him, leading the way onto a small side street—Phelps Place, the sign said—which ran so steeply uphill that half a block away, the street was cut in half by a terrace wall on either side of which were graceful white stairs going up to the next level, on which the paved street resumed.

Malone recognized it at once—no through traffic—as a street on which surveillance would be difficult. The houses were small and set back on terraces of their own; no shop alcoves in which pedestrians could loiter, no commercial buildings or hotels from which to lift the window shades, a perfect street for a cover house.

Because of the bisecting stairs the street had a European air and Malone felt suddenly that he was in Rome again after all, enacting a boy soldier's dream. He had come home with this woman to live with her. Not dream, he realized, but premonition.

She led the way up the sidewalk to a particular house at the point where the street ended in the stairs. The house was white, as if to match the white of the retaining terrace. Like the street itself, it had a Mediterranean air, with its flat roof and its façade dominated by a wrought-iron balcony at the second story. Behind the balcony were a pair of French doors, but they were blank with drawn blinds and so were the first-floor windows that framed the door. The woman withdrew keys from her bag as she approached the house. She moved with authority, but Malone realized from her slight hesitation in selecting the key that this house was nearly as new to her as it was to him.

Perhaps it was in the way he himself was watching her or perhaps just the leftover uneasiness he'd felt when he'd slipped away from the Justice Building as innocuously as he could, but suddenly, despite his initial thought, he felt the presence there on that street of watchmen.

He turned slowly and let his eye run downhill, taking in the windows, the parked cars, the gates; he saw a matronly woman in a wide-brimmed hat pulling a loaded grocery cart, a boy on a bicycle balancing a baseball bat on his shoulder as he crossed Phelps Place on S, an old man with a wooden toolbox walking wearily uphill. As Malone slowly turned to take in the upper street, two schoolgirls in green blazers, each with a hand on a satchel between them, skipped down the terraced stairs. A curtain moved in a window of the house just above the stairs across the street. The breeze that had lifted it now let it fall. Malone caught a glimpse of someone moving behind another window in the same house. He stared until the figure returned: an aproned black woman carrying a broom or mop. No one was watching, he decided. He was only being foolish.

He followed Anna inside. She dropped her keys and bag on a table by the door. She walked through the entrance hall, her heels clacking on the wood floor, into the living room. A carpet muffled her steps as she crossed to the windows to pull the blinds. As she hoisted first one, then the other, sunlight flooded into the room. In that brightness the room seemed suddenly larger. It accommodated two good-sized sofas, one beige and one red, which floated on the edges of the carpet, a deep blue oriental with threads which seemed gilded in that light. There were a pair of wing chairs covered in crisp yellow-flowered fabric and haphazardly abutting—this furniture had yet to be arranged—a square coffee table on which a large cardboard box sat. The box was full of books; other like boxes were stacked along a wall of half-filled book-

cases. Against another wall five matched prints leaned—
black-and-white etchings, abstractions that meant nothing
to Malone—waiting to be hung.

"Still moving in?"

"Yes."

"It's going to be nice." It was going, in fact, to be a
room unlike any he'd lived in. With the clutter of the
boxes removed, and the sofas and chairs aligned, and the
prints hung, it would be a spare, modern room, the
antithesis of the knickknack heaven that he'd grown up
in, stuffy and crowded, but also cozy and reassuring, like
living inside the safe ring of a doily. This room would
contrast also with the uniformly stud-upholstered furnished rooms he'd been living in since the army.

Anna was staring at him from across the room, a cold
detachment on her face, as if to make the point that the
indifference she'd shown him on the street would seem
like affection compared with what she would show him
now that they were alone.

Malone listened for the sounds of the house—a clock,
a tap running, footfalls above—but he heard nothing.

"Whose place is this?"

"I believe it is yours," she said. She looked away;
then, a separate act, she turned to the nearest box of
books, took an armful and crossed to the shelves.

"Mine?" Malone's stomach lurched as he glanced quickly
around. Who would ever believe that this place was his?
"What do you mean, mine?"

She had her back to him now, defiantly, it seemed to
him, and when she did not answer he felt the push of his
anger.

It took him to the boxes too. He crossed back with a
load—some lives of American presidents, histories of
American wars. He waited beside her until, one at a
time, she took the books from him, like bricks, and built
the row. Maybe she was his assistant, a secretary of some
kind. If so, she wasn't waiting for his directions; she
worked efficiently on the shelves, without deferring to
him. Because it was all he could think to do—like a
traveler trusting directions, though he felt lost—he returned to the boxes for more books. Winston Churchill.

American Heritage volumes. He made several trips with stacks of musty periodicals, back copies of *Foreign Affairs*, *National Geographic* and the *Foreign Service Journal*. In silence, for a long time, he emptied the boxes so that she could fill the shelves.

They were just finishing when the door chime rang. His helper, if that's what she was, refused to look at him, so Malone left the living room. He went to the door and opened it as if he *did* live there, as if he expected the newsboy to come and collect his dollar.

It was Minot, holding a pair of large suitcases. A line of perspiration had broken out across his brow, but otherwise he seemed as cool as before. Once more Malone was struck by his gray hair, how difficult it was to be sure of his age. He stepped past Malone and, without speaking, crossed through the hallway and began to mount the stairs. The suitcases were heavy.

Malone realized that he had yet to see the upstairs of the house. Anna had not shown herself, and so he followed Minot.

They came to a bright bedroom, the room with French doors facing the front of the house. The curtains were drawn but translucent. Minot had put both suitcases on the bed, a double bed covered in white. He snapped one open and began to unfold the clothing it held, a man's clothing. He handled the suits and shirts with the efficiency of a valet, hanging the trousers and jackets in an adjacent closet, seams perfectly matched, stacking the laundered shirts on the topmost shelf of the same closet.

That afternoon Malone had been aware of the difference between Minot's appearance and that of the other, more flamboyant agents. But now Malone realized that that difference did not depend, as it would have in Malone's own case, on a lack of attention to his clothing, on a dull uniformity typical of most agents. Minot handled the ties and shirts with an ease that conveyed a familiarity with fine things. The clothing was, in fact, expensive-looking, tailored, not unlike what Minot himself was wearing. Minot held out a tan linen suit to Malone, as if for approval. "Forty long, am I right?"

"What?"

"Size." He opened the jacket so that Malone could read the label: Thomas Nutter, Saville Row, London. "You're a forty long, same as me. Am I right or not?" Minot grinned and Malone sensed unexpectedly, for he was always aware of the older man's rank, that Minot liked him.

"Yes," Malone said, uneasily. "Is that in my file too?"

"Size eleven shoe." He held up a pair of plain-toed brown shoes, not new ones, Malone noticed, but in perfect shape and of a quality he himself had never owned. And then he realized none of the clothing was new, exactly. But of course it wouldn't be. New clothing would be a tip-off.

"Where are my own bags?"

"You'll get your things back when this job is finished." Minot brushed the lapels of the suit as he hung it up, then glanced back at Malone. "If you still want them."

Malone bristled despite himself. "They'll still be mine."

Minot seemed not to hear Malone's statement or the edge in his voice. He removed the empty suitcase and sat on the bed. He lit a cigarette, then withdrew a large, brick-colored accordion folder from the remaining suitcase, and he held it out to Malone. "Meantime, *these* are yours. *This* is you."

Malone took the folder and untied the string. He had carried evidence in such envelopes. He quickly fingered through the papers it held, but all that registered on him in his quick perusal was that they were official-looking documents of various kinds, not in his name. There was a passport, a billfold and a calfskin ID folder, which he withdrew first because it resembled an agent's credentials case. He flipped it open with a practiced turn of his wrist and saw his own photograph on one side and the American seal—not the Bureau shield—on the other.

"You're an FSO now, Peter."

"Peter Ward" was the name under the photograph.

Malone looked quizzically at Minot.

"Foreign Service officer. You've just come back to Washington from Rome. We made your former posting Rome since you've been there. To the extent that we can we want to use what's true about you."

" 'The available truth,' the Jesuits call it."

"Forget the Jesuits, my son," Minot said wryly. He indicated the accordion folder. "Your birth certificate says you were born in Chicago, but you didn't grow up on the South Side. You grew up in Oak Park. Your parents are both lawyers. Your diploma says Northwestern on it, not Loyola. You're not a Catholic anymore." Minot grimaced, a counterfeit disapproval. "They don't hire Catholics over at State." He paused. "That won't be a problem for you, will it?"

Malone was surprised at Minot's solicitousness, and at first he felt embarrassed to indicate that he wasn't the kind of Catholic whose religion factored. *Lukewarm* was the Jesuit word for what he had become. He shook his head.

"Your army discharge papers say you served in Italy, but you were a captain, not a sergeant. You were a ninety-day wonder at Northwestern, an accelerated graduation for OCS. You won the Silver Star at Anzio." Minot stopped and looked away, on the edge of an emotion Malone could not fathom. Then he asked, "You speak Italian?"

"No."

"You're going to have to learn some. You won't have to worry that nobody in Foggy Bottom will have heard of you. You were hired out of the army in 'forty-six and have been attached to the embassy in Rome since, but working mostly with refugees and DPs in the country-side. You're rotating back to Washington now to regularize your standing in the service. It's not unusual. Your ambassador recommends you very highly, and he wants you in Protocol so you can learn the moves, smooth those edges of yours. Your patron's name is Leland, Claude Leland. People will ask you about him. He's a crony of Truman's, and the Foreign Service types disdain him. They will rely on you to confirm their prejudice, but, of course, without being disloyal to the man who got you your plum assignment to Protocol. That wasn't too hard, however, since you are something of a crony yourself because Leland went to Yale Law School with your father. At State they understand about these things. What

they want are competence *and* connections. You were set
to go to Yale Law yourself but you decided to serve your
country instead. We have to give you some hook into the
Ivy League, but we can't claim too much because every
third FSO went to Yale and they'd all want to know if
you were Skull and Bones."

"What's that?"

"Doesn't matter, since you didn't go there."

"Hiss was Ivy League," Malone said, "and look where it
got him."

"It got him a hung jury, and don't forget it. The
Foreign Service is every bit as much a priesthood as the
Bureau is, but the vestments are different and so are the
rubrics. No saddle shoes in Foggy Bottom, my friend."

So Minot had noticed Brigham's black-and-white wing
tips too. "I don't wear saddle shoes."

"Glad to hear it. That's a start. The Robert Hall look
that our friends favor is not what we're after. You are a
guy who wants to be an ambassador. Nothing personal,
but, if that's your ambition, you need a new look, Peter."

Peter? Malone had to deflect a stab of irritation. But
beneath that was a layer of anxiety with which he had no
prior acquaintance. How was he ever going to pull this
off? He said, "You know, it was law school I went to,
not acting school."

Minot waved his hand dismissively. "This is the easy
part. This is the *fun* part." He fingered a deck of silk ties.
"We change who you are on the outside, the inside
changes too. You'll see. We give you a new history. We
give you a new"—he pinched his fingers in front of his
chin self-mockingly—"*je ne sais quoi*." He picked up the
ties and began to hang them on pegs in the closet.

Minot's appreciation of sartorial subtleties, surprising
in an FBI agent, triggered Malone's curiosity, particularly about Minot's own relationship to the distinctions
he was drawing. "So my new suits," Malone said, "they
belong to you?"

Minot stared at him as if to say, You have a nerve to
ask me that. But instead he shook his head. "They come
from my brother. He was a forty long too."

Minot's statement shocked Malone because of the world

to which it referred, Minot's personal world. A brother of whom he spoke in the past tense? A brother whose personal belongings he had now pressed into Bureau service? A brother who had money to spend on British suits? But Minot had money too. Wasn't that one of the differences? Wasn't social class what Minot was talking about?

But it was the personal quality of Minot's statement—the history it implied—that moved Malone. In Anna's company he had felt the sway of the utterly impersonal, and he had begun to adjust to it. Now he reached into the closet to finger the clothing. Minot's brother's clothing. Malone pictured a mustachioed tailor, tape around his neck, brushing the material across Minot's brother's shoulders, then marking it with his disk of chalk. You'll like this one, sir. We'll make it perfect, sir. Malone had seen such tailors at work, but only in movies. They looked like Adolphe Menjou. Minot's brother would have looked like Robert Taylor. Like an ambassador.

"He went to Yale?"

"Harvard."

What had Hoover said about Harvard? A brusque dismissal, but not an eccentric inanity, as Malone had thought—those pinko assholes—but a calculated reminder to Minot that in some place they were enemies. Minot, Malone grasped, had gone to Harvard too, and that recognition brought its own question. Why was he in the FBI? Harvard guys were in Wall Street law firms. But Minot's brother was the issue, and Malone forced his mind back to him. "And he's an FSO?"

Minot shook his head. "He's dead, in point of fact."

"The war?"

Minot considered his answer. "You might say that."

I might? Malone was thrown. He fingered the material of one of the suits; he didn't know serge from sharkskin. "And you kept his things?"

Minot shook his head. "My mother kept them. It comes as a surprise to me to find a use for them."

Malone felt embarrassed for Minot, as if he'd been indiscreet. His mother? Malone sensed a hint of what went on in Minot's family. One brother dead in the war,

even if mysteriously, a wartime martyr—the other a glorified flatfoot who spent the war, as real soldiers would
say, ferreting out fans of the Katzenjammer Kids. Minot,
in his pointedly understated way, had seemed so competent to Malone, so skilled, so profoundly serious. But
now Malone saw a flash of him as a man who'd come in
second. Had he in fact failed at Harvard? Had the OSS
rejected him? Or the Foreign Service? Had the mustachioed tailor sent an assistant to Minot's fittings? Malone
recognized it as a measure of his own small world that he
found it hard to think of the FBI as anything but the
pinnacle of a man's ambition. But even he had instinctively wondered that a Harvard man should join the Bureau. The air that clung to Minot—Malone saw it
now—was one of disappointment. That was what Minot's
rheumy eyes had hinted at, their pearly sadness. That
implication of booze.

"What was his name?"

Minot looked away. "It was Peter. I hope you don't
mind."

Malone hesitated; it wouldn't have occurred to him to
mind, but he felt suddenly drawn further into the mystery
of Minot's life than he wanted to go. "No, sir, it's okay,"
he said, opening the ID again, expecting, despite what he
knew, to see another man's photo there. Robert Taylor's. But the face he saw—the exact photo familiar from
his Bureau credentials—was his own.

Yet he saw it as his father's face, only now his memory
was of his father as another disappointed man, another—
and this was what made Minot so familiar—drinker.

He heard in the back of his brain that smoker's cough
with which his father announced himself home, and he
saw his mother cocking an ear from the kitchen table to
hear if he put down his tools with a careless thud. If he
was drunk, Malone's mother would purse her lips for the
great silence. No matter how he abused her—"You've
the face of a wooden owl, woman! Answer me!"—she
would say nothing. Even when he hit her no sound would
escape her lips. Her silence was more brutal than his fists
were. Malone's brothers would bury their noses, for once,
in their arithmetic and his sisters would huddle in the

same bed, crying. Malone, for his part, would watch his father from the corner of the kitchen, as if his stare could stop him. This was the other image of his father, in addition to the genius door opener, that was fixed in Malone's mind: the cap jutting, the jaw slack, one strap of his overalls unhooked, a stockyarder, blunt but unsteady on his feet before his efficiently mute wife. That image had laid bare the truth of what they were and Malone knew that that was why he'd joined the Bureau. The FBI was his way of fulfilling the first promise to himself he ever made—he made it repeatedly, throughout his adolescence—that he was leaving and never coming back.

Malone felt revisited by that emotion suddenly, and he realized that his first wish hadn't been merely to leave, but to become someone else entirely, with another history, another father, another mother, another past, another future and another name.

Peter Ward.

That urge had laid him open to an anguish he still felt. It had taken him out of the shadow of Comiskey Park, away from the stinking stockyards, into a world in which his drunken father was famous not for his cruelty—this was a transformation of memory itself, for Malone had worked it—but only for having given his son a special way with locks, which in turn—who could have imagined it?—had brought him here. Well, hell, he thought, maybe I *can* do this. Maybe I can do it all.

He dropped the ID back into the accordion envelope and took the passport out, the black passport of an American diplomat. He opened it to see himself yet again, but this time there was no surprise. "Peter Michael Ward," he read. "Date of birth: April 24, 1920. Place of birth: Chicago, Illinois. Nationality: USA."

"So pick out some duds." Minot stood up. "I'll see you downstairs." He walked out of the bedroom. At the door he looked back and said, "You're going to celebrate your new life tonight in the best restaurant in Washington."

When Malone appeared, pausing in the arched threshold of the living room, he was wearing a perfectly creased,

tan linen suit, cut slimly on the British style, a crisp blue
shirt and a yellow-and-blue rep tie. He had shaved again,
more carefully, and his hair was slicked back from the
shower. He stood with his hand in his trousers pocket,
knowing what a pose it was, but he couldn't help it. It
was all a pose, at that point.

He had expected that the woman would be gone, but
she was sitting next to Minot on the beige sofa. The room
had been transformed. The boxes had disappeared, the
chairs and couches had been centered on the carpet,
around the table, and the wall of shelves looked as if its
books had always been there.

The woman too was different. Her hair fell freely now,
past her shoulders, a lustrous black downpour that partly
hid the edges of her face. Where had she bathed to look
so fresh? Where had she changed her clothes? Clearly
there were other parts of the house Malone had yet to
see. Despite his confusion, Malone looked at her openly.
She was wearing a sleek black dress and black high-
heeled shoes. With regal nonchalance, she held a martini
glass in one hand and a cigarette in the other, and she
was looking at him as if she'd never seen him before.
Malone felt ridiculous for having thought of her as someone's secretary, as his.

Minot stood to welcome Malone. With a drink in his
hand he seemed positively debonair, but Malone was
immediately aware of the importance that drink had to
Minot.

"Peter Michael Ward!" Minot exclaimed. "Our own
young lord." He swept an arm toward the woman as if to
say, Allow me.

But her resolute decorum seemed to undercut Minot's
expansiveness. Her silence, combined with that steady
gaze locked on Malone, unflinching but revealing nothing, reminded him of his mother, the face of a wooden
owl. Answer, woman!

The gravity of Anna's eyes, their weight and their pull,
was what Malone had experienced of her as she approached him that afternoon in Dupont Circle. Now he
slipped out from under them, feeling as if he were defy-
ing a law of nature to look away, as he walked with

apparent casualness into the room. What he really wanted out from under was the memory of his mother.

"May I have a smoke, sir?" he said to Minot, reaching for the pack on the table. He had almost never smoked, not even in the army. What he really wanted out from under was the weight of his own history.

When he bent smoothly to Minot's cupped hands for a light, he was Robert Taylor again. Acting school or not, he knew how this was done. He sat in the wing chair opposite the sofa. Minot left the room.

Malone regarded it as Peter Ward's first triumph that in the silence of Minot's absence, the silence, that is, of the woman's presence, he found it possible to smoke that cigarette and say nothing. They sank into themselves.

Minot returned, chattering like a host. "Here you are, Malone, er ah, Peter. It's your highball," he said as if he knew what Malone preferred.

A dark drink, stiff as a snare, brimming. Malone accepted it carefully. Minot had pumped up his own drink too, making it the color of tea. He raised it. "Well, what the hell, here's to Firebird!" He grinned, then went on like an impresario. "The ballet that made Stravinsky famous. The Firebird is the brilliantly colored symbol of everything that is good. It competes with the green-taloned ogre for the soul of the young prince. When the Firebird breaks the evil spell, the prince is released and runs to his betrothed."

Minot bowed toward Anna, then took a generous swallow of his drink. Malone hadn't touched his own drink. He asked coldly, "What are you talking about?"

"Firebird, the classic Russian fairy tale that gave Stravinsky his motif. The prince and the princess and all that rot." Minot smiled with fresh affection, but only for a moment. He cut his mood abruptly. Even his voice changed. This might have looked like the Happy Hour, but it was still a briefing session. "I told you before that there would be a woman involved in the operation, Peter."

"I wasn't Peter then."

"I noticed at the time that, whoever you were, you didn't ask me why there would be a woman or who she would be. Or what she'd be to you. Perhaps you'd like to ask me now."

Malone channeled his insecurity into the awkward stubbing out of his half-smoked cigarette. He remembered Minot's reference, but in that disorienting interrogation room—him a perpetrator, a "perp"—it hadn't really registered. And Minot had not mentioned a woman in laying out the plan for J. Edgar Hoover. The director's attitude was well known, and in the field Bureau policy against "females" participating in anything beyond the clerical was enshrined in the snide dismissal of policewomen as "Dickless Tracys." But it was clear now that Minot's attitudes did not coincide in all things with Hoover's.

Malone said, "I think it would be helpful if you told me exactly what you have in mind."

Minot nodded, lit a cigarette and waved the smoke away from his face. "November seven," he said, "is the day we're aiming for." Suddenly he was all business, decisive and clear in his speech, no cocktail server now. Malone was beginning to understand that Minot was a set of ruses. "It is the anniversary of the Bolshevik Revolution, the *October* Revolution, as we call it because we can't even agree with the Reds on the month their movement started. They date the event according to the old Slavic calendar as opposed to the Gregorian, and that of course pretty much sums it up between us ever since." He leaned forward to put his drink down on the table, as if he'd read Malone's mind about the color of his glass. Sobriety, we need sobriety. "The Russian embassy is like the Kremlin, a walled city, unto itself. Nobody gets inside most of the year, not even diplomats from the satellite nations. The Russian staffers stay to themselves, they're almost totally off the embassy social circuit, as if Massachusetts Avenue is the center of cosmopolitan deviationism. But there is one exception: the gala, old-fashioned ball in honor of the revolution. And ironically it is the most lavish affair on the diplomatic calendar. The Romanovs would feel at home at it. Everybody dresses to the nines. They dance to Viennese waltzes in one of the most elegant ballrooms in the city. They say the walls are mirrored and gilded like Versailles. The food—ten kinds of caviar to start—and the liquor—vodka, of course, but also some of the best wines and champagnes in the world imported from Soviet Georgia—would put to shame anything served anywhere in Washington, not to mention what it would do to the average Russian village—keep it going for a year, probably, or, when the peasants saw how the bosses lived, start another revolution. Talk about cosmopolitan deviationism."

Minot leaned forward for his drink, an interval during which Malone glanced at the woman. From her place next to him on the sofa she was watching Minot evenly; she was immobile like a flat, dark sea. At Dupont Circle, walking toward Malone, she had seemed like a white statue come alive. Her moving body, legs and thighs, breasts and arms, that voluptuous, yet not vulgar, display of silk, moving like wind. But now she seemed made of marble again.

"November seven"—Minot leaned back against the sofa, cupping his drink in both hands—"which in our dispensation this year happens to be election day. . . ." His eyebrows shot up. " . . .our semi*annual* revolution."

"That's what? Seven weeks from now?"

"Six weeks and two days, actually, in which to prepare you, my bull Cinderella, for the ball."

Malone resented the obvious implication, that he had to be retooled to pass as Peter Ward, but he knew it was true. If he was going to pull this off he was going to have to thicken his skin. Minot, at least, had meant no insult. Malone nodded. "So I report to State, join the Protocol Office, in the course of my duties get invited to the Russian embassy. By that time I've mastered Russian locks, have memorized the embassy layout, can make my way from the shindig to a dead space in which to wait until the middle of the night when I emerge, find the code room, know what cipher logs to look for, how to copy them and how—despite the fact it's probably impossible—to get out without their knowing I was ever there."

"More or less, yes, that's it."

Malone flicked his head toward Anna. "Then what's she doing here?"

"For starters, she's how you get invited. I told you. Because of its anomalous—that is, capitalistic—extravagance, this ball is the diplomatic event of the year. Everyone loves the irony of it, not to mention the caviar. Now, what does 'everyone' mean?" Minot began unfurling the fingers of his free hand to keep track. "There are a hundred and fifteen full-fledged ambassadors in this town, their first secretaries, ministers, attachés, trade reps, chancellors, chargés and all their deputies; three thousand accredited foreign diplomats in total, and another three thousand at the UN a few hours north. And they all want to be there toasting Lenin's beard with that vintage vodka. But keep adding: one president of the United States, one vice-president, ninety-six senators, four hundred and seventy-seven congressmen, nine Supreme Court justices, cabinet secretaries, undersecretaries, agency directors, division heads, lobbyists, generals, admirals, several hundred senior Foggy Bottom types and—underscore 'and'—their wives. Not even Russians do Viennese waltzes without their wives. Well, hell, Peter, you're a Protocol officer. Figure it out. How far down on that list do you think you come?"

Malone shook his head. "In Mr. Hoover's office you made it sound like a phone call to Acheson would—"

"Just because Hoover thinks the seas part at his bidding doesn't mean they do. It isn't my job to tell him he's not Jehovah. He gets us a foot inside the door. We have to push it open ourselves. So answer me: how far down on the list do you think a greenhorn FSO, just back from Italy, with no D.C. contacts of his own, comes?"

"How many guests do they invite?"

"Last year twelve hundred and sixty-eight."

"Half of them wives?"

"That's right. The only people from the Protocol Office, from *your* office, were the chief and his deputy. You don't rate high enough even to be rejected. Cracking the code room could be a snap, Peter, compared to cracking that guest list."

Malone said nothing. Minot's persistent use of the name Peter made everything else seem even more unreal. He could purr along inside, his mind humming with questions and answers, but only if the pretense held that Minot's plan was not totally nuts. When the pretense broke, as now, his mind simply went blank and the sinking feeling that *he* was nuts began rising again from his stomach to his throat.

In the silence, the fact weighed on the room itself that the woman in question was sitting through all of this, stark, indifferent, sipping her gin, smoking her cigarettes, watching like Russia. The September day had turned into evening while she sat watching.

Minot smiled gently at her. An expression that said "dear love" softened his face. He spoke with a fresh sobriety, as if the clean sight of her, now that he was looking, made it unthinkable that he had had two drinks already. "We are lucky to have Anna Melnik working with us." Minot's eyes were on her, but he was speaking still to Malone. "Shall I tell you about her? No. I should let her do that." Minot watched her as if he could read nuances of feeling in her face. She lifted her eyes to meet his. No, she was not made of marble. "But perhaps I can tell you about her father. May I?" He waited. When Anna did not respond, either to grant or deny permission, he went on. "Her father was a priest of the Ukrainian Orthodox Church, which was made an arm of the Soviet state in 1931. He was the rector of the great seminary in Poltava. He saw his young priests recruited to serve as spies for the Russian Secret Police. If they refused they were murdered. Rather than train spies for the NKVD, he closed his seminary down. When the authorities ordered him to open it again, he set fire to the great church and monastery and watched it burn to the ground. Though he thought it was a sin to do so he sold the precious icons, chalices and monstrances on the black market and used the money to buy passage out of the Soviet Union for his wife and daughter. They escaped but he remained behind. The authorities of course put him to death—"

Anna Melnik abruptly looked away. Malone could not see her face but he knew it would be, to him at least, as impenetrable as the black veil of her hair.

"His priests refused after that to have anything to do

with the police. As a result the Ukrainian Church was made illegal. That was in 1933. Its last parish was extinguished in 1936. But even now, in Kiev, Kharkov, Odessa and everywhere in the countryside, there are secret shrines, underground churches, in which candles are lit before his picture. In her home country Anna's father is revered as a saint."

Malone was moved by the story, of course. What was the story of his own father compared with it? But he heard it as a type of Catholic hagiography—martyrology—like the gruesome tales the nuns had told him: Saint Sebastian pierced, like a pincushion, with Roman arrows; Saint Damian among the lepers, touching their rotten flesh with his lips. He stared at the beautiful woman in black silk, trying to grasp that such things had to do with her. He focused on the way pleats came to subtle points below her bodice. The points were highlighted with tiny flecks of gold thread. Finally, wishing she would face him, he said to her quietly, "You told me French. You didn't tell me you were Russian."

She turned to him sharply, "I am not Russian. I am Ukrainian."

"Still, you told me you were from France, in response to my direct question."

Minot interrupted. "She is from France the way Peter Ward is from Oak Park. She is from Strasbourg, the capital of Alsace, a city of blurred accents, half French, half German, reflecting the way it has changed hands again and again. Now, of course, it is fiercely French, but the ambiguity remains. An ambiguous place spawns an ambiguous person. The truth between you is full of such mysteries."

Anna faced Minot. "You should not have told him of my father. That does not help him."

Minot stared at his glass. A mistake? He said, "I want you both to understand what you are doing and why. You must trust each other. Your lives depend on it."

"Then explain it to me," Malone said with a fresh authority. When it came time to go operational he would insist on knowing everything or he would pull out, that much was clear. The question now, though, was had they gone operational already?

"Anna will accompany you to various diplomatic functions over the next six and a half weeks. One of them will be a dinner party in the Georgetown home of a British attaché. He will arrange it so that Anna's dinner partner will be one Vladimir Tumark, a Soviet undersecretary. Comrade Tumark has, shall we say, a certain predilection. He will be susceptible to Anna's many charms and he will see to it that she—and therefore you—are invited to the Russian fete. To the consternation of your own office, once the Soviets put you on their list, it will be a matter of strict protocol that you must attend."

"She's coming with me into the embassy?"

Minot nodded. "Every man in attendance will be accompanied. The waltzes, remember."

"But, Christ, I can't look out for her while I—"

Minot raised his hand, silencing Malone. "Don't draw conclusions now about November seven. Everything in its good time, Peter."

"But Mr. Hoover said I would be alone. That seemed essential." Malone fell back on the one thing in all of this that he could trust—Hoover was hovering above them like the Holy Ghost.

"You will be the only FBI agent. But there will be others helping you inside the embassy. Not only Anna. You simply cannot accomplish our purpose without help. Even with it—" He checked himself and shrugged. "Hoover, of course, thinks we agents can do anything. He forgets that we are not all like him or Tolson. Hoover would never approve the details of our plan, because they depend on the help of others, including this woman. But neither would Hoover ever ask to be briefed in this much detail. His method is to embrace ends while keeping his distance from the means." Minot paused, as if to give Malone the chance to rebut him. Malone felt like warning Minot: Don't undercut my faith in the one person I believe. But Hoover didn't need a defense from him. He said nothing.

Minot continued. "His method works for us. As far as our esteemed director is concerned, Anna Melnik is our

Russian translator, safe in the cubicles of our special office in a converted garage on Capitol Hill." Minot's eyes drifted slowly to the woman at his side. She was staring at her gin. "Anna has worked for us in that capacity before, and so has her mother. A translator for us. But for you she is more."

Malone looked at her, and as he did she raised her eyes to meet his. He understood now that they were Slavic eyes. "I am your wife," she said.

4

"The daughter of a priest. I confess, it seems strange to me."

"Strange?" She pulled back to look at him, her white-gloved arm upon his shoulder. They were dancing on the open-air terrace at the Shoreham. Rock Creek Park loomed up from behind the orchestra like a stage-set silhouette of trees. The evening was warm, the stars were enormous overhead, the music was lilting and soft. The trumpet player made his instrument sound like a muted, distant bird in mourning. Others in the terrace restaurant must have thought them the best-looking couple there.

But Malone was acutely conscious that they were not what they seemed. "Foreign," he said and he shrugged. Perhaps he had offended her. He hadn't meant to. "Exotic," he said, and he smiled, hoping she would feel flattered. "Priests don't have daughters where I come from." Then he pressed the small of her back to prepare her for a punch line. "Only sons."

"Like God," she said, but soberly, with an edge of bitterness that deflated Malone, not for the first time that night. He was not capable of softening her. If she was a rigid, unyielding woman, this was not going to work. But was this another test? Was he supposed to know how to open the lock to a woman's heart? Beth Fraser could have told them how little he knew of *those* secrets.

The thought of Beth stung him, and for a moment he closed his eyes against the sadness he felt.

75

Just then a lean gray-haired man twirled past with a chiffon-bedecked girl in his arms, dancing much too fast for the music. But they were a couple, clearly, who did everything too fast. The man gave Anna a quick once-over, then winked at Malone.

Malone turned away, steering Anna clumsily, and feeling completely out of place. He was no dancer. He had no experience of holding a woman's gloved hand as he was doing. Kid gloves had not been a feature of Beth's wardrobe. When Anna Melnik had excused herself to get ready, leaving Minot and Malone in the living room, he was not prepared for it when she returned with both her arms sheathed past the elbows in white. He had realized only then that the simple black dress she was wearing was in fact an evening dress, and that altogether, with her hair loose to her shoulders, her face and lips glowing with subtly applied makeup, the shapeliness of her legs and ankles heightened by her shoes, the impression she made had gone from detached simplicity to formal, studied elegance. He began to think he'd made a large mistake about her, taking as tentative shyness what in fact was the reserved self-possession of a worldly woman. And then he had recognized her for what Minot really intended she should be over these weeks—his personal tutor in a crash course preparing him to become another man entirely.

"If your function is to make me feel at home as Peter Michael Ward FSO, you're off to a bad start," he said. "Unless the idea is to portray a couple whose marriage has already soured. If that's it, we're doing fine."

The music slowed to a stop as the orchestra finished its rendition of "Some Enchanted Evening." The dancers moved in a wave back toward the tables, not dancers anymore but shuffling lemmings. Malone and Anna stood opposite each other for a moment longer than was appropriate, and they realized at the same instant that they were alone in the middle of the polished terrazzo floor. The band members, on break, were lighting up and moving off.

Anna looked directly into Malone's eyes and said without a hint of the defensiveness he expected, but also, still, without a hint of warmth, "Perhaps we should begin again."

Instead of responding, Malone took her elbow and turned to lead her back to their table. Anna slipped her gloved hand inside his arm and followed him through the maze of tables.

The remains of their dinner had been cleared away and coffee cups set. No sooner had they taken their chairs than the waiter appeared to pour coffee for each of them. Anna took a slim, silver cigarette case from her clutch. She put a cigarette between her lips and Malone reached across the table with a match.

As she exhaled she said, "You smoked earlier but only once and not since. Do you smoke or not?"

"No."

"No bad habits?"

"Wild women," he said. He pulled the cuff of his shirt out from the sleeve of his coat. He noticed the stranger's cuff links, gold squares, and he felt a rush of guilt, as if he'd stolen them. As he watched the dark woman opposite ashing her cigarette—a stranger's woman—it struck him that guilt was the appropriate emotion. He looked at the ring finger on her left hand and was sure he saw under the glove the lump of her wedding ring and diamond. He had noticed the rings on the street that afternoon, but they had meant something entirely different then. "Are you married in fact?" he asked suddenly, and before she answered he decided that was it, the source of her reserve.

But she shook her head. "And neither are you. I would not have agreed to do this if you were."

"Why? Since it's only playacting."

"Because it would still involve deceiving your wife; or do you think you would have been permitted to tell her exactly what we are doing?"

"No, I suppose not." Malone absently fished a cigarette out of her case, thinking, are these scruples? He was surprised by an affirmation of traditional morality from a woman who seemed the farthest thing from a midwestern virgin. It was a familiar morality. It was his.

He had begun tapping the cigarette end over end.

Anna lifted her cigarette toward him, offering its cinder,
a natural, unconsidered courtesy. Yet, for Malone, the
gesture felt charged, as if her emphatic propriety was a
façade. To him she was a temptress, suddenly, and his
impulse was to flee. Instead he resolved to be as good a
fake as she was. He bent to take his light. The smoke
seemed as harsh in his throat as it had before, but he did
not cough. Now neither remarked on his smoking. They
sipped their coffee. And he admitted to himself that he
knew nothing—temptress? virgin?—about her.

"You're a translator?"

She nodded. "European languages, but also Russian,
Ukrainian and Slavic."

"For the Bureau?"

She shook her head. "For Mr. Minot." Then she said,
in a different tone, "I have worked most recently for the
Council of Europe in Strasbourg."

Malone nodded once. This was her cover story. But
then he wondered—was it also true?

He said jauntily, "Ah Strasbourg, I remember it well!"
Malone thumbed an imaginary vest. "It's where we met.
I attended a conference on displaced persons, represent-
ing my ambassador, and you were assigned to my group.
We were smitten at once."

"Yes." Anna did not look at him. She refused his
invitation to treat their story lightly. A silence fell between them.

Finally he broke it. "Did you learn so many languages
by—"

"I was ten years old when we left Poltava. We lived in
Vienna, speaking German, then Strasbourg, speaking
French."

"You mean Strasbourg is the truth?"

"It was," she said quietly. "Finally, with the war chasing us, we came to New York. We found a home among
the émigrés. My mother married again. My skill by then,
my only skill, was languages. I enrolled at Columbia."

"And you came to work for Minot?"

She shrugged. "He needed a certain colloquial German—"

"For Amagansett?"

Anna did not react, as if he'd asked her to reveal a national secret.

"And then?" It wasn't national secrets he wanted, but personal ones.

"When the war ended I resolved to have nothing more to do with"—she paused, how to refer to it?—"such things. I wanted to help the people understand each other. Strasbourg is a place in between the enemies. That is why it feels like home to me. When the Council of Europe began, I went there."

Malone realized he had no way of knowing where her truth began and where it ended. He had no way of knowing if the very notion of truth applied. He said, "Minot seemed to have such feeling for you. It surprised me."

"The feeling, I think, is for my mother." Anna looked away abruptly as if she'd been indiscreet. "It was my mother who worked for him at Amagansett. They became friends. It was a difficult time for her."

Malone recognized this for the set of revelations it was. Amagansett, yes: the national secret. Her mother's suffering and her own: the personal. He felt himself drawn to her, really drawn, for the first time. "Your stepfather?" he asked quietly.

Anna did not answer at first. She rolled the tip of her cigarette in the ashtray. Finally she said, "My stepfather had killed himself. He was a wealthy man. There was a scandal. He had come from Kiev at the revolution. My mother was from Kiev. He was proud of the success he had in this country. But he had cheated people for his money and he was exposed. The disgrace. . . ." She shook her head. Now she snuffed her cigarette, then raised her cup, sipping.

He had forgotten the coffee. He put his own to his lips cautiously, but it had grown cold. When he'd lowered the cup, he said, "It must have been difficult for you."

"Not for me. My stepfather paid for my schools and for my traveling, but he could not tolerate me to be near. He could not share my mother even with me. And she had her reasons for accepting him that way." That stopped her for a moment, long enough for Malone to realize that he'd have welcomed such an open rupture with his own parents. Instead, the estrangement he felt had been his absolute secret.

Anna went on. "When the truth was revealed about him I was not surprised, and I was not unhappy, except for my mother. When he killed himself I was relieved because I thought she would be free. But I did not take into account that she loved him."

"And Minot?"

"That next year he came. He was always bringing gifts, simple things, baskets of fruit, as if we were hungry peasants. But the fruits were always shiny and ripe. My mother began to look forward to his visits. She spoke endlessly to him of those years in Poltava. She needed, perhaps because of what happened to my stepfather, to remember my father as a saint. They were stories Mr. Minot loved hearing. He is interested in Russia." She smiled. "He is a student of Russia."

"Was he using your mother to keep tabs on the New York émigrés?"

Anna was shocked by his question and her face showed it. Malone saw that the thought—his first—had never occurred to her. She seemed vulnerable all at once, for the first time, and he realized that from her point of view she had exposed quite a lot to him. He wanted her to know that he would be careful of what she gave him. Minot, he sensed now, was careful like that, which was why, apparently, she trusted him.

"Minot looked at you like a father looks at his daughter."

Anna turned her face away. "He is not a father to me."

"But when he asked you to come to Washington, when, last week?"

"Three days ago."

"You came."

"Not because he is my father. I have no father." A small cry escaped with her words, a hint of pain or anger, some emotion which told Malone that here was a way inside her wall. There was no question whether to go in.

"Do you remember your father? You say you were ten? Can you tell me about him?"

Without hesitating she replied, "You cannot imagine how different things were there, how long ago it was. His distance from me is what I remember, his long beard and the vestments, the hat that made him seem a giant. I always picture him standing before the sanctuary holding the great thurible, obscuring himself in the smoke of the incense, like the Holy Ghost. There is a point in the Ukrainian mass where the priest goes into the holy of holies alone, behind the great gilded screen on which the ancient icons hang. I remember feeling always that he was leaving us, we who loved him, leaving us for God. His loneliness among human beings is what I remember."

But Malone's thought was, Your loneliness.

Silence fell between them again. The waiter poured fresh coffee into their cups. Then Anna said, "I have always felt he could stay behind in Poltava and sacrifice himself to the Soviets because he did not love us."

Malone was watching her eyes, expecting them to tear, but they did not. When he saw that in fact she had closed her eyes, he casually touched the crook of his finger to one of his own, although it was dry. What devastation, to sit in the cold certitude that your father did not love you. Malone wished for a way to say how close he felt to her. How close that devastation made them. But, literally, it was unspeakable.

She sighed, staring out at the dance floor now, where the orchestra was reassembling. "So you see, my point of view on my beatified father is not precisely what Mr. Minot's is."

"Just as well," Malone said lightly, for her sake as well as his own. "Minot brought you on the case to initiate me, but not into holiness."

Color came into her face, light from her skin. "What do you mean?" she asked shyly.

"Teach me what fork to use and how to fold the handkerchief into my suitcoat pocket. You are a Viennese dance instructor of my very own." Malone was speaking breezily, but this was an admission, a point of *his* vulnerability. He added seriously, "I apologize for resisting your assignment earlier. I see that I'm going to need you."

She gave her head a shake. "You dance well."

"But I've never waltzed."

"I can teach you waltzing."

"Who taught you?"

"In Strasbourg, where all the diplomats of the new Europe have collected, everyone waltzes. It is the most natural dance of all. Only in two countries could waltzing seem exotic. Russia and—"

"America," Malone said, nodding, and she laughed. He waited until her face had fallen back into what he'd come to regard as its normal impassivity. "In asking about your dance partners, I guess really I was asking"—he hesitated, then went on—"about the men in your life. What men taught you to dance?" It was unlike him to be so direct, especially with a woman. He watched her carefully, to see if he'd offended her.

"I know that is what you were asking." She stared at him. "And I was not answering."

Did her sensitivity mean that she'd had men or hadn't? Malone cursed himself for a mulish inability to read her after all. Compared with this woman Beth Fraser was sunshine on a meadow, and once more he missed her. He veered from the rebuke, adopting an official tone to ask, "How long have we been married?"

Her eyebrow went up: A quiz? All right. "Eleven months. Our anniversary is October twenty-fifth."

"Do we plan to have children?" No offense, Madonna. Just asking.

"Yes. Now that we are in America we hope to have a child next year." She eyed him evenly, not thrown in the least by his interrogation.

The cold detachment with which she answered his questions gave him an eerie feel for the unreality of their situation. The warmth that he'd sensed between them moments before was gone. Now the image that came to mind was of a pair of shipwreck survivors in a cold, dark sea calling to one another through the night, but with information and instructions—"Top off your life vest by blowing in that tube!"—when all one really wanted was words of comfort and affection. He felt weary suddenly, unsure if he could go on. Two sleepless nights on the train had not prepared him for this. It wasn't three days ago that he'd said good-bye to Beth. He looked at his watch: midnight.

But before he could suggest they go, she said, "So as an FBI agent you can ask any question you like."

"I don't think that's true, no." He looked at her in silence for a moment. It was the sort of comment he expected from left-wing college professors when he was doing a background check on one of their colleagues. The question that always got them was the one about "sexual proclivities." He said, "In any case, we should perhaps both stop thinking of the FBI. Minot said that after tonight we must refer only to our new reality, even when we are alone. I'm in the Foreign Service now." He bowed slightly. "Protocol, don't you know."

"But Mr. Minot also said tonight was our chance to ask questions of each other. You have told me nothing. Tell me one thing at least."

"About the Bureau?"

"Yes."

Malone thought for a moment before he answered. The FBI was the central and most important fact of his life. He had preferred it, hadn't he, to a lawyer's life in Kansas with Beth. Yet he knew better than to think that he could explain the Bureau's importance in his life glibly. "Ordinarily, the main thing they teach us is disgust for the way in which men can seem to be one thing, yet in fact be something else entirely." Malone paused. The hint of cynicism in his own voice startled him; he didn't want her to think that he was critical of the Bureau, because he wasn't. "There's a code of behavior that calls for a kind of boisterous irreverence, as if we're all afraid of being taken as goody two-shoes. You know that expression? Actually that's probably exactly who we were as kids. It's who I was. I don't think I broke a rule until I got in the army and even then the rule I broke was the one against using liquid shoe polish instead of paste. Shinola"—he grinned—"was strictly forbidden, a very big item on the GI black market." For a moment Malone pushed his coffee spoon in a semicircle, remembering the time an NCO mashed his heel down onto his shoe; when the caked polish turned to dust instead of cracking into splinters, Malone's infraction was exposed for all to see. But he had veered from what he wanted to tell her, what he wanted very much for her to understand. Why was it so difficult to talk of this? He shrugged. "Underneath it, the men I've met in the FBI are, well, virtuous. *Virtue* has the same Latin root as *virile*, did you know that? In the army, you tend to feel ashamed of virtue"—he almost said, Like virginity, as if *that* were what he was talking about—"but in the Bureau, well, we don't. And the central idea is this one of being what you seem to be; integrity between appearance and reality. *Integrity*; it's one of the three words they brand on your forehead." He smiled vaguely, watching the handle of his spoon seesaw as he levered it up and down. Then he added quietly. "Not on this job, however."

She might have asked him to elaborate on that and listened while he explored a conflict he was at that point only just beginning to feel. It might have changed the course of these events had he understood sooner what this requirement of circumstance would do to him. But instead she asked, "What are the other two?"

"What?"

"The other two words on your forehead." Anna wrinkled her nose at him, so uncharacteristically that he felt himself freshly charmed. Then he realized she was feigning a squint. "I can't read them from here."

"*Fidelity* and *bravery*." He smiled self-mockingly. "The manly virtues. And what is amazing about us FBI agents is we believe it. Fidelity, Bravery, Integrity. Department of Justice. Federal Bureau of Investigation." As Malone recited the familiar words, the words on the seal, in fact, that hung on the wall behind every desk the Bureau owned, he was afraid he sounded pompous, like an ASAC addressing the Rotary, and so he undercut himself before she could. "I guess we've never stopped being Boy Scouts. Do you have Boy Scouts in Strasbourg?"

"Strasbourg is on the Rhine. They invented Boy Scouts on the other bank of the river." She pushed her coffee cup away. "But over there, scouts were called *Jungvolk* and grew up to be Nazis. It could happen here."

Malone shook his head. "I don't think so." Without meaning to he'd spoken dismissively, as if out of the unthinking Americanism of dull Kansans. Even before Anna reacted, he'd heard the condescension in his voice and regretted it.

Her face filled with color. "You think you are so different?"

"No. But I think Germans are. Hitler was a very special case."

"More special than Stalin?"

Malone forced a smile. "What is this, another test? You want me to rank the bogeymen of history according to degrees of evil?"

"Bogeymen?" Anna repeated the word incredulously. "Are you making light of this?"

"I'm not making light of anything." Malone spoke calmly, layering over the strange push of an anger he could not have justified. "I wish we could leave the Nazis out of this. And Uncle Joe, for that matter."

"Uncle Joe?" Anna pushed back from the table. "How can you say 'Uncle' Joe?"

"Anna, it's how we refer to him."

"But he is no 'uncle.' "

Malone shrugged. "It's an expression."

"An *American* expression." She stood up, knocking the table.

Malone cursed himself for blushing, but he knew couples at nearby tables were staring at them. They would never have believed that her display of feeling—her first, in Malone's experience—came in relation to Stalin, of all things!

Before he could react, she turned, clutching her handbag, and strode away. She crossed the terrace, into the opulent public spaces of the hotel. Malone stared after her, shocked.

He forced himself to look over at the orchestra, pointedly ignoring the adjacent onlookers. Only then did he allow the fact of the music to register, an up-tempo number he did not recognize. On the dance floor the tall, gray-haired man was jitterbugging with the girl in chiffon. When she swirled, her skirts flew, displaying her legs. The sight of that blithe couple now filled him with envy. Why couldn't he and Anna have left it at that, dancing in the dreamy glow of an evening out, crushed—not by the weight of the world's evil, but by the thought that the music might not last forever?

"The hell with that," he said. He couldn't dance that number anyway.

Rather than wait for Anna to return to the table—she *was* returning, wasn't she?—Malone flagged the waiter and paid the bill. He asked where the washrooms were and then casually strode into the hotel lobby. He would get her wrap from the checkroom and wait for her out there.

But when he had climbed the half-dozen stairs into the lobby proper he saw, across the gleaming expanse of polished marble beyond the registration desk and the scattered furniture and the graceful potted plants, the cloaked figure of Anna Melnik—she had retrieved her cape herself—just slipping into the slot of the revolving doors, to leave. The doorman tipped his hat. Immediately Malone quickened his pace, to catch her. She was leaving? What the hell was this?

But then he saw something else. Someone. A man strode out of an alcove behind the registration desk and was making for the revolving door. Even if Malone didn't recognize the man he'd have sensed his purpose. Malone knew the moves too well. Anna was being followed. The man was Kershaw.

Malone nearly yelled at him, You bastard! He nearly began to run.

As quickly as he could, he crossed the lobby and went through the door too. Once outside, along the graceful, curving entranceway, Malone did begin to run. He caught up with Kershaw at the point where the Shoreham driveway intersected the sidewalk on Connecticut Avenue. Anna was half a block ahead of them, striding purposefully toward the bridge that carried the avenue across the deep ravine of Rock Creek Park. Why was she going off like that?

But that was Malone's second question. His first was about Kershaw. He grabbed his fellow agent by the arm. "What is this, Kershaw?" Kershaw whipped around.

"You're *tailing* her?" Malone refused to lighten his grip. "Why are you tailing her? Why are you treating her like a suspect?"

Kershaw glanced past Malone, back toward the hotel, and Malone sensed someone else. "You're tailing *me?*"

Now Malone dropped Kershaw's arm. "What is this?"

Kershaw said nothing and was clearly going to say nothing. It was how agents were trained to respond if "made" and challenged by a subject. Say nothing. Offer no explanation. Do not engage. Back off. But Malone wasn't going to let Kershaw do that. "Tell me, God damn it! Why are you tailing us? Minot knows what we're doing. Minot set this up. Minot *knows* that woman. Why would Minot—?"

But then, instinctively, Malone grasped it. Not Minot. Kershaw wasn't on this because of Minot. Kershaw worked for Brigham. An image of Brigham in Hoover's office, rolling his eyes toward Tolson, a perfect expression of his disdain. Disdain for Minot. It's not me they're watching, Malone thought. And not Anna, either. It's Minot.

"Is that the plan?" Kershaw asked dryly, and he pointed toward Anna, whose figure by then had shrunk in the distance as she strode purposefully away into the darkness. "She goes home from her big date alone? Is that the idea? I thought you two were together."

"We were," Malone said, and he watched her.

Well out on the bridge, one of those high Roman aqueduct bridges, Anna stopped. She faced the stone railing, leaning on it. What Malone saw now was her face and figure in profile. She bent, touching her forehead to her hands.

"What, did you blow it with her already, Malone?"

Kershaw's snide display of satisfaction surprised Malone, and ordinarily it would have prompted him to wonder why his fellow agent had taken so quickly to disliking him, to wanting him to fail. But at that moment the field of Malone's concentration was taken up entirely by Anna Melnik.

How *had* he offended her? What *had* she been trying to tell him? And what was she feeling now? He'd been too full of his own anxiety, his own excitement and his own confusion to see how *she* might be distressed by these events. Kershaw was right. He *had* already failed her somehow, and for once Malone did not measure his lapse against what the *Bureau* expected of him. It was, for a moment, just this woman he was thinking of.

He stared out at her. A striking figure, even at that distance, even in the dark, but then he sensed, as if mystically, the power of her despair.

Despair? Nothing justified his thinking *that* of her. But still. It was as if all his perceptions of her registered now emotionally. It was as if, despite her having fled, he were physically connected to her nevertheless, as if he *knew* what she was feeling. She was bent over in the middle of a bridge, a high bridge, it seemed suddenly to Malone— why had she stopped there?—and very dangerous.

5

"Anna?"

She had not noticed his approach, and his voice startled her. She faced him, but not before he saw her shudder with surprise. And fear? She grasped instinctively at the bridge railing. Jesus Christ, he thought, is she afraid of me?

"I'm sorry," he said, meaning it. But if she'd challenged him, he wouldn't have been able to say exactly what he was sorry for. "I didn't want you to go without me."

Anna shook her head. "It is impossible. I was wrong to agree to be with you. I cannot do this."

"You mean, you can't—"

"I cannot help. I cannot help Mr. Minot."

Malone felt the power of her dejection, and all at once he understood that this was *not* his failure. Anna Melnik had her *own* issues, her own difficulties with this charade. It had been presumptuous of him—and Kershaw—to think that *he* was her problem; *he* hardly existed yet, for her. How arrogant of him to think that his arrogance could be the issue.

"That's your decision," he said. "God knows, you have a right to bail out of this thing, whatever it is. But I still want to understand better what I was missing back there. What all of this means for you."

"What is the point?" Anna's eyes flicked past Malone, back toward the Shoreham.

He turned around to look, quite deliberately and obviously. The sidewalk all along the bridge was empty. There was no sign of Kershaw. He turned back to Anna. "Look, I don't blame you if you want out. I just want you to know that I would have worked harder . . ." His voice trailed off. She was looking so intently at him that he forgot what he was saying. Her eyes probed into him, making him feel utterly exposed. He was surprised to realize how disappointed he would be if, in fact, this was the end of it with her.

After a moment he asked, "What bothered you back there?"

She shook her head and faced out over the bridge railing.

"No, tell me."

"We are so different, Peter. You are American. So *very* American. I am from another world."

"You called me Peter."

She said nothing.

"It sounded strange to me, since as you know it isn't my name. But this is the first time you've called me by any name." He smiled. "I'll take it." He was only trying to lighten their mood, to relieve her of some of that awful weight.

But Anna remained immobile, staring down at the dark ravine, in the grip of the feeling to which she had surrendered.

Still quietly, gently even, he asked, "Would it have come to seem natural, do you think? Perhaps you would have come to call me Pete. My wife would call me Pete."

In a voice he barely heard she said, "You are ignoring me."

"No. I'm trying to respect the depth of your feeling."

"By keeping your distance from it."

"No. I want to be careful with it, that's all. This is my way of respecting what you entrust to me. The question of names isn't irrelevant. Anna, for example. Should I think of that as your real name?"

She nodded. "Anna is my name." She looked up at him. "Anna *Melnik,* which was my father's name. You asked me about my father, what I remembered of him. I remember that Stalin's police murdered him. The one you call Uncle Joe. Uncle Joe murdered millions of my people."

She waited for him to react. He said nothing.

"You think I exaggerate?"

Of course he didn't, but what did "millions" mean? What could he say?

His silence seemed to prompt her, and suddenly she launched into a recitation that, when he remembered it, would seem part diatribe and part confession.

"In 1933 ten million Ukrainians—one quarter of our population and as many as the *total* killed in the First World War—were willfully starved to death by the Soviet regime because we wanted a nation of our own. Those who survived never recovered from the shame of having eaten the food that could have saved the others. To live was to be guilty. Mr. Minot spoke of my father using sacred chalices as bribes, but that was not his shame. He had a fortune in jewels and rings that he stole from the corpses entrusted to him for burial; it was *that* loot with which he bought my mother and me first our bread, then our freedom. I saw him digging up graves at night in the holy cemetery. I was innocent. It never occurred to me what he was doing until later, when my mother showed me the sack of gold rings and diamonds with which she bribed official after official as we made our way west."

Anna stopped speaking, and her eyes clouded over for a moment. Here was something that was true, but Malone wanted to shake his head and say, No, it wasn't like that. It couldn't have been. He wanted to reach across to her, to take her hand. But there were rings on her hand. A diamond.

Anna shook herself, as if remembering Malone. "Mr. Minot spoke of the destruction of the Church, but that was only a small part of what Stalin did. The Ukraine in those years was one vast Buchenwald, and this was *before* Buchenwald. And who has raised a word of protest? Ever!"

Malone realized to his horror that she wanted him to

answer her. And inwardly, he pulled back, afraid. He
could think of nothing to say. She was right to have spit
the word *American* at him. He *was* an American, it was
that simple, and the evils out of which, like a fetid tomb,
the European continent was trying to crawl were abstractions to him, stories, rumors and snatches of grainy news
film. For an instant Anna's stare was like the huge-eyed
stare of a bony camp survivor attacking him from the
coarse photo of her silence. Attacking him for knowing
so little of what she had suffered.

She went on ferociously. "The Ukraine no longer exists. But it exists in me. When I left Poltava with my
mother, traveling by railroad, but also walking and hiring
cars and, at times, hiding in peasants' sheds for days at a
time—everywhere we went I saw people dying slowly,
their bellies bloated, arms hanging like broomsticks at
their sides, their eyes hollow like gargoyles'. I learned
that such sights had become common; I had been shielded
from them inside the cultivated walls of my father's cloister. But on the roads, the dying were everywhere. My
mother tried to keep me from looking but I would be
shielded no more. It was my first defiance of her, to stare
at the dead. I saw horse-drawn sleds piled high with
corpses. I saw people so weakened with hunger they
could not resist when the worms began to eat them alive.
And horrified as I was, and young—I was ten years
old—I swore to myself that I would never forget it, and I
would never forget who did it."

"You mean the Russians?"

"I mean Stalin! Your 'Uncle Joe'! To you he is like
Nero or Genghis Khan. You Americans already make
him a villain of history. But to me, Stalin is the one who
killed my father, and whether my father loved us or not,
I loved him."

Was it possible that only moments before this passionate
woman had seemed unfeeling? The first real feeling she
had expressed, he thought again, and it was in relation to
Stalin! How strange that made her. She was right: how
different they were.

She had barely paused for breath. "Stalin sits with

kings and prime ministers and presidents—who can forget Churchill and Roosevelt flanking him like acolytes at Yalta, or Truman patting his shoulder, like a pet, at Potsdam? They all cluck their tongues over Hitler, over Belsen and Buchenwald and Auschwitz. They create a new nation for the Jews. But what of my people? Who weeps for them? Hitler was no worse than Stalin. I have this advantage over the Jews—the object of my hatred still lives. He exists for me as the source of my defiance, even if he does not know it."

But Malone's thought was, Such defiance is also definition. You have given to Stalin the power to define your life; your hatred is the central fact of it. You have your reasons, yes. But still . . . isn't this *too* personal? Can Stalin really matter like this, enough to immobilize you? To stop you halfway out on this bridge?

But as soon as he asked the old American question Malone saw the new answer—Stalin has the bomb! Malone realized that the oh-so-luxurious American distance not from Europe or the Ukraine but from *history* was precisely what was threatened now. Stalin's A-bomb had brought the Butcher of the Ukraine within an inch of being the butcher of Kansas City, even if those blithely skeptical Kansans and show-me Missourians refused to believe it. They'd believe it when their gingerbread verandas were turned to charcoal.

Anna's emotion was perhaps natural, given her experience, but under the circumstances it seemed also dangerous. Was the purity of her hatred what had qualified her in Minot's mind for Firebird? It had apparently brought her unhesitatingly to Washington all the way from Strasbourg. But would it have let her function? Wasn't she right to have decided that she couldn't do this? Hadn't she intuitively grasped that nothing makes an agent less reliable than an overly personal stake in an operation? Malone realized that if she'd been his partner on the streets he'd have had real trouble trusting her, and not only because of all she'd just told him. He sensed there were things she wasn't telling him too.

"What about your mother?" he asked. "Does she feel these things as strongly?"

Anna shook her head. "My mother—" She stopped herself abruptly. "I won't discuss my mother." And in Anna's eyes, for a moment, Malone saw a hint of an entirely other emotion, something unspeakable. This woman who was so eloquent about her father had nothing to say about her mother. Her mother, of course, was alive. Her mother had something to do with Minot. Her mother, he saw suddenly, had something to do with this. But for now she was the wall before which all movement stopped. Anna was going to say no more.

Malone looked down into Rock Creek Park, hoping to see the serpentine rivulet that had cut the ravine, a gash through the city, a wild scar, eons before. But the moon had set and in the darkness he could see nothing.

Malone thought once more of night survivors wearily afloat in the cold, pitch-black sea, and he understood that in such circumstances a man and a woman would call instructions to each other, however futilely, just to keep talking, just to remember that they weren't alone. In that spirit, though he knew it was stilted, he said, "It's like staring into the abyss." An utterly foreign mode of expression for him; nevertheless, having heard himself say it, he thought, Yes, it's what I've been doing all night.

The hollow eyes of gargoyles, she had said. Worms feasting on living flesh. One vast Buchenwald. But the image those horrors conjured in his mind, finally, was not of barbed wire and pit graves and gas chambers, although his scene too included boxcars. Suddenly he saw Anna's nation as an unfenced, infinite Chicago stockyards and it was all too familiar. Only now the eyeballs distended in panic and the piercing screeches and the cement gullies flowing with blood and the carcasses hanging on hooks the size of lampposts were spread beneath an eye-stinging cloud, the foulest stench on earth, the stench of guts opened and spilled onto floors in closed rooms and left to rot in waste pens—only now it was not cattle and swine, but men and women, boys and girls, old people and babies. What else to measure such things by than a bottomless black hole, sucking like a whirlpool, the blood drain, drawing everything down, down, down, to the no-place that once was thought to be, before this century made it unthinkable, the love of God.

Anna answered dully, her European accent muffling any hint of feeling, "Nietzsche says, 'The abyss stares back.'"

Malone thought, This is the way French stoics speak to each other. But what is that to me? He faced Anna and said, much more simply, "You should know something about me. I feel knocked for a loop by all of this. Until now, I've just been a cop, you know? Nobody's ever quoted Nietzsche to me before."

"I did not mean to make you feel—"

"No, listen to me!" He took her by the shoulders, heatedly. "You said before I wasn't listening to you. But I did listen. And I understand why you want out. You think too much separates us. Maybe you're right. But I can learn from you. I can draw closer to what you've been through. I already understand well enough to know that you should stay with this thing. It's your chance to throw a shoe in Stalin's works." Malone paused. Where had this come from? Hadn't he just decided it wouldn't work with her? She was better out? But he was responding to something deeper than a Bureaulike evaluation of a fellow agent. He was responding to *her*. "If it's me you're worried about, I promise not to let you down."

"If I do this," Anna said, "it is because of Stalin."

"Yes."

"Why are you doing it?"

Malone answered abruptly, "Because I am an FBI agent."

She studied him, and once more Malone felt himself blushing. He knew that he could also have answered her, Because of you.

Anna said, "I'm sorry I left you like that." Her eyes conveyed her steadiness, a fresh resolve. "It will not happen again."

He released her shoulders, embarrassed suddenly to have touched her roughly.

She slid her gloved hand through his arm and turned him, to resume their stroll along the avenue, to leave the ravine, the abyss behind. They walked in silence, but now Malone felt the difference in how her hand closed on him. She wasn't pretending anymore, or not in the way that she had been. He realized with the first relief he'd felt since his arrival that hers had been the most rigorous test of all, and that he had passed it.

Webb Minot was asleep on a sofa of the living room in the house on Phelps Place. Even when Malone snapped the lamp on, Minot did not stir.

Malone looked back at Anna, who hovered in the threshold. "I didn't know he would still be here. Did you?"

Anna shook her head.

Malone approached Minot. An empty scotch bottle lay on the floor beside the couch. Minot was lying facedown. His body moved so little that for an instant Malone feared he wasn't breathing.

"Jesus Christ, he's passed out from drinking." Malone looked helplessly back at Anna. She hadn't moved. He looked instinctively from one window to another, as if the room was being watched, but the windows were black. He felt the headiness of the wine he'd had with dinner and wished he'd had less to drink himself. He pressed his right hand against his hip, that year-old habit of seeking reassurance from the weapon he carried. A pointless habit now that he was unarmed. Still, it was a sign of his nerves and it told him this was dangerous. But why?

As he approached Minot he swallowed hard as if swallowing anxiety. This was the man who was controlling Firebird? A passed-out drunk! Not anxiety, he realized, but anger. This was the man into whose hands he had put himself? This was the man on whose authority he had moved to the farthest fringe of the only world he knew or cared about? This man whose competence and experience and intelligence and judgment were going to, one, lead to the cracking of Russia's most secret espionage operation, and, two, keep Malone himself from being killed! And this man was a drunk? The word was obscene to Malone; a fucking drunk!

Malone's oldest bafflement stopped him. His father unconscious on the daybed in the parlor, the two-barreled stench of the stockyards and booze rising off him, his face and throat flushed red, his mouth open, drooling with every loud, gurgling exhalation until a river of spittle overflowed the edge of the cushion. When his father was passed out like that in the parlor, there was no place else in their home to go but the kitchen, the only other heated room. To Malone that meant no radio, his mother's quarried silence and the unbearable bickering of his brothers and sisters. Once, just before he went in the army, he'd said, Enough! This man whose blood beats in my veins! This man who expects me to be his helper! This man who dares call himself my father! This drunk, this fucking drunk! He'd walked into the parlor and picked up the half-full bottle of rye whiskey by his father's limp hand, and he poured it over his father's flaccid face. His father came to, smacking his lips, wiping the alcohol from his eyes, which focused finally on Malone. "Oh thank God," his father had said, "I was dreaming I was dead."

Malone picked up the empty scotch bottle by Minot's hand. In the way that he'd pressed his hand against his hip a moment before, an old, useless habit, he had an urge now to upend the bottle over Minot's face. Was Minot dreaming he was dead? Lucky for both of them the bottle was empty.

It shocked Malone to realize how much he'd needed to think of Minot as infallible. He had been seduced by the details that had set Minot apart from the other agents, his air of class, his accent, the mystery of his having joined the Bureau in the first place. Malone had instinctively trusted Minot, and had subtly begun to imitate him. He was going to be Minot's brother after all.

His brother! Not his son! Why then did the disappointment Malone felt remind him of his father?

He let the bottle fall to the floor. It bounced on the carpet with a thud that disturbed Minot's sleep not at all.

Anna walked past Malone into the dining room, and on into the kitchen. After a long moment in which nothing else occurred to him to do, he followed her.

She was at the sink drawing a glass of water from the tap. Her elegant kid gloves were in a pile on the table where she'd dropped them. As she tilted her head back to drink, he saw for the first time how the curve of her throat made one continuous turn into the firm line of her breasts. Her profile, from her upturned, delicate face, her hair flowing back from it, to the dazzling black form of her figure, impressed him like a finished work. For a moment he fancied himself the artist, thrilled with what she was, full of longing for her, but also hurt by all she failed to be.

But she was a woman, not an artifact; he chided himself, but knew he was groping for an image that would explain the connection he felt to her.

He felt it more than ever. He was fleeing the old disappointment that Minot's state rekindled, fleeing it in a burst of the old desire.

"Anna," he began, but he couldn't leave the scab of his questions about Minot alone. "You know about Minot, don't you?"

She said nothing.

"Tell me what you know. Why is he an agent?"

She shook her head slowly, still with her back to him. "I think he is—" She checked herself. Why? Then she said, "I cannot speak for Mr. Minot."

"But you know his story. It involves your mother, doesn't it? He doesn't fit in the Bureau. He's not like—"

She whipped around. "He's not like you?"

"No. As a matter of fact he isn't."

Anna stared at him for a moment, then faced away again. She stood with her weight on one leg. Her right foot, nearer him, was half out of her shoe. The seam of her stocking was twisted at her ankle, the only imperfection he could see.

When she looked at him again, it was with resignation that bordered, almost, on that despair.

He veered from it. Minot touched her in places that Malone had no right to push into, and he saw that. The wall of her mother, he thought.

She put the glass down and that was when his eye went to her hand, to her wedding ring, and diamond.

He said, "I noticed your rings on the street today. They're beautiful. I assumed at the time they meant you were married to a very wealthy man."

She turned the rings with her thumb, eyeing them. "These rings are two that my father stole from someone's grave. Mr. Minot offered to supply me with rings when I agreed to be Mrs. Peter Ward. But I told him I had rings of my own, my grandmother's. I did not tell him the truth."

"Why?"

"My mother was ashamed. She never told him. It is not my place to."

"Did you know he had this problem with drinking?"

Anna shrugged. "It does no harm tonight."

All at once Malone felt like a prude. Can't a guy get plastered now and then? Was his anxiety just a way to keep the torture of his childhood going, a trivial version of what Anna was doing with her hatred of Stalin? It was true, what he'd sensed before: despite all appearances, they were not so different. He said quietly, "Why did you tell me? About your rings, I mean."

When she raised them, her eyes cut into him with grief. "Because I see that you are kind."

Malone wanted to answer her, to let her see how touched he was, but all he could think to say—and he knew better—was, You are beautiful.

When he did not respond to her, she turned abruptly away and crossed the kitchen to a door with curtained windowpanes. When she opened it and went in, he saw that it was a small apartment, servant's rooms, and he understood it was where she would be staying.

She came out again carrying a blanket. She walked past him into the dining room and the living room beyond. He understood at once that she was doing what her mother would have done—cover the man against the night chill; his own mother would have added to that chill by becoming ice. To his shame he saw that in his reaction to Minot, he had been exactly like his mother. His temperance, restraint, self-discipline, all his so-called virtues— were they functions, finally, of the rigid contempt he'd learned from her?

But Anna had just told him he was kind. If he was moved and grateful, it was because he feared that he was not. Seeing himself through her eyes—that was the gift that she'd begun to give him.

"Peter!" She reappeared in the doorway, the blanket still in her arms, and a first look of mystification on her face. The mystification he was beginning to take for granted. She said, "He's gone."

6

"Puccini?" he asked. "What the hell does Puccini have to do with the price of beans?"

Malone recognized the note of a cocky pupil's defiance in his own voice, and it embarrassed him. He had intended to greet her with friendly irony, but his impatience and frustration had unfurled themselves against his will. Standing in the living room, a copy of the *Letters of Giacomo Puccini* in his hand, he had confronted Anna before she'd had a chance to take off her coat or to put down her shopping bag or even to enter the room. The surprise of a challenged teacher showed in her expression. It was late in the afternoon, a week into their time together.

From her place in the threshold Anna answered him firmly, but even in her matter-of-fact voice Malone heard a hint of the condescension he had come to dread from her. "In Italy Puccini is second only to Verdi. It is unthinkable that you would have lived there as a diplomat these last three years and not heard all of his operas."

"I feel like I've *lived* them." Malone, to show his unfailing good humor, twirled about mimicking the basso profundo, "La, la la. . . ."

Anna abruptly entered the room, brushed by him to the coffee table, on which she put her shopping bag. Malone felt silenced by her, and once more he felt mystified by the role he was playing. He watched while she drew from the bag another half-dozen books and several

101

phonograph records and inwardly he groaned. She rarely returned to Phelps Place without more of each, books about the cities of Europe, great houses of the aristocracy, the manners of diplomacy, but also apparently irrelevant works of literature—*Anna Karenina,* Joyce's *Ulysses* —and language handbooks that promised easy ways to learn Italian. The phonograph recordings she had brought included Berlitz lessons in Italian pronunciation, but also a full set of the classic works of opera as well as concert performances by musicians famous enough—Rubinstein, Menuhin, Serkin—for even Malone to have heard of them.

Without a sign that his challenge had thrown her, Anna aligned the new books and records on the table in front of her. "Horowitz Plays Scarlatti," he read on the jacket of the topmost album. The topmost book was a biography of Michelangelo. Jesus Christ, he thought, she's prepping me for "Quiz Kids"!

Anna began casually to fish in her purse for a cigarette. It surprised him when, in a stilted, stagy voice, she said, "So please to tell me, Mr. Ward, did you not adore La Scala?"

"Who are you, Marlene Dietrich?"

She smiled, but falsely, and then composed herself to wait for the answer.

He slapped his side with the Puccini volume, and very much as himself, he said, "I *do* see the point of all this . . . I'm sorry. *Mi dispiace.*"

"No, really, Mr. Ward. . . ." Anna found her cigarettes. Malone, in a debonair swoop unusual for him, took the silver table lighter and snapped it in front of Anna. She took the fire, then said through the smoke, "What *is* your favorite Puccini?"

Malone sat down, sensing that her impulse was not born of pique, as he'd feared, but of the more familiar compulsion to rehearse and rehearse and rehearse again. She was as relentless in her sphere as Minot was in his, and once more he relented with a shrug. What the hell, he thought. Marlene Dietrich meets Robert Taylor. He closed his eyes for a moment, trying to picture, say, one of Marjorie Merriweather Post's glittering dinner parties.

When he opened his eyes he was aware of startling her with his fresh expression. "My *very* favorite? Why, I would think the one that makes me cry at the denouement."

"*Butterfly.*"

"But of course."

"I myself prefer *La Bohème*. Will you ever forget Mimi's death in the freezing attic?"

Malone laughed. "Is *that* what she was doing? I thought she was giving birth."

When Anna's expression did not change—her refusal to treat this lightly had, for a week now, been complete—Malone surrendered. "All I mean to say, madame, is that Puccini collapses into mawkishness now and then, don't you think? He depends, really, on mere tunes, rather than on his ideas. Mozart or Wagner, on the other hand. . . ." He opened his hands, to show he had no need to state the obvious.

But Anna pressed him. "Ideas, Mr. Ward?" When she lifted her eyebrows he realized it was to ape not the vacuousness of a trivia-minded socialite but the sharp skepticism of an expert who senses fraud.

All right, Malone thought, time to bring in my homework. "Siegfried, for example. When he defies the old god to forge the sword of liberty, then goes on to wake the maiden from her sleep, he embodies the idea that men *can* act to change the world. Opera at its worst—the flag-waving child, say, in *Madame Butterfly*—is sentimental in the extreme. But at its best, opera dignifies human beings by displaying what nearly limitless stress we can sustain. Rigoletto, for example, whose suffering Verdi pushes to the limit. Puccini would have let Rigoletto escape into madness."

"You seem very sure of yourself, Mr. Ward."

Malone shrugged. "Puccini will survive my failure to appreciate him."

"No doubt."

Malone stared at Anna, wondering if she had just paid him a compliment. She had a gift for keeping herself hidden, and he was never sure when he had succeeded with her. Now he decided to wait her out. This charade had not been his idea.

After a moment Anna said, "You mentioned Mozart. Were you fortunate enough to hear the great performance of *Don Giovanni* at La Scala, wasn't it in 1946?"

"Yes, I was. Mozart's songs, so perfectly pitched to the orchestra, sound as if the human voice was made for nothing else than singing. With Mozart, even in that vast hall, under that incredible chandelier, it is a single human voice addressed to a single listener, one human being to another. It is impossible to come away from Mozart without a sense of wonder at the nobility of man's capacity for feeling and expression."

"Perhaps so," Anna said evenly, "but not in 1946. You should know this. It is a foolish mistake. *Don Giovanni* was not performed until 1947 because the opera house, which was badly damaged by Allied bombing, was still closed in 1946. There was no season in Milan that year."

Malone felt his face redden, and he was suddenly embarrassed not by his ignorance but by all the bullshit he was spouting. He had an impulse to snap back at Anna, What other snares have you laid for me? But he knew she was right. He had to get this stuff down cold.

He nodded. "I should have known that. I won't forget it again." He bowed. *"Scusi."*

Anna exhaled a thin stream of smoke. "Opera defies the drift of our age. Perhaps that is what makes it difficult for many." She eyed him steadily, having no need to cushion her rebuke. "Opera encourages us to take seriously our responsibilities. Opera tells us that the consequences of our failures can be enormous."

And what's *this* opera called? he asked himself. But he knew: *Firebird!* No, *Firebird* is a ballet. The time had come for Malone to say nothing. She was initiating him into bullshit, bullshit, bullshit. But he concealed his irritation. No, he swallowed it.

He reached forward to put the *Letters of Puccini* on the table by the Horowitz album and the life of Michelangelo. When he leaned back against the couch he sensed the difference in both of them, and a voice—not Mozart's—told him that, despite appearances, she was as lost as he was. Shipwreck survivors—the image came back to him—

calling out to each other across the cold, dark sea. He looked for her eyes, but she was staring at her cigarette.

"Tonight," she said finally, "we have tickets for the National Symphony. A mediocre orchestra, but it is all there is." Now she looked up at him. "Washington is a wasteland."

Constitution Hall was the largest auditorium in the city, a Beaux Arts pastiche built to house the annual DAR convention, and when Malone and Anna arrived by taxi, pulling up onto the broad carriage ramp, it was easy to picture the DAR ladies *en promenade,* their long white dresses and colorful sashes enlivening the entrance portico. Malone knew, of course, that for many years this had been a place to which people like him had had access only as servants, yet in leaving the cab, he was also aware that the woman on his arm carried herself with an implicit superiority. The other concertgoers seemed to make way for them. Anna's full, high-collared cape wafted behind them as they strode into the hall, and Malone was aware of it when men and women discreetly eyed her. But they were eyeing him too. That this glamorous scene was exotic and strange to him was his secret. In Peter Ward's clothes but especially in Anna Melnik's company, he looked born to it, and he knew, finally, that Minot had been right.

He wasn't prepared to be bowled over when they entered the hall proper. The festive spectacle stunned him: handsome men and women in evening clothes mingling in a rising tier of open boxes, walls and balconies lavishly decorated with swags of blue drapery, the gold stage curtain framing a gleaming black concert piano and above the proscenium arch the massed colors of battle flags. Over everything hung an excited air of expectation to which Malone responded by forgetting, nearly, the subterfuge that had brought them there.

As they took their seats Malone reminded himself that this was a training exercise, this was part of his education. It was not appropriate to feel this faint thrill—*here* was his secret—this, yes, delight to have come into such a place with such a woman.

But he cut his pleasure short, chiding himself—a
would-be Episcopalian.

When he and Anna were settled, he was aware at once
of the pressure of her elbow against his on the armrest.
She was pointedly studying the concert program. He
pulled his arm into his side, not wanting to trespass. He
opened his program in his lap, but instead of reading it,
he let his eyes drift around the hall. Anna may disdain
the music, he thought, but there is nothing second-rate
about these Washingtonians. He saw them as government officials, agency heads, generals, cabinet officers,
diplomats, architects of the postwar world. Ordinarily
he'd have viewed such men for what they were first—
owners, businessmen, bankers, bosses. He'd have resented them with the old South Side bitterness and he'd
have deflected feelings of inferiority into *his* disdain,
which would have had nothing to do with the National
Symphony Orchestra.

But instead, Malone saw his fellow concertgoers as
something else, as, in fact, the other thing they were:
largehearted, generous statesmen whose response to the
greatest military victory in history had been to dismantle
the war machine that made it possible. For the first time
ever, human beings had turned the mailed fist into an open
hand. These were the men whose monument, the Marshall
Plan, he had begun studying in detail that week, for the
fiction was that Peter Ward had been one of its on-site
administrators. Malone was surprised and moved to find
himself in the company of the men who'd created the ERP.

In the world—the Bible phrase struck him suddenly—
but not of it. He was not here as himself, he remembered, but as Peter Ward, as Webb Minot's brother, as a
man with a woman he had no right to be near.

The audience burst into applause as the conductor
entered from backstage. Not conductor, Malone realized
then. This was a piano recital, and the man in tails was
the soloist. Malone clapped dutifully. Then, unconsciously,
he put his forearm on the armrest next to Anna's, touching her.

When he and Beth Fraser had sat together in the
movies they'd always held hands.

Malone's strong impulse was again to pull his arm back, to leave Anna alone. But she wasn't moving. Was she aware of his touch? The feel of her arm against his—so discreet, so unlike the feigned linking of arms they did for public display—was explosive to him, and he couldn't imagine that it wasn't to her too. Anna, he wanted to say, let me tell you what *else* I'm feeling, that I'm glad to be here with you, that I appreciate the world you are showing me, that I *can* be of it, as well as in it. Anna, I *can* be a man who belongs with you!

He said nothing.

When he looked at her she was still reading the program. She raised her eyes just then because the first notes of music had been struck. The recital had begun.

Malone only now looked at his own program. Chopin, he read, Sonata no. 2 in B-flat Minor.

The title meant nothing to him, but from the first, the composition affected him in a way that such music rarely had before. It was as if Malone was hearing the sharp beauty of the piano for the first time. He quickly left behind the sense of himself as an observer; he was *part* of what was producing this.

He was *part* of the Washington that was rebuilding the earth.

And then, to his amazement, he recognized the heavy, rhythmic notes of the music as something he *knew*. Even *he* knew it. He had heard it on the radio when FDR died; he had heard it at ceremonies at the army hospital in Joliet. But he had never heard it like this.

Exhilarated, he leaned toward Anna, to put his mouth by her ear. "It's the 'Funeral March.' "

She nodded. She looked at him. In her unfathomable Slavic eyes was the deepest sadness he had ever seen.

Malone reported for duty as Peter Michael Ward in Foggy Bottom the following week, and immediately his days were occupied with the clipped routine of a junior FSO. They began with a brisk walk at dawn from Phelps Place down Twenty-second Street past J. Edgar Hoover's alma mater—though why would Ward know that's what GW was?—to the State Department's hulking eight-story build-

ing just above the Lincoln Memorial. For two hours
before the normal workday began, Ward and twenty-
seven other recently returned auxiliary Foreign Service
officers, candidates for regularization, sat in a makeshift
classroom in the basement taking the new entrants' course
as if they had just come in off the sidewalk. Malone had
to pretend to share the affront the others felt to be
treated like novices. They called the course "Brandies
and Ports," resentfully rejecting the implicit idea that
they were social inferiors—"men of the hoe"—who needed
polishing.

Of course, that was just who Malone was, as his private tutelage with Anna Melnik had already begun to
underscore. The unreality of his situation was heightened
in the bunkerlike rooms and hallways belowground by
the steady fooping of pneumatic suction tubes, the exposed overhead pipes through which document-stuffed
canisters zipped from one section of the department to
another. Oblivious of the foops, though Malone never
stopped hearing them, lecturers went on at length about,
for example, diplomacy's ten types of official dispatches
(printed letter, official note, note verbale, *ad decimum*).

The rest of each of "Peter Ward's" days, provided he
didn't get lost in the maze of drab corridors that led two
times out of three to the cul-de-sac outside an undersecretary's office, was spent in the Protocol Office itself.
Twenty-six staffers saw to everything from preparing for
the president's signature letters addressed to heads of
state, to arranging receptions of new foreign representatives, to answering hostesses' questions about order of
precedence. Malone learned that British precedence is a
matter of careful ranking dating back to the Magna Carta,
but the simple American rule is that the higher your
salary, the higher your place at the table.

"It's absurd," he told Anna one night a couple of
weeks after he'd begun. "My responsibility in the office
is known as 'care and feeding of dips'—diplomats. By
virtue of my job I'm called 'the ambassadors' keeper.' "

"Why is it absurd?" Anna asked. It was late at night.
They had just finished one of the regular sessions in
which they endlessly plowed the fields of the history they

supposedly shared. This was his real work, his real "entrants' course."

Anna had gotten to her feet to leave him with his folders—reports of the World Refugee Committee purportedly written by him during his time in Italy. He was going to study and she was going to return to her rooms as she always did. They were like actors with each other. Behind the fallen curtain under naked light bulbs—in Phelps Place—they took off their costumes and makeup in their separate corners, not speaking.

But he had spoken. For a moment he had stopped her. "It's absurd because *my* job is to tell people how to behave in high society." Malone began to laugh. "You know what I am? I'm a *protocolaire!*" He began to laugh uncontrollably for a moment, then reined himself. "Honest to God, Anna, don't you think it's absurd? I'm a pseudo-*protocolaire!*"

He looked at her expectantly. How could she keep this up? She had lifted a corner that first night on the reality of her past—the grief of it. It had seemed to him on that bridge over the ravine of Rock Creek that they had made a kind of promise to each other *not* to be French stoics but to be instead—what? Partners? Like a pair of rookie cops? Since then every overt expression between them had been rooted in a formal, essentially impersonal cooperativeness. Silent partners was the image that occurred now, as if they were investors keeping their distance to deceive their rivals.

But he knew damn well that the undercurrents between them were too intense for that. There *was* an emotional bond, and he was sure that the power of it was what kept deflecting her. Hadn't she resolved that first night not to display such emotion again? Yet it was the *emotional* tie between them that made credible the fiction of their courtship, the courtship of Anna and Peter, which had been, according to the sketch provided by Minot, a passionate month-long *mistral* swirling between Rome and Strasbourg, touching down like a good Kansas tornado in alpine villages and in rooms overlooking the Grand Canal. But whatever the fiction, the undercurrents between Anna Melnik and Christopher Malone were *real*, they were what he wanted to surface now.

"Really," he said, and he raised a suppliant hand toward her. "Can't you enjoy the joke of this situation with me, just for a minute?"

She shook her head. "Nothing here is a joke."

He dropped his hand abruptly, amazed to see that she *could* keep it up. She would. "I know it isn't a joke," he said, suddenly angry. "I know it isn't a goddamned joke. I just thought you might like to join me for a moment in a little circle of what's *real*. All we do, Anna, is pretend or get ready to pretend, or evaluate our pretense after it occurs. Isn't it driving you a bit nutty?"

"You should keep your concentration."

"Is that all you have to say to me? Jesus Christ!" Malone slapped the folders beside him, spilling them to the floor. "I should practice my Italian too, right? *Signorina, c'e una stazione di rifornimento qui vicino?*"

Anna lowered her eyes, saying softly, *"Staz-i-oh-ne.* In Italian one can generalize to say the accent never falls on the ultimate syllable."

"Oh?" Malone nodded slowly. *"Perchè?"*

Anna blushed, knowing he had her. "It is the exception," she said.

He saw an apology in her refusal to look at him. He saw a plea. He imagined her saying, Yes, we are locked apart in the two rooms of our roles, but there are reasons why it must be so. There are reasons why *this* is the kind of partnership we have. Let it be. Let it be.

And what did he imagine himself answering?

That first night when you took my arm on the bridge, I thought it was *you* touching me. But now you never touch me except when someone's looking. At social functions we play the loving couple, and when we return here I feel the chill of loneliness more sharply than anytime since I was a boy. And I see in you an unhappiness I could help with. I wish that we could speak truthfully to each other. That's all.

But once more he couldn't speak, period. He was as silent a partner, finally, as she was.

He felt ashamed of himself. These feelings revealed his

weakness, and suddenly he imagined her reporting him to Minot, who would report to Hoover: Malone can't hack it. Malone is soft inside. Malone chokes.

"Staz-i-oh-ne," he said. "I'll work on it."

Anna still could not look at him. Apparently abject and desolate she muttered, *"Mi dispiace,"* and turned to leave. But at the doorway she stopped and now looked at him directly. "We should both remember what it is we are doing. We are preparing to deceive the Soviets. You are preparing to burglarize their embassy."

"So sing me an aria about it." Malone preferred this fresh flood of his anger to his anxiety. "Maybe then I'll remember."

Anna turned abruptly and left.

Anger at himself, more than her. She was right, and he knew it. She understood, as he had that first night in relation to *her* grief, that all these feelings were the enemy. They simply *had* to block them.

If he was angry at her at all, it was for being here to witness what a fool he was. He pictured her now, collapsed against her door, smoking nervously, afraid of what she saw in him. He pictured wisps of her hair falling over her face like scars.

He forced himself back to the ERP reports, scanning titles above his name—"DP Camps in Calabria and Sicily," "Resettlement Problems Among Rural Populations," "Malnutrition in Molise." But his mind reeled: not *his* name, but Peter Ward's. What had any of this to do with him? Puccini and the price of beans, starving *paesani*, the "Funeral March" sonata, his French wife who was also German, Russian but really from the Ukraine. And who, after all, was he?

Malone was wrong for this assignment, and for the first time in his adult life it occurred to him he was wrong for the FBI. He thought too much; no, *felt*. His feelings were out of their corral. He could no longer keep, in Anna's perfect phrase, his concentration. He was at the mercy of terrible ideas, especially one—that he was wrong for his life.

He stood up. The hell with this. He crossed without thinking to the chair, to the phone beside it. Reaching for it, he checked himself.

Who was he calling?

And then he knew.

No, Chris boy, not here. He looked around the empty room. Not this phone.

He turned his impulse aside, channeling it into a brisk movement to the dining room, to the bottles on the buffet. Minot's bottles. His father's.

He poured a whiskey from one of the gleaming crystal decanters, sipped it and sipped it again, and at once he felt the calming warmth spread through him. Now, slowly, he retraced his way through the living room, snapping off the lights like any householder. He carried his drink upstairs, and once in the privacy of his own room, with the door closed, without a further thought, he picked up the telephone by his bed.

He put his drink on the table and fell back across the mammoth nubby white spread, clutching the phone to his chest. For a moment he lay quite still staring up at the ceiling. Then he put the receiver to his cheek and told the operator when she came on that he wanted Saint Mary, Kansas.

"Beth?" he said when he heard her voice.

"Yes?"

"It's Chris."

He wasn't sure she heard him. She did not respond and in the silence something else hit him. Was the phone tapped? Was someone watching him? Did Anna know he'd made this call? Would she report him?

"Beth, it's me, Chris."

"Where are you?" She sounded drowsy, as if he'd wakened her.

"I'm in Washington."

"Are you all right?" He pictured her sitting up in bed, clutching the flannel collar of her nightgown.

"Yes, I'm okay," he said, and in fact he could feel the tension draining out of his body.

But as if the phone lines had linked up his nerves to hers, Beth suddenly said with alarm, "Are you really? Are you really all right?"

"Yes—"

"Jerry told me that—" She stopped abruptly.

When she didn't go on, Malone prodded. "Jerry told you what?"

She didn't answer.

"When were you talking to Jerry, Beth?"

"He told me not to say anything to you."

"That's ridiculous. Jerry's my friend. You know that. He was my partner." Now it was Malone who felt alarmed. What the hell was Jerry Grant approaching Beth about? "Come on, Beth. Tell me."

"Jerry said you were going away. He said you wouldn't be in Washington after all, and I shouldn't try to contact you."

"Did you tell him you had no intention of contacting me? That from your point of view it was over between us?"

"Yes," she said in little more than a whisper. "But Mr. Shaeffer—"

"Shaeffer? What was he doing there?" Shaeffer was the Kansas City SAC, the Special Agent in Charge.

"He came with Jerry. They both said your assignment was changed, that you're *not* in Washington, that you're doing something else. Weren't they telling me the truth?"

The available truth, Malone said to himself. "I've been sent back for more training, Beth."

"At Quantico?"

"Yes," he said simply. And that was nearly true, since he was about to begin the physical aspects of his preparation at the academy, where he would be spending all his weekends now. But did Beth believe him?

He heard the worry in her voice when she said then, "Mr. Shaeffer told me that if you contacted me I should call him up."

Jesus Christ, Malone thought. This was like having handcuffs slapped on his wrists. Was he a fugitive? He had called Beth instinctively, for a dose of one thing he *knew* was real. But this was nutty too. Everything was nutty.

"Are you in trouble, Chris?"

"No. . . ."

"Why did you call me?"

He closed his eyes to conjure his image of her again.

He pictured himself pulling the hem of her prudish tan
nightgown up along her legs, and then, at the critical
moment, Beth seizing his hand, whispering, Just lie still.
Just hold me.

"To say hello," he told her. "To tell you that—" He
stopped.

"To tell me what?"

Her flat Kansas accent struck him. How unnuanced
her voice was, how lacking in tone, in mystery. He had
felt that he knew everything about her; that she knew
everything about him.

But no more. In fact, she knew less than he did, and
what he felt now was that he knew nothing.

"To tell you that—" What? He missed her simple,
truthful voice? No, what he missed was her ability to
admit the limits of her world and to live within them,
even though that was what had made their love impossible. "—that I understand better now why you wouldn't
come with me." Malone's mind raced ahead with what
else he understood, but could not say: I should have
stayed with you. I belong in a world where what things
seem to be squares with what they are.

"I'm glad you said that."

"I miss you, Beth." But as soon as he said it he knew it
wasn't the exact truth. What he missed wasn't Beth but
the clear, uncomplicated pull of how he'd loved her. No
shadows. No mysteries. The bond between them had
been as uncurved as an arrow shaft.

And it had broken. It amazed Malone to realize how
definitively of the past those feelings were. He pictured
himself covering her ankles again, standing up.

"What's the matter?"

How to answer her? "It's a hard job here. One I
haven't done before."

"Is it dangerous?"

"No." Women always asked that. What would she say
if he told her he didn't even carry a gun anymore? If he
told her that the danger so far was that he might use the
wrong fork? He said, "There's a part of me I haven't
used before, a part that feels like it belongs to someone
else."

"But it's you?"

"Yes."

"Then you can do it."

She said this so matter-of-factly, so certainly, that for the first time that night he thought it was true. "Yes. I can."

There was a long silence then before Beth said, "Mr. Shaeffer told me that when your job there is over you might be coming back to Kansas."

"No, Beth. I won't."

"But why?" He heard that familiar plea in her voice now and he dreaded it. "Especially if the job they gave you isn't what you want."

Malone's eyes traced the seams of the corner where the ceiling met the wall. Anna; it was Anna to whom he wanted to talk, Anna with whom he wanted, impossibly, to lie in bed. But this was Beth, and Beth was the one whose questions always pushed him through his mysteries to the truth. "But this job *is* what I want," he said, and with that admission a blanket of peace settled on him.

There was another silence, then Beth said, "What shall I tell Mr. Shaeffer?"

Malone's paranoia had evaporated. This was the Bureau. He and Shaeffer were on the same side. And so were he and Anna. To his surprise he had let go of the need to know everything, or it had let go of him. "Tell him the truth, Beth. Tell him I called to say thanks for all you gave me."

"And to say good-bye."

"Yes."

7

This was the first of the nights they'd been aiming for and neither Malone nor Anna, so far, had missed a beat. They were at Victor Woolf's, the Georgetown dinner party Minot had said was coming. This was the event from which everything else would flow. Woolf, a British attaché, was apparently a contact of Minot's, though to all appearances this was a typical diplomatic soiree. Peter Ward was the token Yank and the juniormost FSO at a gathering of old hands from various embassies up and down the Row. Woolf prided himself on tagging the circuit comers, and by virtue of Ward's presence at that table, a comer was what the others took him to be. Everyone seemed slightly thrilled to be there, including the targeted Vladimir Tumark, who was seated to Anna's left. Tumark was the Soviet First Secretary for Economic Affairs. For four years now his job had been to negotiate his country's repayment of war loans to America. Minot had said that diplomats liked him for his open acknowledgment of what a sham that negotiation was.

Malone had so steadily kept an ear cocked toward the Russian across the table that he had only half kept up the conversation with the middle-aged women on either side of him. Each was a diplomat's wife, one Canadian and one Irish, and neither took apparent notice of Ward's distractedness. Through the avocado and shrimp and the *coq au vin* they had chattered on in turn. The Canadian was doing so now.

In addition to Tumark, Victor Woolf was another object of Malone's veiled but acute attention. By this point in the meal, when the table was flashing with tulip glasses, small cordial glasses, stout brown cognac bottles and crystal port decanters, other guests were slurring their speech. But Woolf continued to preside at the head of the table, at Anna's right, with verbal agility and flair. He was a gracious, well-tailored man whose pointed gray-flecked beard gave him the look of a professor or a psychiatrist, but he had an infectious laugh and an interested eye. Webb Minot had described him as one of the most popular diplomats in Washington.

Woolf and his wife were unabashedly modern people, classless and charming in a way that English diplomats never were. Even his beard marked him off from his colleagues, both the aggressively mustachioed military men and the pointedly clean-shaven dandies of the prewar generation. So, for that matter, did his wife. Muriel Woolf was a wealthy Jewish woman of Dutch origins whose family had resettled in London after *Kristallnacht*, accommodating themselves quickly to British styles. By now Muriel, with her short hair and her cigarettes and her boyish leanness, embodied, in Washington circles, "the new look." Or so Minot had said. It was new to Malone, that was sure.

Only two of the women at the table were smoking—Muriel and Anna—but the naturalness with which the others had remained to sip their coffee and cordials with the men marked them all as friends of the Woolfs.

But everyone's chatter was interrupted then by the sharp sound of a knife on a glass. Malone faced down the table toward Muriel Woolf, thinking it was she, but the man to her right, Martin Hughes, the Irishman, was holding his wineglass aloft. It was brimming. He'd refilled it himself, crassly. His napkin was crushed on the table in front of him, a lapse of etiquette that Malone might not have noted before Anna took him in hand.

Hughes said, "If I may, Victor." And as everyone automatically raised his glass, the Irishman's went higher. "To the heroes of the Berlin airlift just concluded. . . ." He nodded toward the RAF colonel across

from him, an attaché, Kings Regs moustache and all.
". . . Fifteen grueling months, thousands of air trips, sup-
plying an entire city from the air, a modern miracle—"

"Mr. Hughes!" Victor Woolf interrupted sharply.

Hughes faced down the table toward Woolf, blinking.

Woolf said quietly, "In the presence of our esteemed
guest from the Union of Soviet Socialist Republics, perhaps traditional courtesy would encourage us to refrain
from references to points of dispute between our nations."

Hughes went ashen at this rebuke.

It was Vladimir Tumark who came to the Irishman's
rescue. He leaned toward him, a bit too close to the
colonel's wife on his left perhaps, and gestured with his
own glass. "Here is a toast," he said in his heavy Russian
accent, "to the world's newest republic."

A toast to Ireland? Only two months before Ireland
had declared itself a republic, unilaterally withdrawing
from the British Commonwealth, the first nation to do so.
It was mischievous of the Russian to refer to it. Speaking
of points of dispute!

The table tensed even further.

But then Tumark said, "And as of last week . . ." He
grinned impishly, raising his white eyebrows, which, together with the long white hair obscuring his ears and
curling down over his collar like a violin player's, gave
his face a benign softness that made him seem like a
kindly grandfather. He was about sixty. ". . . the world's
newest republic is not Ireland. . . ." He nodded toward
Hughes and said gently, ". . . Forgive me, sir, for presuming to usurp you, but Berlin is not the only place in which
the footfall of history can be heard." His glass went
high, liturgically. And the authority of the gesture was
so complete that it was like a dismissing aftershadow
of the Irishman's toast. "Ladies and gentlemen, dear
comrades . . ." His smile kept the irony of his address
from seeming sarcastic. ". . . I give you the People's
Republic of China."

Mao had finally conquered Peiping and declared his
government on October 1, the very day the Berlin airlift
ended. The Socialist tide would not be turned back, even
by the indefatigable RAF. Ignoring the general refusal to

react to his toast, Tumark downed his cognac in one swallow.

Tumark, whose wife and daughter lived in Moscow, was there without a spouse, so no one else drank. Everyone was staring at him.

Tumark was a man of manners—Minot had said he was one of the few Soviet diplomats who made himself socially available—but he was also a man of duty, and, whatever he privately thought about the failed effort to strangle Berlin, he could not let a blatant affront to his nation go unanswered. Hence his toast, which, in that company, could only have been received as mordant.

Martin Hughes was relieved to have the spotlight off himself. He put his glass down and sank back against his chair. Malone, as a *secret* Irishman, felt ashamed of him. Why can't they leave the booze alone? he wondered. But the shame spilled back on Malone himself, for being secret.

Before the silence lengthened, but also before his guests could subdivide again into nervous, local conversation, Victor Woolf announced, "One of our guests tonight is intimate with the problems of displaced persons in the Mediterranean, having served until last month as American liaison officer to the World Refugee Committee in Rome. Tell us, Mr. Ward, how you see the situation."

Malone idly picked up his coffee spoon and tapped it arrhythmically, preparing to answer. He knew that Georgetown and Embassy Row dinner parties functioned as initiation rites for new members of the diplomatic community. Despite the show of reined nervousness in his spoon's jitterbug, Malone felt calm. He was ready. Minot had warned him to avoid sounding as if he were reciting. Meander a bit, he'd said, and make your points anecdotally. This is hazing; they know it and you know it. And now Victor Woolf, Minot's friend, has put a fat bottle on the wall for you to hit.

Malone began, "Central and Eastern Europe, of course, are the areas where the refugee problem to begin with was gravest. Obviously, that's because the northern cities were so devastated." Malone stopped abruptly and looked across at Anna. "My wife, as you may have gathered, is

from Strasbourg, which in its city center was forty percent destroyed." Anna lowered her eyes as if to duck the
memory, and anyone could tell from looking at "Peter
Ward" how protective he was of her. The problem of
dispossessed, desperate people was no mere abstraction
to this man. He went on, "Yet the displaced populations
of France, Germany, Scandinavia, the lowland countries
and the United Kingdom have been nearly completely
resettled. ERP funds for that purpose were concentrated
in the most devastated areas, and as you know several
hundred thousand European DPs have become American citizens through other provisions of the plan. But,
really, closing the resettlement camps in the north—and
most of them have been closed—has been a function of
reversing the perilous economic decline." As he droned
on Malone watched himself—watched Peter Ward—with
a detached eye. He was no longer the actor Robert
Taylor, but had become a younger Walter Lippmann,
offering the dry conclusions of a man who'd been everywhere he claimed. "And just in time too. Another winter
like last winter, with the people still exposed, could have
finished the north of Europe."

"And the south?" Woolf asked.

Malone shrugged. "The weather's better. Perhaps that
accounts for the relative lack of urgency." He glanced at
Anna, who was watching him like a dutiful wife. Her
admiration for her wise, promising young husband was
implicit. As was her sense of staggering good fortune to
have snagged her own American.

But Christopher Malone saw it differently, thinking
back to their briefing sessions in which she was the one
teaching him and in which she constantly had to rein her
impatience—at times he thought disgust—with his oh-so-
American ignorance of what the war had really done.

"Or maybe it's a question of leadership," he said. "As
you know Italy lacks an Adenauer or a de Gaulle, not to
mention a Churchill."

"So the camps remain crowded?"

"In Calabria and Sicily alone camps still hold upwards
of twelve thousand people, mostly women and children.

The weather may not threaten them, but malnutrition still does."

Malone let his eyes drift to Tumark, who was looking at him pleasantly, though his nation's leaders had denounced the Marshall Plan—the "Martial" Plan, as Henry Wallace called it—because nothing threatened the Soviet Union more than a recovered Germany. Tumark was smoking a cigarette and just then, to reach the ashtray he was sharing with Anna, he touched her arm, barely and only for an instant, but with a sense of license and familiarity that shocked Malone. In his agent's mind he wondered if the Russian had touched her despite her "husband's" glance or because of it. In his "husband's" mind he wanted to protest, and for the first time he rebelled viscerally at this element of their plan. But he checked that reaction quickly. Everything depended on Tumark's attraction to Anna. The Russian was *supposed* to fall for her.

He looked at Woolf, who, like a stern seminar proctor, was fussing tobacco into his pipe, waiting for Peter Ward to continue. But something told Malone to remain silent.

In a heavily accented voice, a Swede two seats away from Malone said, "Italy has a Pius the Twelfth, however. Could not His Holiness exercise just the sort of initiative Mr. Ward says is so lacking? These are the pope's countrymen, after all. It is one thing for the Church to ignore the fate of the Jews—"

The crack of the front legs of a chair hitting the floor shocked the room. Martin Hughes had sat forward with more force than he intended, but now that the eyes of all were fixed on him again he felt he had no choice but to speak. "The Church did not ignore the Jews."

Once more Malone was embarrassed. He knew that these people took their right to slur the Church for granted. He did not share Hughes's need to defend it. But then he asked himself, had he once? Was he in fact becoming a "Peter Ward" even to himself? Where—he could hear his father's Irish voice asking suddenly—was his loyalty? Judas denied the Lord, but so did the man named Peter.

After a silence that seemed paired with the silence that had finished off the Irishman before, Muriel Woolf said quietly, "Perhaps the fate of the Jews is a topic we could leave aside tonight."

Malone knew from Minot that Muriel Woolf's father had been caught in Amsterdam when the Nazis came, and he was never seen again.

"With due respect, Muriel," Vladimir Tumark said so gently as to call forth an even deeper hush. His eyes were shining at her across the length of the table, letting her see that her heartfelt request had touched him, even if he was about to defy it. "But the fate of the Jews, as you call it, instructs us all. The Zionists were right many years before anyone could imagine it, about what was to befall all of Europe. People now talk of Hitler as an insane aberration, but he was merely an instrument, the focus of a ravaged nation's desperate longing for recovery. Recovery denied becomes a longing for revenge. Now, Mr. Ward has been speaking to us of people who long for recovery. The lesson of the recent past is that we should help them. My country is doing as much in its sphere, and I applaud Mr. Ward's work in doing so in his nation's sphere."

While reaching to pour more brandy in the Russian's glass, Victor Woolf exercised his prerogative as host to tweak Tumark, whether for skirting his wife's request or for assuming the division of the world into spheres neither of which was British. "How is it helping Germany to recover, Vladimir, to flood your occupation zone with devalued currency? Or to cart off to Stalingrad what little heavy machinery survived in German factories?"

Tumark blinked and, like that, his patient smile dissolved. Malone watched the instantaneous but subtle transformation of an apparently compassionate, gentle grandfather into an alien among his enemies. "I was speaking of Europe," he said coldly. "Not Germany." And Malone wondered which was counterfeit, his former warmth or this sudden rigid haughtiness. Or were they both? It would make a humane person insane, Malone thought, to have to defend the positions of Joseph Stalin, looter of half the world and would-be looter of the rest. Had Tumark slipped, seeming to favor a policy of postwar reconciliation? And was he now dropping the proper

colored disk, Politburo-supplied, in front of his kleig? "It
is the position of my government that the German state,
as such, must not be permitted to return to its normality.
Hitler imposed nothing on the German people. Rather
he embodied their normality. That normality must be
thwarted now, forever. The German people, as it were,
must be protected from themselves." Tumark looked
briefly to his right, at Anna. She met his eyes unflinch-
ingly, and Malone sensed her generosity toward Tumark,
and, also, Tumark's need of her. This woman, at least,
understood what he was saying.

As if to prove her sympathy, Anna let her eyes drift
the length of the table until they settled on Muriel Woolf.
Anna softly repeated what Tumark had said before. "The
fate of the Jews instructs us all. As Aristotle said, 'What
has happened, can happen.' "

Malone stared at his spoon. An American Foreign
Service officer in such a situation would feel mortified;
his wife, displaying the parochial Germaniphobia of her
native Alsace-Lorraine, undercutting his own government's
position. The embarrassment that Malone felt had nothing to do with the political issue, however, or his own
supposed relation to it. He was embarrassed for Anna, for
he alone knew what she was doing. In these her first
words addressed to the entire table, Anna Ward spoke
with an authority no one could challenge, as if *she* were a
Jew, a camp survivor, a woman whose mission in life
would forever be to stoke the memory of what Germany
had done. Muriel Woolf nodded slightly, still holding
Anna's eyes. Malone realized that what Anna had done
was transform herself, her memory, her rage. Her Stalin
had become Hitler. Her Poltava had become Buchenwald.
She *had* become a Jew. But Malone knew that Tumark
had become her camp commandant. And she was putting
herself at his feet. A moment before Malone had asked
himself what this charade was doing to *his* loyalty. But
now he wondered what was it doing to hers.

Tumark's affability, thus rescued, slipped back into
place, with his smile. He said expansively, "We have no
disagreement about Mr. Ward's remarks. There is no
place in Europe for malnutrition. . . ."

The Russian spoke with conviction, and as he continued more than one of his listeners felt the knot of fear in his chest loosen. Not all Russians—what a relief to be reminded of this—were strident hardliners. Tumark made the wild hope of East-West accommodation seem plausible.

". . . The great war against Hitler's criminal regime is four years in the past, and even the lesser wars are over: India, Greece, Indonesia, China, Palestine, and also, yes, the dangerous dispute over Berlin—all approaching resolution. In each case no one greets the progress more happily than the people whose fathers are killed and homes ruined. A period of world truce perhaps may now to commence. . . ."

Tumark let his eyes drift slowly from person to person until finally, like a needle finding north, they settled on Malone.

". . . But first, as Mr. Ward reminds us, the people must be fed."

Malone had been discreetly watching Anna throughout Tumark's homily. There was a severity about the deep blue dress she wore, covering her everywhere as it did, except at the nape of her throat, which was all the more riveting for being the only patch of her skin to be exposed. The tight-fitting sleeves of her dress ran to her wrists. Malone had learned the difference by now between the evening dress she'd worn to the Shoreham Terrace and with which long gloves were worn, and a dinner dress like this. It was difficult to imagine, such was the impression Malone sensed she had made at Victor Woolf's table, that the décolletage of the more revealing garment would have heightened the appeal of her sensuality more than this dark modesty did.

Tumark began speaking again, making even more explicit the sensibility his listeners longed to hear expressed. This was why they had him to their parties. "The function of diplomacy is always and everywhere to give support to those factions on all sides that do not want war, but this is especially so in periods of tensions. . . ."

Malone continued to watch Anna. She lit a cigarette, smoothed the tablecloth in front of her, aligned her cup and spoon—all distractedly, so intently was she listening to what her dinner partner was saying. She seemed altogether moved. Malone marveled at her. No one could have guessed that she had ever heard of Joseph Stalin, much less lost a father to him or lived through the beginning of his terror-famine in the Ukraine. How little those others knew of her.

Yes, but how little he knew himself. Malone admitted that the shape of her two brown eyes—her décolletage or lack of it, her kid gloves or sleeves—told him, finally, nothing. Her hair was pulled back from her face, displaying her ears, into which, suddenly, he wanted to whisper all his questions. He watched her breast rise and fall with each breath and he felt that she was drawing him in with the air and smoke. Inside of her it would be night, he knew that much. If she would let him, he would help her bring her sorrow into the light.

But sorrow wasn't the point just then. Tumark had succeeded in lifting the weight from the conversation. Everyone at the table seemed entranced by him. But not Malone. He shuddered with the thought that now, somewhere east of the Ukraine that Stalin had made into one vast Buchenwald, a place named Kazakhstan was one vast Hiroshima. A world truce? No. A Buchenwald truce, maybe. A Ukraine truce! "And who," Anna Melnik had demanded, "has raised a word of protest? Ever!"

By God, I will, Malone thought, even as Peter Ward. He gestured ingratiatingly toward the Russian. "Well said, Mr. Tumark, well said. And I want especially to underscore our point of most profound agreement. *The people must be fed*. From Calabria on the Ionian Sea to Trieste in the Adriatic." Malone stopped abruptly, his words hanging in the air like an unfinished bridge. As he intended they should, everyone heard the last phrase as a key to the most familiar lines of the time. Churchill at Fulton, Missouri: "From Stettin in the Baltic to Trieste in the Adriatic, an iron curtain has descended across the continent. . . ."

Tumark stared at Malone unable, quite, to keep the surprise from his face, as if Malone were a man carrying something on his shoulder.

Not a monkey or a parrot, you bastard, Malone thought, but history.

Tumark, it was clear, intended to make no reply.

Malone glanced at Woolf, who at that moment was sipping from his water glass. It was true; unlike the others he was not drinking alcohol. Alone among the men, excepting Malone himself, Woolf was stone-cold sober. When he lowered his glass he reached past Anna to put his hand affectionately on Tumark's sleeve.

But instead of speaking to Tumark, Woolf drew back, opening Malone's view of Anna again. When Woolf looked at Malone his antagonism no longer seemed covert, and his glance was so steely Malone thought, crazily, He knows I'm Irish.

"We hear, Mr. Ward, that you are the author of highly touted reports." Woolf's smile was sinister. "Tell us, will your reports to Potus now describe malnutrition among us refugees along Embassy Row?"

There were chuckles up and down the table. Malone was relieved that it was not a real challenge, but only more hazing. The trick was to reply wittily.

But before he could, Tumark interrupted. "Reports to whom?"

Suddenly the Russian's interest upped the ante of the question.

"Potus," Woolf answered, while continuing to stare at Malone. "Perhaps Mr. Ward will tell you who Potus is."

It *was* a test, a real one, and Malone knew he was about to fail it. It shocked him to have been so blind-sided. Potus? He had never heard the word before. Was it Woolf's purpose to crack Malone's cover in front of the Russian? Had Woolf decided Peter Ward couldn't cut it, and that this Minot-sponsored operation was impossible?

Potus? Potus? Even while straining to maintain his nonchalance, Malone considered the possible meanings of the word. Report to Potus? Polish Trade? Protocol Office blank blank blank. But why would Protocol receive reports on malnutrition? But the question had been face-tious. Malnutrition on Embassy Row?

Tumark's anticipation was what Malone was most aware of, but everyone was waiting for him to answer.

Finally he said, "Potus is an acronym used in U.S. State Department communications." He smiled disarmingly. "It is not my place to define it here."

Woolf pressed. "It's hardly classified, my dear Ward. Everyone knows who Potus is."

Malone shrugged and let his eyes drift from Woolf to Anna to Tumark. "All the more reason, then, why it is unnecessary for me to define it." Peter Ward, of course, would know what "Potus" referred to. But also, Malone realized now that he had done it, Ward would have refused an Englishman's order to define it in that company too.

In the silence Malone's eyes swung back to Anna. Imperceptibly to all but him, she nodded.

When Malone's glance locked on Woolf's he smiled easily and said, "It's a matter, Mr. Woolf, of being faithful over small matters so that they'll put me over large ones." An ironic Bible quote, Malone knew, was just the thing.

Woolf did not acknowledge the statement in any way, and Malone had to wonder what he'd done wrong. The unpleasant undercurrent between himself and his host seemed all too real.

The Canadian, Hollander, was apparently a man who liked to announce the score, because he said then, "Mr. Ward, you needn't yield to anyone on matters large or small, as far as I can tell. Frankly, the Protocol staff seems a bit of a waste for you. What will they have you doing, folding napkins? That sort of thing?" He leaned down the table. "We should jolly this young man into some wider experience, Victor. Don't you think?"

"My dear James, why do you think I invited him to share the table with you?" Woolf smiled. His charm once more overtook his peevishness. The former tension evaporated. Woolf and Hollander were two old boys sealing the acceptance of a new boy who'd been put through his paces.

Malone didn't buy it for a minute. He recognized Woolf as someone to keep from his blind side, whatever Minot thought of him.

Anna, speaking in the innocuous and—not accidentally—

defusing mode of a wife trumpeting her modest husband, said, "Not folding napkins, Mr. Hollander . . ."

She smiled so winningly, Malone thought at first he was imagining it. In order to look directly at Hollander, she had to lean across Tumark, and as she did the finger of her left hand fell ever so casually, ever so discreetly, onto the edge of the Russian's sleeve. Tumark did not take his arm away.

". . . but serving you and your, you say 'confreres'?"

"Colleagues."

"Yes." She smiled and then, as if reciting from a department brochure, said, "My husband's office protects the rights and immunities of foreign representatives accredited to the United States." Anna looked toward Malone and her first nervousness showed in her face, a look of, Did I say that right, *mon cher?*

Malone laughed and cast his eyes about the table, just one of the guys at last. "So when you get arrested for drunk driving, ladies and gentlemen, I'm the fellow who bails you out."

The RAF colonel crowed, *"That's* why you've invited him, Woolf!" He hoisted the last of his cognac.

"Yes, Anthony. I was thinking of you," Woolf replied to laughs all around, and he stood.

The chill was off the room, as the warmer, only slightly poisoned air of a general exhalation rose to the chandelier. Everyone followed their host's lead, relieved to stand and chat amiably, moving to the library, in groups of two and three.

When Malone faced Muriel Woolf, thinking to accompany her, she excused herself, to see to the help in the kitchen, she said. But Malone sensed some mystery in her. He refused to let it be his problem—yet another failure?—and instead drifted into step behind Anna and Tumark. The Russian had offered her his arm and she had taken it. As they walked Tumark bent toward her ear, speaking animatedly. Malone drew closer to listen just as Anna made her reply, but they were conversing in French. In the library they sat together on a prim settee, where, having received fresh drinks, they remained. They continued their lively exchange, in French, and alone, for the twenty minutes that remained before Muriel Woolf's failure to reappear made clear to the guests that the evening was over.

The ladies' coats were fetched and efficiently donned. In accomplishing his farewells from his place by the door, Victor Woolf held on to Malone's hand for a moment longer than was necessary. Otherwise he gave no sign of their collusion, and Malone left his house wondering, frankly, if Minot had been right to trust him.

Outside Malone and Anna found themselves standing on the narrow, brick-paved sidewalk with Vladimir Tumark. The Russian kissed Anna's hand. When he turned to Malone, he said, "Mr. Ward, I am charmed to know you."

Malone said, "Likewise, Mr. Tumark," but he knew who had done the charming.

Tumark surprised him then. "Mr. Ward, I pride myself on the diplomatic arcane, and I confess to an inordinate curiosity about Potus." He smiled a bit drunkenly, like a man beaming at his bartender. "Won't you consider telling me?"

A man asking his bartender for credit.

But Tumark's meaning was far more loaded than that. Let me bring this small morsel of information back to my cruel handlers—this was how Malone read him—to justify my time with you.

But Tumark had touched an exposed nerve. Whether he was really drunk or not, telling the truth or not, testing Malone or not, he was instinctively tapping against a hollow spot in the wall Malone had built around "Peter Ward." Suddenly he felt that there were watchers on the street, but would they be ours or theirs? he wondered. The shadows threatened.

The dark trees, the hulking silhouettes of automobiles. The city itself, all at once, felt full of enemies, and for the first time Malone was really afraid. He remembered where this lie was taking him, into the Russian embassy itself, a thief. If he failed he was going to die.

But how could he think of that now? "Peter Ward"

would have none of Malone's reasons to feel defensive, and so he worked to keep his anxiety at bay.

Tumark was probably harmless. Infatuated with Europeans and Americans, he had developed a knack for presenting a face westerners loved to see. So they kept him safe by entrusting him with social and diplomatic irrelevancies that he could bring back to Sixteenth Street. "Peter Ward" would surely have found him sympathetic, despite his clumsy flirtation with his "wife," or even because of it. Personal honor was no more an excuse than national security to withhold the innocuous tidbit from him.

But Malone simply did not know what "Potus" meant. He had no choice but to feign drunkenness of his own and cut the Russian because of his overboundary interest in his "wife." But that interest was exactly what they had come to cultivate. Malone could not risk undercutting it now. He stared blearily at Tumark, paralyzed.

Anna took each of them by the elbow—the sober woman—and she pulled them playfully toward each other, like a schoolyard referee. "You can tell Vladimir, darling," she said, and laughed. And then she surprised them both by asking, "Or may I?"

Malone looked at her benignly and nodded, as if yielding the point because she asked him to. It had not occurred to him until now that she would know. "Sure," he said, "what the hell," good and friendly fellow that he was. He slapped Tumark's shoulder.

Even before Anna spoke he felt the Russian's affection flowing in his direction, as it already had, so amply, in hers.

"Potus," she said with dour certitude, "is the president of the United States."

8

Looking up at the gray sky Malone opened his eyes wide and said silently, Here goes.

It was late in the afternoon of November 2, five days before the anniversary celebration at the Russian embassy, and at this meeting the final decision would be made.

"Here goes," he repeated, "or not."

He flattened the collar of his raincoat and looked out from the huge columned portico in which he'd taken shelter. No sign of Minot yet.

This was Malone's first visit to the Capitol itself, and he felt like a tourist waiting for his guide. Minot's message had said simply, "US Capitol-East." What else could that have meant but the east entrance? He was undecided at first whether to go in, but then he thought he should remain where he was, at the top of the broad stairs, easily seen from all across the sprawling Capitol grounds. Through the rain he could see the white splendor of the Supreme Court Building.

It had been drizzling off and on, but the rain had intensified shortly after he arrived by taxi—alarming to him since he was inclined to take the weather as an omen. Nor did he find the stately view before him reassuring. The tall black, nearly naked trees clutched at the sky overhead, but since his perch had him nearly at the level of their topmost branches, the feeling was they clutched toward him.

Being at that height made him think of the rope work
he'd been doing at Quantico, where Marine Corps in-
structors had been taking him well beyond what agent
training had required. By now he had mastered climbing
skills that enabled him to scale the faces of the largest
buildings on the base. Those weekends in tidewater Virginia had been a huge relief, for it was then he concentrated on those parts of this mission that were his alone.
On weekends he was simply Chris Malone again and he
could forget Anna's "husband," if not Anna. He could
be what he was, an FBI agent, with an FBI agent's skills
and resources, his community of support and friendship,
which was nowhere more palpable than at the FBI Academy, where he'd first felt at home in the Bureau. It was a
tidy complex of buildings, athletic fields and firing ranges
all deep inside a sprawling Marine Corps base an hour
and a half south of Washington.

At Quantico it wasn't an imaginary past that Malone
fabricated but his immediate future. He was kept apart
from the other agents, bunking in an isolated building on
the far edge of the academy compound, hardly more than
a shed that in the past had been used as a mock-up
gangsters' hideout against which agent trainees launched
their fierce live-ammo assaults. But even so, it consoled
Malone to be there, and when his eye caught sight of
khaki-bedecked agents in their trilby hats heading for the
firing ranges he wanted to wave. He had never felt the
rare fraternal communion more than now. Perhaps Minot
had brought him out there exactly to quicken that bond,
for it alone kept his otherwise disoriented will from
flagging.

But Minot doubtless had more concrete things in mind.
On that succession of brilliant autumn weekends, while
the solemn trees salted the air with leaves, Malone spent
hours in physical exercise. In addition to the rope work
and conditioning, there were mental exercises too. He
familiarized himself with every make of Russian lock the
Bureau could provide him. He memorized the blueprints
of the reconstructed Russian embassy, with particular
attention to the points of intersection between the main
elevator shaft and the modern heating-duct system that

had been installed throughout the embassy two years before. The contractor who had done the ductwork had met the Russians' specifications, naturally, but also Webb Minot's. It had never been mentioned as a qualification and wasn't now, but Malone understood, as Minot's plan unfolded, that in addition to his skill as a locksmith, and his former distance from Washington, he had been selected for Firebird because he was thin.

The climax of Malone's preparations had occurred when an SE agent named John Hazelton joined him and Minot in Quantico. Hazelton was the agent who had represented Minot in Canada for the year-long debriefing of Igor Gouzenko, the Russian cipher clerk. Using the academy's store of miscellaneous cabinets, as well as cipher equipment from the ASA, Minot and Hazelton transformed the main room of Malone's quarters into a recreation of Gouzenko's Ottawa code room, assuming that the code room in Washington would resemble it. Hazelton went so far as to set the clock on Moscow time and to make a wall calendar on which the days were numbered 1 to 365, with no reference as to month. From the War Assets Bureau Minot had obtained a Czechoslovakian floor safe that matched Gouzenko's description of the code-room safe.

For Malone's first dry run they darkened the room. He had to approach the safe blind, but sight was irrelevant and Malone cracked it—the door had the crucial handle that gave him the necessary pressure on the tumblers—in under forty minutes. Inside the safe he found various volumes and documents that resembled what he would likely find in the real thing. And then, from a key-locked drawer—he picked that lock in seven minutes—he withdrew the prize that Hazelton had promised only the week before—Gouzenko's code book itself. Hazelton had convinced the Canadians to loan the invaluable book to the FBI laboratory for a thorough chemical analysis of its paper and ink, not that it was clear what purpose such an analysis would serve. The book was about the size of a missal, bound in stiff black board, and it felt familiar in his hand, calling up Lenten mornings at mass, those rare times he'd been able to think of himself as a child of

God. But now when he flipped the tissue-thin pages he saw that they were crammed not with Latin prayers but with number groupings and Cyrillic letters, which meant nothing to him.

He handed the book back to Hazelton, thinking all at once that the secret of its Washington equivalent, if he could get it—not to steal but to duplicate, using a palm-sized microfilm camera—would be enough to justify all his lies, even the lie not only of his "marriage" to the strange Ukrainian woman, but the deeper lie, for a lie was what it had become, of his indifference to her.

Malone watched a busload of tourists—Hoosiers, he thought, Buckeyes—filing up the marble stairs, gawking out from under their umbrellas at the massive Capitol. They eyed its pillars—one for every state; its wings—one for each house; its allegories in stone; its statues and pediments and friezes; its crowning dome. When the tourists had mounted the stairs and, folding their umbrellas, began to pass into the entrance, shaking water from their coats, Malone was aware of their shy, sidelong glances at him. Suddenly he realized they thought—or hoped—he was a congressman.

He doffed his hat with the perfect combination of reserve and friendliness, warming their farm-bred hearts. How easily, now, such little deceits came to him. One masquerade after another, but here was the surprise: he was good at it, *great* at it. Others seemed willing—delighted—to accept as true whatever frigging lie he offered them.

Then, alone again, Malone allowed himself to feel what was not a lie, that he had in fact really become different from such people. *This* was true; he was even then in the very act of leaving something behind. He was changing from the outside in, yes; but from the inside out too. For other people's reasons—Anna's, Minot's, Hoover's, even Truman's—but also for his own. And what amazed him was the sense he had that the new person he was becoming at the deepest level was himself.

"This dome is a copy of a cathedral in Leningrad. Did you know that?"

Malone did not need to face the man behind him to know that it was Minot. After a moment Minot joined him, staring out at the rain.

"Saint Isaac's," Minot said. "Eighteen forty-two. The first cast-iron dome in Europe."

Malone glanced at his supervisor. His bleary-eyed visage was no longer a surprise.

"How do you know that?"

Minot shrugged; doesn't everyone?

And once more Malone wondered, Who is this guy? But instead of asking, he said, "I don't suppose the tour guides mention that."

The two men laughed.

Malone consulted his watch. Minot was exactly on time, a precision Malone had come to expect and one that reassured him. Malone hadn't seen Minot passed out drunk since that first night, but the odor of whiskey clung to him. Still Minot always seemed in control of himself. But still, also, Malone felt the tug of his own worry. Couldn't the man leave the booze alone until after?

Minot put a cigarette in his mouth and lit it. "Any wrinkles at the State Department about your invitation?"

"No. Everyone was surprised, of course. Woodward and Muir are the only two who expected to be invited. When I showed Muir my invitation he hesitated. It threw him that it came to me at home. He ran his fingers over it suspiciously. At first I thought he was checking out whether it was real, but he used to be the head usher in the White House, and he was just making sure it was engraved, not printed. Checking out the Russians, in other words, not me. Anyway, once he saw that the chief was delighted that I'd made the Russian list, Muir relaxed. I could see him thinking he should find out more about me, that I was better connected than he thought. Do you know what those guys are? They're valets, they're pants pressers."

"Just don't you start stuffing your handkerchief up your shirt cuff on me. I'll know I've gone too far in making you over."

Malone laughed. "Don't worry. They taught me that *protocol* comes from the Greek and means 'first glue,'

but does it glue people together or gum the works up? I
went with India's new ambassador to the White House
the other day—ambassadress, I should say, since it's Nehru's sister. How's that for taking care of the family? After
she presented her credentials to the president, she had to
walk out of the room backwards, without looking where
she was going. Can you believe it? My job was to make
sure the ushers kept everybody out of her way. I thought
I was going to start giggling, honest to God, like I was in
high school." When Minot didn't respond, Malone fell
silent. Minot still said nothing. How long could they
stand there, staring out at the rain?

High school, Malone thought. Exactly. But now it
wasn't the giggles he feared. Who had he been kidding,
that he was so different now? He began to feel the rising
tide of his old anxiety. To stem it he said, "Madame
Pandit gave Truman a present from India, a baby elephant for the zoo here. She showed him a photograph
and the president said it looked like Dumbo." Malone
laughed. "Truman drives the Protocol people crazy, which
is why I love the guy."

"Maybe before they send you over to the zoo to press
the new elephant's pants, we better wind this operation
up, Pete. What do you say?"

Malone waited for a moment before asking, "So it's all
set?"

"I met with Hoover an hour ago. He gave us the green
light. It seems that in addition to insulting the Nehru
family, our president has been all over J. Edgar's back.
Truman has to decide whether to go forward with the
new bomb—the hydrogen bomb, they're calling it. Now
that the Russians have the A-bomb, Omar Bradley and
the JCS are pushing hard for it, but the AEC is opposed.
Apparently some scientists think after what the A-bomb
did, the H-bomb could blow the world up. Truman does-
n't want to make the decision to start up Los Alamos
again until he knows for sure that Soviet spies won't still
be on board. No point in developing a new bomb if
they're going to get an instant blueprint. However the
Russians were able to read us the first time, we have to
assume they can still do it. We haven't closed in on them

at all; no other leads have panned out, and Hoover knows it. Operation Firebird is the last card he has."

"So did Mr. Hoover tell the president what we're—"

"No. I encouraged him not to. This is strictly 'Do Not File.' We can't have the president approving ahead of time something that's illegal. If you pull it off, then that's something else again. Truman's savvy enough not to make an issue of knowing the details. Hoover told the president we are working up a 'confidential source.' "

"The old Bureau standby."

"In fact, Hoover is totally paranoid about what we're doing. Because of the heat he's getting, Hoover wanted me to move our schedule up. When I reminded him that D-Day is November seven because that's the date of the anniversary party at the embassy, he turned white as a sheet. It had only just dawned on him who was going to be there—not just the Russians, but all the biggest shots in Washington. The guest list includes the vice-president, the secretary of state, Mendel Rivers, Sam Rayburn, two Supreme Court justices and Edward R. Murrow. Hell, the president himself might show up, though not likely, since he can't seem too cozy with the Reds since they just stole the A-bomb from us. And on top of the VIPs there will be all those other ambassadors who will go through the frigging roof if an embassy's—*any* embassy's—sovereignty is violated. When Hoover got the picture that that's who would be downstairs while you're doing the catwalk upstairs, he nearly fainted."

"It makes me a little light-headed myself. You wouldn't be trying to make me nervous about this job, would you?"

"Am I making you nervous, Pete?"

"Yes. Especially when you call me Pete."

Minot shook his head slightly, then said more reflectively, "It may sound strange to you, but it comes kind of naturally to me, to call you that."

"Because that's what you called your brother?"

"Yes."

"What happened to him?"

When Minot brought his face around, Malone saw grief, as he had before, but now Minot seemed not to be in flight from it. Still, he said, "I can't tell you that, not now. I'll tell you another time." He clapped Malone's shoulder with a genuine show of affection. "You were saying I make you nervous."

"Yes."

"Good. I believe in nerves. There's never been a champion yet who didn't want to toss his cookies before the race." Minot gave Malone an easy smile. The man was a master of reassurance, and even now in underscoring the risks involved in the operation, and even in acknowledging the limit to how far he could confide personally, Minot had simultaneously conveyed the depth of his own feeling for Malone. Minot believed in nerves, perhaps, but what Malone saw was that he believed, also, in him.

"We do have a problem, however," Minot said, snapping the ash from his cigarette. He watched as a pair of tourists climbed toward them. Minot smoked in silence.

Malone waited him out. The tourists entered the Capitol.

"It's Woolf," he said finally.

"What do you mean?"

"When I began to sound him out about the part he has to play at the embassy, he balked."

"What do you mean, balked? You know I wasn't thrilled to learn he was in on it from the beginning. Now you're saying he balked?"

Minot flicked his cigarette into the rain. It sizzled even before it hit the ground. "He was in from the start, but not all the way in. I couldn't tell him everything until we were sure we were going ahead. I couldn't tell him you were going to commit B and E on an embassy until I knew for sure we would go through with it."

"But you didn't know that until an hour ago."

"That's right. Which is why we'll be meeting him in" —Minot looked at his watch—"eleven minutes. You have to help me convince him that we can pull it off."

"But Woolf set us up with Tumark and everything else followed from that. What did he think he was doing?"

Minot leaned against the massive stone pillar, putting his back to it with apparent casualness. But Malone sensed that in fact he was as alert as any animal, his eyes steadily scanning the stairs and grounds below them, the benches and even trees and pathways. "Vladimir Tumark is a target of ours, has been for two years."

"Target?"

"We're trying to get him to defect. Woolf and I have been working him together."

A sudden wind whistled up at them, chilling Malone. But had the wind been blowing all along? Had he only just noticed? Tumark and Woolf, he'd accepted them at face value, a pair of midlevel "dips," but the face value of currency in this economy was zero. Was he only just noticing? His gullibility irked him more than the realization that Minot hadn't leveled with him yet either. "So when do I get brought all the way into this operation, Inspector?"

"Woolf's embassy position as minister for commonwealth relations is a sham. He's a deep-cover SIS agent. Not even his ambassador knows it, although I thought you might have guessed it."

Malone felt his face redden. He turned his collar up as Minot looked in his direction.

Minot said, "Tumark is ripe for coming over. All the Kremlin heavies he was close to have been purged since the war. He's identified with the old East-West alliance days. The new hardliners are certain to have him on their list, and he knows it. We've been trying to help him visualize an alternative."

"So Victor Woolf has Mr. and Mrs. Peter Ward to dinner thinking that he's offering Mrs. Ward to Comrade Tumark as a deal sweetener."

"That's right. You don't need to get your hackles up. Woolf knows she's not your wife. He knows you're an agent."

"So he probably assumes that I know what's going on."

"You know what you need to know, Malone."

"I want to know what's expected of Anna."

"Her job is half over. She was to get you invited to the party and she did. Now what she has to do is go to the embassy on your arm and make you look like a good dancer. When the party's over she leaves the embassy and you stay. The logistics of that move are what we are

meeting with Woolf about now. Let's go." Minot abruptly
strode out into the rain, down the stairs, leaving Malone
no choice but to follow him.

Malone wanted to press Minot, but in order to do so
he'd have had to yap at his heels. To keep up with him
he had to close his collar against the rain.

The two men walked briskly away from the Capitol
until they came to the corner of First Street. Malone
thought they were going into the Library of Congress.
But Minot continued past the elaborate, towering Victorian
building to Second Street. Where are we going? Malone
wondered as they crossed this street too. But his question
was promptly answered as Minot led the way up to another imposing edifice—this one a low temple-like, classi-
cal building the shimmering marble of which made Malone
think of the Supreme Court Building behind them. As he
followed Minot up to the entrance and in, he saw, cap-
ping it, a modern sculpted version of the Greek masks of
Tragedy and Comedy, but otherwise he hadn't a clue
what the place was.

Minot ignored a seated guard in the polished marble
vestibule, and the guard seemed content to ignore him
and Malone. They checked their hats and coats at a
counter adjacent to the guard, then crossed through an
inner foyer and through a pair of open, oversized bronze
doors. Now they entered a long spacious hall that seemed
wrong for that building, even to Malone's architecturally
untutored eye. Instead of marble, in here the walls were
oak-paneled, and the arched plaster ceiling took its pattern from wooden strapwork. The floor was rough tile,
not marble. To Malone the place seemed like a guildhall
from the Middle Ages. Along both walls were rows of
display cases, but he didn't see what was being exhibited.

Minot was waiting for him in the middle of the otherwise vacant hall.

"What is this place?"

"The Folger Library," Minot answered. "The Shakespeare Library."

Now when Malone looked around he recognized the
large room as *Elizabethan,* not medieval. The figures
above the display cases were kings and ladies, jesters and

monks, characters from the plays, he guessed. The walls were hung with portraits and banners. There were statues and busts. The cases held books, manuscripts and various other items—jewelry, cups, pieces of costume.

Minot watched Malone taking the place in. Finally he said, "Here they have seventy-nine First Folios. The British Library has five."

"I don't know what that is."

Minot didn't flinch—the man seemed incapable of condescension—as he explained. "Shakespeare's original manuscripts were all lost. First Folios, prompt copies prepared for his actors, are the sole textual source for his plays. Half of them are here." Minot let his eyes drift across the reaches of the hall for a moment. Then he started off again, and Malone followed. Their footsteps echoed loudly as they crossed the room. Malone thought it strange that the eyes upon them were from the paintings on the walls. One portrait was of George Washington, another of Queen Victoria and several were of Shakespeare himself.

Leaving the exhibition hall, they entered a low-ceilinged corridor, and here they passed abreast of several people, library functionaries, apparently, who did not look at them. At the corridor's end, Minot pushed open a stout wooden door.

This room looked more like what Malone thought of as a library. Its walls were lined with books and its floor space was taken up with several dozen library tables, each with a pair of green-shaded reading lamps. At the far end of the room were stacks of shelves, holding yet more books.

Scattered at various tables were readers bent over books, some taking notes. One woman rested her head on her arm and seemed to be asleep. A librarian sat at a raised dais against the near wall, but she had her back to the room, writing. In the silence Malone could hear the scratching of her pen.

Minot set off across the room as if he worked there, making for the stacks. Malone thought it would be better if they meandered, feigning interest in the books. But Minot seemed unconcerned, as if he knew for certain that no one there was watching them. Malone followed him.

Once inside the stacks, out of sight, Malone relaxed.

Now Minot was reading the catalogue numbers on the book spines, and it took him a few moments, wandering up and down the aisles, to locate what he wanted. Finally he withdrew a book from a shelf at a point, in the very corner of the room, where the aisles met. He studied the book, then snapped it closed and efficiently shelved it.

And a moment later he disappeared around the corner. When Malone turned it after him, he nearly bumped into Minot and Victor Woolf, who were standing, backs to Malone, in front of an ill-lit, floor-to-ceiling, lifesized portrait—even Malone knew it at once—of Hamlet, "Alas poor Yorick!," contemplating the skull. A hackneyed painting, Malone realized, consigned to the shadows, a perfect place for their meeting with Victor Woolf.

Woolf seemed mesmerized by the painting. He was standing with the palm of his left hand against its frame. Draped over his right arm was a gray tweed topcoat. In the glare of the cone light above that section of the stacks Woolf's face was pale, his beard flat and unnuanced, false-looking. His eyes were fixed upon the skull as if the thing were real.

He said quietly, " 'Here hung those lips that I have kissed I know not how oft. Where be your gibes now? Your gambols?' "

" 'Your flashes of merriment,' " Minot continued as if the speech were a code, " 'that were wont to set the table on a roar. . .' "

"Yes, where?"

Woolf looked up at Minot and put his hand out. They shook without enthusiasm. Minot indicated Malone. "And you know Peter Ward, I believe."

Malone was surprised that in this remote place Minot maintained the Peter Ward charade. But Malone said nothing and presented his most neutral face when he shook hands with Woolf.

When Woolf then shifted his topcoat to sling it over his other arm, it fell with the label out and Malone's eyes snagged on it. "Thomas Nutter, Saville Row," the same label that marked his own clothes. He understood at once it was no coincidence.

Had Minot lied to him about the clothes belonging to his brother? Had he, in fact, obtained the suits and shirts directly from Woolf or, on Woolf's recommendation, from Woolf's tailor? Had he simply obtained the Saville Row labels from Woolf to give Peter Ward's clothing the proper cachet? In that case Woolf's own suits now would be labelless. Malone understood that, whatever the Saville Row label meant, Minot had yet to level with him about Victor Woolf. "Not now," he'd said about his brother. "I'll tell you another time." Did that apply to Woolf too?

Malone watched as Minot and Woolf stood staring at each other, each rigid and unblinking. But Malone felt that the polished wood floor under his feet was the pitching deck of a ship and any minute its lurch was going to throw him forward and he'd have to grab onto his two stolid companions as if they were banisters. The thought almost made Malone laugh; his job at this meeting was to seem utterly dependable. He was there to make Woolf believe they could pull it off.

"So my dear Minot . . ." Woolf began quietly. ". . . As you were saying?"

Minto did not flinch. "We're sending Ward upstairs as the guests are leaving the embassy. Your role will be to help create a momentary diversion so that Ward can slip away. Then he's on his own and you're finished. But you have to take over Mrs. Ward too, so that her leaving unescorted will not draw notice. Your entire function will take place at the end of the gala and it will require a matter of seconds only, minutes at most."

"Diversion, you say?"

"It's for us to devise now. Something simple, I should think. I have a thought or two. Remember Beograd?"

"But I can't jeopardize my standing with the Soviets now. I can't draw their attention like this, Minot. If I become suspect as anything beyond a Foreign Office functionary, then so does—" He stopped abruptly, then said heatedly, "Good Christ, man, we've just about struck noon."

When Woolf glanced at him for an instant Malone

realized he was talking about Tumark's defection, but the Englishman was not going to refer to it any more explicitly in front of him.

Minot said patiently, "It's a separate operation, Victor. The two things are unrelated and there's no reason to fear shadows from the one falling upon the other."

"It's not shadows I fear. It's light. When our man here gets netted 'upstairs,' as you so blithely put it, the People's State Security kleig will surely be turned upon his wife, which will lead them directly to her new friend. How can you say the two things are unrelated?"

Her new friend? Malone veered from what that implied. He knew he wasn't expected to participate in this debate, but he put his oar in anyway. "My 'wife' will disappear after our operation is over. I won't have come to their notice and neither will she. They won't have any reason to track her."

"They may be already tracking her, in point of fact."

"Why?"

"Because of her weekend walks along the canal. She's at the mercy of her new friend's tradecraft. Who can say if he knows how to shake surveillance."

Minot said, "He shakes us when he wants to."

Woolf frowned, making a show of passing up the chance to slight the FBI.

But Malone's gaze was fixed upon Minot. What he wanted seen was his mystification: What weekend walks? Was Tumark her "new friend"? Why was she at his mercy?

He knew that Woolf's remark would not be explained. Until now it had not occurred to him to wonder what Anna had been doing while he was at Quantico. He was accustomed to thinking that he had functions in this that did not involve her. Now he saw that it worked the other way too. Not that she'd misled him. Her aloofness had been an expression of perfect truth between them. Why, then, did he feel deceived? And why, once again at the wall of Minot's secrecy, was he angry? Anger had no place here, he knew. And neither did the pain he felt to have been kept out of Anna's secrets. Nevertheless anger and pain were what he felt, and if Minot had looked at him then he'd have seen them plain.

Minot remained fixed upon Woolf. "And 'our man here,' Victor, won't get caught." Minot's reference to Malone in Woolf's arch phrase was intended to be sarcastic, a volley back at the Englishman. But to Malone, it was a strangely disembodied statement, made without gesture, without a nod in his direction, as if Malone were invisible. To Malone, Minot's firm assertion was hollow. Unless, of course, he *was* invisible, in which case he could plunder the Russian embassy at will. Maybe that was it, maybe that was what Minot thought.

"What are you after, Minot?" Woolf asked his question of the American like the fierce journalist he once was. "Are you planting a listening device in the embassy? I demand to know what he's going in for! Is that it, a microphone?" Woolf leaned toward Minot, watching him intently.

Minot did not falter in showing nothing, and Malone had to remind himself that his mission had nothing to do with planting a bug. No, it had to do with—what? He looked away from them and found himself staring, alas, at poor Yorick's skull. Didn't that graveyard scene come just before Ophelia's funeral? Why had Hamlet let her die? Why hadn't he put his love for her ahead of intrigue? Malone cursed himself for not knowing, but then what was Hamlet's fate, or Ophelia's, but the make-believe of theater. Theater meant nothing to Malone, no more than opera, no more than Kansas farming. Anna was what he cared about and Woolf had just said that she was at the Russian's mercy.

Minot had put his hand on Woolf's shoulder. "Come on, Victor. You know the game. I'm telling you what you need to know."

"Don't play 'need to know' with me, Minot. Not at this point, not after what we've been through together. I *want* to know. The hell with you."

"Can you keep a secret, Victor?"

"Yes." Woolf leaned expectantly toward Minot.

"Well, so can I," Minot said. And he laughed to have

snagged his British counterpart with the oldest line in the trade. "I can't tell you, Victor. It's that simple."

"Then get someone else to provide our young man here his diversion. Dean Acheson will be there. Maybe even Alben Barkley. Ask them."

"I'm asking you."

"Christ, I *know* what you're after. It has to be the code room. You want the codes. Or is it Fabergé eggs? It's an imbecile idea."

"As I recall, reading enemy mail has served Whitehall well once or twice over the years."

"But we never *stole* the bloody codes; we broke them."

"Ciphers are different now, Victor. This is the age of pure random keys, as you know. I'm asking for your assistance on a matter of utmost urgency to my government. If you don't give it, I am prepared to show you out of Washington myself."

In watching the fierce confrontation between Minot and Woolf, and in seeing how Minot's ultimatum stunned Woolf, Malone thought suddenly that *this* was theater, these were actors in a play. He dismissed an intuition that Minot and Woolf were enacting this scene for his benefit. Malone knew that he *himself* was the actor in this group, he was the one whose job was to make the false seem true. "Really, Minot," Woolf began mournfully, "is it necessary to—?"

Minot still had his hand on the Englishman's shoulder, and now he silenced him by pressing down firmly. "Let me just tell you that we have text that we need to read, and we cannot do so without some clues. And we have to get the clues however we can. If our Russian friend could bring them out I'd happily wait for him to fall from his branch, but he has no access to what we're after. Their security would not trust him with it and as you know their side observes the need to know more rigorously than ours does." Minot smiled, letting his affection show. "I don't want to lose Tumark—"

This was the first reference to their "friend" by name; was Minot's purpose to show Woolf that Malone could be trusted beyond his strict need to know too? Or was Malone still merely invisible?

"—any more than you do, but whether a disenchanted midlevel Foreign Ministry functionary who may or may not be a throwback anti-Stalinist finally defects to our side is small potatoes compared to what I'm dealing with now. Getting my man the invitation which gets him inside the embassy is the most useful thing Tumark will ever have done for us, whether he comes across or not."

"If I'd known you were playing by American rules, Minot, instead of by the rules we'd drawn up together, I'd have stayed out of the game." Woolf turned to be free of Minot's hand.

Malone felt a surge of the same feeling—not that he recognized these rules as "American." If so much had been concealed from him in the beginning, how much remained concealed from him even now? If he had been misled about Anna, that was Minot's doing, he saw, not hers. And that made it worse. In his idea of the Bureau, agents leveled with each other. But in this operation he was not a partner to be trusted with full knowledge. He was a mere technician, exactly like a bug planter. Get in, drop the wire, get out. Or, in his case, get in, crack the safe, snap the pix, get out. Minot was showing his hand only one card at a time. And Malone had a horrible intuition that to Minot, he, Malone, was no more trustworthy than the Englishman.

Minot said, "You have my assurance, Victor, that our end of this will be carried out flawlessly. That's all you need."

Woolf impatiently waved the arm holding his coat, which flapped accidentally against Malone. "It's ludicrous, I tell you. Do you think the Russian embassy is Harrods?"

"No, I don't. I think it is a turn-of-the-century building like hundreds of others in this town. Not Serostlag Prison. Not Potma. Not Spandau. Not a prison of any kind. It's a house with corridors, rooms, doors and windows. The windows are barred only on the ground floor. The doors throughout the building can be opened. We mustn't mystify such places. The Soviets have never had an embassy burglarized anywhere in the world. Their security precautions are aimed mainly against their own people and

consist mostly of surveillance techniques. But against the
outside world their precautions are *pro forma*. They like
thick doors and steel walls but even on their secure
rooms they use locks designed thirty years ago, and their
safes don't compare to what you find in an average
American savings and loan. Look, Victor, we have a
complete set of blueprints for the embassy. We've been
tracking embassy personnel with geiger counters from
across the street. We've been planning this operation for
three years."

Woolf faced Malone directly for the first time, patiently waiting for him to add his assurance. Malone
automatically gave it; "Surreptitious entry for purposes
of microphone installation or mail opening is an old story
with us, Mr. Woolf. We've done it against the Ku Klux
Klan and Communist party leaders, mobsters and even
government offices in connection with HUAC investigations. Breaking into Al Capone's office was harder
than this will be because people like Capone expect it to
happen."

"You're a little young to have taken on Al Capone,
aren't you?" Woolf stared at Malone, waiting for him to
flinch. Malone stared back, by no means convinced that
what he'd just said was true, but the timely appearance
of invincibility was also an old story with the FBI, and he
had no trouble mustering it. Roles on roles, he thought.
Even as Chris Malone, FBI, he was acting now. It shocked
him to realize that in its mundane aspect also, the Bureau
was theater.

Finally Minot said quietly, "He's the best we have,
Victor."

Less because their affirmations disarmed him than because he'd simply reached, as he'd have put it, the end of
that particular lane, Woolf dropped his challenge. "All
that," he said to Malone, flinging his topcoat over his
shoulder, "and your sterling record of service on the
World Refugee Committee. Why, it could fill a man with
admiration." He withdrew a pint flask from the inside
pocket of his draped topcoat, unscrewed the silver jigger,
but didn't use it. He lifted the flask itself—*"Salut!"*—and
took a swig. Then he offered it to Malone, as if his

acquiescence required a liturgical observance, his former reluctance an absolution.

"No thanks," Malone said.

Woolf took another swallow.

What Malone remembered was Woolf at his own table sipping from his water glass. At his dinner party, he had urged the whiskeys, wines and brandies upon his guests but he had drunk less of them than anybody. And yet he was a flask carrier? Like a college boy? A decadent roué?

Without a prelude he handed the leather-covered silver bottle to Minot, who took it automatically. The exchange was one, Malone saw, that had occurred between them many times, a baton between runners.

Despite himself he had to look away while Minot drank thirstily. A picture of Minot passed out on the couch in the living room at Phelps Place was what he saw even as his eyes fell again on Hamlet's portrait.

He wished that the disgust that choked him was for mortality: Alas, poor all of us! But he recognized it as his old repugnance at drunkenness, and he felt afresh the anger of that night in Phelps Place. This man expects me to be his helper? This man who calls me his brother?

But Minot was not his brother, and the rage he felt had its roots in the old neighborhood back of the yards, not in Phelps Place, not anywhere in Washington. Malone curbed his feelings, turning back toward what was real.

Minot is a man whom I can trust, he told himself. And then he added, I trust him because I have to. Does that make me Hamlet? But what the hell do I know about Hamlet except that in being faithful to his father, he failed the woman he loved? The hell with Hamlet, Malone thought, and he turned away from the portrait, saying, Anna. What are they doing to Anna?

Woolf was screwing the cap back onto his flask, and Malone made a mental note that Woolf's attachment to the booze was phony. Roles upon roles: they were *all* actors. This entire operation was a work of theater. Plays within plays.

The one thing Malone could trust as an absolute, as ground on which to stand, was his own investigator's intuition. It told him that Victor Woolf carried a flask of whiskey not for himself but exactly to dispense it to Webb Minot. What *had* these men been through together? What was Woolf's connection—besides a Saville Row tailor—to Minot's brother? In using her to snare Tumark, what had they done to Anna? And which of them, really, was in control?

But Malone's mind came back to the booze. Was it Woolf's role to be there with the regular nip that kept Minot's hand from shaking? Kept him so reliable in daylight? And what of Minot's nights?

And why did it serve Woolf's purposes to have his American counterpart on the juice?

9

Christopher Malone approached the kitchen not intending to be quiet, but with the faucet splashing onto a colander full of peeled carrots, she did not hear him. He stood in the doorway, but she was working at the counter with her back to him.

Slow down, he thought, and he backed away, retracing his steps through the house to the front door, where he hooked his raincoat on the bentwood coat rack. He told himself he had no right to the emotion that had carried him directly to her, and he was grateful that he had not spoken, that she had not seen him in such a state. He had no right to the questions he would have asked her or to the disappointment he felt because he already knew the answers.

Now, as he approached the kitchen again, he called ahead to her. When he came to the doorway she was facing him, poised as always, like a self-accepting diver on a board, a mellow statue. She had turned the faucet off. She was holding a paring knife, twirling it absently. But there must have been some feeling, perhaps even some happiness at his return, for she went slightly up onto her toes when she said, "Hello."

He replied, *"Buon giorno,"* and grinned. Not since that first day in Dupont Circle had he fancied himself an Italian street flirt. He could not use the slang she had taught him without self-consciousness.

She curled her fingers at him—*Ciao*—a hint of the

sarcastic in the gesture, then stood as if waiting for his
next thrust, to parry it, as if this *were* a street in Rome.
Their fencing was always gentle, not pointed, but its
purpose was to keep at their distance from each other.

She wore a functional white apron over a gray woolen
skirt and a V-necked navy sweater that showed her throat,
the white delta between her collarbones. The starched
apron came midway on her chest and accentuated the
normal rising and falling of her breasts.

"You look good in the kitchen," he said amiably,
blunting the stab of desire he often felt on first seeing
her.

"I was at the Pan American Union, that reception for
wives I mentioned."

Wives, Malone thought. She did not look like one.
Even in her demure skirt and sweater, her carefully applied rouge and lipstick, her shoes, which were blue-and-
white high heels, she did not resemble the Washington
women one saw at receptions and restaurants everywhere
in the city. A distinctly exotic air clung to Anna, a
function of her hair, perhaps, so black, so tightly pulled
back from her face, leaving nothing to compete with the
effect of those dark Slavic eyes, their weight, their pull.
Other women spent hours trying to remake their eyes to
look like hers.

"How was it?"

She turned to lower the gas flame under a pot. The
aroma rising in clouds suggested beef, but it was a pungent, sharp smell, not the thin steam of a Chicago boiled
dinner.

Without any particular affect she said, "Ridiculous."
And she began slicing the carrots at the counter again.
She looked slyly at him, over her shoulder. "I did not say
that to them."

Malone felt a wave of defensive indifference washing
over the agitation that had brought him barreling home
to her. How many times had she turned her back like
that, oblivious of what her habitual rejection was choking
off in him? He told himself that he didn't care what she
said to whom.

He turned back into the dining room, toward the buffet, toward the liquor. "I think I'll have a drink," he said to the empty room as he crossed it. At the buffet he lifted the stopper from one of the crystal decanters. Pouring a finger of scotch into a highball glass, his hand shook so that he splashed some of the liquor onto the polished ebony surface of the buffet. He put the decanter down but instead of releasing it he intensified his grip, so that the sharp edges of the cut crystal pressed into his hand. His emotional reactions first to Minot and Woolf and now to Anna shamed him. Why had he wanted Minot to confide in him like a father would in his son? Why did he long now for a sign of warmth, of human feeling, from a woman who was only his co-conspirator, and only his partial one at that?

Conspiracy. From the Latin, "breathe together."

He took a slow, deep breath, then another, then a third, loosening his grip around the bottle while tightening it on himself. The bottle. He stared at it, feeling a shock of recognition at what he'd done. Off the bat of his pain, a line drive, he'd shot to booze. Like his father. Like Minot.

He picked up the glass and swirled the scotch to coat the sides. Jesus Christ, he thought, here goes. He returned to the kitchen. Anna ignored him. After loading the glass with ice, he went to the sink and ran the tap until it was cold, then filled the glass with water. But as he did that he was aware of Anna's eyes on him. Hadn't she seen anybody fix a drink before?

He faced her, raised his glass in the jaunty way Woolf had raised his flask and said, as Woolf had, *"Salut!"*

The watery drink barely registered as he sipped it. Hell, I've got miles to go before this stuff gets its claws in me.

Anna was still watching him and for a minute he thought she was going to ask him to fix her a drink too. How gladly he would have. But instead she turned back to the counter and resumed slicing vegetables—now mushrooms—into the steaming pot.

Malone left the kitchen. On his way through the dining room he splashed another ounce or two into his glass.

In the living room he sat on the beige sofa without

turning the lamp on. When he sipped his drink now he
winced but said gamely, "That's more like it." The drink
settled him and soon he'd purged his mind of thoughts of
Anna and also of Minot and Woolf. In the darkened
room it was as if he'd closed his eyes. He listened to the
rain teeming down outside, the day's cold gray sky still
falling heavily. It was All Souls' Day, he remembered.
The rain blew against the floor-to-ceiling window behind
him, the drawn brown curtains barely muffling it. Rain
like that, to Malone, was like the hum of a car on a long
trip. Cases had taken him on roads and highways all over
Kansas, Missouri, Nebraska and Iowa. In that country, it
was nothing to drive two, three, seven hours to conduct
an interview or to retrieve a stolen car or to check records at a country courthouse, and to do so three or four
times a week. Malone had always traveled with another
agent, but on the open road even men so little given to
introspection invariably fell silent with each other. The
sound of the car's motor, its pitch never changing once in
overdrive, and the endless whirring of the tires on the
smooth asphalt had induced in Malone a blissful vacancy
of mind that had had no equivalent in his time in Washington until now. The drumming rain against the window
four feet away did that for him, and he gratefully surrendered his preoccupations one by one as he sat there in
the dark, until at last he felt a kind of peace.

An hour later Anna came to the doorway. She said
quietly, almost carefully, as if she took nothing for granted,
"Would you come to eat?"

She had taken the apron off. Framed by the glowing
light of the room behind her she seemed taller and slim-
mer than before, a hausfrau no longer. An elegant woman,
but the sight of her for once gave him no pleasure.

"Certainly," Malone said, stifling his resentment. He
would have stayed where he was indefinitely. But this
was the job. He rose and followed her.

The dining room had been transformed, but their evening meals were always formal, and the candles and
gleaming place settings for the two of them did not impress Malone as they had in the beginning. This way of

dining, so unlike anything in his experience, had come to embody the impossibility of their situation. How could their time together be anything but stilted? How could he be himself with her in such a situation? But of course the point was that he should not be himself. Malone was relieved that his earlier emotion—the hurt he'd felt and then his shame at having felt it—had faded. He resolved to treat this meal as if they were in the Federal Building cafeteria.

Ordinarily, at mealtime, she coached him in Italian phrases, but when she passed his steaming plate and he saw what it was, he said, "Beef burgundy! Tonight, *pas Italie, mais la France! Boeuf bourguignon! Très bien!*"

She looked at him sharply. His accent was so crude it was easy for her to think he was mocking her.

But he was grinning like a schoolboy. "Where I come from we call this mulligan stew!"

She could not match his levity, and she seemed not to understand that it was fake. She began to eat in silence.

Malone poured wine into her glass until she nodded. When he'd poured his own he held his glass toward her. She raised hers to meet his, and when the glasses touched, Malone said, "It's a nice meal, Anna. Thanks."

"I hope you like it."

He took a small bite of the meat and after chewing said, "It's good. It's *very* good. Not like stew at all."

"Thank you."

They both ate in silence then and Malone thought that he'd never experienced a slower passage of time. He knew that her mood was even more obdurate than usual because of his initial impoliteness and though he'd resolved not to refer to his former emotional state, he found himself saying, "I think we're both tensing up because, after all these weeks, the big day is almost here."

"Then that is a good reason not to be tense, I think."

"Yes, that's true. I guess I was speaking for myself."

"It is a problem?" Anna eyed him intensely, taking his measure.

He shook his head. "No. Not a problem. Just a passing feeling of, well, I guess you'd call it frustration. It got to me today . . ." Even as his tongue loosened and he heard himself talking to her in precisely the way he'd resolved not to, Malone felt the same sense of peace that had settled on him listening to the rain in the darkened living room. But now he was not alone. He was not tense because D-Day was coming. He was tense because in this woman's presence he had completely stifled himself. And now—this was not a decision exactly, but a discovery—he was going to stop.

". . . that my part in this operation covers such a small corner of it. I've been used to knowing a thing from top to bottom. Bureau work is like that. Where I was before they insisted that you—"

"This is 'Bureau work,' I believe."

"Yes, but not my kind, as you've probably noticed." Malone smiled shyly. He wanted her to know he was admitting something. "On this job, really, I'm just a technician, a combination cameraman and cat burglar, which is all right, I can do that. I don't have any doubt about my ability to do that part. But there've been so many other things I've had to deal with that are *very very* foreign."

"Such as me."

"For one." Malone was startled by her direct statement and by the frankness of her stare, which made him veer. "Foggy Bottom, for another." He sliced through a piece of meat and ate it. He touched his napkin to his mouth, sipped his wine and said, "The State Department is definitely not my—what's that word of yours?—*milieu.*"

"But you have been very successful. There is no reason to think you have not been accepted as Peter Ward. Mr. Minot told me as much."

The pride in her voice pleased him. His success was her achievement too. Hadn't they reversed *Pygmalion?* Wasn't that *their* theater? But Shaw's play was a love story.

He veered from that, saying, "Hell, down the creek, I *am* Peter Ward. It amazes me, but I've done it. I've pulled it off. I really have." Malone felt a blast of his new self-confidence, the prize for having moved into a world that, previously, had simply been beyond his awareness.

This wasn't *Pygmalion* and it wasn't *Hamlet.* It was *Alice in Wonderland,* although in *his* case the adventure included a certain guilty sense that he had claimed his new life at the expense of his old. Out of that guilt he mocked himself now by boasting, "I think I could be first in my class to make ambassador."

"No doubt you could." A smile softened her face for the first time, as if she took some deep satisfaction in having helped him transform an apparent self-doubt. In a few sentences he'd gone from being a mere technician to the first ambassador. She asked him quietly, "Then what bothers you?"

The blurt in which he answered was the only way he'd have dared uncover this: "You do."

"Why?"

"Minot and Woolf laid it out for me today. It's the first I knew you've been seeing the Russian."

Anna's eyes fell to her wineglass in front of her. She picked it up and sipped it rather than look at him, and the light reflecting through the glass from below threw a burgundy mark onto her cheek. All at once she was not a worldly woman but a bruised girl. Malone had a fresh impulse to apologize, to say, Forgive me, I belong on the surface of these things, on the margin of them. I'd happily stay there, but for you. . . .

He said, "Minot made it sound like it's going all right."

She nodded.

He sensed how she had hoped not to speak of this with him, and then he thought, Perhaps she's the one who's kept me out of this part. But why would she do that, unless . . . ?

He asked, "Is it going all right for you?"

"Yes." Her voice was barely more than a whisper.

"Your job is to get him to defect."

Now she lowered her glass and looked at him. The bruise was gone. "There is no word for 'defector' in Russian. There are words only for 'traitor' and for 'emigrant,' and in Russian they mean exactly the same thing."

"Does he know that you are Russian?"

"Perhaps he suspects it. We speak in Russian. But he

knows I am a translator, and I am careful to use a European's accent."

"Is he going to come over?"

"He is vacillating. He has children and grandchildren in Moscow and he is afraid they will be sent to the camps or killed. But his hatred of Stalin is real. The personality cult of Stalin revolts him."

"I thought in order to have a personality cult you had to have a personality." He grinned.

Anna looked at him blankly, apparently unaware that he had made a joke. He felt stupid, a shallow American once more. What he wanted to be was her friend. Malone said carefully, "And Tumark, in addition to hating Stalin, is supposed to have a new motive in his feeling for you? Is that the idea?"

Anna shrugged. "His feeling for me is passing. He simply needs the sympathy of a listener during a time of turmoil. It is difficult to choose when loyalties collide. That he can speak of these things in Russian makes me different. He is an old man. I am a young woman. If that helps him to confide—"

"I'm surprised he trusts you."

"Beria's agents are his only enemy. He knows I am not MGB because I am married to an American diplomat."

"But you could still be MGB, couldn't you? I thought the first rule in this game is: nobody trust anybody."

"What Vladimir feels has nothing to do with trust. Mr. Minot does not expect him to be unafraid of us. Only to be *less* afraid."

"Vladimir." Malone nearly checked himself before going on because he thought she'd hear in his statement the note of disappointment he knew was there. "I envy him that you call him by name."

Anna nodded, as if she'd been waiting for this complaint. "I find it is easier than with you, since he has only one name. At times I am not sure whether the man I am with here in this house is Peter Ward, or is he Christopher Malone? Now, for example. Who is it that is sitting across this table from me, telling me he objects to my seeing another man? But that must be my husband, no? And he is thinking I am unfaithful as a wife. But this man whom I see across from me does not seem like Peter Ward, who nowhere learned to speak as he is speaking, who is too consumed with his own purposes, his ambitions and his causes to think of a wife's unfaithfulness. But if this man across from me is Christopher Malone, my fellow actor, then of what concern is it to him if my duty requires a further masquerade with a sad old man who struggles to leave his slavery behind? You see, I do not know who you are, and that is why I do not address you, using your name."

Malone wanted to say, I don't know either. But he *did* know. He was both men now. And if she was telling him that, after all, who she wanted was the man—the simple man—he'd been before, he was going to rail at her. Why hadn't she said so then? He had to work to keep his voice free of emotion, to declare himself. Both men, yes, but still a man with one heart, one face, one *real* name.

"I'm Chris Malone, Anna."

"Then you are not my husband, and you have no need to know about—"

Malone slammed his hand down onto the table, making the silverware jump. "Please!" He had shouted the word, and now, when he paused, the force of his voice could still be felt hanging above them, like the aftershock of an artillery shell. "Don't talk to me about the need to know. I've had the course on that from Minot. Don't flatter yourself, Anna. My issue about Tumark has nothing to do with marital fidelity, real or otherwise. My issue is more basic and has to do with getting into and out of the goddamn Russian embassy without getting my ass killed, if you'll forgive my fucking French!"

A sharp silence fell when Malone cut himself off. He had just lied to her, and he knew it. Or had he? Was *that* the issue? Just plain old fear of the coming action? He looked away, staring back at the ebony buffet, the bottles of liquor. I need a drink, he thought. That's how I know my name's Malone. I need a fucking drink.

After a moment, Anna said, "Tumark won't get in our way at the embassy. He will have nothing to do with us. Once I think he looked forward to dancing with me, displaying his charms, but not now. He cannot seem overly interested in me in front of his comrades. So there is nothing from him to be concerned about. And as for me, I will be exactly what you need."

"I don't like your having more than one role in this play, that's all. It took me by surprise. I think when the stakes are as high as they are and the mission is as difficult, it's not too much to ask that we each concentrate on one thing." Oh, listen to me, Malone thought. Now I'm Cecil B. De Mille. I'm the director of this melodrama, giving my leading lady tips. "That's the infidelity, see. I don't want you to be bait for some two-bit papa-san defector. I want you to be my wife, period."

"Peter Ward's wife," she said, lightly, trying to temper him, to no effect.

"I don't want the security commissars at that embassy looking *twice* at us . . ." This was his version of the objection Victor Woolf had made. Malone's head was beginning to ache, as if nerves in his brain knotted with each new recognition. ". . . and if they've seen you with Tumark they'll be on us like gum on a seat at the movies."

"They won't have seen us."

"You think the Russians don't stroll down the C and O Canal?"

Now Anna displayed *her* surprise. "How did you know that?"

"Jesus Christ, don't tell me I finally know something! I'll be damned."

"Mr. Minot should not have told you. Now we will have to change it—"

"Jesus, listen to yourself, Anna. I'm the guy who's going inside, what do they call their code room, the *referentura*. I think that gives me the clearance even you need to trust me."

"As I said, it isn't a question of trust."

Malone demanded, "Then what is it?"

"It's how it must happen," Anna said fiercely, "if I am to do this!" And she buried her face in her hands.

Not fiercely, Malone saw, but desperately. She had deep emotions of her own, and he sensed for the first time since she'd spoken to him of Poltava that she was at the mercy of them. Only now those emotions were what made her rigid. His impulse was to stand and go around the table to her, or to reach across, just to touch her sleeve. But he couldn't move. He felt terrible. He'd been too preoccupied with himself to see how awful this was for her. He waited for Anna to lift her face, but when, after a long time, she did, it was to stand abruptly and pick up her plate and the serving bowl and retreat to the kitchen.

She was at the sink, the water running, dishes under it. She turned half away from him. Malone put his plate on the white enamel drainboard. "Let me do the dishes," he said, removing his suitcoat and rolling up his sleeves. "I always do the dishes."

Anna snapped a dish towel from the hook beside the sink and moved away, drying her hands. She returned to the dining room while Malone plugged the sink to let it fill. Ordinarily he filled a pot with hot soapy water so that he could use the rest of the sink for rinsing, but it seemed important now to get on with the washing as directly as possible. He buried the dirty dishes in the suds and while the sink was filling he wiped down the drainboard. Anna returned with the rest of the dishes and glasses. She offered him his half-full glass of wine, which he downed in one swallow. Then he plunged the glass into the water.

He washed and she dried. They did not speak, and from all appearances the silence between them did not become awkward until the last dish was put away. Then Malone stood idly, watching her fold the damp dishcloths over the cabinet door. She straightened and faced him.

"I'm sorry, Anna. I shouldn't be kibitzing you. That's not Peter Ward's job, and it isn't Chris Malone's."

"I know it is difficult for you."

"It was a surprise to me, is all, to find that you are so exposed. It surprised me that I can't do anything to protect you."

"There is a flaw in your assumption." She raised her brow at him.

"That you need protecting?"

"Yes." She eyed him steadily, speaking in a briefer's

monotone, which was itself an assertion of her competence. "Vladimir Tumark is a senior minister, a member of the *nomenklatura*. Before Andrei Andreyevich Gromyko, the ambassador to Washington was a Jewish liberal named Maksim Litvinov. Tumark was his *confidant*. Litvinov was identified with the alliance. It was he who convinced Roosevelt to defend Russia against Churchill at Yalta. But when the war ended he fell from favor. He was too close to the Americans. Gromyko was much harsher and he was suspicious of Tumark. But Tumark, especially since Litvinov's departure, maintained connections in Washington that even Gromyko was reluctant to sever. But now Gromyko has returned to Moscow and there are rumors that he has been demanding Tumark's return also. Before he was in Washington Tumark was head of the International Economic Relations Faculty at the Moscow Institute. He trained many of the present generation of Soviet diplomats. He knows who of them have been trained also by the MGB. If he came to work for our side. . . ." She shrugged. Imagine.

"Why would he?"

"That's the problem. He won't work for us. He very simply wants to come over and to be left alone. Stalin has destroyed his dream of socialism, but he will not trade Soviet slavery for FBI slavery. He wants a defection without publicity and without—what do you say?—confession. The defection is treason enough for him."

"But not for Minot and Woolf."

"They have refused to promise him asylum if he will not cooperate. They expect him to tell them everything, the entire Soviet operation in America. They require him to become a *stukach*, an informer. He rejected their proposition totally."

"And that's when they turned to you."

"Yes."

"Your job is to sweet-talk him—"

"No." Suddenly Anna's face went rigid. "My job is to be photographed with him."

"What, walking arm in arm along the C and O Canal?"

"Yes. Even though it is a public place, they want me to touch him, to seem intimate. I never see the photogra-

pher, but I know that Mr. Minot is getting what he needs
for—"

"Blackmail."

"Yes."

If she could muster such detachment, so could he.
"And Minot laid this out for you? He *told* you that's
what he's after?"

"He didn't have to."

Malone forced a laugh. "God, Anna, maybe you jumped
to a conclusion or two. There's more than one way to get
Tumark over. You've just hit on the most obvious, that's
all. There's more than one way to compromise him. You
don't know what Minot is thinking. Maybe he doesn't tell
you any more than he tells me." Malone stopped. For
once they didn't look away from each other. He wanted
to ask, Why is it that you're doing this? Explain it to me
again. He wanted to ask, Will you do anything Minot
asks of you? He saw for the first time that he and Anna
were alike in playing parts not written for them.

"How about a drink?" he asked. "You're not going to
make me drink alone again, are you? What'll it be?
Brandy?"

Anna hesitated, then said—it was a joke between them
that had begun with his ignorance—"Cognac." In the
beginning he'd thought the two words referred to different drinks.

"Go on into the living room. I'll join you."

When Malone carried the balloon glasses into the living room a few minutes later, Anna was standing over
the phonograph placing the needle arm on a record.
Chopin? Puccini? *The Firebird Suite?* Malone waited to
hear what she'd chosen.

"Jesus, Anna," he said above the sudden blare.

"The Red Army Chorus," she said. " 'Patriotic Songs
of the Revolution.' "

Malone put the glasses on the low table and sat on the
couch. How about Nat King Cole? he thought. How
about "Stardust"? Jesus Christ! The pounding martial
music was too loud to speak over, but she had remained
at the phonograph anyway. She stood with her back to
the room, staring down at the turntable, apparently trans-

fixed by the revolving black disk. Malone had to remind
himself that the robustly sung lyrics would not be meaningless to her, as they were to him. It was easy nonetheless
to picture a field full of young men, red stars on their
hats, singing fervently. Malone heard blood pounding in
the music.

"Would you turn it down, please?"

Anna did so. The martial music faded slowly into the
background. Then she turned and crossed to the chair
adjacent to the couch on which Malone sat. She placed
her hands in her lap and stared at them.

Malone picked up the glasses, gave Anna hers. "I
hadn't noticed Russian records in the collection."

"Vladimir gave it to me. This is the music of his youth.
It never fails to stir his loyalty, he says."

"Does the same for me, a different loyalty, however."

Anna smiled. "He says the revolution was the most
noble event in history, but it was corrupted. He believes
Stalin killed the party as a true political movement."

"And you believe he means it?"

Anna hesitated and Malone saw a hint of—what? An
emotion she had yet to display. She nodded. "The people
who see Russia the way Tumark sees it have mostly all
been killed."

"Then why hasn't he been killed?"

Anna sipped her cognac, then said, "Gromyko protected him until returning last year to Moscow."

"But Gromyko carries water for Stalin. If he thinks
well of Tumark. . . ." Why am I trying to undercut her?
Malone asked himself.

Anna had a version of the same question. "Why does
it offend you if I believe him? What matters is that he
believe me."

"Believe what of you?"

"That I care what happens to him."

"Anna, why do I get the feeling that you do?"

Instead of answering she swished the cognac in her
glass, ever so slightly watching the liquid slide, a small
ocean between two shores.

Malone tried to put this present self-possession of hers
together with that biting passion she'd first displayed in

recounting the vicious story of her girlhood. Did she
believe Tumark innocent of Stalin's crimes just because
he denounced them now? If Tumark thought the brutish
Stalin had betrayed the delicacy of Lenin's vision, why
had Stalin's system rewarded him? What did Anna think
Tumark had done to earn a place on the *nomenklatura*
and then to keep it through the brutal purge that followed the war? Or did she take Tumark's crimes for
granted and then forgive them? But Anna's father had
not been innocent either. He had robbed the dead. And
was Anna innocent if she wore the gold her father had
stolen? What did it mean that she "cared" for Tumark if
she was prepared to blackmail him?

She raised her face to him. "Are you asking as my
husband?"

"I'm asking as someone"—he paused but only for half
a beat, long enough to know that if he did not say this
now he never would—"who cares about you."

The Russian music stopped; the phonograph speaker
crackled as the needle bounced back and forth between
the innermost grooves. Anna, seeming not to hear it,
made no move toward the machine.

Malone found her silence so strange, not to mention
her willingness to forgo even a minimal explanation, that
he began to conjure one himself. He imagined her saying,
"To Minot and Woolf, Vladimir is a mere piece on the
board in their game with the Soviets. To me he is perhaps something else." He imagined her pausing before
an emotional admission. "Vladimir Tumark is like my
father. He is old and caught. It is not for me to judge
what he has done to survive. It is enough for me to sense
his longing now. He wants to be free but he is afraid. I
could not help my father. I will help Vladimir."

And he imagined himself asking curtly in return, "By
blackmail?"

But this was an exchange that did not take place.
Malone had turned back on himself. Where before he'd
resented her feeling for Tumark, now he wanted to believe it was genuine, to believe, that is, that she was
capable of such feeling.

But only he had made such an admission. The words

he had in fact spoken hung in the air between them. He
cared about her, as he'd put it, because she made his
divided self feel whole. In her presence he did not worry
about who he was or what he could do. And he felt that
way despite the formidable, unexplained inhibition that
kept her from responding to him.

Finally she said quietly, "You have no right to say such
a thing to me."

"I'm aware of that." Malone blushed. He'd said so
little compared with what he felt. "I withdraw it," he
said, as if he were an overruled attorney. Then he swallowed enough of the heady liquor to feel it kick the back
of his nose. He stood, crossed to the phonograph, removed the Red Army record and put it carefully into its
envelope, which was covered with closely printed Russian text. Just more coded language I can't read, he
thought. He felt surrounded by secrets. He snapped the
machine off, then went into the dining room for the
cognac bottle, aware of the impulse as a drinker's response, but he didn't care.

When he'd returned to his place on the couch he filled
the well of his own glass. With an impersonal show of
courtesy, he offered the bottle to Anna. She nodded and
so he filled the well of hers too. If you asked him, they
could both do with some lubricating.

He sat back and sipped the stuff in silence. The drink
warmed him pleasantly, so overwhelming the chill that
had fallen between them that it scared him a bit. Maybe
this shit has its claws in me after all, he thought.

And then nothing. For a long time neither of them
spoke. The only sound was of the rain beyond the bay
window. He closed his eyes and listened to it as he had
before, the patriotic music of All Souls' Day.

It took him by surprise when she muttered something.

He didn't understand and asked her to repeat it.
"What?"

"I said I am sincerely sorry."

"You are?"

"Yes."

But did he have the right to ask, What for? Malone
was not indifferent to the changed tone of her voice,

which was purged suddenly of defensiveness, as if she too was ready to acknowledge all they had in common. But then a new question occurred to him, or was it only *his* way of removing the charge from the electric air between them. He wasn't going to invite another rebuke from her real soon.

"The invitation for us to attend the ball at the embassy . . . ?" He smiled thinly. ". . . Mr. and Mrs. Peter Ward?"

"Yes?"

"Did Tumark arrange that before or after you began to meet him?"

"After."

"But it was Woolf who suggested to Tumark that he invite us."

"No. Vladimir would never have seen to our invitation just to please Victor Woolf. Vladimir is resisting Woolf, not trying to please him. It is me he wants to please. I told Vladimir the invitation would be so helpful to your career. He is fond of me, you see, in a fatherly way and he accepts me as an ambitious diplomat's devoted wife."

"Devoted but lonely, is that it? Jesus!"

At last Malone's anger was not at Anna or Minot or Woolf, but at himself for knowing so little how this game was played.

Anna's flirtation with Tumark was for Malone's benefit first, because everything depended on obtaining the invitation to the anniversary gala. If Minot had refused to describe Anna's true function, wasn't it because he assumed that the midwestern Malone would feel sullied? And though he knew it made him some kind of prig, he did. He felt caught in a web of choices every one of which seemed wrong. But hell, who was he to disdain Minot's methods or Anna's cooperation in them? The entire sequence of this operation had begun when, in accepting Minot's initial proposal, he himself had accepted its premise, which involved, at minimum, a serious breach of the law he was solemnly sworn to uphold.

Malone remembered a lean, bald Jesuit with flaking skin, his Loyola professor of moral theology, bellowing from the lecture platform at the head of Xavier Hall, "The ends never, ever justify the means!" What Malone

knew now was that, at some point, he had surrendered
the high ground of that fine ethical principle. What was
the priest's name? Father Walsh. Now Malone imagined
himself raising his hand, then standing to rebut the Jesuit,
as firmly as he could. "If the ends don't justify the
means, Father, nothing does." Then, of course, he would
leave the lecture hall without bothering to collect his
notebooks, boldly, without looking back, like Adam leaving Eden.

"I did not mean you should withdraw what you said."
Anna put her cognac glass down on the table, then took
a cigarette from the silver table tray and lit it with the
heavy, felt-bottomed lighter. She remained hunched forward, considering what to say. Smoke obscured her face,
rising in swirls above her tightly pulled-back hair, making
her seem an exotic figure, like a seer, a reader of cards.
She put her hands against her temples as if pressing in a
language with which to speak. Her voice was barely
audible when at last she found it. "I meant, when you
said to me that you . . . cared for me . . . it puts what we
are doing in a different light. It makes it more difficult to
know how to act. . . ."

"Maybe it would help you act like a wife if you knew
that I—" He stopped. How to say things, was the problem, without saying them.

"But I am not a proper wife." She rocked even farther
forward, dragged deeply on the cigarette and veiled herself again in smoke. "It is not my role to be a proper
wife. I did not mean you had no right to say such a thing
to me. I meant, I have no right to say it to you."

"I would give you the right, if you wanted it."

He watched her hand pressing the side of her face
nearer to him, waiting for that hand to fall so he could
see her eyes. Instead what he saw were her gold ring, her
diamond.

She shook her head firmly: no. "What we are doing is
too important—"

"What we are doing is too dangerous not to be truthful
with each other." Unconsciously, Malone moved forward
to the edge of the couch, mirroring her posture.

She dropped her hands and looked at him. Her eyes were wet. "Are you afraid?"

"Yes. But not of them. Not of the *referentura*."

A tear spilled onto Anna's cheek.

He watched it fall slowly, all the way to the corner of her mouth. She made no sign that she was aware of it, and it was possible to imagine that she had not felt a tear on her cheek in years, since Poltava, since her last glimpse of her father, since the sight of corpses littering the fields she crossed.

"I am afraid of you," he said.

"Why?"

"Because I feel so drawn to you. Because I am drawn to you more powerfully than I've ever been drawn to anyone or anything before. Because you could never feel such a thing for me."

The last thing he'd meant to do was hurt her. Anna's face collapsed. She closed her hands over it, as if her eyes, cheeks, nose, mouth, chin, her lips were what shamed her. Bent double over her knees, she began to sob. Her cigarette fell to the floor, but she was unaware of it.

Malone reached to the floor by her foot to retrieve the burning cigarette, snuffed it in the ashtray, then put his hand on her shoulder.

But for the occasional public embrace, as when dancing, or clasping of hands as the counterfeit married couple, he had almost never touched her. Her body felt soft to him, even though his fingers were pressing through her sweater onto the bone of her shoulder. She who had seemed so hard, who had, in every situation—at embassy receptions and Georgetown dinner parties, State Department briefings and also dangerous meetings with a potential Russian defector—through it all she had looked out from behind a thick veneer of what others took to be worldly propriety but he knew to be carefully layered tradecraft. She who had *succeeded* in being hard, was soft. He wanted to say, You can be soft with me.

The unaccustomed thought that he should be the one reassuring her kept him mute. Still, in the texture of his own hand he felt the depth of her grief, a physical movement through her body, one he was prepared—though God knew how he could be—to receive.

When her emotion eased and she lifted her hand, he withdrew his hand from her shoulder, offered her his handkerchief and said simply, "Tell me."

In wiping them she kept her eyes carefully averted. "I believed that too, that I could never feel such a thing for anyone. And then nevertheless having such a feeling, I believed that I would never speak of it."

Malone stopped breathing. For anyone? For whom?

As if she'd read his question, she looked at him and said, "For you."

An understatement, yet Malone had never heard more explosive words. He offered her his hand, an understated gesture. When she took it, he calmly drew her to the couch beside him and very slowly ran the knuckle of his forefinger along the tracks of her tears, wiping them. Only then did they kiss, a series of small, chaste kisses at first.

He had always thought of her as a woman with a past, but he sensed, as their passion grew in intensity, that she was as new to this as he was.

"Christopher," she whispered, and having opened her mouth she took his tongue into it.

When he heard his name, so unfamiliar-sounding on her lips, he expected her to say, "This is impossible! Impossible!" He kissed her more passionately, in part to silence her before she could list the objections to what they were doing, Minot's objections, Tumark's, Woolf's, J. Edgar Hoover's, his own.

But she had nothing more to say, neither protest nor avowal, not a jot to add to her simple, eloquent "For you." She stayed with him as the pitch of their desire soared. When he lifted her sweater, he felt her hands on the skin beneath his shirt too, her nails cutting him.

They fumbled futilely with each other's clothing until, as if on the same impulse, they stopped suddenly and stood. Malone glanced awkwardly at the draped bay window behind them—were their shadows displayed? Were watchers out there in the rain?

Anna held on to his hand and turned to lead him out

of the living room. He followed her through the dining room and kitchen to the door to her rooms. It was always closed. He had never been inside. Anna opened the door and led him in. She dropped his hand so that with both of her own, even as she walked, she was able to swiftly remove pins from her hair. With one brisk shake it fell free, a raven downpour to her shoulders.

Of her two rooms the smaller was the first. It held a chair and a bookcase, but it was dominated by a large Byzantine icon that hung above the bookcase, gold and deep red, a woman's face, eyes like black stones, and a shimmering circle of golden light around her head. A candle burned on the top shelf of the bookcase below it, the only light; its flickering sent a moving shadow wafting back and forth across the face of the icon. It was the kind of candle his mother had lit every week at the Virgin's feet in Saint Gabriel's, praying, he'd always assumed, for an end to his father's drinking.

Anna crossed herself, right shoulder to left, as she moved past the icon into the other room. There was no door. The room was dark, illuminated only by what light spilled from the votive candle, but in its shadow he saw her narrow bed.

She turned and faced him. He remained at the threshold of the two rooms. The light shifting on her face, which was framed now by her fallen hair, made her seem herself like a figure on an icon, that mysterious but in no way that remote. Her beauty was complete, and so also was her availability.

Slowly, separated by the length of a small oriental rug, watching each other, Anna and Malone undressed.

He was naked before she was but he waited, marveling at the sight of her dark body—her breasts, her finely turned legs, the shadow between her thighs. When she was ready she looked at him squarely, but she was unable to check the shudder that quaked her shoulders, as if she were naked in the rain.

This time it was she who raised a hand to him. "Christopher," she said, though now his name in her voice did not sound strange to him. He went to her, believing, for the first time in too long, in the exact correspondence between what seemed to be true and what was. They grasped each other's hands and knelt shyly, each taking cues from the other with a naturalness that left aside for once any question of ineptness or expertise, any thought of superiority. He eased her back onto the carpet, remaining for a moment on his knees beside her, stunned by the length of her nakedness. When he bent to kiss her breasts she caressed his face, drawing his eyes into hers. He took her fingers into his mouth, her fingers hung on his teeth. He covered her breasts with his hands, reading her nipples, the tiny ridges and protrusions, as if they were the grooved flanges of the dial of a combination lock.

He moved his hands along the curves of her ribs, waist and hips, then stroked the soft skin inside her thighs, brushing the hair at her vagina. When he fondled her there she arched up, opening her legs, all the while staring at him with an expression, pure as any icon's, of longing and fear, but also of something else.

In the votive shadows he could not hold her eyes still enough to see what it was. Another mystery.

But he did not care. "I love you, Anna," he said, as she took him—and as he went—inside of her.

10

Malone had never seen anything like it. The ballroom on the second floor of the Soviet embassy was the size of a gymnasium, and the expanse of its walnut floors peppered with rosewood butterflies gleamed like court parquet. On one long wall, eight floor-to-ceiling windows overlooked Sixteenth Street. The windows were closed against the November night, and they were framed by sweeping blue draperies, but the lights of the street glistened like ornaments beyond the ornate iron balconies protruding from each window. In the center of the room was an enormous multitiered crystal chandelier, an arrangement of shimmering droplets, rods and prisms through which red, blue and gold flashes of light waltzed, as it seemed, to the music of the chamber orchestra that was ensconced on the high narrow balcony on the second long wall opposite the oversized windows. Under the chandelier, the guests too had begun to dance, graceful, tuxedoed men and coiffed women in strapless gowns and gloves past their elbows. Each of the walls at either end of the room was anchored by a large fireplace in which flames too seemed to keep time to the music. Above the fireplace opposite Malone was a life-sized portrait of Lenin, draped in red bunting in honor of the anniversary. He was addressing the crowd at Finland Station.

Not this crowd, Malone said to himself. Lenin would have thought he'd stumbled by accident into a palace of the czar. In a smaller room behind Malone—it had prob-

ably served the original owner of the mansion as a formal
dining room—a long table was spread with a lavish buffet. Guests were steadily grazing, selecting from a dozen
kinds of caviar, duck, pheasant, various roasts, sturgeon,
salmon, salads, pyramids of fruit, cheeses, breads and
hors d'oeuvres made of foods Malone neither recognized
nor trusted. In the hour they had been there, he had
eaten nothing, and was now standing in the arched doorway that separated the dining room from the ballroom.
He held a highball glass half full of amber liquid. The ice
was melted but he had refused every waiter's offer to
replace it. His free hand was hooked in his cummerbund.
To all appearances he was merely enjoying the sight of
the dancers happily whirling about the gilded room as if
they were figures in a *grande dame*'s dream. In fact he
was quite deliberately standing on the brass floor grate,
in size two feet by two and a half feet, through which a
steady current of heat was rising into the room. He had
counted eleven such grates in the two rooms, and had
observed how they were fastened with four brass bolts.
The first trick, if he made it that far, would be undoing
such bolts from under the grate, not above it.

But that was one of the problems for later. Right now
his job was to be fully what he appeared to be, a dashing,
well-connected, jovial, American Foreign Service officer.
He took a swallow of his drink with the careful relish of a
man sipping old whiskey. The waiters circulated steadily
through the crowd with trays holding glasses of Georgian
champagne and also vodka, assorted mixed drinks, especially martinis, which the diplomats favored, and highball
glasses like the one Malone held. But instead of scotch
and water, his contained ginger ale. It had been a gamble
at the crowded bar to perhaps draw attention to himself
by ordering a soft drink, but it would have been a greater
gamble to risk drinking alcohol tonight.

"Hello, darling," Anna said, touching his arm from
behind. She was returning from the powder room.

His smile, when he faced her, was not the counterfeit
greeting he'd been offering others. She was not, by the
standard, say, of magazines, the most beautiful woman at
the gala ball, but to Malone she had never been more

ravishing. Upon having mounted the curving grand staircase on their arrival, they'd found themselves standing
together before a wall-sized, gilded mirror. Malone, who
had never worn black tie before taking up his duties in
the Protocol Office, might not have recognized himself
anyway, but the stunning woman on his arm had made
him all the more a stranger to himself. She was wearing a
black velvet gown, perfectly fit and cut to emphasize her
long, lean figure, plumpness nowhere but at her ample
décolletage. In the reception line, waiting to greet the
Russian ambassador and his wife, Malone had noticed
that most of the other women's gloves were white and he
wondered, *protocolier* that he'd become, if Anna's violated a norm in being black. Their effect, in combination
with the rich black of her gown, was to make her bare
upper arms and shoulders and the curves below her throat
even whiter than they were, which served in turn, as he
saw once he began to look, to emphasize the vibrant
color in her cheeks and the depth of her dark eyes. Her
hair was not pulled severely back behind her ears for
once, like a Puritan lady's, but was swept loosely up from
her nape, and piled in a curving swirl, like the inside of a
shell. Though curls fell at random, gracing her face and
ears, the whole of her hair was held in place at the crown
of her head by the diamond-studded comb of a signorina.
At her throat was a large, tear-shaped sapphire pendant.
Every woman present was wearing her best jewels. Many
were from East Bloc nations, and they were more
frumpishly gowned and their jewelry was garish. Anna's
comb and sapphire were beautiful to Malone because
they were as simple as they were elegant, but to the
others, many of whom did not conceal their admiration,
Anna's jewels were stunning because the diplomats' wives
knew exactly what that sapphire and those diamonds
were. What Malone knew was that he wished he'd given
them to her. He knew also, though he never would have
mentioned it, that her jewels had come from the graves
her father robbed.

"Have you seen him?" she asked.

"Tumark? No. I expect he's here somewhere, though.
He must be."

"I thought he'd be in the reception line."

"No, darling." Malone grinned to display his expertise. "Only the ambassador, the ambassador's wife, *his* protocol chief, his minister counselor and his chancellor. Not a first secretary in the bunch."

"Vladimir was the minister counselor to Maksim Litvinov."

"Well . . ." Malone stopped himself from saying that Tumark had slipped a bit. He disapproved of his resentment toward Tumark.

Anna was casting her eyes about, searching the crowd, a little too obviously.

Malone touched her arm to snag her eyes and hold them. "Victor Woolf is here, however. He was guzzling champagne. Speaking of which, can I get you something?"

"No." She let her velvet clutch dangle from its wrist strap, taking his arm with both her hands. "I thought perhaps we might dance."

"And *I* thought you'd never ask." He grinned. "You *know* how I've been looking forward to it. Let me get rid of this." She released him so that he could cross to intersect a passing waiter, to place his glass on the tray. When he returned he offered her his arm and led her cotillion-style to the edge of the dance floor, where they went into each other's embrace and began to waltz.

To Malone's great surprise the flow of the dance came naturally to him at last, and he actually had a sense of himself as the leader. In the living room at Phelps Place, with the chairs pushed back, he'd finally overcome his lumpishness, but never for a moment had either of them been able to pretend that Anna was not firmly in charge. But now she'd handed herself over so completely that, as it seemed to him, they'd begun to move as one person. No matter how he turned or swayed she was with him. As soon as they began to dance they became one of the couples against whom the others measured their own waltzing. Malone was suddenly and surprisingly enchanted. The magic of the scene, the music, their movement, the elegant couples around them, the flashing light of the chandelier above and the woman of his dreams so lightly in his arms—it was all so perfect, so much his own, that for a moment Malone forgot that this was a world to which he'd gained access dishonestly. He forgot that this anomalous version of it—a Bolshevik gala ball—was itself dishonest. Not even a South Chicago kid—apparently no more than hardened Marxists—was immune to the charms of the civilized rituals of European high society. Look at me, he thought! And the world's envoys did.

And so did Anna. Her eyes never left his face. The simple fact of her love for him was apparent in her expression. Webb Minot would have admired her, thinking she was feigning it; they seemed the perfect young couple whose marriage had yet to lose the edge of passion. But what would the MGB watchers make of her, Malone suddenly wondered, if they had been tracking Tumark after all? *This* woman strolling hand in arm with a senior Soviet diplomat? And with that thought, the spell was broken. Malone missed a step and cut off another couple. He nodded an apology at them, and when he looked at Anna he felt himself blushing. He still had not reconciled himself to her role in the wooing of Tumark. He did not regret it when, a moment later, the music ended.

They drifted away from the center of the room while other couples moved into it. The orchestra stalled, however, before going on to the next number. Without the music, the noise of talkers, who had not modulated their voices, echoed in the room jarringly. Malone, wanting to recover the euphoria he'd felt at first while dancing, scooped a pair of champagne glasses off a passing waiter's tray, and he handed one to Anna.

"To the revolution," he said, clinking his glass to hers.

Anna's face darkened. She pointedly refused to take a sip.

"I was joking," he said at once. "I meant it ironically. Look at us. Look at them. Do you believe these are revolutionaries? It makes me wonder if the Russians aren't just like us."

"They aren't." In her somber face he read the old refrain of her hatred: The Ukraine one vast Buchenwald. . . .

"I know," he said, and then faltered. Sometimes this waltz partner of his made him feel utterly inept.

The orchestra had stalled because something else was about to happen. On no signal Malone had noticed, people had begun to drift in from the adjoining room, and the waltzers had fallen out of their twosomes and were turning now, slowly, but perceptibly, again as if a signal had been given, to face the balcony. The members of the chamber orchestra were pushing their chairs and music stands aside.

"Wait until you hear this, old boy," Victor Woolf said as he joined Malone. He took Anna's hand and bent to kiss it. "Hello, my dear."

"Hear what?"

"The toast."

"We have to drink to the October—?" Malone was thinking of Anna, that she would refuse.

"No, of course not. To peace." Woolf grinned leeringly. "We dips only drink to peace."

Woolf lurched slightly. Whiskey poured off his breath. He was drunk, but Malone was not alarmed. This man who had sipped only water at his own table at that first dinner party was supposed to be drunk tonight. He was acting. We're all acting, Malone reminded himself, and inwardly he shuddered.

Woolf said, "But the ambassador is required to read the venerable party chairman's statement and it's a masterpiece."

"Stalin's?"

Woolf gave Malone a dismissive look: Of course Stalin's.

And the two men stared at each other unpleasantly. Malone had not forgotten Woolf's uneasiness with this plan, or the fact that, at their meeting in the Folger, Minot had invoked the need to know, as if he didn't trust Woolf. Then he'd had to threaten him with expulsion. And then Woolf, for reasons of *his* own, had offered Minot whiskey. Woolf teetered before him, making Malone worry suddenly that the Englishman was all *too* far gone. Woolf began fingering his beard, an absentminded, nervous gesture. A line of perspiration had broken out on his brow. But no, Malone realized, Woolf was just good at this. He'd better be.

Silence descended upon the room as the Soviet ambas-

sador appeared on the balcony. He was a stocky man
with heavy eyebrows that met on the bridge of his nose,
making one black line across his face. His name was
Valentin Gubichuk, and when he'd replaced Gromyko it
was taken as a bad omen in Washington that he'd never
served outside the Kremlin, even in the alliance years.
After Litvinov and even Gromyko, he was regarded as a
throwback Russian bear. But if this party was any indication, this exquisite Viennese rendition, he was not the
insecure Russian xenophobe whom Washington had been
deriding. As the crowd fell silent, he smiled and nodded.
In Russian fashion he wore medals on the breast of his
tuxedo—"Black tie and ribbons," the invitation had read,
but except for military only the East Bloc diplomats
displayed their honors. He greeted his guests in Russian.
Then, raising his glass while reading from a folder that an
aide held for him, making Malone think of an acolyte at
mass, he went on in heavily accented English. "We do
not want war . . ." he began.

Woolf whispered to Malone and Anna. "This is Stalin's statement. He's required to read it."

When Malone glanced at Woolf, he saw that Muriel
had joined him. With her short hair and her dress, a
shapeless white chemise, the line of which fell unbroken
from her shoulders to her ankles, and an unusual silver
necklace sculpted to resemble a string of bird's eggs, she
seemed dangerously unconventional for a diplomat's wife.
She was carrying a bejeweled cigarette holder, but it was
empty. At functions like this one, women did not smoke
standing up. She smiled at Malone, but her eyes were
cloudy.

" . . . Let no one imagine, however, that we are intimidated. The Soviet government possesses the atomic
weapon. . . ."

An abrupt and tangible nervousness swept through the
crowd. Malone's eyes, like nearly everyone's, fell automatically to the figure of Dean Acheson, who was standing, glass in hand, erect and immobile on the front edge
of the assemblage. His face was an impassive mask.

" . . . But war does not frighten us. World War One
brought the noble Bolshevik Revolution, which we com-

memorate today. . . ." Gubichuk plowed through the
statement doggedly, without inflection, without betraying
in any way what his own attitude might have been to the
words he was uttering, or even if he had an attitude.

". . . World War Two brought socialism to Central
Europe and now to China. A third world war will be the
grave of capitalism. Hence we are not afraid of war. But
from time immemorial the Soviet peoples prefer peace
. . . ."

Malone glanced at Anna. She was staring at her
champagne.

Georgian champagne, Stalin's champagne. Malone's
mind swerved back from the waltzing romance to the
harsh fact of what he was doing here. If they prefer
peace, he thought, why are they already at war with us?
He felt a fresh blast of terror that these people too, led by
Stalin, had the atom bomb now— But wait a minute! Who
was he kidding? If he felt terrified at that moment, it
wasn't for the fate of the world. He was about to burglarize
the fucking Russian embassy! *There* was the terror.

He stared rigidly up at the ambassador, trying to shut
the gate on all his feelings.

". . . And on the solemn anniversary of the noble
Bolshevik Revolution we dedicate ourselves to the cause
of peace everywhere in the world." Gubichuk stopped. A
second aide—acolyte?—handed him a champagne glass—
cruet?—from which he drank unceremoniously, without
so much as a glance down at his guests.

The diplomats from East Bloc countries and a few
others—Mrs. Pandit, for one—sipped dutifully at once.

The others all had their eyes on Acheson, the tall
stately American whose white hair and moustache seemed
a part of his evening attire.

On this occasion Acheson was not required to speak.
He allowed a moment to pass—just enough to underscore the difference between those who drank on the
Russian's cue and those who drank on his—before slowly
raising his glass to his lips. He barely kissed it, hardly
sipping any of the liquid at all. Then the diplomats of the
West, and then their well-trained wives, did likewise. At
this party no one was unaligned.

"Sodding bastards," Woolf muttered, ignoring his wife's having taken his arm.

"Hello, Mrs. Woolf," Malone said. She didn't offer her hand and he didn't reach for it. She might have expected him to kiss it.

"Nice to see you, Mr. Ward." Muriel Woolf gave him a brisk smile, then pressed into her husband. "We should go, darling," she said, but her obvious meaning was, You've had quite enough.

"Wasn't that *the* most gracious word of welcome you've ever heard in your entire life?" Woolf grinned stupidly at Malone.

Muriel Woolf was in on the plan too. Despite Malone's objections it had proved impossible to proceed without her, and in fact, in rehearsals, she had seemed utterly competent. Her role now was to play the part of the nagging, sober wife, which would begin to underscore Woolf's drunkenness. Malone sensed their dislike for each other, and he recalled that at their dinner party she had disappeared before her guests had departed. Who was Woolf to grouse about the Russian's bad manners? What about his wife's? If he was faking drunkenness, was she? Were they really capable of cooperating? Their part in the operation was small but crucial.

Malone felt a surge of his familiar anger that Minot should have made him so dependent on fools like this. Minot himself had refused to trust Woolf fully in their meeting at the Folger. "Can you keep a secret?" Minot had teased. "Well, so can I." But now Malone was supposed to trust Woolf with his life, and, for a moment, with Anna's.

Anger at Minot was what Malone felt, Minot the Deists' God who'd wound up the clock of his creation in the beginning, then had gone away to let events run down without him. And if the clock broke? Malone tried to shake these feelings off; but better anger than anxiety. He knew damn well that what he was really feeling was plain afraid. Stop it, he told himself; everything depends on staying steady.

Besides, Minot hadn't gone away at all. Even now he was in the National Geographic Building across Sixteenth

Street. Malone glanced at the wall of windows, at the
lights outside. But Minot would be in darkness, staring
across at this very room with binoculars, with spyglasses.
Malone knew that Minot was the one predictable factor
in this equation. If the Woolfs and Anna did their part to
get Malone upstairs, Minot was going to get him down.

Woolf gingerly removed his wife's hand from his sleeve,
and, muttering with mock solemnity, "I shall return"
—mocking Americans—he walked unsteadily away. Muriel Woolf turned on her heel to go in the opposite
direction in search, Malone guessed, of a corner where
she could smoke.

"Those two don't seem to have to pretend to dislike
each other. They give a young married couple something
to look forward to."

"She is sad, I think," Anna said softly.

Malone sensed that she was thinking of Muriel Woolf's
lost father, Hitler's victim in the Netherlands, and what
therefore they had in common. He said nothing, but only
arched his eyebrow somewhat callously. He looked at his
watch. "We have twenty-seven minutes. I hope Woolf
can stay on his feet. Christ." What was it Minot had said,
how athletes feel sick before the big event? But do they
feel afraid?

To rein his anxiety, he began a systematic check of the
room, of the faces of the men and women, as if eyeing
them for suspects. Mostly the men were talking with
considerable concentration, their faces revealing nothing
except their seriousness, their high degree of interest in
the subject at hand. The women, mostly, were silent,
standing on the edges of the animated clusters, looking
about with a common, abstracted air. Now that the toast
had been offered—even that one—protocol allowed the
guests to depart, but, except for Acheson, who'd gone at
once, few had begun to do so. The waiters had reappeared with fresh drinks, and in the dining room coffee
and an elaborate assortment of desserts had been brought
in. On the balcony above the throng of distracted heads,
the orchestra was reassembling. No one seemed in a
hurry to leave. Malone checked his watch again: twenty-
five. The plan depended on there being a crowd of peo-

ple leaving simultaneously. Was twenty-five minutes too soon?

When Malone brought his gaze back to Anna it seemed two nights were looking at him from deep inside her eyes, a strange conceit for a man like him. Two nights? Did that make him the day?

"How are you?" he asked quietly.

"I am afraid for you," she replied, even more softly.

The music began again, not a waltz now, but a slow, sweet tune, a ballad.

Malone took Anna's hand and led her into the center of the floor. As they began dancing, slowly, amid the other couples, he said, "If you'd told me that night at the Shoreham that I'd soon find dancing like this so natural, I wouldn't have believed you." He smiled. "The dancing has been the hard part for me, Anna. The rest is easy. The rest is what I do." He put his mouth by her ear. Maybe it was true. "So don't worry."

They danced without speaking.

Only when he was holding her in his arms did Anna's presence in his life seem unambiguous. The shadows in which she continually disappeared ceased to exist when her body, merely by his holding it, became part of his body. Then she became part of his own fixed position, the absolute given that was the base of every experience. Looking at her from across the small room where they made love, watching her stepping from her bath, a bar of light falling the length of her body, the icon glowing in its golden light behind her, making her nipples shine like petals—not even that sight of her was free of the shadows in which he lost her. When she turned away to towel herself, it was as if she dissolved into the patterns of the wallpaper and was gone.

He pulled his face back to look at her and waited until she looked up at him. She was here now, no shadows. "I guess even at the Russian embassy a husband can tell his wife he's in love with her."

She nodded, pleased, and said, "If his name is Peter Ward."

"Even if it isn't." He laughed and pressed her close as he twirled her with happiness. His anxiety had completely fallen before the sure knowledge that once this Firebird shit was over he could be with her as himself. No, *more* than himself: as the new man he was becoming. That realization, in fact, reversed any nervousness he might have felt, making him *want* to get his job done.

But he sensed it immediately when she stiffened. He looked at her and saw that she was staring over his shoulder, an expression of surprise on her face, and something else. A shadow.

He turned to follow her eyes, and he saw who she was looking at. Tumark. Vladimir.

The Russian was standing on the edge of the room, framed by the huge gilded mirror in such a way that Malone saw both Tumark's figure and its reflection, both his face and the back of his head. Even at that distance and despite the dozens of men and women between them, constantly interrupting their line of sight, it was clear that Tumark was staring as fiercely at Anna as she was at him. His long white hair, curling onto his collar, onto the black of his tuxedo, gave him the air of the court composer, the one who'd written all that stately music they'd been dancing to, come now to take his bow.

Come now—this was the feeling Malone had suddenly —to take Anna.

When he released his grip on her hand she stopped dancing, still staring at Tumark. Tumark took a step or two toward them, and Anna seemed to take that as her cue. She grasped Malone's hand again to lead him through the crowd toward Tumark. Malone hesitated. "I don't think it's a good idea," he said.

Anna flashed him the most natural, relaxed smile he'd seen on her face that night. "But of course it is," she said. "We must thank Mr. Tumark for putting you on the guest list so that we could come to this splendid party." And with that, she turned, thinking to lead him to Tumark.

But he stopped her, pressing her hand to the point where she winced. "No, darling," he said firmly. "We should go and get our coffee."

She pulled her hand free of him. "You can get mine for me," she said, all at once imperious as any wife in the place. "I'll be in the corner."

When Malone saw the degree of her determination he realized he had no choice. He was no Hamlet. He was not going to let Ophelia die. He said, "I'll come."

"As you please." She took his hand again, lightly, a lover's clasp, and they moved as a pair toward Tumark.

Tumark was smiling broadly when they joined him, and he greeted both, warmly shaking Malone's hand, calling him "My dear Mr. Ward." After bending to kiss Anna's hand, he called her, simply, "My dear," as if there were nothing in the world for him to hide.

He said to Malone, "And how do you like our Georgian champagne?"

"Nearly as well as your fine Georgian toasts." Malone grinned easily, knowing it was the kind of jibe diplomats permitted each other.

Tumark laughed, clapping Malone's shoulder, and he said, "Ah, but you do not understand what a primitive place is Soviet Georgia. Permit me to quote from our great Georgian *vozhd,* our chief . . ." This was Tumark's jibe; he paused, long enough for Malone to think the chief to whom he referred was Stalin. But he announced, ". . . Mayakovsky!" and laughed before going on. " 'Jackals used to creep right up to the house. They moved in large packs and howled terribly. It was there that I first heard those wild piercing howls. We children could not sleep at night, so our mother would reassure us. "Don't be afraid, we have good dogs. Our dogs won't let the jackals near." ' "

What, Malone wondered, was Tumark telling them? Stalin's dogs, but Truman's jackals? He nodded as if the recitation had clarified things, and he said, "Mayakovsky. Isn't he the one who killed himself?"

"Yes," Tumark replied laconically. "A woman he was in love with rejected him."

"Oh. Is that why?"

"Why else?"

"I thought perhaps his dogs had failed him in the end." Malone had instinctively adopted Peter Ward's tone and attitude again. It jarred him to hear such ritual banter in his own voice, but it seemed to satisfy something in Tumark.

The Russian turned to Anna. "You know Mayakovsky's work, Madame Ward?"

Anna nodded. " 'Such a word,' " she recited, " 'sets in motion/Thousands of years and the hearts of millions.' "

"Ah yes. 'A Cloud in Trousers.' " He raised a finger like a professor of literature demanding the attention of his distracted students.

In Malone's assessment, no one was paying attention to them. Apparently Tumark had been holding forth like this all evening, living proof that Russian charm could survive the chill of the Cold War. Malone, from his secret place behind Peter Ward's façade, had become a man searching behind appearances. It was the advantage *his* appearance gave him.

Tumark began reciting the poem in Russian, and at once his voice became more inflected as he gave himself to the highly accented and rhythmical language. His recitation seemed offered like a gift for Anna, and he was so focused upon her as line after line flowed from his mouth that Malone saw that for Tumark his performance was taking place exclusively in her mind. It was easy to imagine the old man as a declaiming virtuoso, and to picture an enchanted Anna upon his arm as they strolled through a gentle rain of October leaves along the derelict towpath of the canal, and for a moment Malone sensed in Tumark, without understanding a word he was saying, what drew Anna to him.

When Tumark finished he clapped his own hands, clearly astonished by the poetic vision he had just laid bare. Malone saw him even more acutely then; he saw a flash of the man's capacity to be affected, the depth of his passion. And he grasped intuitively that the core of the Russian's passion, despite his joviality, was sadness. Malone believed for the first time in Tumark's disaffection, but, as with Mayakovsky, who could say whether its origin was personal—the love of a woman—or political— the hatred of a system?

But then Malone thought, If I can sense his disaffection, so also can the MGB *rezident*. He looked warily around but still no one seemed to be listening to them or noting their encounter. Couples had begun to drift out of

the ballroom, toward the cloakroom at the head of the
grand stairs.

Sadness. Malone looked at Tumark again, wanting to
see into him. Malone knew that sadness had no place in
the world of men, and that finally was what made Tumark
vulnerable. But he also knew that sadness was a kind of
arch through which women passed to embrace such men.
Anna, despite her refinement, stared at Tumark with
what Malone recognized—and could others?—as an expression of attachment. What did she know of his sadness? The separation from his family? The destruction of
his dream, if not for Russia, perhaps for peace? However
layered and complicated were her motives—blackmail?—it
was clear that to Anna, Tumark had ceased being a mere
enemy.

Once more her physical presence—not the lines of her
face or her silhouette, but the quality of her patience, her
calm—resembled the presence—not the color or the
pose—of an icon figure. A Russian icon. Its serenity, he
understood for the first time, is rooted in passion. Instinctively, he let his eyes drift from Anna's face to the
face of the icon hanging on the far wall above the fireplace. He had never seen it as such before, the face of
Lenin, but it was a Russian icon every bit as much as the
forgotten face of Christ was. Anna—when he looked at
her again, he said this to himself, having long forgotten—is
as Russian as Lenin.

It was like stepping between them when he spoke.
"What is that poem about, Mr. Tumark?"

Tumark blinked at Malone, as if he were a stranger
who had approached him on the C&O Canal. "Oh the
poem," he said. He was an old man whose powers came
and went. His face fell easily into its habitual smile, and
he adopted once more the tone of declamation, but now
in English with its unsuitable rhythm. " 'It could be that
only five undiscovered rhymes are left / In all the world,
and those perhaps in Venezuela. / The trail leads me into
cold . . .' " He stopped and touched his temples lightly,
shaking his head, as if he'd forgotten. Malone saw that
his eyes, under the cover of his hands, darted left and
right, to see who was standing nearby. Then he said, "It

is a poem about the lengths to which every poet must go
to find his truth." Tumark smiled again. "You know the
Russian proverb, Mr. Ward. 'One word of truth out-
weighs the world.' "

Tumark's eyes shot left again as a bemedaled dour
Russian approached. For his benefit, Tumark gently poked
his finger between the studs of Malone's shirt, saying,
"And the world is not divided in two with all lies on the
one side and all truth on the other. That is the Mani-
chean view, Mr. Ward, one long since discredited even
by your own best philosophers. Please tell that to Mr.
Truman for me, would you?"

Malone laughed easily, showing no sign that he'd seen
the eavesdropping Russian approach. "I didn't expect a
lesson in Thomas Aquinas from you, Mr. Tumark, and
President Truman would not accept a lesson in philoso-
phy from me. Unless, of course, it was in Aristotle. I do
recall someone quoting from Aristotle at the British minister's that night. 'What has happened, can happen.' "

"Yes." Tumark nodded solemnly. "We were talking
about the Nazi murder of the Jews."

At that the second Russian leaned clumsily in to whisper in Tumark's ear. Tumark listened, then nodded with
a sigh of slight exasperation. The second Russian withdrew. Tumark said, "I'm sorry to excuse myself. The
new Polish ambassador has asked for me. He wants to
know a restaurant probably. I shall tell him Duke
Ziebert's." He laughed. "I always tell them Duke Ziebert's." He kissed Anna's hand once more, but perfuncto-
rily, barely bringing his eyes to her face. And he shook
Malone's hand in the same curt way, a man whose body
took its leave less efficiently than his mind already had.

When he was gone, Malone looked at his watch. "We
should get our coats," he said.

Anna and Malone walked casually out into the spacious
black-and-white-tiled hallway that funneled into the descending grand staircase spiraling down beneath yet another mammoth crystal chandelier. To one side was a
cloakroom, before which a growing throng waited to

claim wraps. Mr. and Mrs. Peter Ward joined the line like everyone else.

A pair of dour-faced Russian men handled the coat line from their places behind the counter, receiving the number slips and retrieving the garments. Most of the male guests had apparently arrived coatless, because the items handed over all seemed to be ladies' fur coats. Malone watched the coat-check workers carefully, even as he drew closer to them in line, looking for signs that they were what he knew them to be, agents of the MGB. But they were as impersonal as they were efficient.

Woolf was nowhere in sight and neither was Muriel.

After Malone handed over his ticket and received Anna's cloak, a sweeping black zamarra, he helped her into it. But they made no move, once away from the counter, to leave. Instead they looked about distractedly, like novices on the diplomatic circuit trying to identify the dignitaries surrounding them, as if unable to disguise the self-satisfied thrill they felt to have been part of such an event. Now they simply did not want it to end.

In fact, with their gawking, they were maintaining their places on the edge of the crowded coat line. Had Woolf missed his cue?

Malone took Anna by the elbow, preparing to move her with apparent purposefulness from one edge to the other, but then, from the far rear side of the gathering came the sound of a loud thud, followed by quickly stifled screams and a wavelike surge in the crowd as the people moved back, like a single creature, away from whatever had happened. Malone, still holding Anna, pushed through the people, coming quickly to the circle that the onlookers had instinctively opened around the sprawled figure of a fallen man and a lone woman kneeling over him. Victor Woolf, passed out drunk, and Muriel, frantically tugging at his black tie, as if that had anything to do with his condition.

Malone went to one side of Woolf and Anna went to the other, joining Muriel.

One of the embassy waiters appeared beside them then, and it was immediately clear from his brisk self-assertion as he edged the two women aside that he was no mere kitchen servant. Malone recognized the methodical scanning movement of his eyes, the efficient poking and touching maneuvers of his hands as he checked Woolf over. The man was trained.

When the Russian looked up at Malone, Malone said, "I am Peter Ward, U.S. Protocol. It is within my purview to take care of him."

"One moment, please." The Russian glanced quickly around for one of his seniors. But the circle of diplomats and their wives had closed even tighter. Concern had given way on their faces to a certain smug disdain. Two things you judge a man by, went the old foreign service saw; the other is how he holds his liquor.

There were no Soviet officials in the circle of onlookers because the Soviets weren't in line to get their coats.

When Woolf showed signs of coming around, Malone put an arm under his shoulders to lift him. He said to the waiter, "Give me a hand here, please." The waiter did.

They lifted Woolf unsteadily to his feet. "Good Lord," Woolf said groggily. As he lurched forward, his flask fell out of the inside pocket of his dinner jacket. Malone picked it up in one motion and slipped it back into one of Woolf's coat pockets.

The other guests turned aside at that lurch, at the sight of the flask, as if a border had been crossed, bad form spilling over into malfeasance.

Woolf was trying desperately to find his keel again, but he couldn't quite. When he shook Malone off he nearly fell once more, so that when Malone grabbed him then, Woolf clutched back at him.

The Russian waiter had hovered at his other side, unsure what to do. When Muriel took her husband's other arm, opposite Malone, the waiter stepped away from them.

Malone said to the man, "Surely there's an elevator. He'll need the elevator."

The waiter looked at him blankly.

Just then a tuxedoed man wearing a pair of medals on his breast approached, the same functionary, Malone realized, who'd interrupted earlier with a message for Tumark. "My dear Mr. Woolf," he said unctuously, but he had barely contained his agitation. If the Englishman's condition grew any worse—if he vomited, for example—the dignity of the entire event would be undercut and once more Washington stories would feature Russian—not British—barbarism. The man seemed to take Woolf's *faux pas* as his responsibility, though he carried himself with the palpable insecurity of one who had just enough rank to realize it wasn't enough.

Woolf grinned somewhat foolishly at the sound of his name. He opened his mouth, then closed it without speaking as all expression left his face. Perhaps he *was* going to be sick.

Malone said to the second Russian, "I am with U.S. Protocol. I am responsible here. Would you show us to the elevator, please? He requires the elevator. Don't you think we should get him out of here as quickly as possible?"

"Yes, but of course," the Russian said, but then he too, like the waiter before him, looked about for someone of yet greater authority to ask. But unfortunately the decision would apparently be his.

Should he dispose of this embarrassment at once by letting the American—a Protocol officer after all—take the pathetic Woolf away? Or should he risk prolonging the embarrassment for all by making them wait until one of the ambassadorial deputies could be summoned?

Malone helped him make his decision. "I insist," he said. "The man is ill."

The Russian raised a finger at the waiter, who joined him—no mere waiter, therefore—in leading the way through an adjacent door, down a narrow corridor at the end of which a large young crew-cut man in an ill-fitting brown suit sat rigidly in a straight-backed chair. The man's body ached to be in uniform. He stood as the tuxedoed Russian approached ahead of the others. The first Russian addressed him abruptly, and in response he turned to the door behind him, opening it to reveal the small cubicle of a domestic elevator.

It had the cramped aspect of an elevator that had been shoehorned into a shaft that had originally housed a servants' spiral staircase. The tuxedoed Russian and the elevator guard stood aside for Malone and Woolf.

Once Malone had Woolf in the cubicle, propping him against a wall, the guard moved as if to join them, but Malone said, "I'm sorry, my friend. If you please. . . ." He nodded toward Anna and Muriel, who were still standing in the corridor, and he held an arm out to them. Muriel was holding her collar closed at her throat. Tears were freely running down her cheeks. Anna had her arm around her. Muriel Woolf belongs on stage, Malone thought. We all do! And his relief doubled when the Russian guard stepped aside for the women, who entered the small elevator, filling it.

The guard looked uneasily at his superior. When that man said nothing, the guard tried to enter the elevator, but he'd have had to tread on the ladies' shoes. He looked again at the diplomat, then at the waiter. Finally the former gave him a clipped order. The guard withdrew a single key from his pocket, leaned an arm into the elevator to apply the key to the lowermost of the seven round locks that served as floor buttons. The elevator would not operate without that key. On each floor a guard with such a key was stationed at the door of the elevator, controlling it absolutely. Having turned the key in the first-floor lock the guard withdrew it and pulled clear of the elevator car, which could go now only to the first floor.

The door began to slide closed.

But Malone reached between Anna and Muriel to stop it, demonstrating that, while he wanted to get his British colleague efficiently out of his humiliating predicament, his hurry to do so was by no means inordinate. In fact, he was improvising now. His confidence had soared. Everything was happening exactly as planned.

"What are your names, please?" he asked, apparently addressing all three of the Russians. "I intend to have my chief inform Ambassador Gubichuk of your graciousness. Discreetly, of course."

The three Russians exchanged glances. Even though they were men of widely differing positions, their anxiety at that moment was the same. It could be exceedingly beneficial to be brought to the ambassador's attention in such a way, but only if they were not in the process, even now, of making a mistake.

The tuxedoed man addressed a clipped Russian sentence to the waiter and the elevator guard, each of whom nodded. Then he said to Malone, "Gorin, Tupalev and Evaschevsky. We thank you."

"Not at all," Malone said. "Thank *you.*" And he let the door slide closed.

Only moments later the elevator door opened again, but now on the first floor of the embassy, in an alcove behind the main entrance foyer. Yet another elevator guard was seated there. Their arrival took him by surprise—the elevator was not to be used by non-Soviets, and of Soviets, only by certain officials—and he came awkwardly to his feet.

Victor Woolf emerged from the elevator unsteadily. Anna was holding one of his arms and his wife was holding the other. He was so clearly sick, and the elegant women so distressed, that the guard did not challenge them. Instead he watched as the man staggered away, nearly falling as he turned the corner into the embassy entrance foyer.

Out of habit the guard looked back into the elevator, and he was satisfied to see that it was empty. He had not authorized the elevator's use and he could see with his own eyes that it was still secure. So nothing bad could happen to him. As the elevator doors slid shut once again, he resumed his seat.

The embassy foyer, like the hall upstairs, was crowded with departing diplomats. At a small desk adjacent to the ornate Gothic entranceway sat a man in a navy blue business suit, also ill-fitting. His impassive silence bordered on the morose as he watched the guests file out, as if he were an usher watching mourners leave a funeral parlor.

When Woolf and the two women slipped into the main line of those who were moving slowly from the staircase to the doorway, the desk man saw it and he openly began to eye them.

Despite his unsteadiness Woolf was walking now on his

own steam, depending on his companions only for balance. He smiled sheepishly at the Russian, laying bare his humiliation as if expecting the man to sympathize, one lush to another.

The telephone on the security man's desk rang. The sound was nearly lost in the loud bustle of all those well-oiled professional talkers, but the man heard it and he picked it up. As he did Woolf, Anna and Muriel drew abreast of him. He listened for a moment, then held his hand out, indicating they should stop.

They did so.

He listened for another moment, then put the phone at his shoulder and asked in a gruff, uninflected voice, "There are four of you?"

Nearby diplomats and their wives fell back, knowing better than to involve themselves with the Soviet security man. The space that opened around Woolf and the two women made it very clear that there were not four of them now.

Woolf slumped, too sick to deal with this. Muriel leaned with him as she took his weight.

It was Anna who said simply, "My husband went quickly ahead to bring our car to the curb for Mr. Woolf. My husband just went by you a moment ago." She peered out through the door, stretching her full height to catch a glimpse of him. "There he is." She looked down at the security man again. "Didn't you see him?" She asked her question evenly, the way a supervisor would. And she stared at the guard until he dropped his eyes uncertainly.

He put the phone to his mouth, spoke a few words, then hung up. Once more he adopted an air of glum indifference, not looking at the three again, as they left the embassy.

11

A cave, he thought. The bottom of a mine, the belly of a whale, a grave, Yorick's grave.

Nothing moved for moments at a time, not the air and not the stone around him. The silence was like stone except when the machinery snapped to life. Then, instead of silence, the narrow shaft reverberated with echoes of the motor's noise. There was a whiff of electricity, an aroma that reminded him of his electric train, and at that memory of his claustrophobic boyhood the space, the utter lack of it, pressed down on him. The motor in the recessed canopy far above sent its shudders whipping down the girders, cables and counterweights every time, at a key's command, the elevator began to move.

Malone froze at those moments, gripping the iron handholds even harder, keeping free of the running cables. He wanted to remain unheard and undetected, of course, but also to concentrate his own hearing, to penetrate the clacking, whirring mechanisms through to the human sounds he knew were there. The elevator did not move except to admit and discharge people. Its passengers conversing curtly in Russian stood only a few feet below Malone, who was crouched on top of the car, his knees pulled into his chest, his hands clutching at the protruding ironwork, his feet upon the trapdoor through which Woolf, Anna and Muriel had hoisted him. They had perfected that deft maneuver, working at night, in a similar small elevator made by the same company and installed in another converted mansion in Washington.

The elevator had been regularly in use when Malone first perched on it, for though the departing diplomats and their wives had not used it, the musicians had, and once all the outsiders were gone the embassy cleaning crew had hauled their equipment in it, up from the basement and back down again. As various Russian officials completed their duties through the evening, they used the elevator in leaving too. Many of them seemed to be drunk.

Throughout these raisings and lowerings, from ten o'clock until after midnight, Malone rode the car undetected up and down the elevator shaft, and all that time he worked at keeping his mind clear, focusing on the plans he'd memorized, the building blueprints and contractor's specs that Minot had provided him. He wanted to study the walls of the shaft, looking for signs he knew were there, but it was too dark. Mostly he succeeded in maintaining his concentration. It did not flag except for those moments when, as with the whiff of electricity when the machinery first fired, claustrophobic memories ambushed him, and not just of his boyhood. He remembered once spending hours in cramped motionlessness inside a jammed panel truck, a surveillance of a Kansas City hoodlum who had killed an FBI agent. He remembered sleepless nights in Italy spent under army trucks because the endless rain had saturated their tents. He remembered waiting for the priest to slide back the trapdoor on his side of the confessional; how he ached to finish the recitation of his sins.

As long as he remained motionless, he was safe. The one precaution he'd been rehearsed to take was that whenever the elevator rose above the fourth floor—and he could tell when that happened because at four the hulking counterweight which was apparent despite the darkness, drew even with and descended below the car—he curled himself around the pulleys, gears and cable housing, flattening himself as well as he could because the air space between the top of the elevator car and the bottom of the steel motor frame hanging from the ceiling at the seventh floor shrank to twenty-one inches.

In fact, the car rose to the seventh floor only once, and that at midnight, for a shift change involving a new guard and a new communications clerk. The Russians replaced one another exactly on the schedule that Gouzenko, the defector from the Ottawa embassy, had described. That first confirmation of Gouzenko's information so relieved Malone that only then did he realize how insecure it had made him to know the entire operation depended on what Minot had learned from the defector. If he was right about the shift schedule, maybe he would be right about the code room and the safe and the book. But until then Malone had not allowed himself to think that Gouzenko's information could be false or inaccurate or outdated. If Minot could depend absolutely on Gouzenko, so could Malone. He wasn't going to start second-guessing either of them now.

Instead he concentrated on what he knew about the seventh floor. In the eaves of the building its ceiling was low and, near the walls, sloping. It had half the square footage of the floors below because of the building's swept-back mansard roofline. Unlike the other floors its guard was posted twenty-four hours a day, and just beyond his station outside the elevator was the door to the *referentura*.

The *referentura* consisted, first, of the communications room, a radio station that an operator manned at all times. Midnight in Washington was eight in the morning in Moscow, and the clerk could expect to be busy with incoming traffic through the night. His job was only to receive the messages and reply with his acknowledgment. The task of decoding them belonged to the cipher clerk— Gouzenko's role in Ottawa—and, except for the rare occasions when a message came in coded red, requiring immediate analysis, the cipher clerk did not report for duty until 5:00 A.M., which gave him time to have the overnight cables deciphered by 7:30, when the embassy day began.

The cipher clerk did his work in the *referentura*'s second room, the code room, to which not even the communications clerk nor the guard posted at the elevator was permitted entrance. The code room could be entered only through the communications room but it was separated from it by a steel door with a peephole and by double walls with an air space between, through which low music played continually so that the sounds of the cryptographic equipment could not be heard. There were no windows in the code room, and so once he was inside it and had taped the peephole in the door Malone would be able to work without fear of giving himself away with light or noise.

Presuming he got inside, of course.

At 2:45, exactly as planned, he began to move. He had long since removed and pocketed his tie and shirt studs, but he was still wearing his tuxedo and street shoes. Now he raised the legs of his trousers to roll down from his calves a pair of rubber sleeves, which he slipped onto his shoes for traction. He lowered his trousers to his thighs, where he had taped a pair of nubby-surfaced rubber gloves, which he donned, also for traction, and a small cup-shaped flashlight attached to an elastic band. He turned the flashlight on—it cast a narrow, faint beam—and fit it flat against his forehead, securing it with the band, miner-fashion. And then, from the top of the elevator, which had come to rest for the night at the first floor, he began to climb.

The seventh floor was his second objective. His first was a niche in concrete, a foot-square shelf hidden in the north wall of the elevator shaft midway between the fourth and fifth floors. He climbed using as handholds and footholds barely protruding bricks and cinder blocks that broke out of the rough surface of the walls in a pattern that was only apparently random. Every eight or ten feet he could prop half his weight on metal brackets that secured the main vertical heating duct in the south-west corner of the shaft. The ductwork stretched all the way up the narrow space like the trunk of an espaliered tree from which branches extended in perfect symmetry, other smaller ducts going right and left, bringing heat throughout the building. Though the heating system was new three years before—when his light fell on the ductwork the aluminum gleamed—he had been instructed that the braces holding the metal column would not take his entire weight, so it was a question of propping himself gingerly, using the heating ducts more for balance than support. He had also been warned against grabbing the cables that ran down the center of the shaft. They were strong enough, since they carried the elevator, but the pulleys and gears from which they hung would squeal under his weight, and the noise could give him away. But he did not need the cables. Minot's contractor had done his work, and as Malone found it possible to ascend the shaft efficiently—in exactly the way he'd practiced at Quantico—he felt himself relax. He was relieved to have the thing under way at last. This is what I do, he'd told Anna. This is easy, he'd said.

In the beam of his light Malone found the niche set in the bricks just where it was supposed to be. As he propped himself in the angle between the walls to reach into it, his hand fell, just as it should have, upon the rough canvas of a sturdy black bag, navy issue, with strap, the size of a salesman's satchel. And at that he felt an overwhelming sense of gratitude toward Webb Minot, the man who'd said so little but who did what he said.

Malone was awed at what Minot had pulled off here, in the spinal column, as it were, of the Soviet embassy itself. For years Minot had been planning this operation and now Malone felt his own selection for it as a staggering stroke of luck. Minot operated on the Bureau's shadowy margin, where Malone had never expected to find himself. He'd never appreciated what was happening out here or with what finesse men like Minot made their moves. He remembered the implicit disdain with which Brigham, Tolson and even Hoover had treated Minot, as if his lack of black-and-white wing tips had somehow disqualified him. But Hoover had been forced into the shadows too, now, and it was to his great credit that, however he disdained him, Hoover already had a man like Minot ready to go. Firebird put to shame everything else Malone had seen or heard of in the Bureau, yet that "everything else" was what had prepared him, physically and mentally, to pull this off. This *is* what I do, by God,

he thought. At last the posing and the lying and the
pretense had come to an end. If only all things were as
simple, he thought, as moving up these walls. But as he
brushed the dust from the black bag, the emblem now of
his deceit and, yes, his crime, he realized for the first
time that subterfuge was as central to his mission as it
was to a burglar's. He *was* a burglar. But here was the
difference: he was acting not for himself—he had a powerful sense of this suddenly—or for the Bureau or for the
nation, but for the world. Stalin's threat rang in his ears.
". . . War does not frighten us," Gubichuk had read, "it
will be the grave of capitalism." Stalin will make a
Buchenwald of the world. *That* was what Malone was
moving to prevent. Nothing less.

He slung the bag over his shoulder, careful not to
knock the flashlight at his forehead. And he began to
climb again, catching glimpses, in the wedge of narrow
light, of the footholds and handholds he needed when he
needed them. The feeling was he couldn't miss. He was
invincible. One after another the crevices and protrusions
in the masonry and the thin metal braces of the ductwork
appeared in perfect synchrony, making him feel like a
creature of the trees. Yes, this was easy. He was born for
this.

Malone knew from the plans that there was a roof
hatch at the very top of the shaft, above the motor and
through which mechanics had access to it, but the hatch
was sealed shut from the inside, so that not even slivers
of the relative light of the city night came in. The darkness outside the small cone of light above his eyes was
absolute, and that undercut what sense of height he might
otherwise have had, even as he climbed higher. He felt
no danger, had no thought of falling. His mind was given
over completely to the particularity of his hands and feet,
the rough surfaces and narrow ledges to which he gave
his weight, although never all of it at once. Move after
move, step after step, pull-up after pull-up, an endless
sequence it seemed, and even if each single exertion
required a painful vising of his fingers, the process of
scaling the hollow inner core of the Soviet embassy seemed
in the doing to be utterly simple. When his fingers threat-

ened to cramp, he said to himself, "Open them," and realized that was what Minot had said in their first encounter, about those handcuffs. "Open them," he heard Minot's words as a kind of motto finally, a kind of charm.

Near the top, just above the lintel of the sixth-floor elevator door, he forced himself to stop. He had no sense of being winded, of his breathing being audible, but he had to be certain of it because on the other side of the next door up was the *referentura* and its guard. Malone waited, calming himself, listening first to the sounds of his own body, then to the walls around him. Nothing.

He switched off the flashlight; near the seventh-floor door he could not risk it. He waited for his eyes to adjust to the darkness slowly. The black forms took shape in front of him, the cables, the bulk of the heating ducts, the rough-surfaced walls. He held his hand in front of his face until he could see his fingers distinctly.

Then he made the mistake of looking down, for now that his pupils were dilated he discerned enough in the telltale convergence of the shaft's rectangular lines to have a sudden, visceral experience of the shocking height to which he had climbed. That the bottom was indistinct, a black nothing far below, only made it worse, transforming that elevator shaft into an abyss.

Malone pressed back against the wall, shutting his eyes.

But it was too late. Fear choked him. His left foot slipped. He clutched at the nearby section of heating duct with too much weight and felt it begin to give. He let go of the duct and found a protruding brick for his left hand, then his foot found its ledge again. Now he *was* breathing audibly. Had there been other noise? Had the guard heard him? He felt a slick perspiration inside his gloves. Involuntarily, he looked down again, and now the abyss was staring back. He thought of Anna, heard her quoting Nietzsche.

It hit him that he was seven stories up, as precariously perched as a would-be suicide on a ledge.

His mind veered from suicide and clutched instead, as if it were a railing, that phrase, *seven stories,* and clung to

it. *The Seven Storey Mountain* was the title of a book
he'd seen in the stores, and he thought of it now as if the
mundane facts of books and stores would rescue him
from the unreality of a nightmare world built around a
bottomless hole. But that hole was sucking him down and
the phrase turned on him, making him feel suddenly that
though he couldn't see it, he *was* on top of a mountain,
no mere building ledge, and he was going to fall.

And to his horror he did.

He fell away from the narrow outcroppings on which
he'd been balanced, and for an instant there was nothing
but the black air between him and the unforgiving steel of
the elevator roof eighty feet below. Or was he falling into
the abyss, that nothing which he knew was the very core
of himself?

Now his thought, again, was of Anna. Hadn't she
touched him there, in that place, and made him feel that
he was not nothing? Hadn't he fallen like this, but into
her?

His face hit the cables, the forbidden, oil-coated cables!

Grab them! Grab the cables!

He thought for an instant that that's what he had done
and he listened for the alarm of squealing pulleys and
gears and then the shout of the guard who was just
beyond the door above.

But his conscious thoughts were now irrelevant. He
was acting from pure instinct. He had so internalized
Minot's warning about the cables that, as if they were
white-hot rods, he'd dodged them, hurling himself directly across the five-foot shaft, brushing the cables, but
not stressing them. His hands hit the second wall before
his feet left the first, leaving him spread-eagled, the black
bag dangling under him, between one side of the elevator
shaft and the other. He did not move.

In the silence that followed he realized two things: The
referentura guard had heard nothing. And the feeling
he'd had of not being able to miss, of being charmed by
Webb Minot, was goddamned dangerous.

Creature of the trees, shit! he said to himself as he
painstakingly worked his way back to an upright position
in the angle of two walls. Even though his hands shook,

that he was chastened now meant he would be more careful. For fear of it happening again, he did not allow himself the luxury of time to recover his calmness. Perhaps calmness had become the luxury.

He took a penknife from his pocket, opened it and put it between his teeth. Then he set off again, climbing the remaining feet in a few swift moves to the point below the seventh-floor elevator door that was his objective. He knew it as such even in the dark because of the obvious twin branches in the heating ducts just there. Below the level of every floor the airways split off horizontally from the trunk. Each one was two feet square and it ran between the ceiling struts of one story and the floor-boards of the other. Once the heating ducts branched into the walls where the supports weren't visible, they were reinforced to carry a man's weight. My weight, Malone thought.

He removed his gloves and pocketed them. Then he ran his hands around the edges of the heating duct and quickly found the panel he was looking for just at the point where the horizontal ducts broke from the larger vertical one. He slid his penknife under the panel seams and popped it at each corner, then took the knife back in his teeth. The panel came loose without a sound, exactly as the one in Quantico had. It hung on hinges that were concealed inside the joint.

When Malone swung the panel open a blast of hot air hit him full in the face, but he felt it as if it were cold, as if he were kneeling before a meat locker at Swift and Company holding his father's bag of tools. But now the strange vision was of the freezer slowly swinging open to reveal his father's body lying there, not drunk this time, but dead. He died because his son the apprentice lock-smith had not been able to get the door open in time. His father's eyes were open, staring through the lens of tears that had frozen solid.

Malone snapped his own eyes shut.

It was hot air, not cold, and he welcomed it for reasons that had nothing to do with meat lockers at the stock-yards, nothing to do with his father, who in reality had died in bed. He welcomed the heat because it was a

physical sign that Webb Minot's people had done their
work. The makeshift hatch gave him access to the air
duct that brought that heat to the rooms of the sealed-off
referentura. First the heat, now him.

Pushing the black bag ahead, he snaked into the air
duct, turning onto his back as he did so. Once he was
well into the tube he froze and listened. Above and to his
left he heard the faint thud of chair legs striking the
floor, as if the guard had sat forward alert. Malone
waited, not breathing. In the heat he'd begun to perspire
freely and he had to resist an impulse to wipe his upper
lip. A moment later he heard the same sound again, the
chair softly striking the floor. And then the sound repeated itself. The guard was rocking back and forth in his
chair, balancing on its rear legs, tapping first the wall
behind him, then the floor, then the wall again in the
classic mindless movement of a bored watcher.

Only now did Malone allow himself to reflect on the
eerie vision he'd had moments before of his father dead.
What concerned him was not the image of the frozen
corpse or the bizarre notion that he himself had caused
his father's death. What worried him was that now, in
this circumstance, when he needed more than anytime
ever in his life to be cool, steady and unemotional, he
should have been ambushed by such feelings. It wasn't
his father's corpse haunting Malone, but his ghost. Now
the image in his mind was of the old man not dead but
alive, his face bloated red with booze, his hand on Malone's shoulder squeezing him hard and telling him step
by step how to crack the safe. And Malone knew cracking the safe was impossible, because he could not concentrate, because the pain in his shoulder from his father's
squeezing was too intense.

Perspiration had begun to pool in his eyes. Now he did
wipe it. He pulled the black bag onto his chest, a tight fit
in that space, and he began to snake through the heating
duct again.

Very quickly he became aware, as he expected to, of
light spilling back toward him from a grate in the floor
above him, the opening through which hot air rose into

the radio room. Passing under that grilled opening would
be Malone's moment of greatest danger.

He moved very slowly, pushing with his hands at his
sides, flexing his buttocks in a kind of peristalsis, staring
at the riveted sheet metal inches above him, watching
color spread on the aluminum as light from the grate
filled the tunnel as he approached it.

He stopped just shy of the grate to listen.

But he heard nothing.

He listened without breathing, but he heard nothing.

The clerk was up there. He had to be.

Malone felt the familiar stir of anxiety in his chest, but
he clamped down on it. He was not falling! The ghost of
his father was not here! A rivet in the aluminum just
above his eyes struck him and suddenly there was a
change of scale in his perception, and he saw the rivet as
an immense bruise on the skin of the metal, the result of
a fearful blow, the noise of which had left him deaf.

What if he simply could not hear the man? Or what if
the man had already become aware of Malone in the
heating duct under his floor? What if even now they were
stuffing rags into the ends of the tubes, to shut off his
air? That was it, he realized! He was suffering from lack
of oxygen! The heat! The closed space! The constriction
in his chest! He could not breathe!

He was locked inside a chest, and his father was outside frantically manipulating the delicate tools of his trade
to free the lock, to save his son! Dad! Dad! I can't
breathe! Hurry, Dad! Hurry!

A sound cut short his panic, saved him from it.

He listened, clutching at the black bag on his chest,
channeling his anxiety into the tension of his fingers.

He heard it again, the rustling of fabric, followed by
the creak of stretching canvas. The sounds fell into a
picture of a man turning over on a narrow cot, a man
sleeping or trying to sleep.

The image was enough to free him. He began to move
as quickly as he dared. When the grate appeared above
his face he did not pause to look through it, but pushed
past it, glimpsing the ceiling and the edge of a hulking
piece of wooden furniture, a filing cabinet perhaps.

And then he was in the darkest part of the heating duct again, sliding through it like a worm, but now toward the grate that he would not see coming because it opened onto the code room itself, which, if Gouzenko was correct, would at that hour be completely dark.

It was. His moves came quickly now, and when he sensed a change in the air on his face he put his hands on the metal above him and pushed with his feet until his fingers came upon the grid of the opening into the code room.

He pushed up on it firmly and the pseudo-bolts snapped out of their grips.

Moments later he was on his knees inside the room with the black bag open before him. He had taped shut the peephole in the door, and then had snapped on the flashlight on his headband and removed short lengths of tubing from the bag. Now he assembled the tubing into a tripod to which he attached the small cone of a portable spotlight. He plugged its cord into an adjacent electrical outlet and the spotlight went on so brightly that the dim beam from the flashlight on his forehead was washed out completely.

He looked quickly around the room. The light was falling directly on an oversized wall clock that read 10:57.

He recalled coolly that the clock was set to Moscow time. He looked at his own watch. Two fifty-seven. Exactly twelve minutes had elapsed since he'd begun.

He picked up the spotlight to turn it, and instinctively he knew where to aim. He'd been in this room with its desk, cipher machines and cabinets many times before, for the code room was the authentic version of the mock-up Minot and Hazelton had made for him in Quantico.

The light fell directly onto the floor safe, which was where it was supposed to be; it was of the size and shape—twelve cubic feet, half a ton of steel, the bulk of a refrigerator—that Malone was rehearsed to expect.

But something was wrong and it took him a moment to realize what.

The safe had no handle on its door, only the number dial.

No handle.

Malone carefully placed and adjusted the light, trying
not to admit to himself what he already knew. He stared
at the black door as if he had just noticed the oddest
thing. When the light was set he stayed still for a moment, as if waiting for the handle to materialize before
his eyes. He had never seen a safe of this size without a
door handle. That there wouldn't be one had never seriously occurred to him.

The Czechoslovakian floor safe in the mock-up of Gouzenko's Ottawa code room was supposed to duplicate the
Russian safe in all aspects. Minot himself had assured
him of that. All aspects, unfortunately, but one. In the
first Quantico dry runs Malone had cracked the safe in
under forty minutes. But he wouldn't need that long
now. He wouldn't need any time at all because he could
not do it.

No handle meant no pressure on the bolt. No pressure
meant no tiny clicks as the bolt fell into notches on the
separate disks. No clicks meant no way to break the lock.
No copy of the code book. No clues, therefore, to the
crucial Russian cable traffic from the weeks before
Hiroshima. Hiroshima. Only a bomb, Malone thought
bitterly, would get me inside this safe.

He felt numb. No sensation of falling now. No clau-
strophobia. No panicked visions of his father. Instead a
simple, rare sense of failure began spreading in him. He
was going to have to tell Minot that he had not succeeded, and all at once he felt a full blast of the depression this failure was going to leave him with. It felt worse
than the dream of having left his father inside a freezer,
because this was real. He liked to think of himself as a
man whom life had rarely thwarted, but he knew the
truth was different. From the moment in his youth when
he realized that his own family were people to whom he
was not particularly attached, to the night a few months
before when Beth Fraser had simply refused to unlock
her heart to him, Malone had carried as a note of his
identity a vague but powerful grief, one shrouded not in
the usual darkness but in his accomplishments, which, as
long as they followed one upon the other, protected him
from the disappointment he felt in his own life. But there

was no protection now. He had been kidding himself about becoming someone new.

He slowly approached the safe, his eyes fast upon the combination dial, as if it were a hypnotist's locus.

No handle. He still hadn't quite accepted it. How could Minot have made this one mistake? All his other ingenious tricks were for nothing. Now instead of numbness he felt anger at Minot! The outrage of it, once more to have been at the mercy of someone who could not quite deliver, like his parents, like Beth, like Anna.

But her name in that litany shocked him. How had she fallen short? Malone was certain of nothing if not of her love. Yet, now, approaching the Russian safe, he was as certain that he would lose her as he was that he could not open it.

And whose fault was that? Finally it was no one's but his, not his drunken father's and not drunken Webb Minot's either.

Without a handle, the mammoth door would have to be swung open, once the combination had been worked, by a firm pull on the dial itself. The dial served as the knob of the spindle connecting to the latch. He closed his fingers around it, an unthinking act.

And the feel of the grooved metal against his skin made him think of the old safecracker's trick, looking for the numbers of the combination on the hidden side of an adjacent file cabinet or the inside cover of the dictionary, anyplace a forgetful secretary might have scrawled it.

But he knew there was no point in doing that here. He closed his fingers firmly on the dial, taking its ridges into his skin, and he had no impulse even to fiddle with the thing.

It is also possible, safecrackers say, to guess the combination from significant dates in the owner's life, birthdays, anniversaries, national holidays.

Like the Russian Revolution.

He laughed. An American safecracker, thinking of the *October* Revolution, would get the date wrong.

This was November. Eleven seven seventeen. Or was it, in the European style, seven eleven?

His fingers had not moved. The dial was immobile

between them. The Russian code clerk was an officer of
the MGB, not an intimidated secretary who needed memory aids. Malone simply stooped before the safe like an
aborigine before a totem, handing himself over utterly to
the disaster of this bad luck.

He gripped the dial the way earlier he had gripped the
edges of bricks in climbing the walls of the elevator shaft.

Instead of turning the dial he pulled it toward him, and
to his amazement, like that, the perfectly balanced mammoth door swung open.

Not for more than a moment did he allow himself to
think about the fact that the safe had not been locked,
but for that moment his dread was intense. He had to
resist the urge to look over his shoulder as if someone
were there, watching him. This is a trap, a fucking Russian trap! How else to account for this unthinkable event?
He was barely breathing. He forced himself to consider
the possibilities. The Russians had deliberately left the
safe unlocked because they'd known he was coming and
they wanted him to open it? No. It couldn't be a trap.
What possible sense could a trap make! The explanation
had to be far simpler. The clerk must have neglected to
twirl the dial after closing the safe. A breach of procedure, a violation of security and, for Malone at that
moment, not a trap, but a miracle enough, nearly, to
make a Catholic of him again. He pushed his near panic
aside and opened the heavy door wide.

The key-operated interior compartment was not open,
and he smoothly turned back to the black bag at his feet.
It contained a length of rope, a small grappling hook, a
figure-eight descender, a body belt, a plastic press and a
thirty-five-millimeter camera the size of a wallet, but
what he was after was the set of lockpicks, a four-inch-
long tool resembling a pocketknife but with six folded-in
steel picks, each variously fashioned with grooves and
edges. He took the set, unfolded one blue steel pick and
turned back to the safe, positioning himself so as not to
block the light. *This* is the easy part, he thought. *This* is
what I do. He inserted the pick into the lock, jiggled it

past the successive pins and tumblers and snap—the lock was open, and this door too swung open.

Open on a set of drawers, the top one of which, as Gouzenko had said it would, held the code book. He took it, and set it inside the clear plastic wings of the book press, open to the first page of text, Russian words and corresponding numbers. He arranged the light above the book and efficiently began to photograph page after page of it. Thirty-seven minutes later he was finished. He put the book back in its drawer, closed the interior compartment, locking it, and then swung the heavy door of the safe shut. He did not lock it.

He disassembled and repacked his camera gear, slung the black bag over his shoulder, cleared the tape from the peephole and left the room the way he'd come in, leaving it exactly as it had been. Moments later he had climbed to the top of the elevator shaft and worked his way past the exposed gears, belts and cables of the motor to get at the roof hatch. He threw off the snap bolts that secured the hatch, turned his flashlight off and then pushed the hatch open. The cold night air hit him like freezer air and for the first time he realized that he was soaked through with perspiration.

Once on the roof he softly lowered the hatch back again and pressed it down until he heard the faint clicks of the inside snap bolts locking in place again. Those were the first sounds he'd heard and, as if they'd un-clogged his ears, suddenly the night noises of the city struck him. He was out! He looked up at the sky full of stars and he felt exhilarated! He was out! And he had the code book on film! And the Russians would never know! Like that, his dread uneasiness at finding the safe un-locked was gone. And so was his sense of himself as a failure. Now he could not wait to get to Minot and, yes, to Anna.

He crept to the edge of the sloping roof, attached the rope to the grappling hook and fed it through the figure-eight descender, a climber's tool that would enable him to control his slide. He donned the body belt and gloves and clipped the figure eight to the belt, then cleared the rope's coil to throw it. Only then did he look across

Sixteenth Street at the National Geographic Building. His eye went unhesitatingly to the second-floor window from which Webb Minot was watching. Malone took the flashlight off his forehead and, holding it before him, snapped it on and off twice. He waited, then did it again. When the same signal came back at him, he put the flashlight in the bag and secured it, then crept to the south side of the embassy roof. He reached up to attach the grappling hook to the lip of the chimney, then he flung the coiled rope as far away from the building as he could. It fell into the darkness. A moment later his end of the rope took a sharp tug as the rest of its length went taut, held in a steep angle that ran from the roof's edge to the shadows of an alley that separated the embassy grounds from the neighboring building.

Malone did not look down this time. He climbed over the edge of the roof and pushed off backward as the rope ran between the iron figure eight in his hands. He slid down it like a circus performer, silently, away from the embassy, a bit faster than he'd done it in training perhaps, but not for a moment out of control.

The arms that received him, breaking his momentum, belonged to Hazelton and Minot. When he was down they held him in their embrace for longer than was strictly necessary.

Malone was the one who spoke. "I got it," he said, and he grinned, feeling a fresh dose of what Minot meant to him.

"You're my man, Chris," Minot said, and Malone felt anointed.

They snapped the rope free of the chimney lip and hauled it in, grappling hook and all. Then they silently slipped away.

Malone thought that once they were in the car he would tell Minot everything.

But as they approached it, several blocks from the embassy, the car door opened, and he saw a figure in the shadows of the rear seat.

Anna. It would be Anna. Suddenly fear washed over him, fear at what he'd been through, fear at what had nearly happened and, then quite explicitly, fear that the operation had gone wrong after all, and because it had, he would lose her. The safe had been unlocked! For the second time the impossibility of what had happened hit him. Malone did not believe the clerk had simply forgotten to twirl that dial! The safe had been left unlocked for a reason; and that he could not possibly imagine why was what made him afraid.

His dream had been that once the embassy operation was over he could come out into the light again, leaving the dark layers of deceit behind and beginning an open life with the woman he loved and who loved him. But now he realized, as he approached the car ahead of Minot and Hazelton, that he had not yet left the realm of mystery. There was a new secret, the unlocked safe, and if it was his to fear, he resolved suddenly, he would make it his to penetrate.

He went to the car, to *its* open door, knowing he could bring his fear to Anna, if to no one else.

But when he bent into the car he saw that the lone figure in the corner was a man, not a woman.

The man did not speak. Malone got in next to him, trying to control a wave of disappointment that threatened, finally, to demolish the thin grip he had on himself.

Minot opened the door in front, tossing the black bag in ahead of him and craning back toward the man as he got in. He said, "We got it, Mr. Hoover."

J. Edgar Hoover put his hand on Malone's arm, calming him at once with a dose of his own composure, and pulling Malone back to his central purpose, his own fundamental loyalty, fixing him in it—or so it felt— permanently, when Hoover said firmly, "Well done, son."

PART TWO

12

During the first month of the second half of the twentieth century American fears about the Soviet Union stopped seeming paranoid. Joseph Stalin had just turned seventy but the empire he presided over had never seemed more powerful than the day in January when he received the triumphant Mao Tse-tung in the Kremlin. The American successes against the Communists since the war—the Truman Doctrine in Greece, the Marshall Plan in Europe, the airlift in Berlin—all seemed undercut suddenly by the humiliation in Asia. In the popular mind this grievous defeat of the American client—Chiang Kai-shek had received more than two billion dollars since V-J Day—was linked with the autumn nightmare of Stalin's A-bomb. The "loss" of China and the loss of the nuclear monopoly fed on each other, so that what had begun as a bizarre obsession of "ultraconservatism" became in one short season the central truth of all American life.

Thus in the new Hiss trial, Dean Acheson's former protégé, whose innocence had seemed incontrovertible to some members of his first jury the summer before, was quickly and unanimously found guilty by a second jury within a few days of Mao's visit to Moscow.

That same week Omar Bradley and the joint chiefs of staff began the public debate about the hydrogen bomb by exaggerating the menace of the Russian A-bomb, thus contributing to the growing national hysteria. Bradley was trying to force the hand of what he saw as an ambivalent president who still had not ordered the building of the new superweapon.

But ambivalence had never been Truman's problem. He had delayed his decision to reopen Los Alamos for the new crash weapons project out of fear that the secret of the H-bomb would be compromised from the start by Soviet spies. Truman was not a victim of hysteria. He was not worried about Harry Dexter White or other anglophile dandies who'd spent their youth under the sway of Oxbridge leftists. Nor was he worried about Alger Hiss or other Roosevelt protégés whose wartime commitment to an antifascist ally—for that's what Russia was—made them vulnerable now to attacks by superpatriot businessmen whose real motive was the destruction of the New Deal. Nor did the nation's security seem to Truman to be particularly threatened by the simpleton labor leaders and movie stars who were being hounded by right-wing vigilantes for having attended cold-water-flat cell-group meetings in the 1930s.

The president *was* worried, though, about real Soviet agents who had in fact penetrated the most closely guarded secret in American history. So intent upon deceiving the Russians had the Manhattan Project directors been that right up until 1945 the United States had continued to ship uranium to the Soviets rather than risk alerting them to the mineral's new significance by halting the shipments. Of course HUAC now took those shipments as yet another signal of Soviet infiltration. HUAC was Truman's nemesis, wanting, for example, to nail J. Robert Oppenheimer as the Soviet agent in Los Alamos. Truman knew that the charges against him were stale. Not even J. Edgar Hoover, whose men had compiled a file on Oppenheimer measuring four and a half feet, still believed that the physicist was the spy. Hoover might have tossed up Oppenheimer's name anyway—his brother was a Communist and hadn't his fiancée been?—but Truman had made it very clear that what he wanted was not more rumormongering but hard evidence and arrests.

And in the first week of February—the same week, as it happened, in which an obscure Wisconsin senator said at an airport in West Virginia, "I have here in my hand a

list of names . . ."—hard evidence and an arrest were
what Truman got.

KLAUS FUCHS, BRITISH PHYSICIST, CONFESSES AS SOVIET A-SPY.
The headline marched across the top of the front page of
the early edition of the *Evening Star*. Christopher Malone, still posing as Protocol Officer Peter Ward, stood
with other staffers around a table near the entrance of
the State Department cafeteria. The news was such in
those weeks, particularly about the Hiss trial, that the
arrival of the early afternoon edition had become something of a daily Foggy Bottom event. These men had just
finished lunch when the papers came in, and now they
huddled over several copies, reading avidly.

The news story identified Fuchs as a German-born
scientist who'd fled the Nazis to England in the 1930s and
become one of the most important figures in British
physics. As a researcher at Edinburgh University he had
mastered crucial aspects of so-called uranium science, and
in 1942 he was assigned as a member of the British
mission to the Manhattan Project. In confessing his espionage for the Soviet Union he admitted to being a Communist since before fleeing Germany, and he defended his
turning over research documents to his anonymous contact, a man whom he knew only by the code name
"Raymond," on the grounds that in 1944 and 1945, when
he did so, the Soviet Union was an ally. Now that Stalin's
regime had been exposed as equal to Hitler's, Fuchs
claimed to have repented his treason and he promised
full cooperation in the effort to track down "Raymond."

Malone read every word of the article, noting that
though British authorities were reported to have been
tipped off to Fuchs by information supplied by the American FBI, no explanation was offered as to how the FBI
had obtained *its* information. The article did identify
Fuchs as one of the scientists who had been expected to
play a key role in the development of the hydrogen bomb
if and when Truman ordered it. If he had not been
exposed he'd have been in a perfect position to betray
the superweapons project too. Truman's instinctive re-

fusal to go ahead until the spy was exposed had been clearly correct.

"Jesus Christ, a Brit!" one of the FSOs near Malone muttered. "Brit security has gone to hell in a handbasket. London should have known the guy was a Commie."

"London doesn't care," another said. "They just recognized Red China, didn't they? Of course the spy would be a Limey. We never should have let them within a mile of the Manhattan Project."

"Klaus Fuchs? Limey? Doesn't sound Limey to me."

Malone turned away from the group without speaking, but one of the others took his sleeve. "What do you think, Ward?"

Malone blinked. Me? A forks and knives and napkin setter? He shrugged self-deprecatingly. Learning what attitude to strike among his colleagues—American brilliance achieves its effect by refusing to draw attention to itself—had been like learning how to dress as if he'd spent his youth at Baltimore cotillions. An FSO's feigned indifference to the impression he made was deliberately undercut by the way his perfect necktie knot rode serenely above his gold collar pin.

"I'm glad they nabbed the guy," Malone said. "But as for London, I do not intend to turn my back on our English allies." He looked at them deadpan.

For a moment the others did not react at all, then they laughed, shaking their heads and moaning. That Peter Ward could be one cruel son of a gun.

Malone was demonstrating the irreverence proper to a junior FSO, but he had skirted a boundary, for he was spoofing their own beleaguered Dean Acheson, who had stunned Washington two days before by using exactly those words, not about the British but about Alger Hiss. In the corridors of Foggy Bottom, Hiss and now Acheson's defense of him were delicate subjects on which feelings ran deep. Everyone who knew Hiss liked him and everyone else felt besieged along with him. At worst, some wanted to know what was he guilty of? Being a premature antifascist? Secretary Acheson's loyalty to Hiss in the face even of his conviction seemed noble to them. But still there were questions. Whittaker Chambers may have been a psychopath, as a Harvard psychologist had testified only the week before, but he had still produced notes in Alger's handwriting and stolen State Department documents typed out on Alger's machine. What could they do but what Ward had done, layer over their mixed feelings with knowing cracks?

Christopher Malone's real feelings were far from mixed, of course, and he often had to check his impatience with the smug self-indulgence of State Department assumptions about Alger Hiss. Did the man's social standing or his Ivy League accent or his Brooks Brothers tailor exempt him from the normal requirements of decency? Acheson's diehard loyalty to Hiss had its admirable aspect, but what about a sworn official's loyalty to his nation? What would Acheson say if Alger's middle name turned out to be Raymond?

Malone returned to his office as if the Klaus Fuchs story, lacking a direct link to Foggy Bottom, were only of passing interest to him. For three months now he had simply maintained his cover as a Protocol officer, responding to routine requests from the various embassies, arranging for ceremonies involving foreign dignitaries and attending the endless round of receptions along Massachusetts Avenue. The work seemed trivial to him, as if he'd become a kind of shipboard social director, but he carried out his duties with energy and panache, with a casual grace that made it seem he was born to be a diplomat.

It had surprised and disappointed him after his November seventh success that Mr. Hoover had still wanted him in place at Foggy Bottom. Malone understood that what Hoover wanted, in fact, was distance from him, deniability, in case the operation and his role as embassy burglar became exposed. And it made sense that Minot would want him in Foggy Bottom, because the burglary might have to be repeated. If Minot's cryptanalysts were unable to break the Soviet cable traffic, despite the purloined code book, or if the plaintext turned out to be innocuous, then it was conceivable Minot would want Malone to go back into the Soviet embassy for other cipher material or to plant listening devices that might provide new clues to

the Soviet penetration of Los Alamos. Malone knew that
beyond the needs of Firebird, it would also serve Minot's
long-term purposes to have an agent in the Protocol
Office indefinitely. It was the ideal perch from which to
watch not only the Soviet embassy but also the embassies
of the other Warsaw Pact nations. Malone had apparently succeeded in establishing himself as Peter Michael
Ward, Claude Leland's protégé, not only among the for-
eigners he mingled with at ceremonies and receptions but
among his peers and superiors at the State Department.
But his successes at Foggy Bottom meant nothing to
Christopher Malone, for he hadn't signed on to this falsi-
fied life indefinitely, and the moment Firebird broke
open he fully intended to remind Minot that he wanted
out. He was not going to be the Bureau's dirty little
secret forever.

Well, maybe that moment is now, he thought as he
returned to his office, a small cubicle off a crowded
hall-like room in which rows of stenographers' desks
were arranged between rows of filing cabinets. Malone
closed his door and went to his window, which overlooked the sterile winter courtyard. Since the burglary of
the Soviet embassy the weather had seemed perpetually
gray and damp, as if the earth too were waiting to be
released. The windows of the north wing opposite were
uniformly empty, reflecting the dull sky, looking like a
wall of sockets from which the eyes had been removed.

Malone was trying to empty his mind, to picture the
face of Klaus Fuchs when the arresting officers burst in
upon him. "But how?" Fuchs would have cried. "How
did you find me?" And for the first time since the night
of his crawling through the holes of the embassy he
allowed himself a moment's satisfaction. He had never
fully shaken the fear he'd felt when the Russian safe had
proved to be unlocked, the intimation of disaster, of a
trap, of some secret that, eventually, was going to ex-
plode under him. When he'd told Minot about the open
door, Minot had seemed to think it meant nothing and
chalked it up to the cipher clerk's carelessness. Malone
had never accepted that, and Minot's nonchalance about it
left Malone with the uneasy suspicion—certainty almost—

that Minot simply was not leveling with him. But now it didn't matter. The code book was real and the cable traffic it enabled Minot's people to read revealed just what they'd hoped it would. The proof was in the paper today. No explosion under Chris Malone. The atom spy had confessed.

Malone was startled when the phone rang on his desk behind him.

"Hello?"

"Peter, darling?"

"Anna?"

And Anna. Here was Anna.

In those months they had found it possible to live in near normalcy in the house on Phelps Place only because their peculiar double lie—to their neighbors and his colleagues they were husband and wife; to Webb Minot and, through him, to the puritanical Hoover, they were chaste secret agents who scrupulously slept apart—served as the structure of the irresistible truth between them. The truth of their love.

"Did you see the newspaper?" she asked.

He heard the reined excitement in her voice. She too felt the thrill of their achievement. He remembered her unfettered happiness when she'd welcomed him home that night in November, how gloriously she'd swung in his arms.

"Yes. I just read it."

For a moment she said nothing. Then, "I knew you would want to know as soon as possible."

"Yes." Malone faced back to the window. Now the wall across the courtyard seemed full of eyes no longer blind. He felt watched. He had no reason to think his phone was tapped but he and Anna had always kept up their pretense when talking on it. But this time he had to rein the urge to blurt out his true reaction. "It's good news, don't you think?"

"Very good news. Have you spoken to our friend?"

To Minot, he understood. "No. Not in weeks. He was going to get in touch with me, remember?"

Again Anna fell silent. And Malone stood immobile at the window, the phone at his ear. He wanted her to ask him something else. What happens now? Is it all finished? Can we use our own names yet? Can we find our own place?

"I thought he might have called you."

"No."

"But—"

"I imagine he has other things to worry about, darling." The identity of "Raymond," for instance.

But now in the silence the insult of his marginality hit Malone. Why should he, of all people, have had to read about the arrest of Klaus Fuchs in the afternoon paper? And what *was* his role to be now? If Minot hadn't contacted him before this, if only to give Malone the news of their triumph himself, why should he contact him now?

As if in that silence she had read his thoughts, Anna said, "Perhaps we should go to him ourselves."

Malone realized at once how they were different. She was not an FBI agent and therefore lacked the inbuilt reticence of one. Reticence not toward criminals or Communists—agents were men of solid ego, of nerve, as they'd have put it themselves, when it came to adversaries and perpetrators—but toward their own hierarchy. Agents craved the approval of their superiors and dreaded their indifference, so of course, once the line was drawn, they toed it. Malone's orders had been simply to maintain his cover and wait for Minot's initiative. He had done exactly that for months now—protecting his cover, yes, but also, of course, protecting the Bureau by staying away. Minot's contacts had been infrequent, always unannounced late-night visits to Phelps Place that had sent Anna scurrying down from Malone's bedroom to her own. Minot's purpose, since he never had information or instructions for them, had apparently been merely to reassure them as agents in the field, but those encounters hadn't really done that either because Minot invariably arrived reeking of whiskey. Still, Minot's authority was absolute, and it had not occurred to Malone to approach him on his own. Why? Because of that agent's reticence. But also because Minot's drinking had combined with the length of time that had passed and with the nagging fear of that opened safe to make Malone afraid that Firebird was leading nowhere.

But it had led to Fuchs!

Wasn't a contact between an agent and his control appropriate now? And why not on the agent's initiative?

But how? Minot's Firebird offices were outside the FBI, someplace else in Washington, and Malone had no idea where. He could leave word with the SE desk at the Bureau asking to be called in, but notice would surely be passed along to Hoover, tagged to indicate urgency. It was Minot Malone wanted, and at last he admitted the need to himself, admitted its urgency, even if Hoover would never see it as such.

"I don't know where our friend is," he said. It felt pathetic to him, another admission, but he said it anyway. "I don't know how to reach him without involving the Bureau."

"I do."

"What?"

"I know where Mr. Minot's offices are. We could go there." By referring to Minot by name Anna was indicating her readiness to speak directly, even on this telephone line.

Malone felt the same urgency. And what reason was there, finally, for thinking that the phone was unsafe? *"How* do you know, Anna?"

After a moment's silence in which he pictured the indecision in her face, she answered him. "I worked there in December and part of January, helping to translate the cables from Russian once they broke the code."

"You didn't tell me that."

"Mr. Minot said I shouldn't. And between us it seemed unimportant."

"I had my work, you had yours."

"That's right."

"The difference is you know all about mine. I tell you everything." Malone felt a wave of disgust, but at himself for not being like she was.

"I tell you what matters," she said.

"You tell me what Minot says you can tell me."

"No," she said firmly. "Mr. Minot and Mr. Woolf told me not to discuss Vladimir with you, but I did."

Tumark. She hadn't mentioned him since before Christmas, but at that point she had told Malone that Minot and Woolf had dropped him as a target. The Russian had made his decision finally, and it was a decision in favor of his Moscow-bound family. He was never going to defect. He was never going to work against his country. Malone had sensed at the time the depth of Anna's feeling about it. He knew that she had identified Tumark in some way with the memory of her father and he assumed that Tumark's rejection of the West had to seem to Anna, however well she understood his motives, like a rejection of herself. But she'd refused to discuss it in those terms. She'd seen Tumark for the last time at the New Year's reception at the embassy of Czechoslovakia, and Malone had seen her eyes brim when the Russian, having kissed her hand, walked away from her. That Anna had shared her experience of losing Tumark and the disappointment she'd felt about it had made Malone believe that she'd begun telling him everything. But now she was telling him that she knew where Minot was. Why hadn't she told him that before? Because, he thought bitterly, he had no need to know? What other secrets had she kept from him? It was a question he hadn't asked himself in months.

"I could pick you up in a cab," she said. And then she added softly, "Christopher, we should tell Mr. Minot that the time has come for us to stop. . . ."

It was her use of his real name that decided Malone. He looked at his watch. It was just past two o'clock. He had a meeting at the Belgian embassy but it was with a junior diplomat, one of his own rank, and their purpose was to plan the itinerary for the Belgian queen's visit during the April Cherry Blossom Festival. It could wait. "I'll be in front of the Lincoln Memorial. Come quickly."

By the time she came for him Malone had, unfortunately, been able to think twice and three times and ten about their impulse. Whatever approaching Minot like this meant to Anna, it was an unprofessional act for Malone, an unprecedented one in his Bureau career. He had resolved to reverse their decision and send her home.

But then she came. She was in the backseat of the Yellow Cab, looking at him, as it pulled over to the curb. Malone crossed around behind it and got in, and when she kissed him—a brisk, wifely kiss, but one that conveyed nevertheless her rare emotion—he knew that she was right. Fuchs was arrested. What remained was the legwork, routine investigations and running down leads that would smoke out "Raymond" and any others who had conspired with them. Operation Firebird was finished. It was a triumph. But, because of it, Malone and Anna had held themselves in check in every way but physically. They had not dared to give expression to their longings except in the clipped language of their bodies. But that was no longer enough.

Malone kissed her again, now passionately, as the cab pulled into traffic, and when he pulled back from her face, holding it lightly in his hands, he knew finally what all of this was about. "Anna—" he began.

But the driver interrupted him. "Where to now, folks?"

Anna's eyes darted away from Malone, toward the driver, who was watching them in the mirror. The cab was stopped at the traffic light at Constitution Avenue. To the left, up the steep incline of Twenty-third Street, were the stucco buildings of the CIA, a yellow acropolis enough removed from the rest of the city to seem not part of it.

Anna said to the driver, "The Library of Congress, please."

And then she faced away from Malone, looking out her window as the cab turned onto the avenue and began to cruise along Washington's elegant main axis. What, to look at sights?

Malone felt a rush of anger at her, how from the beginning she had withdrawn from him at crucial moments, dropping a veil between them as if the pain of her history or the burden of her secrets were simply too much for a bantamweight like him. He stared at her, angry at himself for being unable to speak, to force her to deal with him, to ask her the question that at last he'd understood was the only question left.

The wind feathered wisps of her prim hair loose and

they danced around the edges of her neck and the quarter of her face that he could see. Her face was dark. He couldn't read it.

They passed the Ellipse and the White House, which was obscured by scaffolding as workmen restored its façade. Malone thought of Harry Truman slapping Mr. Hoover on the shoulder with his "Damn fine work, Edgar!" They passed the Labor Department and Internal Revenue and, in the heart of the Federal Triangle, Justice itself. How grateful Malone felt that Hoover's office overlooked Pennsylvania Avenue on the far side of the building. The director would need only the barest glimpse of Malone to read him, or so Malone felt, a condition of his being suddenly transparent to himself.

"Anna?" He touched her shoulder. She was wearing a Navy cape, had it wrapped tightly around her, as if to keep herself together. Her mood surprised him. He had not expected to see in her such gravity, such disappointment. "What's wrong?"

She said something, but since she'd remained turned away he didn't hear.

"What?"

She faced him. "It's over," she said. "I wanted it to be over, but I . . ." She stopped: I didn't want it to be over with you.

The moment had come finally when Malone could say what he felt. "It doesn't have to be over with us."

She fell upon him, dead weight, and he simply held her. He sensed her acquiescence, her acceptance, her relief. Yes, give yourself to me, he thought.

The cab came thudding to a stop at a light. The driver glanced in his mirror, caught Malone's eye and his own darted away.

"We should put it into words, don't you think?" Malone whispered. "We've stopped short of words for too long now."

The cab swerved into the circle at the foot of Capitol Hill, leaving a brooding General Grant on the right, more gray than blue, and then careening up the incline so fast that Anna even in his arms swayed back against the seat. He propped her up and made her look at him.

She shook her head slightly. "It still seems impossible to me."

"No, no, that's what I'm telling you. Now we can think of ourselves. When we started out I had a hundred questions, a thousand questions. Now I only have one."

"What?"

"Will you marry me?"

"Oh, Christopher," she said, and she seemed about to tell him everything that she was feeling, when the cab stopped and her words just fell back down the well of her throat and it seemed he could hear them hitting the forgotten water deep inside her.

"Library of Congress," the driver said. "Two-fifty."

Malone paid the driver and then they got out. They stood facing each other on the chilly damp sidewalk. Beside them, straddling an elaborate fountain, a broad staircase swept up to the triple-arched entrance of the ornate library building, which, with its ribbed copper dome, resembled a huge gray lantern. Clerks and secretaries passed them, ascending and descending the massive sandstone stairs.

Anna hugged herself and stared at the ground. Her cape clung to her body like a cocoon.

They had never discussed marriage. They had never discussed a future with each other. Now he had asked her to put her feelings into words, and suddenly he was afraid of what she was going to say.

When she looked up at him, her eyes were brimming. "I want so much to be with you."

"But will you marry me?"

In the moment it took her to know how to answer, Malone thought, How strange this is, to be on a cold street, not touching each other.

Anna said, "We should wait before speaking of that." Tears spilled onto her cheek. She made no move to wipe them.

"Wait until what?"

"Until we are finished with Mr. Minot. Until we know this is over."

"But it *is* over, darling. They have Klaus Fuchs—"

"Then let us go right now. If we finish . . ."

"We can begin?"

She nodded. Malone had never seen such an expression of feeling from her, certainly not in a public place, and suddenly it seemed thoughtless of him to have pressed the issue, to have *proposed*, in that setting. How could he have possibly expected her to respond? She's right, he told himself; one thing at a time.

But also he sensed more in her reticence than a need to tie up loose ends. What wasn't she telling him?

Suddenly he thought of Beth, sunny, sweet Beth, who had answered this same question much more simply, by saying no. But if Anna said no—

He snapped his mind shut on the thought. "Okay," he said. "Let's finish Firebird. Lead the way." He gestured with a princely sweep of his arm.

Anna turned and they walked side by side up the stairs. As they entered the library, Anna took the lead. They cut across the grand entrance hall to the main reading room, the great rotunda, above which was suspended the lantern dome. Scores of mahogany desks were arranged in concentric rings around a central distributing station. Supreme Court clerks and congressional pages and schoolboys and attorneys and scholars and idling old men sat with their books and papers and inkwells. No one glanced at Malone and Anna as they cut through the reading room and out a modest doorway on the far side that led to a secondary set of circular stairs. A few moments later they were outside again, crossing Pennsylvania Avenue, leaving the Library of Congress behind.

Pennsylvania Avenue at that point was a broad street still, but not grand. It was lined with shops and luncheonettes, and as Malone followed Anna striding away from the stately buildings of Capitol Hill, he felt a certain relief to be reentering the world of ordinary commerce. He glanced at the reflection of Anna's image in the shop windows and thought that in her blue cape, moving so purposefully, she resembled a Victorian nurse.

Two blocks down Pennsylvania Avenue, near Seward Square, she turned onto a side street. The third building from the corner was a modest service garage that had seen better days. A pair of Amoco gas pumps sat like sentries on the sidewalk. Anna pushed through a spring-hinged hatch in the garage door, and when Malone followed her, he saw a lone mechanic bent over the motor of an old Ford. When the mechanic straightened to look at them Malone saw that his face was acne-scarred and grease-stained. He wore overalls, a soiled painter's cap turned backward on his head catcher-style, and in his eyes an expression of weary vacancy. Nevertheless Malone recognized him as one of the agents who'd picked him up at Union Station in September. The agent from the Shoreham. Kershaw.

Anna ignored him. As if the grimy, cluttered garage was turf of hers, she crossed between its soiled boxes and oil drums, not brushing up against them but also not taking particular pains to avoid doing so. Like that nurse, she seemed indifferent to the contrast between her pristine grace and the sores through which she moved, but Malone wasn't. He had awakened only that morning clasping her hand, his leg across hers, aware of light shining on him that at first he thought was winter sun but then realized was the warm glow of her white skin. She had still been asleep. For once there had been no mystery in her silence. The language of their bodies had seemed enough.

Now she was moving away from him into the darkest corner of the garage, and for a moment it seemed mad, as if she were about to deliberately trap herself in the angle between two walls. Why had she led him here? But why had she done any of it? In the beginning it had seemed clear to him that she was motivated by a powerful personal need to lay to rest the ghosts of her people, especially of her father. Or he assumed it was her father. What about her mother? And her mother's connection to Minot? She had refused to speak of it, but her silence itself confirmed the continuing importance of that connection. Was her mother the source of her reticence now, her inability to speak of the future?

It was the past that haunted Anna, and had been from the beginning. Then it had seemed that her partnership with him had become central, as if their collaboration

itself, more even than secrets of her past or than larger
national purposes, was what justified the uncertain and
ambiguous situation they shared. And hadn't their partnership become more than mere collaboration? It was a
bond turned back on itself repeatedly until it had become
already the physical and moral union he had just invited
her to join him in declaring. As far as Malone was
concerned, as if his name *were* Ward, they were already
married. But Anna was not ready to affirm that with
him. And he admitted now that in refusing, she put him
at the mercy again of his doubt. Not doubt in her, but in
himself.

He saw the obscure door in the dark corner—a toilet?
—and as she approached it a buzzer sounded, unlocking
it. She opened the door without hesitating, fluttering a
pinup calendar that hung nearby. She went through the
door, then stood holding it open for Malone.

Kershaw leaned over his carburetor again, having shown
no sign of recognition and no interest either. Handsomely
coiffed women and men wearing gold collar pins and
fifty-dollar shoes crossed through his dirt every afternoon, sure they did.

The doorway led to a spiraling metal staircase. Malone
climbed it behind Anna, then followed her through a
door at the top that opened on a narrow vestibule so
brightly lit that it hurt his eyes. A man in a white shirt
and a tie, and wearing a holster on his hip, sat on a stool
in front of a glass panel angled at the level of his knees in
such a way as to serve as a window on the garage below.

Kershaw was still working on the car.

The panel was a one-way mirror, and it shocked Malone to realize he had not noticed it above the rear wall
of the garage, and that made him feel that he'd lost his
edge. For the first time in months he touched his jacket
where agents kept their credentials, missing them. He
pressed his hand against his hip, wanting the bulk of his
gun. He remembered how he'd reacted when Beth Fraser
had rejected him: he'd told himself it didn't matter as
long as he had the Bureau.

"Hello, Miss Melnik," the agent said. Around his neck
was a silver chain that held a plastic ID card with his

photo on it. To his right was a small table along the edge
of which a row of buttons was aligned, and next to it was
an upright gun rack holding a long-barreled shotgun.
"I'm sorry but you're still required to show your pass.
And you too, sir."

Malone decided to let Anna handle it and said nothing.

Anna opened her purse and lifted her pass. "If you tell
Mr. Minot I am here. And this"—she glanced at Malone
and for a moment a rare insecurity showed in her face—
"this is Mr. Ward."

The agent had barely shifted on his stool, yet still he
had managed to keep an eye on the scene in the garage
below. He nonchalantly rested his hand on the table
beside him, but Malone knew he was pressing one of the
buttons.

The second door opened at once. A woman in a prim
tweed suit stood with her hand upon the knob. She too
wore a laminated pass around her neck.

"Miss Melnik is here," the guard said.

The woman nodded at her, but without friendliness.

The guard continued, "She and Mr. Ward want to see
Mr. Minot."

The woman stared at them for a moment, then disappeared behind the door, which closed noiselessly.

During the moments it took her to return the guard
watched Kershaw below, Anna stared at the seam of her
cape and Malone felt his anxiety begin to climb.

When the woman returned she held the door wide for
them.

Anna and Malone filed past her into a large, high-
ceilinged room, the entire floor of what had been a
warehouse once perhaps. There were no windows but the
room was bright with unadorned white walls and rows of
fluorescent fixtures hanging from the roof beams. Under
the tubular lights was a parade of desks arranged in
columns of four, several dozen of them. Men and women
were bent over their work.

As they filed down one aisle behind their tweed-suited
escort, Malone saw that the papers piled neatly on each
desk he passed were covered with nothing but numbers,
row upon row of them in groups of five digits, and he

realized it was the intercepted cable traffic. The men and
women, some wearing eyeshades, some wielding pencils,
some with calculators in front of them, were cryptanalysts.

The unsung cryptanalysts, he thought suddenly. With
the arrest of Fuchs and a confession forced no doubt by
material they had deciphered, these ordinary-looking men
and women had scored the cryptanalysis coup of the
decade! Hell, maybe of the century! But you wouldn't
know it from them, so fiercely concentrated were they
still, as if the crucial secret had eluded them. What else,
he wondered, were they trying to learn?

He noticed then that the dozen desks in the farthest
aisle were mostly empty. Three were occupied, and Malone sensed that the two men and one woman were doing
something different, not manipulating numbers, but checking reference works, speaking into Dictaphones and actually writing. On their desks the books and pages were
covered with letters that, even from a distance, registered
as Cyrillic. They were Russian translators. Anna had
been one of them, and one of the empty desks was hers.

The woman was leading the way to one of two glass-
enclosed cubicles, Minot's office, directly ahead. In the
second cubicle opposite Minot's sat a white-haired old
man hunched over his desk as over the steering wheel of
an automobile he was no longer sure of. Light glinted off
his spectacles as he strained to see what was printed on
the page before him. Even Malone could see that it was
digit groups. The old man's concentration made Malone
wonder again what they were working so hard to crack.

Then he saw that the old man was wearing a rumpled
black suit and a clerical collar and Malone realized this
was Father Abetz, the scripture scholar whom Minot had
described to Hoover as the most brilliant cryptanalyst in
Washington.

Minot was standing by his desk when the woman showed
them in. Malone hadn't seen him in more than a month
and he was shocked by Minot's haggard appearance. He
was coatless. His white shirt hung loosely on him, as if
he'd lost weight. His tie was knotted clumsily because his
collar was too big. His face had the gaunt, sunken look of
an exhausted man. The veins stood out in his neck. But

his usually rheumy eyes were clear, sharp and focused—a function, Malone suddenly realized, of his anger. He was staring coldly at Malone, ignoring Anna.

But once the tweed-suited woman had withdrawn, closing the door between Minot's office and the larger room, it was Anna who spoke. "Klaus Fuchs confessed. It is in the papers."

Minot hadn't moved and his eyes were still hard on Malone. "What are you doing here?"

Malone realized what a mistake he'd made. This was what the knot of anxiety constricting his chest had warned him of—a major deviation from what was expected of him as an agent. How could this have happened to him, whose responses for years now had been so finely calibrated? But of course he knew. And now, he thought, am I to tell Minot the truth? That I am here because for a moment—or a day or a week or a month—I allowed myself to think that nothing mattered more than that I love this woman? I am here because, having held my breath for all these months—all these years—my lungs have burst.

What he said, with a placidity he did not remotely feel, was, "I came here to find out what my responsibilities are now."

"Your responsibilities?" Minot's voice rose sharply, but the glass walls of the small room seemed to contain the sound. Malone had the strangely divided sense both that he was about to be humiliated in public— before all those cipher clerks and translators—and that no one was paying the slightest attention. As if the walls were steel. As if they were inside a safe.

A safe. For a reason he could not have explained Malone thought of the safe in the Russian *referentura,* of that open door, and once more he felt the anguish of that mystery. No doubt he called to mind that image as a way of defending himself against Minot's anger. There was a release in surfacing what he'd never been able to quite forget, that Minot had never really leveled with him anyway. It wasn't as if he'd violated Minot's trust.

Minot said, "Your responsibilities are to maintain your cover until told otherwise. How dare you come here like this!" At last Minot faced Anna. "How dare you bring him here!"

She did not flinch. "I brought him here because I want him to hear this when I tell you I am finished."

"What do you mean?"

"You asked me to work for two purposes. The first was for Tumark and that purpose failed when he refused to come over to us. The second purpose is accomplished now. Is that not what this confession of Fuchs means?"

Minot didn't answer at first, and Malone sensed it when Minot decided he had to handle this differently. His tone changed and even his rigid posture softened somewhat when he said, "Not quite."

"What, then?"

"We have Fuchs, yes. But he had helpers. Go-betweens. Someone else at Los Alamos, and others."

"This guy 'Raymond,' " Malone said.

"That's right. For one. Firebird isn't finished until we have them all."

"But that is not my work," Anna said evenly. "That is police work."

"That's true." Minot looked at Malone with more than an implication: *Your* work, you son of a bitch. "All right, Anna," he said, still eyeing Malone. "If you're ready to wind up your part in this, then we wind it up." He paused, slowly facing her. He seemed utterly unmoved by her resignation and by the intense emotion with which she'd offered it. It was hard to see them as people who'd shared a bond of intimacy.

"So why don't you wait outside, Anna? Chris will be out in a minute, and you can leave together. Isn't that what you want?"

"Yes."

"Then just go have a seat at your old desk. We won't be long. Chris is still on the case." He glanced at Malone. "Right, Chris?"

"Yes, sir."

Anna was reluctant to go; she looked at Malone with uncharacteristic helplessness, but he refused to raise his eyes to her. She turned and left.

"Sit down," Minot said, taking his own chair, and

hooking his leg over one of the desk drawers. Malone did as he was told. The massive desk was between them.

Minot studied Malone in the silence, like a headmaster trying to decide whether to cane his mulish pupil. Finally he said, "She's a girl with a guilty conscience, you know."

"No, sir. I don't know that." Malone was aware of the defensiveness in his voice, but he didn't care.

"I don't mean guilty because of you. Her falling for you is the good part." Minot surprised Malone by smiling suddenly. "You're the all-American boy, for Christ's sake." His voice was infused with a nearly paternal warmth. "I expected you to fall for her. Hell, who wouldn't? Sharing a posh house and a high-paced drill with a beautiful woman who plays your damn wife? I expected you to fall hard! I didn't think she would. I guess that's what happened, eh?" He stopped, but Malone said nothing. "I was depending on Anna to keep it professional with you two."

"Whatever happened between us didn't stop us from doing the job."

"If you were doing the job, Malone, you'd be across town right now wearing Peter Michael Ward's inbred air of superiority instead of sitting here in my office looking like you're about to throw up."

Minot let the weight of his rebuke accumulate in silence for a moment, while Malone realized that throwing up was exactly what he felt like doing.

Minot swiveled in his chair to look out at his team of cryptanalysts and translators.

Malone glanced across at Father Abetz, who was bent, as before, over a stack of pages. From here Malone saw that in addition to yellowed cable paper, the priest was working with sheets of graph paper.

Minot's gaze moved slowly toward Anna's desk, then settled on her. She was impassive in her chair, faced away. Her cape and gloves were on the desk in front of her.

The filmy cloud had returned to Minot's eyes, as if only anger could clear his head of its boozy weather, but at least the moisture made him seem familiar again, the unlikely counterspy whom Malone had trusted because of his unlikeliness. Now Malone did sense Minot's feeling for Anna, the old affection having swamped the impersonal steeliness, but there was also a new note of worry for her.

Seeing the worry in Minot prompted Malone to blurt, "I just asked her to marry me."

Minot showed no surprise. "What did she answer?"

"Nothing. She led me here."

Minot nodded. "She couldn't answer you until her slate was clean. She came here to wipe the last of the chalk off." Minot swirled back to Malone. "Unfortunately, it won't come clean that easy."

"What do you mean?"

"She's still in it. She has to be. We won't let her go."

"Why?"

"Because we may need her yet with Tumark."

"But Tumark is out. He refused to defect. He shut it down."

"No, he didn't. Tumark didn't defect because we didn't want him to. Not yet. He's more valuable to us where he is. Tumark is working for us. He has been for months."

"Impossible. Anna hasn't seen him. Tumark told her he's too worried about his family and then he refused to see her again. I know that for a fact! Anna told me."

"She had no business telling you that."

"But you can't tell me that it's not true. I don't believe you. I believe her. You've never leveled with me anyway." Malone had never intended to speak so directly, and in part of himself he was horrified that such words had come from his mouth to an Inspector of the Bureau, to the man who controlled his future.

But Minot was unfazed. He said evenly, "I've told you what you needed to know."

"What about the open safe? I've never believed you about that, and it's something I *did* need to know. You claim that the code clerk left it unlocked by accident, as if you believed such crap! Not a coincidence, a goddamn miracle! But now I see that you knew ahead of time that the safe would be open. I've been afraid all this time it meant there was some kind of Russian trap. I mean, if you didn't arrange for it, then *they* did. But Fuchs confessed! The code book actually turned up the spy, so I see it wasn't a Russian trap because it did the trick. They sure as hell wouldn't turn Fuchs in, especially not if he's set to work on the H-bomb. So therefore you are the one who arranged to leave the safe unlocked. It was your show. And of course you were the one—maybe the only one—who knew I couldn't crack the safe if it didn't have a handle. And so you just had somebody leave the damn thing unlocked."

"That's right," Minot said evenly.

Malone stared at Minot, having seen it. "Tumark."

Minot nodded slowly. "Tumark."

"Then why in hell did you send me in there? Why go to all that trouble? Not to mention what could have happened to me . . . ."

Malone felt the nausea rise inside him and for an instant he was falling again into the black abyss of that elevator shaft, into the bottomless hole of what he did not know. Terror seized him so sharply and so abruptly that it cut the hallucination off cold, like a safety clamp that grabs the cables when an elevator car begins to freefall.

Still, as with that fall in the black shaft, the feeling left him spread-eagled over nothing, straddling what he feared most, staring into it and seeing, unfortunately, the shadows of everything.

"You could have had Tumark bring out the code book."

"No, we couldn't have."

"Why?"

"It's not for you to know that."

"If he could leave the *referentura* safe unlocked he could have copied the code book, same as I did."

Minot stared mournfully at Malone, who understood that if his supervisor answered this question he would have to answer them all. And he wasn't going to do that. Why? Because he was the supervisor, that was why.

As it was, the story about Tumark didn't click on the pins; Malone's locksmith's instincts were what kept him from accepting it without questions.

He said, "Anna told me Tumark loves his wife and daughter too much to work for us. She believed him and

I believe her. I don't know much at this point, Mr. Minot, but I know she would not lie to me."

Unlike some people I can think of, he added to himself.

"It's not a question of her lying to you. She doesn't know, that's all. We had Tumark break off with her months ago. Once we had him hooked, we didn't need Anna holding the pole. Anna was bait."

"But she *believed* him. And so do I. The man hates Stalin, but he's deeply Russian. His hatred of the regime could prompt him to defect maybe, but not to stay in place as a spy. Why would he work for us?"

Minot was rigid for some moments, perfectly focused on Malone, judging him. Finally he leaned forward and opened a drawer. He withdrew a manila envelope and threw it onto his desk in front of Malone.

Malone stared at it.

Minot said quietly, "Klaus Fuchs is one of several people in the Russian atomic spy ring. He's the key, the source of the scientific documents. And you're right. The documents we deciphered here, with the key you provided to Father Abetz, are what led us to him. But we have to get the people Fuchs depended on. And we have to do whatever the hell is required to get them. The secrets they stole were all funneled to Moscow through the Soviet embassy, and Tumark was there. He's *still* there and that is where we need him until we crack 'Raymond' and the rest. Tumark is crucial. Don't ask me to say more than that."

The two men stared at each other. Malone knew an order when he heard one, and he nodded.

Minot continued, "And Tumark has a reason of his own for working with us as long as we need him to." He stopped and waited. Malone had refused to recognize the envelope as being meant for him.

"Open it, Chris. You wanted me to level with you."

Finally he did it, upending the envelope, freeing its flap. A dozen eight-by-ten black-and-white glossy photographs fell to the desk.

He recognized her at once, of course, the woman whom he'd just asked to marry.

He recognized her breasts, flattened on her chest as

she arched back toward the headboard of the bed, her legs hooked around her partner's waist. It was impossible to see who the man was in that particular photograph, but there was no doubt about the woman. He recognized that scissors grip of hers, having felt its blissful pressure around his own hips dozens of times. He remembered how unbreakable it was, those long legs of hers, how she clung with them to stay hooked to him through everything.

In another photo he recognized the way strands of her hair caught in her teeth. In the heat of passion her mouth would gnaw on anything.

In yet a third photo, one in which Tumark's face was clearly visible, framed by his long white hair, his eyes somehow pathetic with the ache of his overwhelming passion, her dark fingernails were what Malone saw of Anna, pushing into Tumark's shoulders. But something about the photograph struck him as wrong. What? That the Russian was too old to be at such an edge of desire? It exploded Malone's illusion—the illusion every lover clings to—that Anna had pressed her fingers so desperately only into him. He stared at those fingernails, thinking, So this is what that perfect pain—he had felt those nails digging in his back, but obviously had never seen them—looks like.

"I don't think Comrade Tumark appears that worried about his wife, Chris. Do you?"

Tumark. The ambivalent, distressed, old wartime alliance diplomat. But not that old, clearly, and not that ambivalent, and if there was distress in those photographs it was Anna's as much as Tumark's—distress that their mutual, passionate, naked ache might not last forever.

He looked at the first photo again, of Anna fiercely gripping the headboard behind her. And then he recognized the headboard as part of his own bed. His bed in Phelps Place. She had brought Tumark into the bed they'd shared.

Without thinking, Malone crushed the photograph, balling it in his two hands violently. Then he threw it against the window of Minot's cubicle, and the thing fell to the floor. Malone slammed his fists down on the desk, about to curse Minot, but the other photographs were lying there, and he couldn't stop himself from looking at them. Gradually a kind of numbness spread through him.

In the half-dozen others, Tumark was pictured with Anna in various public settings—a park, a street, a dinner party—which in the context of the sexual images clearly took on the aspect of rendezvous, lovers hastily exchanging glances, slight caresses, plans for their next meeting. Malone himself at numerous receptions and at the Russian embassy itself had witnessed some of those exchanges, but now he was seeing them as for the first time. The glass of his naïveté was shattered.

Tumark was the man she told him was like her father. She was like his daughter.

Tumark's access to the *referentura?* It ceased being a question, given his access to Anna. Anna. Tumark. He flipped through the photographs silently, a bare inch above his rage. Tumark. Anna. Tumark fucking Anna.

He raised his eyes to Minot. Minot looking all at once exhausted and old—older than Tumark—and unhealthy. The disease he had was his job.

Minot said, "We can't let Anna go, Chris. You have to keep her here, whatever you have to do or say. Tumark has to know she's still around, showing up at embassy parties as Mrs. Peter Ward, so that, if we have to, we can produce her as an American agent"—he gestured at the photographs—"and not just some hooker he poked on Ninth Street."

Poked? It was a verb Malone had never heard before. Was he this stupid? This green? He forced himself to reply. "Produce her for the MGB's benefit, if Tumark balks, so they'd know the full extent of his treason. The Russian has a lover whose so-called husband is with the FBI." Malone released his breath in a faint, admiring whistle. "You've really hooked the bastard, haven't you."

"I'm glad you appreciate it."

"Yes, Mr. Minot," Malone said with a calmness that seemed eerie even to him. "I truly appreciate it." Malone put his hand on his hip where his gun should have been. With his free hand he gestured at the spread of pictures.

"You lay this out for Beria's boys and Tumark's dead."

Minot nodded, coldly. "I hope we don't have to."

"And so is his wife and daughter."

"Right."

"Jesus Christ, Minot." Malone's rage, having turned to numbness, had now become nausea. He felt like throwing up, exactly.

When he looked through the glass wall, past the still bent Father Abetz, toward Anna, she was staring back at him coarsely, as if he and Minot were the crude subjects of an obscene photograph.

As to Malone then they were.

They all were.

13

Malone waited for her on a bench in the near corner of Seward Square. He sat with his hands plunged into the pockets of his coat, his eyes fixed upon the passing traffic, but his mind focused, despite himself, on what had happened.

After Malone had left Minot's glass-enclosed corner office, Minot had surprised him by asking Anna to step inside. Anna? Wasn't the point—her point?—that Anna and Minot were now finished with each other? But she had docilely walked past Malone into Minot's office, like a person in a trance. After Minot closed the door, he sat at his desk, looking at her for a long time, saying nothing.

Malone had retreated awkwardly to a corner near the second glass-walled office, the cubicle occupied by the chief cryptanalyst, the old priest, Father Abetz. If there'd been a window, he'd have stood with his back to the room, its desks and people, but the blank wall was no solace. Should he have stood facing it, like a punished child? But perhaps he should have, because when he let his gaze drift instead across the room it went right to Minot's cubicle again.

Just then Minot had reached across his desk to touch Anna's hand, a gesture of such apparently deep-felt concern that, given what Minot had just revealed of his true attitude toward her, Malone felt shocked at the man's hypocrisy, and regretted witnessing it. He felt like a voyeur and he wished that the walls of Minot's office were made of wood. He felt a ridiculous rush of resentment at, of all things, the FBI itself, for its cookie-cutter office layouts; there was no reason why Firebird had to occupy space identical to a field-office squad room, with its uniform rows of desks and its glass-encased supervisors' corners. He resented the need Bureau chieftains had, not to watch their underlings through those glass walls, but to make their underlings *feel* watched.

But now he had become the watcher. He wished that he knew nothing of Minot's history with Anna and her mother. If Minot had befriended them how could he now have so cynically exploited Anna? Where was Minot's friendship in his use of those photographs? In his need for them in the first place? What was Minot but a desperate pimp to whom even the daughter of a friend was just another jane to be corrupted? The photographs were what made Malone feel like a voyeur.

"Anna, dear Anna. . . ." It was as if Malone could hear Minot's words. Even from the distance he sensed Anna's gratitude, and whether he'd known of their history or not, he could feel it in the way they bowed toward each other. All at once Malone remembered churches in Italy in which the confessionals were not sealed off behind curtains. What a violation it had seemed to be able to see the penitent kneeling before the priest even if their whispers were impossible to hear. It stunned Malone to think, even momentarily, of Anna and Minot in such a context, and the image heightened the outrage he felt, not at the Bureau now, but at his patron. The bastard was using every trick he had just to keep Anna on the job, including, Malone said to himself, me.

He might have continued to successfully deflect the loathing he felt away from himself, but at that moment he noticed that the old priest was staring at him from inside *his* cubicle. His glasses had slipped to the tip of his nose, which glistened with moisture. He was fumbling in a pocket for a handkerchief, the reason for the break in his concentration, but his eyes, having fallen upon Malone, bore into him. Malone tried to focus on other things, the dandruff dotting the shoulders of his worn black clerical suit, the gnarled hand holding the stub of a

pencil, his outsized, ancient ears. But the priest's eyes
held him. All at once Malone felt their accusation, as if
the screen in his confessional had just been opened. He
resisted the Catholic boy's impulse to look down.

Because he did, he saw a change come over those eyes,
or was it only a change in his own perception? Now
Father Abetz was looking at him with an intense but
knowing kindliness, as if he knew everything about Firebird and everything about Malone's relation to it. Malone's momentary impulse was to cross to the priest's
office, to kneel beside him and tell him everything. It was
a ludicrous idea, but he knew that, on one condition, he
would have done it—that the old priest tell him everything
in return.

Instead he crossed to Minot's secretary's desk, told her
he would wait for Anna Melnik across the street, and he
left.

The chill air of the dank winter afternoon made him
think how different this was from the first time, that
warm September day, he'd waited for her in a small
Washington park. Seward Square was cut into quarters
by the intersection of Pennsylvania and North Carolina
avenues, unlike Dupont Circle, where the avenues, running in respectful circumference, formed a tiny border to
the park. Seward Square lacked the elegance of Dupont
Circle, therefore, but its triangular patches of grass and
shrubbery were not the less precious—or, to Malone, less
evocative—for that.

The thought of that first sight of her in Dupont Circle,
how her dress flowed elegantly around her body, carried
with it another image—her unclothed body next to him in
bed. He thought of the unselfconscious grace with which
she slid out of his embrace, out from under the sheets to
cross the bedroom for cigarettes. How natural it had
come to seem, her standing before him naked, lighting
her cigarette, hugging herself against the chill, going up
on her toes with pleasure as she inhaled a lungful of
smoke, then doing a quick pirouette out of sheer joy
before skipping back to the bed, to him. She was the first
woman in whose presence he took nakedness for granted,

his own as much, nearly, as hers. Anna's body, in revealing its secrets to him, had revealed his own. Despite the stranger's clothes and the stranger's house and even the stranger's bed in which so much of this occurred, Malone, in her company and because of it, to his great amazement, had become himself.

But now his picture of Anna's nakedness was a picture that included Vladimir Tumark.

And he knew that no matter what happened now he would never see her in that simple way again, her back arching, her breasts pressing upward, her white throat exposed, her face coiled in that particular expression of sexual excitement, without also seeing the pale shoulders and the half-turned head of another man.

Now his thoughts of Anna condemned him to the status, again, of voyeur. But unfortunately not a disinterested one, for he had been usurped. He was condemned from now on to watch in his mind the man who had taken his place. A stranger, it turned out, owned not only his clothes, his house and his bed, but also his heart. Whoever possessed Anna possessed him. And now the possessing stranger had a name. Vladimir Tumark, passed-over diplomatic hack who lacked the courage either to be loyal to his country or forthrightly to betray it. Vladimir Tumark, a pasty-fleshed old man whose high-minded love of political principle shriveled in plain old blood-pumping lust. Yet curiously it was not Vladimir Tumark whom he hated for this, nor Anna, nor even Minot. He hated himself.

He stood up and tightened the belt of his trench coat and began to walk along the periphery of Seward Square. The carillon of a nearby church began to play the melody of a hymn. It was familiar but he couldn't name it. He stopped walking and stared at the stone belfry of the church, wondering why there was religious music on a weekday afternoon. Then he thought of Lent, its panoply of observances, and it shocked him to realize he had no idea whether Ash Wednesday had come yet or not. Once the smudge of ashes on his forehead had been as much a part of his year's calendar as Christmas or Thanksgiving. But now his feeling was, Who needs it? As if his mild

mental blasphemy carried across the square, the carillon
music stopped with the scratch of a jarred record needle.
The church warden testing his loudspeakers? Malone resumed walking.

At the intersection of the two broad avenues it was
apparent that the day's-end congestion of automobile
traffic had begun. He stood on a curb, staring at the
passing cars as if hypnotized by them. As an exercise of
mind he imagined who the drivers were. Senior officials
didn't leave work quite this early, so they were clerks and
stenographers and Civil Service slot fillers. They were
congressional librarians and Capitol Hill staffers in their
Fords and Chevies and Studebakers, heading east in a
halting flow, a honking glacier sliding toward Suitland
and Anacostia. He conjured the map he'd memorized and
pictured the blue patch of Bolling Field on the Potomac, the dotted boundaries of Saint Elizabeth's Hospital.
When the light turned and the traffic in front of him
stopped, he studied the drivers of cars, solitary men
going home to their new little houses in Seat Pleasant
and Hillcrest Heights, where their wives and children
waited to greet them. A red-trimmed silver bus hissed to
a stop in front of Malone—A, B, and W, the eye-level
letters read—and the field of his concentration was taken
over by the passengers, in the windows, women's heads
in profile, like a row of pearl cameos. Tight-lipped ladies
who, though oblivious of him, sat like they were always
being looked at. They were going home to their tidy
garden apartments where they would devil up some eggs
for the girls who might come over for a rubber of bridge.

Malone turned away from the intersection to walk
back across the square toward Fourth Street. In the con-
fines of the deserted small park, away from the bustle of
the avenues and their powerful intimation of normalcy,
their suggestion that people had other cares than what
had befallen him, he felt a rare wave of self-pity.

Punctuating it was the sight of Anna coming toward
him through that gray little patch of lifeless earth. Now,
instead of elegant and self-possessed and beautiful, she
looked, in the way she walked, in the way her cape hung
from her shoulders, in the way she held herself or refused

to, defeated. A drained fountain, he thought, becomes plugged with half-frozen leaves, so that what threatens it most, finally, of all things, is the rain.

Will you marry me? He stopped where he was and watched her approach, trying to remember the shape of feelings that had prompted such a question. What a fool he was! Malone was aware of it when she raised her eyes and saw him, and he was surprised that she did not break stride at the sight of him or seem thrown off-balance. Instead she continued toward him as if she expected Malone to open his arms.

He waited impassively, unable to blot from his mind the sound of his own voice, a sharp memory of those words. I had a hundred questions, a thousand questions. Now I only have one. Will you marry me?

Had he really said such a thing to her, and, after all these months, had he said it only an hour ago?

He sensed that she was coming to him now as if the feelings prompting his question were still alive. Yet he knew that, whatever had happened to the feelings, that question was gone with all the others. His hundred questions, his thousand, were like those leaves exactly, frozen in congealed lumps blocking gutters and drains. When he had asked her to marry him, ludicrously, in front of the Library of Congress, a true Washington buffoon, Anna's demurral had made him feel that he'd misjudged her. And hadn't Minot's revelation confirmed that in spades! Like a shrapnel-packed grenade, his outrage had exploded, leaving him in the grip now only of this numbness. A clogged gutter in his heart.

When she drew close enough to read what was written in his face—no questions, not a one—she stopped. For a moment they simply stood looking at each other across a distance of a dozen yards. When she saw that he was not going to move toward her, she continued toward him, but slowly, with none of that great verve he associated with her public walk.

She said, "What just happened in there?"

"You don't know? Minot didn't tell you?"

"No. I thought *we* were going there to tell him something."

"That we wanted out."

"Well, that *I* did."

"I wanted out too." Malone felt the pressure behind his eyes of the emotion he would not show her.

"But you aren't out, are you?"

"No. I'm still on the case. Klaus Fuchs is just the beginning. There's 'Raymond' and there are others. I'm in this until we catch them all." Malone's tone was as cold as the air that carried it. What he wanted now, above all, was to end this scene without telling her how she'd hurt him. "You said it's just police work from here out, but Minot seems to think the 'police' still need a certain backup. We gave them the lead they needed. And they might need—"

"I don't believe it. Why does he need us as Mr. and Mrs. Ward? You *gave* them the code book and it provided the key. What else is there for you to steal? Why else does he need you on Embassy Row? Why won't he let us stop?"

Anna had drawn close enough to touch him, but she didn't. He was rigid, unyielding. He sensed her disappointment. Had she really expected he would simply fold her into his arms? There was no give in his voice when he said, "But he told you that you could stop. He said your part was over if you wanted it to be."

"But I don't believe that either. Mr. Minot is not telling me what is true. I can feel it."

Malone stared at her, but it was as if he was seeing himself, his *own* perplexity, his *own* confusion. Minot had told her she could leave, but he'd told him to keep her on the job; Good Old Minot with his double and triple messages, his lies. It amazed Malone, how much he'd trusted Minot, how much he'd needed him.

Anna lowered her eyes and asked quietly, "If I left Washington now, where would that leave you?"

Malone shrugged with a casualness he did not feel. "I'm still Peter Ward, U.S. Office of Protocol. Minot said we can arrange it simply that you had to return to Strasbourg, for example, to care for your dying father." With a stagy sadness he said in a mock accent, "My dutiful wife is an even more dutiful daughter." He paused waiting for her to look at him, but she didn't. "Your absence would be accepted. Even your permanent disappearance would—if the thing went on that long. It would square with the air of mystery that made you exotic to all those other Foggy Bottom wives, those Bryn Mawr girls." When she still did not raise her eyes, he asked in his own voice, "Why don't you believe Minot?"

She kicked at pebbles, shaking her head slightly. "He asked me to stay in Washington, but he couldn't give me a reason. There is no purpose for me now."

"I suppose he thinks your purpose would be to help me."

She raised her eyes finally. "No, he doesn't think that. He knows you don't need me now. He hasn't told this to me but I know what it is. He wants me here because of Tumark."

Malone stared at her for a moment, as if trying to parse the meaning of her statement. Finally he said, nodding, "Tumark. That's right, darling. Tumark is the issue, and of course he always has been, even if one of us didn't know it."

The truth splayed itself between them. Now that he saw it, the fact of her relationship with the Russian seemed so obvious that Malone felt it as a fault of his own that he had not caught on before. But before, this "obvious" truth would have seemed preposterous.

Watch it, he warned himself, as he felt his anger coming back. And with the anger, hurt.

"Tumark," he said again, his eyes locked on hers. He could not speak the man's name without seeing—as if it were an image burned into the dark center of her eyes, into which he was staring—the pasty flesh of Tumark's shoulders, and a woman's fingers pressing into it. Hers. The pain rose from his stomach to his chest to his throat. Oh, Anna. The pain was behind his eyes now, making him—to his utter horror—want to cry.

He veered from her, from the hurt, back to Tumark. Tumark, the bastard. How he hated him. And wasn't hatred so much easier to handle? It calmed him enough to go on with their discussion. Only their discussion would keep him from collapsing, there on the street, in tears,

He said, "In fact, darling, what I said before is just the cover line. You see, now we have cover lines with each other. It isn't the 'police' I'm backing up by staying under. It's you. As you say, there is nothing for me to steal. My job isn't to break into the embassy again, but just to keep bringing you to parties, to keep you visible, to keep you on the scene. Our roles are switched. I'm the helper now. You're at bat, not me, or at least that's what Minot's hoping. That's why he asked you to stay and why he told me to use my influence with you too." Malone laughed. "He thinks I have some."

Anna's face showed that she did not know what to make of his bitterness, and so he checked it. He said matter-of-factly, "I'm staying on as Peter Michael Ward, FSO, to protect your cover so that Minot can keep the pressure on Tumark. Remember what I told you about how to crack a safe? In this case you're the handle we push down on to pop the proper pin into place, to open the lock."

"But Mr. Minot is wrong," Anna said wearily. "We have been over this and over this. Vladimir Tumark will never come to our side. He will never work for us."

Malone turned away from her to look across the square toward the crowded intersection, to keep her from seeing the confusion in his face, to think for a moment.

Tumark left the *referentura* safe unlocked because it had no handle and there was no way to get the pressure he needed.

Anna was displaying ignorance that suggested, despite his conceit a moment before, that she was no handle either.

Was Tumark's role in the *referentura* a secret he, Malone, had to keep from her? Was Tumark's entire role a secret from her? But how could it be?

Or did she think she still had to protect the secret from him?

The anguish he felt was about her, nothing else. What an earthquake it was to discover that he could not trust her. He could not trust his Anna.

It was like making fists inside when he told himself, Think of her as an agent! She is not your fucking Anna. She is an agent. *Now* ask your questions.

Why hadn't Minot prepared him for this? What to tell her and what not to? His assumption had been that she knew more than he did. But if she truly did not know that Tumark was *already* working for Minot and had been since autumn, then Webb Minot had reasons not to trust Anna with the central fact of her own involvement.

But, hell, until today, he thought, Minot hasn't trusted me! And I'm his goddamn agent. Suddenly he felt exhausted, incapable of maintaining the pitch of emotion any longer.

"Look," he said, surrendering for the moment, "it's cold and it's about to rain and it's been a rough day, and I think we both could ease off a bit. Let's find a bar and get a drink. What do you say?" He looked into her eyes now, determined to see nothing of Tumark or even of himself. What was going on with *her*? Could he put his feelings aside and look at Anna? Just Anna. Not *his* or Minot's or Tumark's. Where was *she* in all of this? "Maybe a drink would help us tell each other the truth," he said quietly. "Don't you think it's time we did that? Even if no one else will do it, don't you think we should?" Now her eyes made him think of that icon hanging on the wall in her room and before which her candle always flickered. "Isn't that what we owe each other now?"

She nodded.

The Neptune Bar and Grill on Pennsylvania Avenue, across from the Library of Congress, was crowded with junior lawyers and Supreme Court clerks, congressional aides and library workers, young men and women who were pleased with themselves for having come to Washington at the time of its triumph. For the privilege of administering that triumph, which reached after all across what was called the entire free world, they had left behind places named Sharon and Dayton and Glenn Falls and Southbridge. If the truth be told, their work in low-ceilinged offices or in cavernous file rooms or in the cramped corners of Quonsetlike tempos was tedious and unrewarding, but there was a thrill in being among such people as gathered after work in the watering-holes up and down the length of Pennsylvania Avenue from

M Street in Georgetown to Capitol Hill. Each one's illusion was that though his or her own piece of Washington was as mundane as any hometown insurance clerk's Main Street, the rest of Washington where these others worked had the glamour proper to the capital of the western world.

The Neptune was crowded with people, in other words, who felt great about being there. It wasn't the work they loved or even the city, but this rare, jovial camaraderie. Four rows of green leather booths, separated from each other by frosted glass panels, gave the room the feel of a staid bar and grill, but its patrons called to each other across the partitions and made cracks at the waitresses and argued good-naturedly at the jukebox, like the college kids or GIs or bobbysoxers they'd been until not that long ago. No one paid attention to the man and woman sitting quietly in a rear corner booth below the draped fishnet that gave the decor—Neptune's kingdom—its underwater motif. The noise and bustle of the room at large, in a curious reversal, provided Malone and Anna with solitude and privacy. No one could overhear them. No one cared to.

Malone toyed with his empty shot glass. He'd thrown the whiskey down in one gulp, then took his first sip of beer immediately, as if he always drank like that. It was his father, not him, who had taken such double-barreled hits on the way home, yet when the waitress had asked him what he wanted, he'd answered automatically, and when she'd served it, he drank without ceremony.

Anna's beer sat before her untouched, the pilsner glass glistening with condensation. She was looking at her hands, absently twirling her wedding ring.

Malone leaned back into the booth, letting out a sigh. "You were going to tell me about your friend," he said gently, "and about what he's meant to you."

Anna looked up, though she continued to twirl her ring, the ring that Peter Ward was supposed to have given his wife, but that in fact a priest had stolen from the corpse of his dead parishioner. "You said we should tell each other the truth. Everything I have told you about Vladimir is true."

"But there are things you haven't told me."

Anna opened her mouth to answer him, then closed it.

And then Malone thought, Why should she level with me, since I haven't yet with her? "You didn't tell me that Tumark is working for Minot, and has been for months."

"But I do not know that." The incredulity in her expression seemed real enough. "I do not believe it."

"Minot just told me that. It was Tumark who left the *referentura* safe open for me that night."

"But how could he? The code-room safe? He is first secretary for *economics!* He would never know the, the . . ." In her agitation, she'd lost the word.

"The combination," he said, shrugging. "All I know is the safe was left unlocked. Minot wanted me to think it was a lucky break, a coincidence. I never bought that, and today he told me the truth. Maybe Tumark had the combination because in fact he's an MGB officer. Maybe he's the *rezident.* That would explain why Victor Woolf was so anxious to snag him that he didn't want to risk him on our black-bag job."

Anna slowly shook her head. "Then everything he told me would be a lie. He *hates* the MGB."

"Minot *convinced* me, Anna. He *proved* to me that Tumark had good reasons to work for us." Malone waited for the color to rise in her face, since those reasons were photographs of her.

But she continued to shake her head. "I just don't believe it. He would not defect for Mr. Minot. I've told you that. Because of his daughter. Nothing Mr. Minot or Mr. Woolf could do would have changed that. I *know* that."

"But you, darling. What about what you did?"

Anna, hearing the hint of accusation—more than hint—stared at him coldly.

Malone suddenly wondered, Was it possible she didn't know about the photographs? About the blackmail?

He decided it was not.

"Do you want to tell me? Or shall I tell you?"

Anna opened her mouth to speak, but no sound came. She fled into the business of fishing in her purse for a cigarette.

Malone felt a surge of impatience, and despite his resolve to let her be the one to lift the veil he said, "You told me Tumark reminded you of your father, that your talks with him were part of how you were finishing with your father."

She nodded nervously while lighting her cigarette, then said through the billowing smoke, "That's true, that's true—"

"Is that why you make love with him? Because he's like your father?"

She fell back as if she'd been slapped. "What are you saying?"

"The truth. After all this time, the truth."

"But that is not true. That is—" She shook her head, unable to speak.

And for an instant Malone thought he must be crazy, that he had imagined those photographs, that he had dreamt what they portrayed in some awful nightmare. But no, the photographs were real. Tumark and Anna were lovers. And if she could genuinely deny it, then *she* was crazy.

"Well, you *did* make love with him, then," he said, as if the tense of the verb mattered.

"No," she said firmly. Her dark eyes did not waiver. "I have not deceived you. Vladimir was like my *father* to me. To him I was like his *daughter*. His daughter is the center of him. And his wife. *They* were what we spoke of. *They* are his last loyalty. And as I listened to him, it was always as though *my* father was speaking of me in such a way, and of my mother, with such love, and such longing. Vladimir helped me think it is time—"

She stopped for her first breath, and her face softened as if, only then, she realized who he was.

"And you . . ." she said quietly. "You know this if no one else does. *You* are the man I make love with."

The ground shifted under Malone. Despite everything— Minot's word, the evidence of those photographs, the logic of Tumark's role inside the embassy—he felt himself slipping into the crevice of his inability to doubt her.

But that she was telling the truth was impossible. There were two truths here and they were opposites.

His mind clutched at a way to make sense both of what Minot had revealed and of Anna's fierce assertion. He said, "You mean, you haven't made love with him since you and I became—"

"Never!" Both of her hands came down on the table, making her beer glass jump, spilling it. "Never!"

He remembered how at the Soviet embassy that night he had subtly forbidden her to cross the ballroom to Tumark. But she had gone anyway. And he had seen in her exchange with Tumark the meaning of her own Russian origins, that she was bound to Tumark in ways he had barely grasped. And Tumark also; Malone had seen in his recitation of a poem a flash of humanity that had drawn Anna to him in ways she had not perhaps intended. The core of the Russian's passion, Malone had sensed, was his sadness. Anna had attached herself to him because of it.

But in what way attached?

"I'm sorry, but I'm sure of it," he said firmly. "You've been with him in that way—"

She shook her head so sharply the movement cut him off. Her eyes filled with tears, but she refused them, dragging deeply on her cigarette, hugging herself, pressing her head back against the booth, so that the crown of her head touched the frosted-glass partition. She closed her brimming eyes while she exhaled a stream of smoke.

Then, in that posture, she said, " 'In that way,' as you say it, I have been with only one man in my life."

She opened her eyes. Her head was tilted now over her right shoulder and there was the tranquillity of utter resignation in her voice as she continued. "And that is you, of course, my darling."

She waited for him to react, but he didn't move. She had never spoken of her sexual past; he had never dared to ask her. How far he had come from his South Side Irish Jansenism, that this revelation of her virginity was what stunned him.

Finally he said, "But I thought you were so . . ." His voice trailed off. He hated himself for blushing. He'd stopped himself from saying, You seemed so experienced, so lustful, so free of the inhibitions I take for granted in myself. But would she hear it as an insult if he told her he'd assumed he was only one of many men to be with her, as he'd put it, "in that way"? He hated himself not only for speaking in such euphemisms but for thinking in them.

But she was lying, wasn't she?

He'd seen those photographs. She did not know he'd seen those photographs. He said carefully, "When I looked at you from Minot's office, from inside that glass partition, I saw something in your eyes that makes me think— Oh, Anna, why did you think I was looking at you like that?"

"Because you had just asked me to marry you. And I had not answered. And I thought you had told Mr. Minot. And he made you think you were a fool. . . ." Tears spilled from her eyes. She made no move to wipe her cheeks. Despite her sadness, she sat there so calmly, so free of regret at her show of feeling, that Malone felt a calm of his own. For a moment he didn't care what the truth was. Her sadness was the truth, the arch through which, then, he went to her.

"Why didn't you answer me when I asked you?"

"Because I could not believe you meant it."

"Why?"

"Because I was so afraid it is impossible."

"Because of Tumark."

She leaned forward, wiping her tears with one swift movement of her hand. "You refuse to believe me!"

"I—"

"No!" She cut him off absolutely. "Listen to yourself. You ask to marry me! And I say I fear it is impossible. And this is why! Because when I tell you solemnly that you are the only man I have been with, ever, you do not believe me! Instead you believe what? What is this strange, bizarre business about Vladimir? And how can you prefer it to what I tell you? To what I swear to you!"

"Don't swear. I'm not asking you to swear."

"But what does it mean, that you think I lie? Yet you say you love me? What is this love you have?"

Her sadness was gone, swept away by anger. Now he did glimpse the truth of her past, even if he'd missed it before. She was convinced he couldn't love her, and that was why she'd fled from him. And now he was proving that she was right.

But she was lying, wasn't she?

He was about to say, I've seen photographs, when he realized how it would destroy her to learn that Webb Minot had done such a thing to her. Malone knew about Anna's emotional dependency on Minot because, however the origins of their feelings differed, he shared it. He knew that, with her mother, Minot was the only person Anna trusted fully.

And Minot, by laying her out as bait for Tumark, had betrayed her. No wonder Minot didn't want her to know about the photographs. If Malone showed her the extent of Minot's betrayal, then her conviction that no one could really love her—could want to marry her—would be confirmed.

The damning photographs were still in Minot's drawer. Minot's boys had been photographing Anna's trysts with Tumark from the start, and now, much as each would want to, no one of the three could deny what they had done.

Malone could not deny it either.

But Minot would defend it all. Hadn't Tumark enabled Malone to get the code book that even now was leading to the exposure of the Klaus Fuchs spy ring? And Tumark was still in place, a permanent crack in the wall the Russians had so ruthlessly built around their secrets.

The question nagged again at Malone: Why hadn't Tumark simply copied the code book himself? Why the extraordinary risk of sending Malone into the embassy?

But Minot had his reasons, that was all. No doubt he regretted exploiting someone he cared about and for whom he was implicitly responsible. It was necessary, that was all.

If you asked Malone, Anna had been poorly served by these two surrogate fathers of hers. Of course she was lying to him. If he felt a certain sympathy for her nevertheless, wasn't it because he understood why she'd made that mistake, trusting both those men because they promised to give her what she'd lost as a child? Malone's interest in her, on the other hand, had been as a woman.

The photographs came back to him, the undeniable, hateful photographs. Webb Minot had seemed so detached when he'd displayed them, yet he knew better than anyone the violation they were—those images of Anna's beautiful face distorted with passion, her lips open, abandoned to those primitive, guttural sounds of hers, her hair only half unpinned, her eyes sunk into the perfect innocence of her sad ecstasy, her fingernails—

Her fingernails! All at once Malone realized what had jolted him in that particular photograph—Anna's fingernails sunk in the flesh of Tumark's shoulder. They were dark, in the photograph, black, clearly coated with a deep red polish.

He immediately dropped his eyes to Anna's hands, one of which was resting by the narrow cone of her pilsner glass, the other of which was holding her cigarette at the ashtray. Her fingernails were clear! In the four months Malone had known her, she'd never worn fingernail polish! That woman in that photograph—Tumark in the delicious white heat of her clutches—was not Anna!

It was as if an elevator that had been rising slowly inside of Malone from his groin to his throat now dropped suddenly.

He forced himself to hold on. He forced himself to think.

The woman was not Anna. All right. But how—? And then his mind tossed up the answer, a picture of the FBI darkroom and the skillful technician bent over his equipment, over those images—legs and arms, eyes, shoulders, breasts, lips, fingernails—merging them, deleting and adjusting, blurring focus. The technician, a master forger and counterfeiter, would be a cool character who wouldn't feel a qualm, who, despite what he was seeing, wouldn't even whistle to himself. Malone had been there. He saw it clearly.

So that one picture—those fingernails—was not of Anna.

But some of the photographs certainly were of Anna in the throes of lovemaking; there was no faking her face, her Slavic eyes, her mouth—

And then a cloud removed itself from the sun.

The naked man whose arms and legs were entwined with Anna's—was Malone himself.

Minot had been photographing him and Anna all this time in the second-floor bedroom at Phelps Place.

The photograph he had crushed into a ball of Anna fiercely gripping that familiar headboard! How it had enraged him to think that she would bring her Russian lover into that bed. But of course she hadn't. Of course she wouldn't.

Anna had not lied to him.

Minot. Minot was the liar. Worse than liar. From the outset Firebird had included this element, and Malone had done just what he was supposed to do. And more. For he had fallen in love with her. Was that the plan too? "I expected you to fall for her," Minot had said, hinting at this grotesque strategy.

How could Minot have expected as much of Anna?

Malone's mind clicked from question to recognition, one after the other, clicking like Minot's hidden cameras in Phelps Place, silent lenses that gave the lab technician pictures of their lovemaking from every angle. Hundreds of photographs. Thousands by now. Many more than enough to clip and reshape and graft onto similarly stolen, though necessarily fewer, photographs of Vladimir Tumark with some other woman, perhaps that Ninth Street prostitute to whom Minot had referred.

Presented in the context of the other, unretouched pictures of the real Anna offering her hand to the Russian in the park along the C&O Canal, of the Russian with his hand through Anna's arm on a street, of Anna whispering in the Russian's ear at a fancy dinner table that Malone had recognized as Victor Woolf's, of the pair of them exiting a taxi outside the Mayflower Hotel— the intimate sexual scenes had convinced Malone utterly. How much more convincing would they be to an MGB officer who had none of Malone's reasons to question what he was seeing.

And Malone had questioned instead whether Anna was telling him the truth.

It revolted him that he had ever thought well of Webb Minot, that he had come to think of him, after all, as a brother. Now it wasn't Minot's betrayal of Anna that staggered him, but of Malone himself. Minot was the

Bureau and the Bureau was his family of brothers. In Malone's mind Minot was linked with Hoover, and therefore, it was not too much to say, for Christopher Malone was a deeply convinced FBI agent, with God.

Anna was still waiting for his reaction. She had asked him about his love. What thin soup it had proved to be. He said, "I'm sorry, Anna. I do believe you."

He reached across the table to take her hand, those fingers with unpainted nails. His eyes fell to her chest, her breasts, and as he often did when he felt the stirring of his lust, he pictured her naked. But now, instead of seeing her as she always was in his embrace, he saw her, as in those photographs, with Tumark.

And the outrage of the thing hit him, what Minot had done, not the mere betrayal but the sacrilege! Minot had turned this sacred secret of theirs—his and Anna's—into pornography. Their sexual caresses, perfect expressions of the love toward which they were both struggling, had become obscene in being photographed. Minot had made the most private moments of Malone's life a public show. And he felt an overwhelming impulse to go back to Minot's garage, to storm up to the crypt-trans section, scattering the clerks with his war cry, upending their desks, flinging the pages of their holy writ—all those encrypted numbers—to the four winds. In his fantasy he was upsetting also the trays full of developing fluid in the lab darkroom and he was yanking down the clothesline full of drying photographs. He was smashing the glass windows of Minot's cubicle, and ripping the drawers from Minot's desk until he found those first photographs, which, instead of merely crushing, he tore to pieces in Minot's face. And when Minot began his speech about this *war* we have with Russia and the extreme measures it requires, how it even makes us turn against each other and how it even forces us to betray the very people we most care about—then Malone viciously slugged Minot in the face with his fist.

And that old priest, with his rimless spectacles, was there watching from his cubicle and Malone left saying, "Shame on you, Father. Shame!"

* * *

"What?" It was Anna asking. She was squeezing his hand.

Malone blinked at her, surprised that, in fact, he hadn't moved from the booth. Around them the young Washingtonians were slickly circling each other up and down both aisles of the Neptune, but—that undersea motif again—they seemed like skittish fish to him, afraid to touch each other. The jukebox lyric was "Don't sit under the apple tree with anyone else but me, no, no, no . . ."

"You said, 'Shame.' "

"I did? Jesus." *What's happening to me?* he thought. He looked at his two glasses, the beer and the shot, both empty. He wanted a drink. For the first time in his life he felt that thirst without being afraid of it.

"What's wrong?" She pressed his hand in both of hers. He saw her rings. Her fingernails.

"I said 'shame,' maybe, because I am ashamed of how I made you feel." That was true, but his shame ran even deeper than how he'd failed her. He'd been failing himself. "When I asked you to marry me, I meant it. But I think it also seemed a way out of the confusion, out of the mystery. I'm a very simple man. You know that now. I really wasn't built for this stuff. But since I'm in it. . . ."

As he spoke he was aware of a new determination, a resolve he hadn't felt before. Compared with the fantasy of storming into Minot's office, a real response to what he'd learned would be much more difficult, more dangerous. A fantasy attack would make it easy for Minot and it would answer none of Malone's questions.

There was the shame he felt. He had a string of questions and its first knot was still that open safe in the *referentura*. Now there were large knots in that string, one each for Minot and Tumark and Victor Woolf and a small one, even, he realized for the first time, for Father Abetz. He was ashamed that he had been so easily deflected all this time from his string of questions. What else does an agent have to go by? Instinctively he sensed their relevance to the mystery of "Raymond" and the rest of Klaus Fuchs's spy ring, but at bottom his ques-

tions were all the same question: What could possibly
have justified Minot in deceiving him like this? Malone
decided the time had come to find his own answers.

" . . . I want to see it through," he said. "You and I
are one thing. What we're part of is something else. I
hope we can finish together with the one so we can start
with the other. That's why I want you to stay, Anna. Not
for Minot's reasons, but for mine. Not because he needs
you, but because I do. You are the only person I trust."

He hesitated, aware that he had not told her about the
photographs. But how could he?

She read his hesitation, but wrongly. "A few minutes
ago, you did not believe me."

He nodded, thinking, If I don't tell you everything
even now, it is to protect you. He said carefully, "Minot
was rehashing the contacts you'd had with Tumark. I
didn't know he hadn't leveled with you about Tumark's
working for us, and I read too much into all those sur-
prises because, well, because I was afraid, after I'd asked
you to marry me, that you wouldn't—I was afraid that
you didn't—"

He stopped, unable to complete the sentence, but not
because of her. He could barely control the rage he felt
at Minot. But Minot wasn't the issue now. She was.

When she said nothing, he lifted his shoulders, "But
then, in your simple, irresistible way, you told me to
believe what you were saying on the evidence that it was
you saying it." He smiled. "Not enough evidence for
most FBI guys, but enough for me. I *decided* to believe
you, Anna. And when I did, I began to see things differently." Her fingernails for starters. In this first real surrender of his life, Malone felt his first real self-acceptance
too. He saw himself differently. For one thing, he knew,
how he saw the Bureau would never be the same.

"What do you see?"

"I see a mystery." He tilted his head to one side,
admitting to himself that he was drawn to her in the first
place because she'd been at its center. But no longer. She
was on the edge of it now with him. "A mystery about
the Bureau, for one thing. I thought I understood how
the Bureau works. But I don't. At first I felt sent forth by

Minot, but now I feel cut loose. I feel—" He stopped himself from saying "abandoned." This was not Anna's problem. He returned to what was. "And I see a mystery about Tumark. You don't believe what Minot said about him? I don't either. If Tumark would leave the safe open for me, why wouldn't he just copy the code book? Why go to the extraordinary risk of sending me in? Minot wouldn't answer that question, and I thought it wasn't my place to press it. But I'm the only one who has the question. And maybe a few other questions. I want to ask them now without Minot knowing that's what I'm doing." Malone stopped, barely able to believe what he was saying. He was an FBI agent! He was cutting *himself* loose. By what right? No right, he answered himself. He was acting from pure instinct. But at a certain point even an agent must do that. They *train* you to do it once you draw your weapon. An agent's instinct becomes his absolute. So he was acting now—how he still needed to believe this—*for* the Bureau, not against it. "And I want you to help me."

"Without telling Mr. Minot?"

"Yes."

"Why?"

As lightly as he could, Malone answered, "Because in the Bureau, if you don't stay snug in the hole they dig for you, you get a nasty letter from the director or maybe you get fired. You don't want me to get fired, do you?" He grinned.

She hesitated, then said quietly, "I love you, Chris."

"You've never told me that before."

"But you knew it."

"I *hoped* it."

"I also was afraid. I was not sure before if you were—"

Now when she didn't finish her sentence, he finished it for her. " . . . If I was using you somehow?"

She lowered her eyes.

"You're right to be afraid of that, Anna, but not with me. Look. . . ."

When she brought her eyes back to his it made him feel as if he had the power to call the sun up in the morning. He felt suddenly more certain of himself than ever before.

Now looking at Anna, images surged back; not the observed sexual passion that in photographs always looked hackneyed, but the gentle, spontaneous movements of lovemaking that, between them, had seemed utterly original. In her nakedness Anna had seemed unique to him, as if she was the only creature in the world with such a body. The images he could call up so easily depended for their power, even in his imagination, on discreet insinuation, not the crude explicitness of Minot's photographs.

That bastard—Malone felt his rage again. But it went as quickly as it came, for Anna was at the center of his feelings now, not Minot.

He saw her opening herself, her arms, her legs, opening to him. And because he saw such images not from the distance of those photographs but from inside the act, inside his memory and his dream, there was nothing lewd in them. He felt a fresh rush of pleasure at what he'd had with her and what, now, he could have again.

Leaning forward, he hooked her fingers with his, and raised them to his mouth. He eyed her steadily but spoke with her fingers at his lips, as if they would take his words directly to her heart. "I love you too."

He grinned happily. "Let's get out of here and go buy a night's worth of champagne and get a hotel. We'll make love until we can't do it anymore. And we'll drink all the champagne. And we'll hold each other while we sleep."

"Without going home?" She pulled her Navy cape onto her shoulders, watching him.

She didn't know about the cameras. She didn't know about Minot. He would never tell her. "Let's go someplace where no one knows it's us."

14

"This is the biggest espionage case in the history of this country," the one-time chicken farmer said, holding up a tattered manila folder. "And I am here to announce that I have penetrated this government's iron curtain of secrecy."

It was February 20.

His fellow senators hadn't thought Joseph R. McCarthy was there to announce anything. Rather, hadn't they summoned him to appear before the quorum in this extraordinary session to substantiate the sensational charges he had already made weeks before in Wheeling? The august members of the United States Senate eyed one another uneasily as the bull-shouldered, rumpled newcomer hauled one folder after another out of his battered tan briefcase. Perspiring and half muttering to himself, he seemed a figure from a bus station.

"I am here to denounce all the . . . the . . ." McCarthy looked around the Senate, but his eyes refused to settle more than an instant on any man. Suddenly he lunged forward as if to propel his words, and his mouth sprayed those in front of him as he found the words he wanted. ". . . the egg-sucking phony liberals whose pitiful squealing would hold sacrosanct those Communists and queers who sold China into atheistic slavery. . . ."

The visitors' and press galleries in the quarter-moon balcony above the well of the dome-ceilinged Senate chamber were packed. The reporters were so numerous that the sergeant at arms had allowed the overflow to stand in the aisle of the press section, though no such exception was made in the sections reserved for the general public. Every seat was taken, but in fact, once McCarthy began to speak, a man dressed in a carefully tailored gray suit and a subdued tie of maroon silk did take up a position alone behind the last row of the visitors' gallery. Present several rows in front of him were his charges, three touring members of the British House of Lords. The three were dressed alike in dark double-breasted suits that emphasized their leanness. One was bald. The other two wore their gray hair longer than American men, curling over their collars, and they held themselves with an implicit hauteur, as if they'd come not merely to observe but to judge. When they had learned they were to be present for the address of a senator they had never heard of—instead, say, of a Taft or a Tydings—they had expressed disappointment. Now, however, they were leaning forward, hypnotized by the sight of the unkempt Irishman pounding his fist on the unsteady pile of dossiers on the desk before him.

Their escort, standing alone at the rear of the gallery, was an American Protocol officer known to the British lords as Peter Michael Ward.

" . . . A conspiracy," McCarthy was saying, "so immense and an infamy so black as to dwarf any previous venture in the history of man."

If Malone was skeptical of McCarthy's charges against the State Department, it was not because he took the patriotism of the well-bred Foreign Service for granted but because he knew that, as an extension of the four-year-long Hiss investigation, the Bureau had checked out State more thoroughly than any other branch of government.

That was why the senator, in his heated opening on the Senate floor, reminded Malone of an ill-prepared defense attorney seeking to impress a jury with verbal bombast and a flamboyant display of what appeared to be evidentiary material, but had yet to be admitted as such. Tricks of the country courthouse, he thought.

"Here they are," McCarthy said. "Eighty-one cases in which—"

But the sharp sound of a gavel resounded across the chamber, cutting McCarthy off. From his place on the dais, the presiding senator peered sternly out across the room. "Indulge me, Senator. You say eighty-one. What relation does this figure have to the two hundred and five you spoke of in West Virginia?"

McCarthy blinked toward the senator on the fixed mahogany bench, which dominated the chamber like the prow of a ship. There was a schoolboy's whine in his voice when he said, "I do not believe I mentioned the figure two hundred and five. I believe I said 'over two hundred.' "

A silence followed that reply. McCarthy used his forefinger to wipe a line of perspiration from his upper lip.

The presiding senator pressed his point. "And I believe that in Salt Lake you said the number was fifty-seven."

"Yes, well they're included here. . . ." McCarthy lowered his eyes and leaned wearily on the pile of dossiers, as if he hadn't expected his colleagues to badger him.

"All fifty-seven," he said. Then he looked up sharply. "And I'm giving you"—he paused, moving his lips silently around the arithmetic before adding with a triumphant flourish—"twenty-four more cases besides."

"Cases of what exactly, Senator?"

McCarthy leaned forward suddenly and hissed, "I am only giving the Senate cases in which it is clear there is a definite Communist connection. . . ."

"Cases of persons presently in the employ of the United States government?"

". . . Persons whom I consider to be Communists in the State Department! This man, for example!" He lifted up the first folder, and when a photograph fell out of the folder he picked that up, looked at it briefly, then waved it over his head. "Look at the uniform he's wearing! The uniform of the Russian Secret Police!"

Malone leaned back against an adjacent pillar, thinking, Oh brother. The reporters to his right were furiously noting down every word. Malone looked for even one quizzical face among them—a man wondering, for example, if the MVD wore uniforms, or, if so, whether they posed for photographs. But every reporter was too busy writing to ask such questions, and Malone realized that, whether McCarthy knew it or not, they were his real audience, not the skeptical senators.

McCarthy began to plow through the cases represented by the files spilling now over the two desks in front of him.

Several times he was interrupted as senators tried to test his claims against reason, but he ignored the questions. He recited a litany, not only of security breaches, but of rampant homosexuality, adultery, bribery, embezzlement, perjury and even the forgery of school transcripts and military records. Such wildly unprovable assertions were familiar to Malone, as they would have been to any FBI agent who'd done background checks.

When McCarthy, red-faced and gasping, finally stopped talking, it wasn't clear whether he was finished or simply exhausted. He slumped into his chair.

The other senators sat in silence. For long moments no one moved in the entire chamber, and for once the reporters were not writing in their notebooks.

Malone's thought was that the Communists had lucked out again, for this new, self-appointed nemesis of theirs, like Martin Dies and John Rankin before him, was a total fool.

But McCarthy was not a fool to members of the visitors' gallery in front of Malone. Some of them were legionnaires, who followed their leader in starting to applaud. The sergeant at arms bolted down the aisle to shush them, but the green-hatted veterans ignored him. Instead they came to their feet. Each wore an armband that Malone was now able to read: "The Sons of I Shall Return." They applauded more loudly still, and the tourists around them began to do likewise, coming to their feet. Reporters in the adjacent press gallery began to stand too until half of them, at least, were on their feet, applauding.

The presiding senator banged his gavel, but the entire gallery, at the mercy of its zeal now, ignored him.

Malone crossed past those immediately in front of him to see if the British lords had come to their feet. No. And, judging from the stiffness of their backs, he sensed their firm resolution not to, despite the prominence of their first-row chairs.

The senator banged his gavel repeatedly, but to no avail.

One by one the other senators turned their faces up toward the balcony with expressions that suggested they'd never seen this before. And then McCarthy himself raised his brimming eyes to those ordinary Americans who had heard him, even if his esteemed colleagues had not. Not yet.

It was just twilight as Malone drove the lumbering Packard up Massachusetts Avenue. Two of the British lords were in the rear seat, conversing quietly, and the third, the bald man, was next to him in front, silent.

In dealing with foreign dignitaries Malone usually felt the detached indifference of a bored tour guide, and he had developed a way of describing the tripartite workings of American government that was like pointing out the sights along the Mall. But not this evening. He had no capacity for affable chatter now. Instead of resenting Joseph McCarthy for the buffoon he'd made of himself or McCarthy's admirers for behaving like fanatics, Malone resented the British peers for having witnessed the spectacle. He knew that the pair in the backseat were harrumphing at the primitive Americans.

As Malone slipped the car into a lower gear, approaching Dupont Circle, the man next to him touched his arm. "Tell me, Mr. Ward, what did you think of your Senator MacArthur?"

Inwardly Malone groaned, speeding through a yellow light. He realized how anxious he was to dump the Englishmen at their embassy. He wanted to get home. He wanted to be with Anna.

He said absently, "I think the senator's main point is a good one. His name is McCarthy, by the way. MacArthur is our general." He glanced at the man to smile ingratiatingly.

"A good point, sir?" The British lord stared at Malone.

Malone felt a rush of irritation to be pressed. Did they really expect him to defend McCarthy? McCarthy had reminded Malone of a stockyard's shirker. But this Englishman was reminding him of Lord Hawhaw. He said, somewhat officiously, "Given what's been happening, it's hard to be too careful on matters of security. Don't you agree?"

"How is that, Mr. Ward?"

"Security, for example, concerning the atomic bomb. As I recall it, our Atomic Energy Act of 1946 requires FBI checks on anyone who comes in contact with restricted data."

"That seems only prudent."

Malone looked across at his companion. "Do you think, sir, such a law would apply to British scientists assigned to participate in American research? That they would be checked by the FBI, I mean?"

"One presumes British scientists would be vetted by British security."

"Yes," Malone said coldly. "One *does* so presume."

"You're thinking of Klaus Fuchs, Mr. Ward." Once more the Englishman touched his sleeve.

"Yes, Your Lordship," he said, looking at the man briefly, causing him to blush and remove his hand. As an American Protocol officer he was supposed to make a point never to use that undemocratic salutation.

Malone went on, "I *am* aware that Fuchs, as a young man, had quite an open history with the Communist party. He listed his affiliations himself in his *curriculum vitae* when he was appointed at—where was it, the University of Edinburgh?"

"You seem to know well enough, Mr. Ward."

"Yes, Edinburgh," Malone said, making a show of remembering. "I just thought that a Senator McCarthy, or even a MacArthur, in either house of Parliament might have helped British security penetrate the man's published biography—not mere rumors or gossip—before he was assigned to the Manhattan Project."

"We all regret Klaus Fuchs, Mr. Ward. Although I must point out he is native German, not English."

What a dodge, Malone said to himself. "Is that why your courts sentenced him to fourteen years? It doesn't seem much for treason."

"Fourteen years is the maximum under the Official Secrets Act," the Englishman replied. "I agree with you. He should have been tried under laws governing treason. But he wasn't. I don't know why. Fuchs should be hanged."

Malone said nothing. In point of fact he knew that if Fuchs had been charged with a capital offense, British law would have required that the crucial decrypted Soviet cable traffic—Fuchs's own descriptions of the gaseous diffusion process for obtaining large quantities of high-grade uranium—be introduced as evidence. The Russians would have known at once that their cipher system had been broken. They would even now have been replacing the permanent code book, eliminating Father Abetz's and Minot's ability to read present and future traffic. The Russians would even now have been hunting down the traitor in their Washington embassy—Tumark—who would not have gotten off with fourteen paltry years. It had been Webb Minot's insistence that Fuchs be charged and tried without indicating what had led to him, and the circumspection allowed in an Official Secrets trial was what made that possible. Malone knew better than the British lord, in other words, that Klaus Fuchs wasn't the beneficiary of famous British decadence, but of the need to protect the secret of Operation Firebird. Still, he shrugged and said, "In this country you get fourteen years for robbing your first bank."

"Ah yes, Mr. Ward," the Englishman said with a supreme—and deflecting—condescension, "bank robberies! Tell us about your Al Capone."

The British embassy anchored the northwest end of Embassy Row, an elegant counterweight to the Russian bulwark three miles away. This was a meticulously maintained compound of Georgian buildings set among tidy lawns and geometric flower beds in a private corner of Rock Creek Park. The two largest buildings were the chancery and the residence, both cut off from Massachusetts Avenue by a formidable iron fence.

Malone drove through the gate, waving casually at the guard, who recognized the blue license plate of the official American car. When Malone pulled across the white gravel apron, bypassing the larger chancery building to stop in front of the ambassador's residence, he thought the bay-windowed English house with its double-height entryway and, over that, a painstakingly gilded pediment seal that featured the familiar unicorn and lion, had the grace and weight—the gravity—of a Mount Vernon or a Hyde Park. He felt as he had before in coming here—reduced by the place, as if its purpose were to remind him of the dingy South Chicago tenement in which he was raised. But the ambassador's residence cast its shadow over more than Malone's origins, for he realized that, with even the White House smothered by scaffolding, this was perhaps the stateliest house in Washington.

Malone, like a chauffeur, hopped from his seat to open the rear door. The Englishman on that side used a walking stick, but Malone sensed that he carried it more as an item of apparel than as medical equipment, and so he refrained from helping him to his feet.

Each of the three aristocrats shook Malone's hand warmly. He'd served as their general factotum now for three days and they seemed genuinely appreciative. All at once Malone regretted his previous resentment because it seemed to confirm his status as their inferior. His sole role was to resent; theirs was to be gracious.

He watched them make their way up the curving walk to the residence entrance. A butler opened the door for them before they raised the knocker.

He climbed back into the car, which he would have to return now to the garage beneath the looming Foggy Bottom building. He looked at his watch. If he took a cab from there he could be at Phelps Place in half an hour. He put the car in reverse, throwing his arm over the back of the seat to watch as he swung around. But a figure among several in the distance caught his eye, a man with his topcoat collar up against the chill, crossing from the chancery building to the parking lot behind a low hedge of boxwood. He knew at once that it was Victor Woolf, despite not having seen him since the anniversary celebration at the Soviet embassy. He realized, without knowing precisely why, this was one of several moments that he'd been waiting for.

Very slowly he began to back the Packard up, watching as Woolf got into his own car.

When Woolf pulled out of his parking space, Malone pressed the accelerator to the floor. In reverse gear, the motor of his car whined, and gravel began to fly as he suddenly sped backward into the path of Woolf's oncoming car, cutting him off.

Both autos stopped abruptly.

Woolf lowered his window and yelled, "I say, what are you doing?"

Malone got out of his car, crossed to the passenger side of Woolf's and got in. "Hello, Mr. Woolf."

The English diplomat stared at Malone as if he expected upon the moment to be robbed.

But Malone offered his hand.

"Ward! Good God, dear man, you nearly caused an accident here!" Woolf took Malone's hand, but only as a matter of minimal courtesy. They shook brusquely, without warmth.

"I'm sorry, sir. I was pleased to see you. I didn't want to miss you."

"I wasn't leaving in point of fact. I was pulling over to the walkway to await my wife. You needn't have cut me off like that. It was utterly unnecessary."

"Oh, I am sorry, sir," Malone said. But a vague question about Woolf's wife began to form itself in the back of his mind. He was watching Woolf now—and everyone—with the hidden eye of an investigator.

"What brings you to the embassy, Mr. Ward?"

Malone grinned, less deferentially. "I thought I'd break in, to see how it compares." He glanced back at the formidable brick chancery building. A healthy crop of ivy gave it the air of a university lecture hall, and the staffers leaving it singly and in groups of two or three were like professors and graduate students heading to their rooms. Lights in several windows switched off while Malone watched. He said absently, "Getting inside there would be a snap, don't you think, Mr. Woolf, compared to certain other establishments we could think of?" Facing Woolf again, he said, "How's the stomach?"

Now when he grinned, it was genuine. It amused Malone to think of this staid Englishman drunk and sick at the Soviet embassy, and he marveled that Minot had convinced him to so sacrifice his dignity.

"What do you want?" Woolf stared at Malone icily.

"I just dropped off three members of Parliament. I've been showing them the sights. You recall my position with the Protocol Office?"

Woolf nodded, barely.

"We've just come from a remarkable session at the Senate where something happened that I'd like your advice about. . . ."

Now when Malone smiled it was less to ingratiate himself than for the pause it gave him. He knew his phony nonchalance was getting him nowhere with the skeptical Englishman, but it was the only mode he seemed able to call up, since he had no conscious idea, yet, what he wanted from the man. What he wanted was a chance to see what questions surfaced, to see how he would ask them and how Woolf would answer. It was a gumshoe's instinct, but his cover job at State had also made him something of an expert at improvisation. Often, as now, he began sentences without knowing how they would end.

" . . . Apparently we're on the brink of a major new investigation into State Department 'fellow travelers.' This time it will be the U.S. Senate doing the investigating."

"This peculiar man McCarthy?"

"Yes. And if what I—and your three lords—saw this afternoon is any indication, he'll turn over every stone in the Foggy Bottom swamp until something real crawls out. He wants another Alger Hiss."

Suddenly Malone saw his plausible problem—what could have brought him like this to Woolf—and he saw also that it could be real.

"And guess what?" he said.

"What?"

"You're looking at him."

"What in the world are you talking about, Ward?"

"The new Alger Hiss. The new State Department pinko. The traitor in our midst. Me."

"Nonsense. You're an FBI agent."

"You know that. So do J. Edgar Hoover, Webb Minot and maybe six others in this town. But as far as the rest of Washington is concerned, I'm Peter Michael Ward, and my State Department file runs a mile wide but only an inch deep. The snoops will come to me like a hound to blood."

"Your position is secure."

Malone shook his head. "You haven't been paying attention. There are alarms going off all over this city. I know men at State who want it out of their file that they went to Yale. And my record? It won't bear a second look. My supposed mentor, for example, is our ambassador in Rome, a man named Leland. His association with Acheson alone—he's one of his closest friends—would draw the light to me. Acheson and his circle are about to be destroyed, especially after Acheson's defense of Hiss. But even if I survive that, what about my service on the World Refugee Committee? That's part of UNESCO now, and McCarthy says UNESCO is run from Moscow. And what about my wife, Mr. Woolf?" Malone stopped cold, staring meanly at the Englishman.

"What about her?"

Now the question Malone wanted to ask was an echo of the old HUAC question, the Hiss question: Are you now or were you ever part of Webb Minot's pornographic photography operation?

But Malone saw that of course he was. Woolf would have been essential to it, for Woolf, not Minot, was in a position to meet Tumark, to blackmail him. Minot was surely known to the MGB, but Woolf could meet the Russian openly on the diplomatic circuit. Woolf, not Minot, would have been functioning as Tumark's control. Woolf would have been the one to put the doctored pictures of Anna and Tumark into play. Hell, Woolf would have been the one to think up the idea.

Malone shrugged. "My wife has been intimate with a Russian diplomat. What if Senator McCarthy comes across that?"

"How would he?"

Malone shrugged again. "It's a small town, Mr. Woolf. And once McCarthy's people start beating the bushes, the next thing they learn is that this newly suspected Foreign Service officer's wife is *herself* a Russian."

"Your wife is a Strasbourgeoise!"

"Spare me the show of surprise," Malone said brusquely. "You know who Anna is. And you know how it would look if the Red baiters found out who she is." Malone ran his finger along the grain of the gleaming wood of Woolf's dashboard. "Look, the reason I stopped you is because I just realized this afternoon that McCarthy could become a problem for us. He spent two hours reading material that could only be the State Department's own internal security data, raw files, probably, left over from the Hiss investigation. McCarthy has sources in Foggy Bottom, maybe somebody who wants to help him bring down Acheson. Whether you think so or not, Peter Michael Ward is vulnerable. And if he is, the whole operation is."

"You should be taking this up with Minot, not me."

"Minot would just pull the rug out from under Tumark when he saw this problem. He'd have to, to protect the FBI, *and* to protect Firebird. Hoover would call a press conference to show how he'd infiltrated the State Department as a way of snagging a *real* Commie. Is that what you want? A senior Russian diplomat defects, but by handing himself over not to the British SIS, which cultivated him, but to the FBI?"

Woolf stared at Malone, obviously trying to decide what he knew.

For his part, Malone felt like a witness with cataracts, watching shadows move in front of his face, but required to describe them as if he saw them clearly. All he knew for certain, from that November day in the Folger Library, was that Woolf and Minot had different notions of how Tumark was to be played. Into that difference just now, he had instinctively pushed the thin angle of his wedge. Woolf had spent years developing his relationship with Tumark, and he was damned if he would let Minot force his defection in such a way that the FBI could claim sole credit for it.

Malone went on, "And it isn't only State Department sources we need to worry about. There are people in the Bureau who will welcome McCarthy's crusade. They'll give him anything he wants. Not Hoover and not Minot, but zealots in the file room maybe. Hell, it could be that those reports McCarthy read from today were *Bureau* files! It was to stem just that kind of hemorrhage that Minot cut his operation off from regular Bureau channels, took it to a converted garage on the Hill, instead of leaving it in Justice or Ident. But still, Firebird involves a couple of dozen agents and clerks, especially now in the flatfoot phase while they track down the leads they get from the Russian cables. Minot may not be able to control it."

"But these are problems your supervisors would expect you to bring to them. Why are you talking to me about it?"

"Because I want you to set up a meeting for me with Tumark." Malone made this impulsive thrust without breathing.

"That's impossible!"

"No, it's not. You set me up with him before, at your fabulous dinner party. Just bring us together again. Otherwise I'm going to tell Minot to reel him in. And close the operation down."

"Minot won't do that until he has 'Raymond' and whoever else worked with Fuchs. That's what Minot wants."

"He'll get 'Raymond.' He'll get them all. Don't you worry. Your concern should be with whether the British will ever get credit for their part in this operation—your part. You and I know how central Tumark has been, and you and I know that you are the one who turned him, making him available for Firebird in the first place. But no one else knows. The world already thinks that the American FBI alone tracked down Klaus Fuchs, even to London, using its incredible, infallible, scientific investigative techniques. And of course Mr. Hoover—and therefore Minot—would like the world to keep on thinking

that. Publicity like that is how Hoover keeps the Joe
McCarthys away from us, but it's also how he extends his
authority into new areas. When Hoover finally goes public with Firebird, he will want to show that it took Americans to ferret out British traitors, not because he's vain
but because he wants the power to run his own security
checks on all British scientists who come into contact
with secret American research. You can hardly want
Hoover having that power, can you?"

While he waited for Woolf to react, Malone realized
that he'd used the verb *ferret,* and he remembered the
rodentlike cartoon of Hoover and its caption, "America's
Ferret." If Hoover had had a problem with that cartoon,
wouldn't it have been because he wanted to be the world's?

"Why do you want to see Tumark?"

"Because of Anna."

Woolf faced away from Malone to stare out his own
window.

A soft February rain had begun to fall, and so had the
night.

Malone said, "She became attached to Tumark. It
became personal with her, very personal. . . ." The available truth, Malone said to himself. Tell him the available
truth. " . . . And frankly, because of that, it's become
personal with me. I know this is unusual. And I know
you're saying to yourself, This is one of Minot's men;
why isn't he looking at this thing from the Bureau point
of view? It's because I've started looking at it from hers."
Malone paused, then said, "You could finish me as an
agent by reporting this conversation to my boss. But I
hope you don't."

Woolf said nothing, only continued to stare out his
window forlornly. And it occurred to Malone that Woolf
was afraid of a trap, as if Minot had put Malone up to
this, to test Woolf. Malone wanted to grab his shoulder
and shake it, saying, Listen to me; I'm telling the truth!
But with a shock he realized he wasn't. The truth had
nothing to do with the words Malone was using.

He said, "Anna hasn't seen Tumark since the new
year. He told her then that he was going to have nothing
further to do with you or Minot, and by then she was

relieved that he had decided that, even though it meant she herself wouldn't see him again either. She knew that if his cooperation with the West became known to the MGB, it would certainly lead to the murder of his wife and daughter, and she didn't think that Tumark, even if he was safe in the West, would survive that. For reasons of her own, having to do with her own history, she had begun to value Tumark's family loyalty more than a change in his political loyalty. She saw Tumark as sacrificing his own conscience—his opposition to Stalin—for the sake of two people he loved, and she found that choice of his to be noble, and I guess I did too. But obviously, Minot doesn't see it that way, and probably you don't either."

Malone paused to give Woolf a chance to comment. Woolf said nothing. But there was gravity in his silence. He was listening very carefully.

"This is what happens, I guess, if you lose a grip on your professional distance and get too involved with a subject. The subject becomes a man."

"Or a woman," Woolf said, turning slowly to face him now. "No one could blame you for becoming involved with Anna."

"What can I say?" Malone smiled. "She's my wife."

Woolf nodded, then faced away again, indicating that he expected Malone to resume his explanation.

"Then, two weeks ago, the day that J. Edgar Hoover announced the arrest and confession of Klaus Fuchs— that FBI triumph—things changed. Anna and I thought it was time for us to come up for air, and we confronted Minot about ending our undercover work. But then Minot told us about Tumark, that he's been working for him and you right along. Anna didn't believe it at first, because it meant that Tumark had lied to her, but obviously he just couldn't bring himself to tell her about the photographs. And neither could I. She still doesn't know."

Woolf turned slowly back to face Malone, as if he was going to interrupt with a question, but still he said nothing.

Malone felt the knot of a warning in his chest, but ignored it. "It's obvious to both of us that Minot is preparing to bring Tumark over. That's why he needs

Anna on the scene, to threaten to produce her as a bona
fide agent. If Minot demands it, Tumark has no choice,
of course, about defecting and now even Anna knows
that. But he has a choice about how he does it, and Anna
wants to talk to him. She wants to encourage him to put
himself in your hands, not Minot's. She wants him in
London, not Washington. With the hysteria here, the
Hiss case, Klaus Fuchs and now McCarthy, a Russian
defector would be led around this city with a ring in his
nose. Even if Minot wanted to, he couldn't protect him
from congressional subpoenas, and the committees on
the Hill would be lined up with knives and forks to get
slices of him. Anna is certain such a public humiliation,
after the deaths of his wife and daughter, would destroy
the man; and after what I saw in the Senate today, I
think she's right."

Woolf shifted abruptly to look at Malone. "But how
can you cooperate in preempting your own agency like
this?"

The available truth. "Because of the photographs."

"What photographs?"

Woolf's question stunned Malone. A hint of Woolf's
ignorance was what Malone had felt in his chest moments
before. Was it possible that Woolf did not know what
Minot had done? Was it possible that Woolf did not
know what power Minot had now over Tumark? That
those photographs were what would enable him to force
the defection? But how would Minot have gotten to
Tumark, if not through Woolf? Who else was working
him?

Malone stared at Woolf with all these questions, and
he realized that all of it was possible. Woolf might not
know anything. Instinctively, Malone veered from the
truth without flinching or hesitating. "Those pictures Minot's people took in the fall of Anna and Tumark walking along the C and O Canal. Evidence like that put
Anna in unnecessary jeopardy. I wanted Minot to leave
her out. I'm trying to *get* her out."

Woolf seemed to accept the man-in-love tremor in
Malone's explanation, though Malone himself knew how
thin it was. Woolf said, "Not to undercut your resolve to

see things from my side, which I do appreciate, but your young woman is in no jeopardy and neither is our Ukrainian friend because of her, if the concern is with those encounters of last fall." Woolf didn't miss a beat, but Malone fell behind him for a moment. Ukrainian? Had he said Ukrainian? Anna was Ukrainian. Did that mean something?

Woolf was droning on, having fallen into a briefer's voice. "Tumark is a past master at exploiting the considerable latitude of the traditional diplomatic social scene. As you've doubtless noticed by now, every embassy party has its canine aspect, those corners of heat where the nose-to-tail sniffing abounds. Even our otherwise reserved Communist friends have been known to partake of the ritual. Everyone does to one degree or another." Woolf snorted. "It's why embassy wives are regarded as essential accouterments to the profession. They are expected, at very least, to sniff back." Woolf paused pointedly, hauling himself back from his digression. When he resumed talking his voice was more subdued. "We arranged Tumark's meetings with . . ." Again, he paused, to lift his eyebrows with a how-to-say-it? He nodded to Malone. " . . . with Mrs. Ward as a routine Embassy Row flirtation, an aging diplomat beguiling a young FO wife with his war stories, but always in public, always in company, as I daresay photographs along the canal would establish. I didn't know you FBI people were taking pictures, but I assumed at the time that the Soviets were. The trick was to make the meetings only slightly surreptitious. Real hidden rendezvous, in safe houses or washed hotel rooms, would have been far more dangerous. Tumark was probably reporting his meetings with Mrs. Ward to his superiors himself, with tidbits of information gleaned in the service of Mother Russia." Woolf shrugged, toying with the steering wheel, rocking it. "This particular Russian's flirtations are famous for coming to nothing. He had one with my wife too. All he seems to want is a well-turned ear to bend with the torment of his overlarge Russian soul."

But Malone, still thinking of the real photographs,

pushed Woolf. "I gather Tumark is famous also for certain indiscretions along certain blocks of Ninth Street."

Woolf shook his head dismissively. "Means nothing. There aren't that many women assigned to any of the East Bloc embassies, and the ones who are happen to be moustache ladies." Woolf grimaced. "So certain traditions of the otherwise decadent West become accepted. And then *expected*. Take my word for it, Comrade Tumark would be suspect if he did not avail himself of your famous Ninth Street hospitality." Woolf grinned suddenly. "At his age, of course, he'd only be expected to do so once a week."

As Woolf spoke, Malone saw, despite himself, the familiar images once more. In fact, he'd only laid eyes on those photographs for a few short moments but in the weeks since, like the icons of an anchorite's memory, the figures of those lovemakers had ambushed him, in his own memory, again and again.

She was never with any man in that way but him. Yet the disjointed images from Minot's photos had haunted Malone as if they portrayed some truth about her. He had just exaggerated her attachment to Tumark as a way of manipulating Woolf, but suddenly Malone sensed anew the strength of the bond between them. Perhaps Tumark was the key to more than one secret, to a secret of Anna's—what did it mean that they were both Ukrainian?—as well as to a secret of Webb Minot's.

Malone knew that Woolf was deciding whether to help him or not. Had he given the Englishman reasons enough?

Woolf flicked a switch on the dashboard and the windshield wipers began to snap back and forth in front of them. He turned on the headlights; in the twin yellow cones of rain a woman was approaching from the direction of the chancery building.

She wore a man's fedora, the brim overhanging her face, obscuring it. Her black wool coat was belted snugly at her waist, but otherwise she seemed unprotected, coming toward them in the rain, like an apparition.

She went to Malone's side of the car and, without hesitating, opened his door.

Woolf leaned toward her. "Hello, darling."

It was Muriel Woolf, the dark planes of her gaunt face making her look so modern, and also sad. Malone remembered how at that first dinner party, she had disappeared before the guests had left.

Malone got out of the car. "Hello, Mrs. Woolf. I'm Peter Ward."

Muriel Woolf looked at him with a vacancy that startled him, as if she were in a trance. Then she took his place in the car.

Malone thought, What is she doing here? Did the British embassy provide offices for socialite wives?

Woolf leaned across her to say to Malone, "So it's settled, then. You'll come to Georgetown a week Friday, and Mrs. Ward, of course. We'll have an even more interesting collection for you than before. And some of our own favorites too. Right, darling?" Woolf's eyes stalled on his uncommunicative wife. "I'm so pleased to have run into young Mr. Ward. I was just telling him how we've missed seeing him."

Muriel Woolf looked up at Malone and said dully, "Yes, it's true."

She was no ordinary dip wife. She had, after all, been part of Woolf's drunken ruse at the Soviet embassy. She had helped boost Malone himself into the elevator shaft. If there was tension between her and her husband, there was also trust. Who was she?

"A week Friday, then," Woolf said. "Cheers!"

Mrs. Woolf shut her door as her husband put the car into gear and pulled past Malone's black Packard.

Malone watched the car ease past the guardhouse, through the pillars of the formidable gate and out into the evening traffic of Massachusetts Avenue. He watched until he could no longer distinguish their car.

The guard in the doorway of his cubicle was watching him.

Malone turned back toward his own car. The sight of the chancery—its office windows darkened now—stopped him. Suddenly what had before appeared to him as a straightforward tidy brick English building seemed shrouded in mystery as if it were a manor house isolated on a remote heath, abandoned by the heirs of the lord who

built it. Only the veil of rain, he told himself; but still the
place reminded him in the early darkness of the scene of
a Gothic horror story. What were its secrets? The frivo-
lous lords, the devious Woolf, Woolf's neurotic Dutch
wife all seemed of a piece with the strange British
scientist—Fuchs—who was also German. All these English people abhorred what Fuchs had done—the world
would be infinitely more dangerous now—but they also,
each in his own way, reflected the national slackness of
spirit that Fuchs had exploited.

The chancery, he focused on it: four stories high with
large, multipaned, mostly casement windows, though on
the second floor, French doors, each with its small wrought-
iron balcony. All the windows that he could see were
snugly shut, presumably locked. There was the guard
behind him. There would be a regular foot patrol throughout the compound. But they would carry themselves with
that British slackness too. This building was sealed not
half so well as the Soviet embassy had been. Sealed
against him.

On first seeing Victor Woolf moments before, what
intuition was it, exactly, that had prompted his joke?

That he'd come to the British embassy to break into it.

15

In the front hallway of his Georgetown house, Victor Woolf held Malone's coat open for him.

Malone kept trying to catch his eye, hoping for a signal that this wasn't how the evening was to end.

Vladimir Tumark had not come to the dinner party and throughout the meal and cordials afterward Malone had been alert for something to explain the Russian's absence. Nothing had. The other guests were midlevel diplomats and their wives. The talk had been animated but innocuous, and every time Malone had tried to engage Woolf in conversation, the Englishman had smoothly deflected him.

And now he was holding Malone's coat, but refusing to look at him, chatting absently with one of the other departing guests.

Malone glanced at Anna, who was waiting by the door, already in her wrap. He turned his back on Woolf to put his arms into the sleeves of his tweed topcoat. There should be an elevator, he thought. Someone should get sick.

When he turned around again, Woolf took his hand and shook it warmly. "My dear Ward, thank you ever so much for coming."

But now Malone had his eye, and he held it. "I hate to leave. The evening seems incomplete."

"Better to leave wanting more, don't you think? I'm so glad you enjoyed yourself. And you, dear Anna. . . ."

Woolf turned and took Anna's hand and kissed it. "Good night." And he opened the door.

Malone's impulse was to stand where he was until Woolf dealt with him. But the cold wind whistled into the house. The other guests were waiting for their moment with Woolf. Woolf again refused to look at him.

You bastard, Malone thought. And then he realized that now he would have to assume that Woolf had not taken his bait. Worse, he would have to assume that Woolf had alerted Minot.

Once outside and walking along the uneven brick sidewalk, Malone shuddered, only partly with the cold. He slipped one hand through Anna's arm, whispering, "He fucked us."

But at the same moment he plunged his other hand into his coat pocket for warmth, and at once his fingers closed on a slip of paper that had not been there before.

He said nothing until they were two blocks from Woolf's house, when he stopped under a streetlamp. "Wait," he said. "Woolf left a note." And he withdrew it, carefully unfolding the slip of paper only to find that its tiny letters were Cyrillic.

He handed it to Anna. She studied the note for a moment, then looked up at him quizzically. " 'Large collapses'?"

"What?"

"That is what it says. 'Large collapses.' "

A Russian proverb? A cryptic warning? More fucking code. "Is that all?"

She looked again. "Tuesday, oh-six-hundred."

"Then it's a meeting," Malone said. "Tuesday morning at six. 'Large collapses'? What else could those words mean?"

Anna stared at the paper. "Huge," she said. "Or great."

When she looked up now there was an expression of worry in her eyes. "Great Ruins?"

Malone stared at her, but he was picturing his map of Washington. Where? Where? And then he saw it. He understood. Nodding, he said, "Great Falls."

It was just after dawn, a windy raw morning in March.

This was the third Tuesday in a row that they had come, and it was as if by now neither Malone nor Anna expected to see him. It was as if they were a pair of bird watchers or, given the weight of Malone's ruminations, itinerant Russian mystics.

Trekking along the dilapidated canal, at that point so overgrown and collapsed upon itself that it seemed merely an abandoned ditch, he felt once more the overwhelming melancholia of the lost world such remains implied. Here and there he and Anna passed sections of the ancient, unmortared retaining walls that still held, and about a quarter of a mile from where they'd left their car they came to the ruins of the main Great Falls lock.

The branches of the trees were tipped with green, if you looked closely, but the forests on both sides of the path seemed more like the black walls of a barren canyon. Ground fog rose from the damp floor of the woods, giving the scene an eerie unreality.

At the lock, the ditch, though dry, was shored up by stout timbers, and it was wide and deep enough to imagine it as a waterway a century and a half before. Rusted iron gears adorned the wooden beams, and beneath the vines and brush it was possible to see the mammoth wooden gates that had once opened and shut around laden barges.

Or had been built to. The lock, after completion, had hardly been used. Malone, when his attention was drawn to this place, had done his research. This was the C&O canal again, along which Tumark and Anna had rendezvoused in the fall. But this site was in the Maryland hills, more than a dozen miles northwest of Georgetown where those meetings had taken place. Great Falls was the barrier that had defeated the canal as a commercial venture. It had been the most ambitious engineering project of eighteenth-century America, intended to run all the way from Alexandria to Harpers Ferry, opening up trade with the trans-Appalachian interior. But the canal, for all its locks, couldn't climb into the mountains. Great Falls, where the waters of the Potomac fell in a glorious cascade down from the foothills of the Cacotin chain onto the coastal plain of Virginia, stopped it. The canal and its locks had been sliding into ruins—some said nature—ever since. Great Falls, Great Ruins, both.

Perhaps that was why—wasn't melancholia a Russian trait?—Tumark seemed attached to it as a place for his melodramatic meetings. In Georgetown, where fetid green water still filled it, the canal had always attracted city strollers whose use kept the towpath from becoming over-grown. Tumark could meet Anna or anyone there with-out its seeming predetermined. But this place was remote, rarely visited, despite the grandeur of the falls. The tow-path of the canal, for example, was passable in this stretch because CCC laborers had hacked it out of the forests a decade and a half before. They had done so not for the canal's sake, as if donkeys would ever pull barges along it again, but to give the public access to the Poto-mac and its dramatic waterfalls toward which Malone and Anna were walking now. Neither dared wonder aloud if Tumark would show, but Malone had already decided that if he didn't they would not come here again.

They followed the path as it veered away from the vestige of the canal. It cut through the misty woods toward the river itself. As they approached, they could hear the steady rumble of the torrent. Great Falls, in fact, was the point at which several mountain streams intersected the Potomac, even as the riverbed narrowed from three quarters of a mile to two hundred feet. Once it roared through the boulder-strewn gulch, dropping hun-dreds of feet in less than a mile, the Potomac broadened out again, but now as a major river, settling into the broad meanderer that lent its dignity, far downstream, to the capital of the western world.

Here, though, the river's attribute was not dignity, but rage. They heard it grow louder and louder as they approached. The tiny, bud-tipped branches of the trees through which they were walking glistened now, not with the morning dew, but with river spray. The forest floor was alive with fresh-sprouted mosses, fiddlehead shoots and the first spears of skunk cabbage.

Coming around a last curve in the path, they emerged from the forest suddenly to find themselves on the edge of the cliff. The sun was not above the trees yet, but the light off the broad expanses of white, tumbling water was so much brighter than in the dark woods that it stung their eyes. The cliff on which they stood was fifty feet above the water, which had cut a similar bank two hundred yards across from them, on the Virginia side of the falls. Upstream to their right, the river came tearing down over rocks, past islets, between stone chutes, like a herd of panicked, white-maned stallions, and, as it had the first time he'd seen the falls two weeks before, it made Malone marvel that the river itself—as if it *were* a fragile, living thing, a thin-boned thoroughbred—could survive such violence.

He scanned the vista, looking for signs of Tumark. Across the river, in Virginia, was a picnic grove, overgrown and disused, apparently, for years. Malone guessed it was a vestige of the CCC era, with its central lodge built of logs, a dormitory, probably, also now abandoned, and its scattered, partially upended, mist-enshrouded picnic tables. Upstream, a hundred yards from where Malone stood, suspended above the narrow neck of the river at the lip of the waterfall, was a rickety footbridge, swaying in the wind. It was made of rope and slats, no doubt another CCC relic built in the early thirties not for the public, but for the laborers who'd worked both sides of the river. The footbridge had not been built to last and now, with its ropes frayed and slats rotted or missing, it was closed, as Malone and Anna had already discovered, with a faded sign marked, Condemned, Danger, Keep Off.

It had not been possible to know from Tumark's note whether he was proposing as a rendezvous the Maryland side of Great Falls or the Virginia, but roads from the District were far more direct in Maryland, and when Malone had realized that the C&O canal—Tumark's choice in Georgetown—was a feature of the Maryland side, his instincts told him to come here.

But as if his eye was drawn across the river by that old footbridge, he found himself watching for a figure to appear on the Virginia cliff.

"Virginia," he said to Anna. "It was the capital of the South in our Civil War. If the canal had worked, getting past these falls, Virginia would have been tied to the North economically. Robert E. Lee would have commanded the Union army. The Civil War would have been very different. It might not have happened at all. Except for these falls. Think of that."

He was speaking loudly, above the noise of the river, and the strain of his voice made him feel as if he'd begun a lecture. It was not knowledge personal to him anyway. And it was probably bullshit. If Great Falls hadn't blocked the canal, he'd also read, the advent of the railroad would have soon made the waterway irrelevant anyway.

"This is the North," he said, referring to the ground they stood on, and pointing across, "that's the South. And look at the violence in between."

But Anna said nothing. What was the American Civil War to her?

Her silence prompted in Malone a second thought as he looked across the river. Violence, yes, but not much distance. He could have thrown a baseball to the other shore.

He thought of George Washington and that silver dollar, and he suddenly felt a dose of the warmth of his grade school classroom where he'd first learned to love such stories. Eli Whitney and the cotton gin. Abe Lincoln doing his sums on the back of a shovel. And, always, the G-men chasing down Capone. That was radio, not school, but it was the same warmth. The warmth of his love, yes, for his country. And what he loved about it was the majesty implied in those stories, the grandeur, the spaciousness—the 'forty-niners panning for gold. Those stories made him feel that the world *was* larger than the cramped rooms and dark streets of his parents' world, and that, because he *could* picture himself as young Eli or Abe or even Eliot Ness, there was a place in it for him.

And now here he was, a South Chicago boy on the edge of an exotic wilderness with a beautiful woman from the far side of the globe—if the North and South had been enemies, how much more were Russia and America! Yet what separated him from Anna? She was an aristocratic woman and he was what her people would

have called a prol. But issues of class had no weight
between them, any more than nationality.

What separated them? he asked himself again. Not
violence and not distrust. Not suspicion and not fear.

He took her hand and pressed it, wanting to make her
feel his gratitude. He said above the noise, but more
gently than before, more personally, "I was just thinking
of George Washington standing by a river like this and
throwing a coin across it. They say he did that. The
Delaware, I think. And it makes me wonder what kind of
stories they tell children in Russia, to make them love
their people. The czar freeing the serfs, or something?"

"No. The stories are always about Lenin. Only Lenin.
In the fighting at the Winter Palace, he climbed to the
pinnacle of the great building himself and he seized the
white-and-gold imperial flag. It was a crime for an ordinary citizen to touch it. The flag was sacred. Yet he
began to tear it into pieces, strips of white cloth. The
fighters thought he was enraged, but that wasn't it. He
brought the strips of cloth, made from the flag, down
into the great plaza where the wounded lay dying. And
Lenin himself used the cloth strips as bandages, caring
tenderly for the fallen Bolsheviks and palace guards alike.
When the soldiers of the imperial army heard what he
had done—Lenin loved *all* Russians—they refused to
oppose him. And when we children tied our kerchiefs
round our necks we were to think of those patriots whose
blood—Russian blood—turned the white flag red."

"It makes him sound like Christ."

"Which is the idea. That's why his face is everywhere
in Russia now, in place of the Pantocrator, the face of
Christ." Anna shrugged. "Lenin is one thing. Stalin is
another."

"Are there stories like that about him?"

"No." There was a definitive note in her voice, and
Malone realized it was naïve of him to think her relationship to history, like his, was a matter of cartoons, comic-
strip narratives, radio shows or even icons. Anna's silence
about herself was not a function of reticence—Beth Fraser's shyness—but of her direct experience of all that is,
literally, unspeakable. Malone had come to treasure her

silence because it, more than the words she used in all the languages she knew, was what drew him close to her. And when he was close to her, she spoke for them both, saying everything, in the language of her body.

She was staring out across the river, and Malone thought the conversation was at an end. But then she said, "My father, when he referred to Stalin, called him 'The Seminarian.' He knew how it embarrassed Stalin that he'd studied for the priesthood, and that the Church had found him wanting. My father loved that." She smiled slightly with the memory of her father, but then she sobered and added quickly, "But, of course, it's why Stalin hates the Church so and why he . . ."

As her voice trailed off Malone finished the sentence to himself: why he killed my father.

His own father had died of liver disease. Anna hated Stalin. Who was Malone supposed to hate? Jim Beam?

They walked along the cliff, hopping boulders, balancing on the turned-over lip of earth, moving playfully, like truants, first downstream, then up, remaining pointedly as visible as they could be. They held hands, though also they separated, negotiating a narrow place or mounting a boulder, or examining the odd tossed-up piece of driftwood while above them the air brightened. Even before it appeared on the sill of the trees the sun grew stronger, evaporating the mist, lending far more definition to the spray off the falls, softening, though not eliminating, the otherworldly eeriness of the place.

After an hour of moving in this way up and down the rugged Maryland shore, always looking, always showing themselves, they came to an outcropping above the footbridge, which reached out over the water. Upstream of the main chute of the falls, the river was flatter, not calm, but quieter. They made their way carefully out onto the windy finger of rock to sit in silence, content to wait for another hour, hoping this would be the day that Tumark showed himself.

It was.

Downstream from them a man appeared on the opposite shore, near the footbridge, free of the shadow of the woods behind him. For a moment he stood immobile, like the senior actor having made his entrance. The wind tore at his coat.

Or rather, his cape. He began to move along the cliff's edge, toward the footbridge. When, in order to take hold of the bridge railing, he let go of his grip on his cloak, the wind lifted it, making it fly behind him, like a black wing.

The man's long gray hair flew too, and that was what convinced Malone that it was Tumark. Hair like a violin player.

"It's him, Anna. He's coming across."

"But that bridge—"

"It's all right," Malone said, as much to reassure himself as her. He watched the Russian carefully, and in fact once Tumark had adjusted to its rhythmic swaying, he moved smoothly out onto the bridge. "They would never have left it up all this time if it was really dangerous. They just don't want kids playing on it. That's why they put those signs up."

Tumark had to hop across the occasional gap where the footboards were missing, and he held firmly to the rope railings. But he seemed to have no trouble keeping his balance. He negotiated the bridge with an agility and grace that belied his age, and with the cape soaring dramatically behind him he was a striking, erect, romantic figure.

A man a woman would be drawn to. Malone's mind threw up those photographs of Tumark's naked body, and what Malone recalled now about his mode as a lover was his air of self-acceptance. Not that age had not touched him—wasn't there a slackness of flesh that a second examination of those pictures might have revealed, setting Tumark's body off from Malone's—but the years had made him a man of depth and feeling. That quality was what a woman would want to cling to. Even if she had not been with him sexually, that quality was what drew Anna.

The substance of the man, his bravery, his resolve, was evident in the way he made his way across the river. Malone thought of George Washington standing in the prow of a boat, *his* cape flying.

"Let's go meet him," he said.

They moved off the outcropping onto the shore and turned downstream. Anna got ahead of Malone and began to run. He could not quite keep up with her.

She and Tumark came to the edge of the bridge at the same time and without hesitating they went into each other's arms, across that low barrier marked Condemned. Their embrace, while full of feeling, was not the embrace of lovers. Malone imagined her turning back to him and saying, This is my father. I could not tell you before.

Instead, when he joined them, Tumark pulled away from Anna, reaching across her to extend a hand to Malone. "Thank you for coming," the Russian said.

Which surprised Malone, for he was the one to have asked for this meeting.

Tumark pressed Anna's shoulder, but he held Malone's eyes. "I wanted to warn you. Victor Woolf suspects Anna of being MGB. Be careful of him."

"MGB!" Anna said.

Now Tumark looked at her. His face towered over hers. He smiled. "They think, of course, that because we are Russian, we are without moral sensitivity. Without freedom. Woolf thinks you have been assigned to trap me. He thinks you have fooled your husband."

"I'm not her husband. I'm an FBI agent."

Tumark's face whipped around with surprise that Malone was sure could not have been feigned. "Does Woolf know that?"

"Yes."

Tumark stared at Malone, calculating. "But he warned me about meeting you. He said it was one last chance for my enemies to ensnare me. My *Russian* enemies."

"Woolf thought I would try to make you defect on our terms. On *American* terms, I mean. He wanted you to suspect me, because he wants you to defect on his terms. You're not caught, Mr. Tumark, between East and West. You're caught between British operatives and American."

Tumark shook his head. "I am not caught between anything. I am returning to Moscow tomorrow." He turned back to Anna. "It's the other reason I wanted to see you. To say good-bye."

Anna nodded. This was what she expected all along. There was no question of Tumark defecting, hadn't been since, with her help, he'd decided to return to his family. She'd been sure of it.

But Malone knew still that it was impossible. After a moment he said, "But Woolf and Minot won't let you go. Once you're in Moscow they can't get to you. They can't use you anymore."

"They can't get to me *here,* Mr. Ward. I said no to them months ago."

"But you've been working for them. For Minot."

Tumark shook his head. "I have been deceived by them. By you." He looked at Anna. "So you are not MGB, but are FBI?"

Anna lowered her eyes.

Tumark sighed, more resigned than disappointed.

Malone said carefully, "But what about the pressure they applied to you?"

Tumark shrugged. "The offer of a fancy house? A pension? What is that to me? If there was 'pressure' it was from myself."

Malone had no choice but to refer to them. "No photographs?"

Tumark stared at him blankly.

It was Anna who demanded of Malone, "What are you talking about?" And then she said something in Russian to Tumark.

"Don't speak Russian!" Malone ordered.

Anna looked at Malone coldly. "I told him that you were informed he and I were lovers."

"What photographs?" Tumark asked.

"You really don't know, do you?" Malone could not imagine that Tumark was telling the truth now, but his perplexity seemed utterly genuine.

"What photographs?" Tumark demanded angrily. At last anxiety had surfaced in the man. Malone felt it too, precautionary anxiety, a warning of something coming. Tumark and Anna were waiting for him to explain. Despite the roar of the river below them, all seemed quiet suddenly.

He should not be doing this, meeting with this Russian

without permission, talking to him, telling him what Minot had done. These were secrets. Until now it had never occurred to him that he would know more of what was happening than Tumark. Should he tell him? This might be treason. What if *Tumark* was MGB?

Anna's face, now haggard and afraid, cut short his FBI agent's scruple. "What photographs?" She asked with a numbness that she'd put in place, clearly, to deflect the blow.

Malone had no capacity now not to answer. He looked at Tumark. "Minot has photographs of you and Anna in bed together."

Neither Anna nor Tumark looked away from Malone. Each was waiting for him to explain how such an absurd assertion could be true.

"Minot told me that he was using the photographs to blackmail you into working for us."

Tumark raised his shoulders and lowered them. He said quietly, "It's not true. Nothing of it is true."

"I saw the photographs. They are composites and they were doctored." He looked at Anna. "They had photographs of you and me. . . ."

Anna stared at him with horror and for the first time Malone felt ashamed to be an FBI man. Even the anger he had felt toward Minot fell short of what this deserved.

Tumark said, "This is why I am going home. You are all the same." He turned and prepared to go back across the bridge, but Malone grabbed the fold of his cape.

"The photographs fooled me. They would fool your police."

"Are you threatening me now?"

"No, but the photographs exist. I don't know what Minot . . . He told me—"

"*This* is the blackmail!" Tumark's rage flared. "Produce them! If you have threats to make, make them!" He faced Anna. "And to whom do you report when I surrender?"

Anna shook her head soundlessly, horrified at what was unfolding in front of her.

Malone felt he was seeing through the lens of Tumark's anger into the truth about him, the truth to which Anna had clung. He was a decent man who had made the most of the choices given him. A man like her father.

"No," Malone said. "You're wrong. Anna is—" Malone pulled Tumark around to him again. "You haven't been working for us at all? Not for Woolf *or* Minot?"

Tumark shook his head no.

"But you left the door open."

"What door?"

"The door—" Malone checked himself, aware of the tingling in his hand, the surprise that had registered physically, even to the tip of his fingers, when the door to the *referentura* safe had popped open at his touch. But if Tumark truly had had nothing to do with that, then Malone could not now explain it to him. He wasn't MGB, but he was a Russian. Here was the secret with which he could go no further.

He saw clearly now that Vladimir Tumark, alone of everyone he had encountered since Firebird began, was exactly what he seemed to be. He was an aging, meticulous, conscience-bedeviled diplomat who had to balance his political hatred against his personal love. However he had indicated his disenchantment to Woolf and Anna, his fundamental loyalty had held, and even to his enemies within the party he could justify his behavior in Washington as essentially routine.

Tumark may have gotten the bright young American Protocol officer invited to the Soviet celebration, but who had known that Peter Michael Ward was an FBI safecracker? Perhaps in some fatherly way Tumark loved Ward's "wife," but did that make him a traitor? Tumark did not know that the Soviet code room had been burglarized; he'd had nothing to do with it. Minot had lied.

And that left Malone back where he was in November. Who had left that safe open and why?

The question was the same, he knew, but the man asking it was not.

Malone and Anna stood riveted to the boulder at the edge of the footbridge, watching Tumark push out across it. The wind was behind him now, so that his cape wrapped him like a curled leaf instead of flying out behind, but he moved nimbly, back toward the Virginia shore, more quickly than he'd come over.

Malone dared to look at Anna, finding her face only after some seconds and barely recognizing it, so distorted by incredulity were her eyes and mouth. Things should not have changed between them, but Malone knew they had. Anna was feeling the horror he had felt on seeing those photographs, on seeing, that is, evidence of her corruption. No matter that the evidence was false, or rather that it was evidence, instead, of Minot's corruption. Anna, Malone knew, had seen his.

A loud crack, like a gunshot, rang out in the air above them.

Not a gunshot, Malone knew at once, sensing the alteration in the rhythm of the snapping footbridge. Every step Tumark had taken had registered all along the bridge as a jolt, but now the bridge had fallen sideways, and its rope was groaning.

The center and right support ropes were groaning, he saw, because they were taking a new burden of weight. The third, leftmost support rope was slack, having broken somewhere out along the bridge.

Tumark was perhaps halfway across. The bridge, cock-eyed now, at an angle, had nearly dumped him into the river. He was on his knees clinging to the side ropes and to the floorboards both, struggling to get free of his cape, which he now hurled away. The wind took it and it soared from the bridge before settling, this time like an open leaf, on the swirling surface of the river. The river sucked the black shroud under at once.

Malone instinctively lifted his leg to climb over the barrier in front of him, to go to Tumark. But he stopped. Those three supporting ropes were most likely worn equally. If a single man's weight had snapped one, another man's weight could snap the second or third. Malone watched Tumark. As long as the two remaining ropes held, the Russian could make it. But Tumark wasn't moving. He was curled over the slats, clinging to them while the wind bounced the skewed bridge arrhythmically.

Malone cupped his hands around his mouth. "Get up!" he cried. "Keep going!"

Tumark didn't react. He remained frozen, hunched over, his face hidden. But Malone sensed that it was not panic or fear that immobilized him. The Russian was a man meeting his fate, bent before it, awaiting it, and that recognition made Malone's stomach contract and a curl of the coffee he'd had two hours before shot into his mouth. "Get up!" he cried again, and now he did climb over the barrier.

Anna, behind him, grabbed his coat. "I should go," she said. "You are too heavy."

Before Malone could answer her, a second bolt rang out, a second support rope snapping somewhere along its hundred-yard length, and now the bridge lurched and tilted wildly, twirling on its last remaining support and losing its form as a bridge altogether, becoming instead a long, useless tangle of wood and line.

Malone fell back from it, taking Anna, mostly to thwart the impulse to leap onto the span, as if that would help. Both kept their eyes fixed on Tumark, who dangled upside down, clinging to the suspended wreckage with his hooked legs and arms, like a sloth, bouncing slowly ten feet above the water. Tumark's face was turned away from them.

"Vladimir!" Anna screamed, and then another word, something in Russian that Malone did not understand. She repeated it at the top of her voice and began to struggle against Malone, to get to the bridge.

He had to fight to hold her. "It'll collapse," he said. "It won't take your weight!"

When she understood, she relaxed against him, repeating the strange Russian word over and over again.

Tumark craned back to look at her. But just as his face, pale and shaken, came into view, he lost his grip and he fell without a sound. He sank beneath the surface of the water, appeared once a few seconds later a dozen yards downstream just at the lip of the falls, and then he was gone.

The sounds of the river closed over them, broken only by Anna's hysterical repetition of the single Russian word.

"Uncle," she answered.

They were sitting now on a rock shelf back from the river, overlooking the falls but well above them. It was an hour later. They'd spent the time frantically hiking along the bank of the cascade, futilely looking for some sign of Tumark. At last they climbed to this vantage and collapsed on the rock, exhausted. For a long time they didn't speak. Then Malone asked her what the word was that she'd been crying.

"Uncle," she said again softly.

"He was your uncle?"

"My father's brother." Anna looked at Malone with a pain in her eyes he had never seen before.

He said, "Tell me about it."

And when she began to speak now, it was utterly without her usual reticence. "When this began I hated him. He betrayed the people of the Ukraine. . . ." Wasn't this the last part of her story, her last secret? It was as if, by handing it over to him, she could get free of it at last. Her hesitation fell away as she went on. "As the daughter of a priest I was forbidden by the Bolsheviks to go to school, so when I was seven—this was 1930—I left Poltava to live with my uncle in Kiev. I was there for three years, during the beginning of the terror-famine. I was too young, of course, to understand. But later I learned. My uncle was an economics professor at the Institute and he became a member of the Ukrainian Economics Commissariat. It was this council which implemented the grain plans of 1932. That was the year the famine began and it began in Moscow. Stalin demanded that seven million tons of grain be delivered to Moscow from the Ukraine, knowing full well that the best total harvest ever before was only six million. Because my uncle's commissariat did its work so well, nearly five million tons of grain were collected and shipped out of the Ukraine, leaving nothing for my people to eat. Millions would starve. And do you know what happened to the grain? In huge pyramids, it was left to rot.

"My uncle was promoted. He became the head of economics at the Institute. My father came for me and in my presence he denounced my uncle. He cursed him. He

called him murderer. And my father took me away. I
didn't see my uncle again until this year.

"In 1936, the year my mother and I left and the year
my father died as a criminal, my uncle was appointed to
the Foreign Ministry. His role was to go abroad and
denounce the reports of the famine as Hitler's propa-
ganda. He did this very well. He enabled British and
American friends of the Soviet Union to deflect criticism
as the carping of émigrés. The famine, as you know, was
discounted, and the worse it became the more stories of
the horror were dismissed as coming from Berlin. My
uncle was the author of the famous report that President
Roosevelt referred to in announcing the American alliance with Russia. The report said that the population of
the Ukraine increased over the Five Year Plan period by
two percent, and that it had the lowest death rate of any
Soviet republic. 'Plump Babies and Fat Calves' was the
name given to that report. The truth was that in that
period twenty percent of the population starved to death.
And my uncle made it possible."

"But you don't hate him now."

Anna shrugged. "I agreed to be part of this because
Mr. Minot told me that once my uncle defected he would
be charged under Nuremberg with war crimes."

"But they're not charging Russians."

"Mr. Minot said this would be the beginning. After the
standards already set at Nuremberg the world would
have to pay attention finally to what Stalin did."

Malone marveled once more at Minot. He would say
anything to achieve his ends. There was no chance—zero—
that Nuremberg would tackle any war crimes but German, and surely Minot knew it.

"But it ceased to matter because . . ." Anna hesitated.
How could such things cease to matter? But they had.
". . . because my uncle . . ." Anna raised her face to
Malone, as if to her confessor. "My role, according to
Mr. Minot, was to encourage my uncle's defection by
making him think that I loved him, that I had forgiven
him. And to my surprise . . ." Her voice trailed off.

"You did love him. You did forgive him."

She nodded, and said in a whisper, "He hated himself.

He has always hated himself. He hated himself enough for both of us."

"And you began to fear for him if in fact he did defect. You didn't want him brought to trial in Nuremberg."

"No."

"You wanted him to go home."

"Yes."

"And you wanted his wife and daughter to be spared."

"Yes." Anna's face was streaked with tears. "He and my father were opposites. One a priest, one a believing Communist. My uncle truly believed in the revolution. He worshiped Lenin. But he told me that when my father was put to death, his faith broke. He admitted the truth of what my father had said, that he *was* a murderer, one of Stalin's murderers. He applied to the Foreign Ministry as a way of getting out of the commissariat, but then as a diplomat he had to deny what it had done. What *he* had done. For fifteen years his life as a Communist was a lie."

"Did you tell him that if he was to defect he would be charged with the terror-famine?"

"He knew that he would be expected to prove that it had happened. He saw clearly what he would have to do if he came over."

"And he couldn't do it."

"No."

Malone let his eyes drift upstream to the dangling remains of the CCC footbridge. If he'd been Tumark, faced with such a choice, he'd have been tempted just to drop into that river and end it all that way. Maybe he had.

And then Malone realized that, given his history, there had been no chance that Tumark was ever willingly going to defect. Especially with someone like McCarthy on the loose, he'd have been eaten whole. Anna saw it and surely Tumark would have. Was that why Minot had sought to increase the pressure with the phony photographs? But Minot hadn't used them yet. Tumark may have built a life around a lie, but he was telling the truth, Malone was certain, at the end.

Minot. Minot was something else.

Malone's eyes followed the twisted line of the bridge
across to Virginia, and he realized—it shocked him, as an
investigator, that this hadn't occurred to him until now—
that he would have to go over there and look back on
this scene from its other side.

Look back for what?

He didn't know. All he knew—and he knew it viscerally, the way a cop does—was that this was the scene not
of an accident but of a crime.

"I have to go over there," he said, pointing. When he
looked at Anna her eyes were full of dazed questions,
and he imagined how she would lie in bed next to him,
not asking them. They would be awake all night, each
sifting through the silence for pieces of the bitter truth.
Tumark's death and what had been laid bare before it
would surely make their love impossible. But today, tonight, they would not speak of that. Then, tomorrow or
the next day, or the one after that, he would wake to find
her gone, and he would have a worthy reason, at last, for
what he admitted now was his hatred of Webb Minot.

"I don't want to report what happened until I've seen
what's over there. Do you want to come? Or I could take
you to town."

"How will you get across?"

"Chain Bridge. It's most of the way back to Washington anyway."

"No, I would come. But . . ."

"What?"

"Who do you think is over there? Did you see someone?"

"No. But we don't know if he came alone, do we? We
don't know if he was followed. We don't know much."

She lowered her eyes, as if ashamed, and then he saw
that she took his ignorance as an accusation. All this
time, despite all they'd said to each other, she had still
kept her secrets back. But hadn't he? He said, "There've
been things you haven't told me. There've been things I
haven't told you. You think of me as a man whose house
has oil paintings and leather-covered books. But I have
nothing to do with a place like that. My rooms have
always had kitsch on the walls. Everything I own fits in
two bags. Your story stretches back through great events

and across the world. My story is full of timid, disappointed people whose lives are small. I have been pretending that I am not one of them, that I'm like the fancy people at Victor Woolf's dinner parties. I've been pretending that I'm like you. But I'm not. You know what I am? I'm a cop, that's all. And I want to live again without all these levels of meaning, without all these goddamned secrets. And I'm going to start by crossing this river and doing what a cop does. Asking questions when they occur to him instead of trying to read minds. If I'd done that before, your uncle might still be alive."

When Anna looked at him he sensed that she too now grasped what Tumark's death, in addition to everything else, had done to them. That's why it surprised him when she said, "I want to go with you."

"All right. Let's go."

More than an hour later they pulled into the barren picnic grove on the Virginia side of Great Falls. Pine needles blanketed the ground and it wasn't clear where the parking lot ended and the picnic area began, so Malone drove as far as the first stone barbecue pit.

Sharing an instinct, he and Anna closed their doors quietly. The familiar roar of the waterfalls hung thickly in the air above them.

Anna began to walk directly toward the footbridge, but Malone remained standing by their car, as if listening.

"What is wrong?" she asked.

"Where the hell is his car?"

Not listening; he'd been staring at the soft, covered dirt. A dozen yards away were the fresh tire tracks of a single automobile, a pair of shallow gullies in the pine needles. But the car was gone.

Anna said, "He must have come with a driver. An embassy car."

"Did he ever do that when he met you before?"

"Yes. It was a way of making the MGB think he was hiding nothing. He knew the driver would report him. And the driver knew he knew that. So if he took an embassy car, it guaranteed that his business was innocent."

Malone crossed to the auto tracks themselves, bent to finger them, then straightened and turned. He went to

Anna, took her arm and led her across the picnic grove,
past the lumber tables and the log-cabin lodge. Here,
where the underbrush had been kept clear, there was no
path to follow, but Malone took them directly to the near
edge of the forest, upstream. The soft, mushy earth gave
way to rocks and boulders and smooth granite shelves as
they approached the river, and when they came to its
bank, looking now across to where they had stood before, Malone was struck by how the falls looked against
the pale green backdrop of the sharply rising Maryland
hills.

The remains of the tangled bridge were farther upstream yet, fastened on this side in the thick, uncleared
woods above them. They climbed to it, finding the ropes
of the footbridge, both its handholds and the three stouter
slat supports, secured not by iron stakes in boulders as in
Maryland, but around a pair of large oak trees that stood
well back from the river's edge. Trees behind which,
Malone realized, a man could easily hide.

He stood, an arm still linked in Anna's, looking out
across the river, along the line of the ruined bridge. He
pictured Tumark dangling from it.

"There is no warning sign here," he said, looking
about, as if he expected to find it in the brush. Someone
disposing of a board marked Danger, Keep Off would
simply have tossed it into the river. Tumark would have
crossed out onto the bridge unsuspecting.

Tumark dangling, craning back to show his face.

Had this really happened?

Malone pictured that snapping wave, how it sent the
rope and slats recoiling, the bridge sagging at an odd
angle, then bouncing, nearly spilling the Russian diplomat. One rope gone.

Malone pictured that other rope snapping, how the
bridge on its remaining line had begun to spin in tight
little circles, how the slats had folded together length-
wise, like leaves of a fan, how Tumark had clung to the
one remaining rope.

And when Tumark fell, had the man behind the oak
trees been about to cut that last rope as well?

Malone dropped his eyes to the ground and saw, even

without stooping, what by then he fully expcted to see, the remaining ends of the two broken support ropes. Not broken, but cut, sliced cleanly through.

Had the man expected the bridge to collapse of Tumark's weight?

Had the man expected Malone and Anna to be on the bridge too? Was their entire rendezvous supposed to have taken place above the raging river?

Malone caressed the back of Anna's neck with his hand, saying quietly, "Someone cut these ropes. Someone killed your uncle."

"It was MGB," she said dully, as if anesthetized.

But to himself Malone rebutted her; the MGB would have just packed Tumark off to Moscow. The MGB would never involve American authorities. The MGB had no reason to kill me or Anna.

Now Malone did stoop. He lifted the broad branch of a scrub evergreen and found what a flash of glinting light had hinted was there, a small silver cup, an oversized thimble. It was a whiskey shot, grooved along the inside of its lip to screw, as a cap, onto a flask.

Malone held it for Anna to see. "Maybe this is why the killer didn't cut the third rope right away. He took a drink to quell his panic. And then, when Tumark fell, he didn't need to cut it."

Anna stared at him with a look of such fresh horror that he realized she was only now grasping what had happened.

Suddenly she faced away from him, toward the river, and began to shriek, a shrill, endless sound that pierced the permanent dull noise of the waterfall. It took him a moment to realize that her scream had the form of a word, a Russian word.

When Malone touched her coat, she bolted, and began running like a scared child. Going after her he slipped, so that, by the time he followed her back into the picnic area, she was well ahead of him. She continued screaming as she ran, that same word, and he felt he was chasing her back through the nightmare of her own past.

When he caught her in the middle of the desolate grove, near a rusted-pipe A-frame from which the chains of a swing set no longer hung, he was no more immune to that frantic desperation than she was, but in him it caused a plunge into the carnal. She pulled away from him and ran as far as the car. When he grabbed her there and when she fought him he pushed her against the rear fender and began to kiss her. He was drowning, drowning.

She tore at his coat, kissing him back with a burst of passion, in flight still from her grief, perhaps, but now fleeing into a violent oblivion that surpassed his.

Despite the cold they flung their clothing off. Their abandon had become absolute, a raw, instinctive pushing back against death and terror, and it continued absolute until they were naked inside the car; it continued absolute as they clawed each other and then as he pushed into her, beginning nearly at once to ejaculate while she once more cried out against his cheek words he did not know, words of Russian.

The storm of his own orgasm passed but Anna continued coming. Her intense, endless spasms astounded him and the strength of her grip on his neck hurt him, and she never ceased whispering into his ear what he did not understand. It was as if he had never been with her before, or with any woman. It was as if he were seeing their white bodies entwined against the gritty car-seat upholstery in a photograph.

With a shiver, he slid out of her, and he heard another voice—that cop's voice that he'd resolved to listen to because it was his own—and it said, You're a fool to trust her.

16

It might have been a replay of the September meeting in the director's office, but certain minor things were different now. What had set Malone apart before were his rumpled khakis and open shirt; now it was the British cut and superior tailoring of his dark double-breasted suit.

It was late in the afternoon of the day on which Tumark died. At noon Fairfax County police had recovered his body two miles downriver from Great Falls. Minot's agents had spent the afternoon combing both sides of the river, above and below the tumultuous cascade. The first thing they had done was dismantle completely the remnant footbridge, which was sent into the FBI laboratory on Tenth Street.

In September Malone had felt a novice agent's panic in this office, but now more than his tailoring and grooming had changed. If his appearance was marked by the refinement of his self-possession, it wasn't only appearance. He felt the calm of a man whose job was only to observe, which was nonsense. He was going to have to explain himself and he knew it. He was going to have to admit meeting both Woolf and Tumark without Minot's approval, and he was going to have to accept at least indirect responsibility for Tumark's death. Yet, standing next to Minot, who had, unaccountably, avoided him until now, Malone felt detached because he was, even here, still at work.

As before, Tolson was standing behind Hoover; he was

paler after the winter, but his hair was slicked back and his trousers were perfectly creased. Now, however, Malone recognized Tolson's suit—there was a faint sheen to the overpressed material, his collar did not lay flat against the line of his shoulder—as an outfit off the rack at Robert Hall.

J. Edgar Hoover was studiously ignoring them, bent over a stack of letters, signing his name then flicking up the bottom inches of each page without looking at it, to sign the next. Since Minot and Malone had entered the room the only sound had been the scratching of Hoover's fountain pen.

Finally he worked his way to the bottom of the pile, and still without looking up he pressed the button on the left side of his desk, then began to align the edges of the stack of letters. Miss Gandy entered the room and crossed to Hoover's desk soundlessly. Hoover handed her the stack without a word. She retreated and closed the door behind her.

Then he looked at Minot. "Brigham called from London?"

"Yes, sir."

"And?"

"We have positive identification, sir. Fuchs confirms that Gold is definitely the man he knew as 'Raymond.' "

"And Fuchs will testify?"

"That's the deal, sir."

Hoover slapped the desk in front of him and swung around in his chair to exchange a triumphant glance with Tolson. A grin spread across Hoover's round face, as if despite himself, but by the time he turned back to the men in front of him, it was gone. He said, "I want an arrest, then. Bring him in. Charge him with espionage. What's his name again?"

"Gold, sir. Harry Gold. My boys nabbed him an hour ago in New York."

"You arrested him already?" Hoover's face darkened at this preemption.

"As you know, sir, we've had him under surveillance for a week. There was no question that this was the man who met with Fuchs. We already had identification from

Fuchs's sister in Cambridge. And Gold, as a chemist from Drexel in Philadelphia, matches 'Raymond's' history as we pieced it together from the Soviet cables. And I'm told we found a map of New Mexico in his apartment—"

Hoover waved impatiently. "So where is he?"

"In the lockup at Foley Square."

"Do the newspapers have it yet?"

"No, sir. The arraignment is scheduled for nine tomorrow morning. I thought you could make the announcement at eight-thirty. Brigham said Scotland Yard was present for the interview with Fuchs, and they could conceivably go to the press before us. But it's not likely, sir. It's already night there now. London never heard of Harry Gold before today. They'd look foolish, trying to scoop us."

Hoover looked back at Tolson. On cue Tolson asked, "Would the director have to take questions?"

"No, sir." Minot kept his gaze fixed on Hoover as if the director had been the one to ask the question. "Pending the indictment, questions would be inappropriate. You'd simply make the announcement that the mysterious courier who served as go-between from Klaus Fuchs to Anatoli Yakovlev of the Soviet consulate has been taken into custody by agents of the Federal Bureau of Investigation. Your statement would refer to leads developed from interviews with Fuchs, even though, of course, Fuchs gave us nothing. It was the cable traffic that led us to Gold, but we can't refer to that, of course."

"You'd write the statement?"

"Yes, sir. I'll have it on your desk at seven."

"The director will want it tonight, Minot," Tolson said.

"I meant tonight, Mr. Tolson." Minot raised his eyes to the associate director for the first time. "I meant seven P.M., Mr. Tolson."

The two men stared at each other, not disguising their disdain.

Malone, despite himself, felt the pull of his old alliance with Minot. He had been confused at first by the unexpected news of "Raymond's" arrest, and he still had not figured out how it related to what had happened at Great

Falls. It explained at least Minot's unavailability through
the afternoon. Tumark's death, to Malone's great surprise, was an event of secondary importance that day.

Hoover said, "And what about this Russian?" He looked
at Malone for the first time. The director's face was an
impassive mask, and for a moment Malone felt a surge of
the old panic. What was he supposed to say? He understood implicitly by now that Minot had habitually told
Hoover as little as he told everyone. Minot was the
keeper of secrets and he doled them out like gumdrops,
even to J. Edgar Hoover. Malone, therefore, had an
automatic impulse to defer to Minot, but he checked it.
"I was with Vladimir Tumark this morning, sir. It was a
prearranged rendezvous at Great Falls, the purpose of
which was to determine whether he was working for us."

"Of course he was working for us!" Hoover barked.
"What the hell do you mean?"

Malone's fragile resolve collapsed before the blast of
the director's anger, and suddenly the rank arrogance of
his own suspicions struck him. Hadn't his self-important
questions sprung from nothing more, really, than a junior
agent's ambition? From his resentment at being, for all
the flash of his State Department position and his fancy
wardrobe, on the periphery of this crucial operation? He
realized what a grievous error he had made in thinking
the rules of need to know did not apply to him. And
because of it, Tumark was dead. And now he was going
to be rightfully and severely—

Minot surprised him utterly by saying, "Malone was
doing what I wanted him to do. He wasn't following a
blueprint of mine, but as you know, Mr. Hoover, he's
had to work on his own. And in fact he developed some
theories that he wanted to test out. For example, that
Tumark was a double agent, which he wasn't. But I gave
Malone his head because the Russian liked him, and my
hope was that eventually Tumark would agree to let
Malone replace the SIS man, Woolf, as his control. That's
why I wanted the meeting to take place today."

Minot looked at Malone evenly. Malone was stunned,
trying to make sense of what he was hearing.

But Minot wasn't finished. "What I didn't count on,"

he said, "was that the Russian was in a mood to commit suicide."

"Suicide! That's impossible!" Even as he spoke Malone realized how out of place his spontaneous, emotional response was in that office. Nothing was ever said there that was not calculated, self-concealing and self-promoting. For some reason Minot had concocted a rationale that absolved Malone and he'd offered it convincingly to Hoover. But Malone was not convinced, and this statement—that Tumark had killed himself—was too much. That the man had committed suicide was impossible and it was impossible now for Malone, *who had been there*, not to protest such an outright lie.

Minot eyed him coolly. "You haven't had the benefit of the lab report, Chris."

"But the ropes were cut! I saw them! I saw them myself!"

"Yes. Microscopic horsehairs from those same ropes were found on the blade of the penknife that was itself found in the pocket of the coat on Tumark's corpse. He sliced through those ropes, probably to within an eighth of an inch, himself. The third supporting rope was similarly sliced. It was supposed to break too, but it held. That's why he dropped." Minot faced Hoover again. "There's no doubt it was a suicide, sir. The man arranged it to look like an accident, probably to avoid drawing postmortem MGB suspicion onto himself and therefore reprisals against his family in Moscow."

"But what about the car?" Malone said. "It was gone. Whoever drove him there just left. How do you explain that?"

Minot shrugged. "An embassy underling doing as he was told. Obviously Tumark sent his car away before the fact."

Malone stopped himself from giving voice to his further objection, his last one. As he had stopped himself that day, for a reason he still could not explain, from referring to or turning over the silver cap of the whiskey flask that he had found in the brush beside the footbridge. Instead he calmly said, "Do you have the lab report with you, sir?"

"It's on Mr. Hoover's desk," Minot said, nodding toward an unopened manila folder.

Malone looked at Hoover. "May I, sir?"

Hoover blinked, communicating his permission.

Malone stepped to the edge of the desk, opened the folder and flipped through its pages until he came to the list of effects found in the pockets of Tumark's clothing: no flask.

He turned to the autopsy, the report of substances in Tumark's system: no alcohol.

Malone casually put his hand in his coat pocket as he stepped back from Hoover's desk, but his finger was secretly closed around the small silver cup.

Hoover watched Malone with narrowed eyes until Malone had resumed his place beside Minot. Then Hoover said, "So what's the conclusion, gentlemen?"

Minot answered, "A simple suicide, Mr. Hoover. It's the risk in dealing with these people. They are under duress. They are traitors to their countries, after all. Tumark could not bring himself to defect, but he also could not face going back to a totalitarian Russia made worse by the fact that his patrons have lost power. Frankly, he did us a big favor in going out the way he did."

"What do you mean?"

"Even though our man was present, we're not involved. Deniability up and down the line. The Fairfax police report makes no mention of Malone. The *Evening Star* has the story in the second section as the accidental drowning of a midlevel Soviet diplomat. The initial conjecture of acquaintances on Embassy Row is that he fell into the river while bird-watching. The Great Falls area is famous—"

"Bird-watching!" Malone cut in. "That's ridiculous."

Minot held himself rigidly, still addressing himself to Hoover. "He was wearing binoculars. A copy of a bird manual was found in his coat pocket." Only now did he slowly face his subordinate. "The man was known to be an ardent birder."

If there were binoculars on Tumark you planted them! Everything in Malone made him want to rage at Minot, to spit his accusation at him. Minot was speaking for

Malone's beloved FBI, and what he was saying was a lie!
The man was a total liar! What he had done in planting
binoculars was a crime, and now he was deceiving Hoover!

Everything in Malone made him want to rage, that is,
except his instinct as a cop. Even now Malone found it
possible to ask, What is Minot doing? In order to find
out, he knew, he had to hold himself in check. And by
some miracle of restraint, he did.

Minot had continued smoothly. "Tumark obviously prepared himself well—not to fool us or the press, but to
fool his own police. Apparently he succeeded. The Soviets have claimed the body and there's no indication there
will be any kind of inquiry beyond what was conducted
today. The State Department has already sent condo-
lences. The affair won't impinge on you at all, Mr. Hoover. Everything will be handled out of Foggy Bottom."

"Out of the Protocol Office, presumably," Malone
said briskly, recovering. If he was still playing this game,
then he'd damn well better play it. What he wanted now
was a neutrally worded reassertion of his competence.
What he wanted, above all, was a way to see this mystery
through. "I'll be able to keep the Bureau informed since
that's my office at State."

"*Was* your office, Mr. Malone," Hoover said. "As of
now, you're in the Bureau again."

Tolson reached into a box on the table beside him and
withdrew a bulky manila, cord-secured envelope, placing
it in front of Hoover.

Malone felt blind-sided once again. He stared at the
envelope thinking, Now what?

Hoover unwound the string fastener and opened it.
He took out Malone's leather credentials folder, his gold
badge and his gun and holster, and he pushed the lot
toward him across his desk. Hoover's blank face told him
nothing and Tolson remained impassive behind him.

Malone approached the desk, pushed the gun, badge
and credentials back into the envelope. How inconceiv-
able it would have been to him a year ago that his
attitude toward those objects could be so complicated.
Once they were the simple, pure emblems of his commitment and he had carried them without ambivalence. Now,

receiving them back, he felt compromised and manipulated. He remembered how Anna had looked at him that very morning when she'd heard him describe the photographs. Minot's photographs, the bastard. How sullied he felt. Still, he said, "Thank you, sir."

Despite himself, when he turned back with the envelope under his arm, his eyes went right to Minot's, and he was sure his bitterness was apparent.

But Minot said in a kindly voice, "Firebird is being wound down, Chris. We're closing up shop. That's what nabbing 'Raymond' means."

"The whole operation?"

"That's right. Phelps Place. The Garage. Everything."

"The Garage? But why stop the cryptanalysis?" This was the part of the operation that Malone's burglary had made possible, but in fact it was the loss of the house at Phelps Place—his life with Anna—that threatened him. He remembered his earlier conclusions, that nothing would be possible between them now, after Tumark's death. But Malone knew he simply could not think of Anna here—not if he was to keep his hands off Minot. He focused on this other question. "Father Abetz has used the code book to crack the Soviet system. Can't he keep on reading their traffic indefinitely? Why stop that?"

Minot exchanged a quick look with Hoover, more than an expression of their mutual displeasure at a young agent's impropriety. Hoover, Malone realized, was taking cues from Minot. The implicit disdain with which Hoover had treated Minot the autumn before—his sneering crack about Harvard—was nowhere in evidence now. Malone sensed how indispensable Minot had made himself and now he sensed that Minot was prompting the director from a script he had written himself.

Hoover unwound the string fastener and opened it. quiry of an off-base journalist, "The FBI is not in the cryptanalysis business. That's what the ASA is for. What we did here was on a temporary, emergency basis, at the direction of the president. The cryptanalysis operation will go back over to Arlington Hall, where it belongs. And my people . . ." Hoover opened his hand and at once

Tolson put a folder into it. Hoover opened the folder in front of him, a list of names several pages long, the roster, Malone guessed, of Minot's shop.

"All of you who were part of Operation Firebird are to be commended. . . . Unfortunately I can't put anything on paper. . . ." Hoover looked up at Tolson with a sudden helplessness.

Tolson said, "You could issue letters of commendation without referring explicitly to the operation. Administrative achievement, for example."

Hoover nodded. That's what he would do.

Malone was mystified, as if it mattered whether letters of commendation could be issued, and it shocked him to see in Hoover such a petty preoccupation. But then Malone realized that Hoover had merely deflected him from the unbelievable revelation that the FBI was getting out of cryptanalysis in deference to another agency. Hoover deferred to no one.

What Hoover was doing was indulging at last his bright mood. His boys had done their job, by God, and now *his* job was to pat them on their backs. Hoover ruled by chastising and rewarding, and it wasn't true that he vastly preferred the former. Letters of commendation, Malone saw suddenly, weren't petty matters at all. They were instruments of the man's control.

"First Fuchs," Hoover said, tapping his desk expansively. "Now this fellow, Gold." He looked sharply at Minot. "They're both Jews."

"Fuchs is widely thought to be a Jew." Minot paused, then said mournfully, as if he agreed that this was bad news, "In fact he is not."

Hoover shook his head. "He probably *was* a Jew."

Malone wanted Minot to say, But so what? Instead Minot confirmed with his silence Hoover's obvious assumption that it was important to portray the spies as Jews. Malone's rage rose in his throat again, threatening to spill out as speech: What in God's name does their being Jews have to do with it? Is this the Bureau, he wanted to scream, or is it Buchenwald?

Hoover was nodding sagely, mulling over his own

assessment of Fuchs's bloodline before dismissing it with a shrug. "Well, anyway, it's good work. Damn good work, Inspector. President Truman's going to be pleased. First the master spy. And then his messenger. The missing link. The men who stole the A-bomb." Hoover suddenly leaned toward Minot. "Can I tell the president that this guy Gold will confess like Fuchs did?"

"Once we face him with Fuchs's identification, what else can he do? Plus we have his map marked with Los Alamos—"

Tolson leaned forward suddenly, putting a hand on Hoover's desk, and with a snarl that contrasted sharply with his usual impassivity, he said, "Don't let the bastard think it'll go easier on him if he talks. They let Fuchs off the hook in London, but this one is ours, and he has to fry!"

Minot replied calmly, "We can't introduce the cables in evidence, Mr. Tolson."

"Then get that confession!"

"We fully intend to, sir."

For a moment no one spoke. It wasn't clear if Hoover had anything else to say about Gold. He sat with his fingertips steepled at his mouth. "In that statement, Minot, I want you to give me a way to talk about what they did, what it means, stealing the A-bomb, giving it to Stalin, breaking their sacred trust as scientists. Gold's a scientist?"

"Yes, sir. A chemist."

Hoover nodded. "I want to talk about this thing in a way that John Q. Public will understand."

"Yes, sir. I intend to do that. Now that we've cracked the case I think you can expand quite a lot on it, and I think I know how you should characterize it."

"How?"

"As the Crime of the Century."

Hoover did not react.

But Malone did, inwardly. Was this true? Fuchs and Gold—the Crime of the Century? For a moment Malone thought, Christ, what's wrong with me? Why is it *Minot's* crime I'm obsessed with? Minot has captured Fuchs and Gold. That's the point, isn't it?

Tolson leaned forward to whisper in Hoover's ear.

Hoover nodded, then said to Minot, "I want that statement on my desk before I go home."

"Yes, sir."

Malone half expected Hoover to say, " 'Crime of the Century,' I like that." But he didn't.

Minot read the signs of their dismissal. "Thank you, Mr. Hoover," he said and he turned to go.

Once more, on instinct, Malone risked an impropriety that would have been unthinkable months before. He said, "If I may, Mr. Hoover?"

Minot stopped, displeased.

Having just been handed by these men what he knew was going to be a tremendous personal coup, Hoover was feeling generous. "What is it?"

"I was wondering about my assignment, sir." All Malone knew for certain was that he had to get out from under Minot. But he also had to stay in Washington so he could pursue his questions on his own.

Hoover looked at Minot. "Why haven't you discussed it with him?"

"There hasn't been time, sir."

"I can see that. . . ." Hoover shifted toward Malone, preparing to explain what he intended to do.

If what Malone had done before had been unthinkable, what he did now was, by Bureau standards, unspeakable.

He interrupted the director to tell him what *he* wanted. "When I was sent from Kansas City in the summer, it was for the bank-robbery squad in the Field Office here, sir. I hope you'll see fit to let me take that up." Malone smiled as ingratiatingly as he knew how. "You remember, sir, that I have an interest in safe-cracking."

Their moment in the backseat of Hoover's car that night—Malone successfully evoked Hoover's memory of it, Hoover's sense of what he owed this brave young agent.

He said with rare kindliness, "I know you do, son. And I know damn well that this entire operation depended for its start on you. And the Bureau owes you one. . . ." He looked at Minot. "I don't see why we can't—"

Now it was Minot who interrupted, saying far too fiercely, "Impossible, sir! Malone has to be gotten out of Washington, and for the same reason we have to close down the Garage on Capitol Hill. There are too many snoops in this town now. Malone had a very visible position at the State Department. He can't be dusting for fingerprints at the Riggs National Bank after traipsing around at Embassy Row receptions all year. Unless you'd care to explain to Senator McCarthy or Drew Pearson why you had an undercover man in the State Department during the Alger Hiss trials." Minot stopped abruptly to let Hoover imagine one or two of *those* questions. Then he went on more calmly. "And secondly, sir, whoever drove Tumark's automobile to Great Falls this morning may well have seen Malone across that bridge. We know that Tumark deliberately used MGB drivers to emphasize his innocence, so we have to assume that the driver this morning was MGB."

What bullshit, Malone thought. The MGB would never have left Tumark alone. Tumark might have met Anna with his embassy driver watching, Malone thought, but he would not have met me.

Minot, however, was emphatic. "The Russians never caught on to Tumark, that he was working for the FBI. . . ."

Bullshit! Bullshit! Malone had to clamp his teeth shut to keep from yelling, don't believe him! Tumark was not working for us!

Minot hadn't missed a beat. " . . . Do you want to give the Russians a free shot at doing that now by putting Malone in an office where the MGB stakeout will photograph him routinely?"

When Minot stopped talking the vacuum of silence in the room pressed at Malone's ears. To his great surprise what Malone sensed was Webb Minot's fear—fear of him. Clearly Minot and Hoover had earlier agreed to send him off to Seattle or to Butte or to Memphis, Tennessee. The point was to get him far away from

Minot's operation, which, whatever happened to Phelps Place or the Garage, Malone did not believe for a moment was winding down.

The debt of gratitude that Hoover had once powerfully felt toward him gave Malone a last card, and before Minot could call, he played it. "I see the point, Inspector," he said politely, shifting the envelope with his gun and badge from under one arm to the other. "And, given the urgency of getting me out of Washington, I'd like to request immediate assignment to the SE Squad in New York."

In New York Malone could still track down the answers to his questions, and without Minot on his back. But there was another reason. Wasn't New York where Anna's mother lived? With Phelps Place shut down, wouldn't Anna go there?

The thought of Anna stopped him. He simply refused to think of losing her. His first instinct that morning had been that Tumark's death, her *uncle's* death, would make their love impossible. But now what seemed impossible—was this the result of events here, in Hoover's office?—was life without her. Malone was simply not going to play any of this—not Firebird and not Anna either—the way Minot wanted. For what Minot wanted, clearly, was for Malone to disappear. He looked at Hoover. "If I can't do what the Bureau first had in mind for me, Mr. Hoover, I'd like to finish what I've started with Firebird. I'd like to be part of the team that works on Harry Gold. I know how important it is to get his confession. I'd think of myself as your representative, since Mr. Minot's duties"—now Malone faced Webb Minot, expecting an open expression of resentment but finding instead a blank impassivity—"will keep him here in Washington."

"Good idea," Hoover said. "All right with you, Inspector?"

"Yes, sir," Minot said without flinching. "That's fine."

Malone and Minot stood together in the crowded elevator. It was five o'clock and Bureau clerks and secretaries left work as punctually as they arrived. Malone was grateful that the press of employees made talk impossible. But when the elevator doors opened on the ground floor, Minot touched Malone's elbow, indicating he should wait. The others hurried off, leaving them alone. Minot pressed the hold button.

"You have a car?" Minot asked.

"Yes. A State Department car. I have to get it back to Twenty-first Street."

"I'd be grateful for a ride. I have to get up to my desk, to write the boss's press statement."

"Sure," Malone said, but his heart sank. As they went out into the corridor together, heading for the courtyard, he said with a counterfeit jocularity, "But aren't you afraid of being seen with me?"

Minot not only made no reply to that crack but kept his silence until they had driven past the Capitol grounds and veered onto Pennsylvania Avenue toward Seward Square. If he felt that he'd been outmaneuvered by Malone he didn't show it, and Malone relaxed enough to realize how different things were going to be now.

"What do I tell Anna?" Malone asked.

"You don't have to tell her anything. She's already gone." Minot turned in his seat to look at Malone.

Anna? Gone? Malone refused to show him any reaction, but inwardly he felt as though he'd been shoved from a cliff. Gone!

It was what he'd feared, of course—Minot's intervention. But it was also what he'd sworn would not stop him.

When Malone didn't react, Minot said carefully, "That's why you asked for New York, isn't it? Because of her?"

Malone held his breath; Minot thought his only issue was with Anna, that his maneuvering and his impulsiveness and his resentment were the excesses of love. Harmless excuses. Was it possible Minot wasn't tuned to his suspicions, his questions? Maybe Minot wasn't afraid of him after all. By asking for assignment to New York, Malone had given Minot a way to relax about him. "Yes," he said, gambling now, looking for confirmation. "I knew she'd be going there to be with her mother."

Minot didn't deny it, and Malone knew at once that he

had the lead he needed; she *was* going to her mother. Malone pretended to concentrate on his driving.

"I think you've made a big mistake by falling so hard for Anna, Chris. But maybe you have to learn the hard way."

"I gather you made a mistake like that yourself once, with Anna's mother." Anna's mother, Malone repeated to himself. He needed clues now about her.

Minot faced away, fixing his eyes on the storefronts they were passing.

Malone said, "Anna came into this thing thinking you were the other person in the world, besides her mother, whom she could trust." Malone let his implication hang in the heavy air between them: Not anymore.

Minot said quietly, "Anna is out now. She has nothing further to do with us. I don't want you to see her again."

"Just like that, eh?"

Minot brought his steady gaze around. "Just like that," he said coldly.

Malone held Minot's eyes a bit longer, given that he was driving through rush-hour traffic, long enough to have yielded nothing.

After a few moments of pointed silence Malone said, "I'd like to ask you a question."

"What?"

"Did you know Anna was Tumark's niece when you put them together in those pictures?"

"Yes."

"And what did Tumark say when you showed them to him?" As he asked this Malone recalled Tumark's face, utterly credible, only that morning as he'd denied any knowledge of those pictures.

"He was disgusted." Minot looked at Malone. "Who wouldn't be?" He waited for Malone to answer. When Malone said nothing he added, "I know *you* are disgusted, Chris. I don't like it any more than you do, but there have been good reasons for everything. . . ."

"You don't have to explain that to me." Malone bristled. Was he a teen-age boy? Having been forbidden to see his girl, was he now to have the harsh realities of life laid out for him? "Those wonderful pictures," he said coldly. "What happens to them now?"

"I destroyed them all immediately after I showed them to you. They'd already served their purpose, getting Tumark to come across. Once we had him hooked, we didn't need the pictures anymore. It was a mistake for me to hold on to them. It was a mistake for me to show them to you. I didn't want Anna to know."

"Then why did you show them to me?"

"You just seemed so damned . . ."

"Suspicious."

"Yes." Minot's face fell for a moment into an expression Malone had seen only on his father's face. What was it but the self-hatred of a man seeing in his own son the certain signs of disdain and contempt? Whenever Malone's father showed him that forlorn face, he was already on his way to getting drunk. Malone sensed Minot's thirst and it was easy to imagine how his hands would shake opening the locked drawer of his desk where he kept his bottle. And it panicked Malone to feel a blast of that thirst himself. He swallowed but his dry throat rebelled, and his voice cracked as he repeated the word, "Suspicious." Without speaking further he took the flask cap from his pocket and offered it to Minot. Minot stared at the thing without moving.

At last Malone said, "I found this at the bridge."

Minot took the cap and eyed it calmly. He said, "It's Tumark's, from the flask we found on his person."

Malone didn't flinch. "Is that the case, sir? And no doubt you've asked Victor Woolf to keep it for you, since it makes a pair with his."

Without a further glance or word, Minot put the oversized thimble in his pocket, then faced away.

A few minutes later Malone turned into Seward Square and stopped, a block away from the Garage. Minot got out, but instead of slamming the door at once, he bent back into the car. "Look," he said, "I'm sorry about some of what had to happen."

"Me too. I'm sorry about Tumark."

"Yes." And then Minot closed the door and, pulling his coat closed against the March wind, he walked away.

Malone watched him for a moment, then put the car in gear and drove slowly off, looking for a place to turn around. He had to make a complete circuit around Seward Square to get back to the avenue.

As he turned into the downtown flow of traffic, he saw, in the middle of a sidewalk bus-stop queue, the tall, black figure of Father Abetz. Instinctively Malone pulled over. He couldn't have said exactly what he was after, but he knew that the priest was closer to the center of the Firebird mystery than he was, and it was into that center that he now had to find a way to move. He stopped the car and leaned across to open the passenger door. "Hello, Father," he called in his best former-altar-boy voice. "Can I give you a lift?"

The old priest bent toward him. Malone discreetly slid his credentials folder out of the manila envelope and let it fall open on the seat. "I'm Chris Malone." He grinned. "We met a few times at the Garage when we were having our cars worked on. I see you're still busing it. I'd love to give you a ride. I'm heading out toward Catholic University myself."

Father Abetz studied Malone's friendly face, bouncing his eyes off the credentials on the seat, then got in, moving slowly, a man inflicted with arthritis.

Once they were folded back into traffic Malone said easily, "Actually, you saw me in Mr. Minot's office a few times. Most recently, the day that Klaus Fuchs was arrested."

"You were only there once. That was the only time."

"I guess you're right. I've been holding up another end of the operation." Malone paused, then said, "It's classified, but I guess there are no secrets from you. I became an undercover agent, Father, so that I could obtain the code book you've been using. You probably wondered where it came from." Malone grinned again. He was working fast. This frontal assault on the man's reticence might backfire, he knew, but there wasn't time for subtlety. "I guess I'm not supposed to tell you how I got it."

"You burglarized the embassy."

Malone nodded, satisfied that they'd established their security clearances with each other. "Maybe the ends do justify the means sometimes, eh, Father? Not that my Jesuit ethics prof at Loyola would ever have said so."

"Which Loyola?"

"Chicago."

"I taught in the scripture department at Loyola of Baltimore before here," he said in his heavy German accent.

"I know you did. Ancient Near Eastern languages, isn't that your field? Mr. Minot brags that you are the world's leading authority on ancient Aramaic."

"Hardly the world's. The Church's perhaps. And we don't say 'ancient Aramaic.' It is a redundancy, as there is *only* ancient Aramaic."

Malone nodded pleasantly, but he felt as if he were back in a sterile, crucifix-ridden classroom suffering the mean stare of a nasty Jesuit who salted such picayune corrections with blizzards of dandruff. It was a feeling Malone plowed right through. "I loved the Jesuits at Loyola, Father. I almost joined up, not that they'd have had me."

Father Abetz smiled and his pale, wrinkled face softened in this first show of warmth. How they loved their priests manqué. "If the Bureau took you, the Jesuits would have."

"You're kind to say so, Father." Malone slowed the car for a traffic light, and when he'd stopped he leaned back easily. He pointed across to Union Station a block away. "The Baths of Diocletian," he said. "I heard from a train conductor my first day here that Union Station imitates the design of the famous Roman baths."

"It is fantasy. The original looked nothing like that."

These priests, Malone thought, never pass up a chance to demonstrate their superiority. But Malone knew that his Catholic-boy resentment would not serve him now. He tacked, saying amiably, "I arrived on that train half a year ago. We set up Firebird in, what, September?"

"Yes, September."

"And you were recruited because you had done cryptanalysis during the war?"

"Yes."

"And since then?"

The priest raised his shoulders, grimacing. Age had so betrayed him that he couldn't even shrug without pain. Malone sensed how it infuriated him that his body was failing his brain. It was easy to read his grim silence. Catholic U., like colleges everywhere, would have been overrun with students on the GI Bill, students such as Malone himself had been. Relic professors like Father Abetz had been swept aside, and for the first time their fate seemed cruel to Malone.

In the face of the priest's depression, Malone felt an urge to be radically upbeat. "I have to say it certainly is satisfying to have been a part of something so successful and so important as Operation Firebird. I guess you heard, today we nailed 'Raymond.' "

"Yes," he said, but gloomily. How could he rejoice at the end of the project that had redeemed his time?

"We're all aware, Father, including Mr. Hoover, that we succeeded by using leads that you gave us."

The priest accepted the accolade, nodding. But then he surprised Malone by reciprocating it. "If you provided the code book, it's you, son, who deserves . . ."

"I guess we all deserve credit. Not that we'll get it, of course." The light changed and Malone gunned up North Capitol Street. "You'll be going back to teaching Aramaic now, I guess. Is that right?" He was ingenuousness itself.

"I'm retired."

"Oh." Malone shifted gears easily and said while changing lanes, as if he had only the vaguest interest, "So will you be moving over to Arlington Hall then, now that Firebird as such is shutting down?"

"Arlington Hall?"

"The Army Security Agency. To continue your cryptanalysis, using the code book to keep reading the Soviet traffic."

"The code book is useless now."

"What do you mean?" Malone asked casually, but his

heart had begun to race again. Here was a hollow spot in the wall if ever there was one.

"The Soviets stopped using it right away. They only used it that one summer, in 1945. We've read everything they sent in that particular code."

"You mean they *changed* it?" Careful, he told himself. Don't show him how this confuses you.

"They changed their central code twice." The priest seemed unaware that he was astounding Malone with this revelation. "They began using that code book the first week in June, and they abandoned it in August, to begin using another one."

"But, forgive me, I thought the point of a double-cipher system was that by changing the one-time pad every day, they could use the same code book for years. Isn't that what Gouzenko said? They wouldn't change it unless they thought it was compromised. And it wasn't compromised at all then."

"That's all true. Nevertheless, this particular code book, the one you obtained, was used, at least from the Soviet embassy in Washington, only for that period of ten weeks."

Jesus Christ, Malone thought. Even if he couldn't figure the meaning of this yet, the wire to every alarm he possessed was tripped. *Here* was the question to push through! *Here* was the opening!

The rush of excitement he felt was almost sexual. Control, he told himself, control! And as calmly as he could he went on with his, yes, interrogation.

"Was this code book used from other embassies or consulates? Did Minot give you traffic from that period from the UN Mission or their embassy in Ottawa?"

"No."

"But if this code book was just used in Washington . . ." Malone could not formulate his question. He had the sense, suddenly, also familiar from those Jesuit class-rooms, that his mind was not quite sharp enough for this. He took his eyes from the road to look at the priest. "So all that other cable traffic that we intercepted remains unbroken?"

"Given what we have, it's unbreakable."

"And no part of your operation is moving from the Garage over to ASA?"

The priest shook his head. "Our work is finished. We learned what we set out to learn. As for the rest"—he continued shaking his head, sadly—"ASA could not do any better than we have done. Only if you were able to obtain for us the code book in use since August of 1945 could we read the material we have intercepted. Fortunately the cables which pointed us to Fuchs and Gold fell within that ten-week period."

"That is fortunate."

"Indeed."

Malone appeared to give himself over to driving for some moments, but in fact he was concentrating nearly entirely on the problem of that code book. If in fact the Soviets had abandoned it, why wasn't it destroyed? Or shipped back to Moscow? No procedure would have justified leaving an inactive cipher key in a working *referentura*, much less in its unlocked safe.

Once the flow of automobiles slackened, Malone picked the conversation up again, quietly. "August, you said."

"Yes."

"As I recall, the exceptional volume of cable traffic that drew our attention in the first place doesn't drop off until sometime in September."

"That's true. September ninth."

"So from sometime in August to September ninth, the Soviet embassy kept up an urgent pace of communication with Moscow, but we can't read it."

"That's right."

"What day in August? Do you remember the exact date, Father?"

"I know the exact date very well. I have spent weeks trying to read the intercepts from that one day when the new code book went into use. In the beginning I did not understand that to be what had happened. I thought the code clerk had made some mistake, and I worked that day's material for weeks. I could not bring it into clear."

Malone sensed how it had wounded the priest's pride that the cipher had defeated him. But then he sensed that it was more than pride, as if he hadn't been able to reconstruct the very words that Jesus used. It was as if his faith was shaken. Whatever it was to him, the priest had been deflected into the pain of that disappointment, and he had fallen silent.

"What day, Father?"

"August seventh."

"The day after Hiroshima. That was the day after Hiroshima."

"Was it?"

"Yes." Malone looked over at Father Abetz and suddenly saw that his brilliance was a matter of numbers and letters, of alphabets and schemes of numerical probability, of abstract calculations and theorems and formulae. Had he really never considered that the messages he was trying to read, messages known to have originated in Los Alamos, might have something to do with Hiroshima? Why had the Russians changed their code on *that* day?

Did the priest not understand that the entire project of Operation Firebird had everything to do with another August explosion? Had he not gathered that because of *these* messages, *these* numbers, *these* marks on paper, the barbaric Russians had the goddamned A-bomb? The Firebird itself.

Apparently the priest hadn't asked these questions, any more than priests ask why their brilliant pulpit abstractions about proper human behavior are taken in by sexless old women and no one else! If men like these, Malone thought angrily, are the barometers of our morality, no wonder we've fallen prey to men like Minot who will do, apparently, whatever comes to mind.

Father Abetz surprised Malone by touching his sleeve. "Could you?"

"Could I what, Father?"

"Go back into the embassy and get the current code book?"

Malone nodded automatically. Why not, what the hell? If only everything had been as simple as those first lies were, he thought. Let's do whatever occurs to us, without regard for its meaning or its consequence. Wasn't

that what he had happily done himself, taking his cues
from Webb Minot, to start this runaway process rolling?
"I could get back in the embassy, sure . . ." he said, but
he let his voice trail off as he realized that this time he
would not find that tidy black book waiting for him in an
unlocked safe, and not because Vladimir Tumark was
dead. This was what Malone's instincts—that goddamned
open door!—had been warning him of all along.

At last he saw it. The safe had been left unlocked
because the Soviets *wanted* him to get that code book.
The Soviets *wanted* Father Abetz to bring those cables
into clear. *That* was why this code, unlike all their other
central diplomatic codes elsewhere in the world, had
been in place for mere weeks.

But why? He cursed himself for his puny, uncompre-
hending mind.

It wasn't until they were crossing Rhode Island Avenue,
approaching the northeast corner of Washington, in which
dozens of Catholic seminaries and convents nestled against
America's only pontifical university like whelps at their
bitch, that Malone thought of a way to put the crucial
question. "If I couldn't get you the proper code book,
Father, what else could I do to help you read those other
cables?" The cables intercepted, that is, after August 7
and before September 9.

This was a question the priest understood. It was one
that, in his passion to solve the riddle of those ciphers, he
had asked himself repeatedly. He answered at once, "Plaintext. Bring me plaintext. Even fragments of the original
plaintext. Presuming the second code book, once they
went to it, remained constant, I could reconstruct the
system, working backwards, if I had a sizable fragment of
the material they were encrypting. I reconstructed the
Hammarubic alphabet from the inscription on a single
tombstone."

"I can't get you a tombstone, Father, but . . ." Malone
paused to calculate, but he was operating on instinct and
there were no numbers for him to add or subtract. He
was at the mercy of another kind of abstraction than the
old linguist's, the abstraction of a detective's hunches.

". . . Maybe I can get hold of documents the Soviets might have had reason to send home that month."

"Yes! Get me documents!" The priest's eyes flared. "Even a few paragraphs of the right documents, and I could begin from there."

"Has Minot . . . ?"

"He said it is impossible."

Malone nodded. "He told me the same thing, but I don't agree." Now who was Mr. Bullshit? What was he going to do? Burglarize the Pentagon? The AEC? And then he realized, Yes. The AEC exactly. "If I could come up with something, would you be willing to work with me on this unofficially?"

"Not telling Mr. Minot, you mean?"

"Well, not until we had something. You and I would have to step outside normal Bureau procedure."

"But after today I will have no copies of the *encrypted* traffic. Mr. Minot said now that we have caught both Fuchs and 'Raymond,' we have no further need of that other material. . . ."

"But who knows what it could tell us? Don't you want to finish what you've begun? Imagine breaking the Soviet cipher without the key to help you. That would make your achievement with the Hammarubic alphabet look simple. Maybe I could come up with what you'd need, Father. If you're game, I am."

The priest did not reply. A lifetime of rulekeeping inhibited him. Malone remembered a Jesuit saying, I keep the rule and the rule keeps me. While Malone waited he felt the burden of what he'd just proposed gather mass. He had just offered, in effect, to burglarize the FBI. The cop's voice drummed in his head: You've lost yourself this time, bud. All you just offered to deliver are the originals, which you don't have, of secret messages, which you don't have, to an aged priest who's looking at you like you just promised him guilt-free sex in heaven.

He thought of Anna again. Had she really simply left without speaking to him? *Would* he be able to find her? If she had left, simply because Minot told her to, didn't

that mean the warning voice was right—that he *was* a
fool to trust her?

But he couldn't think of that now. Firebird. Go deeper
into Firebird. To find the truth, yes. And then he understood, that at the center of this mystery, he would find
her.

"What do you think, Father?"

The dark Gothic hulk of Catholic University loomed
on the hill above them so oppressively that Malone was
not surprised to hear an abject note of gratitude in the
old man's voice when he said, "All right, yes."

Gratitude. Malone felt a dose of it too. His visceral
anticlericalism evaporated in the warmth of his relief. He
had a plan now, and he had an ally.

17

Malone had rushed back to Phelps Place that night, but even before getting there he knew for certain that she would be gone and she was.

To his amazement he realized that he had always secretly expected that she would eventually disappear from his life as abruptly as she had entered it.

He was not, finally, surprised to find her room stripped of her belongings, her worldly clothing, her books in four languages, her burdening jewelry, everything. Not surprised. But still stunned. For a long time he stood in her vacant room, heartbroken.

Hadn't the depth of her silence always been, in part, a signal of her ultimate unavailability? And wasn't he kidding himself to think that now he would find her? He would find her again if it was only Minot who didn't want him to. But what did she want?

Her rooms were tidy, the bed neatly made, but they were, with one exception, as impersonal as a room at the Y.

The exception? One thing remained—the icon of Mary and the votive candle flickering under it. That timeless face, its infinite sorrow, the woman before whom Anna had maintained what Malone had come to envy as an unbreakable self-communion. More than once, after they made love on her narrow bed, when he had roused himself to look at her, he had found her gazing into the Madonna's eyes, and for the first time in his life a religious object had come to seem openly erotic to him. The votive candle itself had filtered the shadows of their nakedness, heightening its mystery and wonder exquisitely, so that, time and again, when they had fulfilled their desires, it seemed they had done so with the icon's blessing.

That night, alone before the Virgin, Malone understood it was only their own blessings they had withheld from each other, despite their efforts not to. Malone admitted that, for his part, he *had* refused to trust Anna totally. Was that the cause of this, the worst loss of his life? Had she been right to leave him?

He drew closer to the icon, as if it would answer his awful questions. If in some mystical realm the Russian Madonna had seen them coupling, it was not as a voyeur, like the cold eye of Minot's camera, which had driven Malone from the violated bedroom on the second floor, but as an omniscient, loving third partner. Because Anna had felt no self-consciousness in front of an image of God's mother—no self-consciousness, certainly, with him— Malone had found it possible to let go of his inhibiting, Catholic-boy reticence, experiencing sexual love for the first time as pure benevolence. And the icon, that figure of stern asceticism, became a sign of that benevolence, that ultimate acceptance in which Anna and Malone had found repose but that, for their separate reasons, they had never quite bestowed upon each other. Therefore he understood, when he came upon it still in her room that night, that she had left the icon with its wavering candle as a sign of her love, intending him to take it. He picked it up carefully, as if his unconsecrated hands were not worthy of such an object. The Virgin's eyes were full of pain, but also acceptance. He had to look away from them. He had never felt such hurt before, such desolation. Oh, my Anna, my darling Anna! He turned the icon over. Along the bottom edge of its back was a line of Cyrillic letters, a pair of Russian words whose meaning he could not measure. Another mystery.

Yes, she left this as a sign of her love. But it was also a sign of what separated them. Not Minot, but Anna herself. It was a sign of farewell. Anna intended, he understood, never to see him again.

By now he had been in New York for five weeks. He had been assigned to the team of agents interrogating Harry Gold, but Gold had steadfastly refused to admit even knowing Klaus Fuchs, much less to being "Raymond," the courier who'd brought Fuchs's crucial stolen data to Yakovlev. Malone knew that the Firebird cables identified "Raymond"—a Drexel-trained chemist, born in Switzerland of Russian émigré parents, raised in Philadelphia, active in the Young Communist League, recruited to Soviet espionage after earning his doctorate *summa cum laude*—in ways that could only apply to Gold, but not even Malone's fellow agents in New York knew that. Firebird was an operation the New York agents had heard rumors of, but Minot's Washington circle had remained closed. No one outside it knew of the cables.

In New York, the agents assumed that Hoover's obsession with getting a confession from Gold resulted from the circumstantial character of their evidence—that map showing Los Alamos—and from the unreliability of Fuchs's identification. In fact, some of the interrogating agents had begun to have their doubts that Gold was even the right man. Nevertheless, they worked in four-hour shifts, twelve hours a day, five days a week, pushing their questions at the mouselike, simpering chemist as if he were Al Capone.

"Tell us, you bastard," Malone muttered to himself one day as he watched from a corner of the interrogation room. The urgency of his need to know what lay at the center of the Firebird mystery had not eased in all these weeks, despite his distance from Washington. He hadn't figured a way to follow through with Father Abetz, and Anna's absence only made him hate his own ignorance more.

He watched Harry Gold, who was, finally, his last real link with the truth. Not that Gold looked like anything of the sort. He was a thick-faced, dark-featured man with sallow skin and pitch-black, wavy hair. He was thirty-nine years old. Malone thought he looked like a baker's assistant, a man who had nibbled too much uncooked dough.

After listening for hours to the futile, pointless interrogation that day, Malone pushed away from the wall and crossed to the table, interrupting one of the other agents, who was halfway through the Drexel questions for the hundredth time. "Forget it, George," Malone said. "We all know how much Mr. Gold loved Drexel. That's neither here nor there." Malone towered over the suspect. Seated next to Gold was his lawyer, a man of no distinction who'd been appointed to the case by the court.

"What we want to know about," Malone said in an explosion of anger, "is the Russian who sent you to Fuchs!"

To his own surprise, as if released by that emotion, Malone's mind leapt to its next question, what he could never ask: Was the Russian who sent you named Vladimir Tumark?

But he knew it wasn't Tumark. This was a measure of his desperation, that he could no longer keep his questions straight.

Gold simply shook his head. He was exhausted and sick. His eyes filled up and he seemed about to weep. "I've told you and told you," he said hoarsely. "I don't know Fuchs. I don't know Fuchs."

Gold's lawyer put his hand on his client's arm. "I think, gentlemen—"

Malone interrupted him. He was exhausted too, and now his anger had him by the throat. "Make sure your client understands that he's going to be in this room every day for the rest of his life until he tells us! You make sure he understands that!"

At that Gold did begin to sob. He lowered his face into his hands, as his shoulders shook. The lawyer moved away from him, embarrassed, but he cast a resentful glance at Malone. "I hope you're satisfied."

But Gold's wimpering only made Malone angrier. "I won't be satisfied—"

"All right, Malone," one of the other agents said with undisguised disapproval, and everyone fell silent.

The agent told Gold and his lawyer they could leave. Once they were gone, he turned to Malone. "You're out of line, Malone."

"Why, because the SOB cried?"

"Maybe because he's not our man."

"Don't be ridiculous. He's just well trained, that's all."
The other two agents exchanged a look, then the second
one said, "Maybe you guys in Washington made a mistake. Has that occurred to you? I've never seen anybody
who was guilty stand up to interrogation like this. There's
nothing left of that bastard. What makes you so sure he's
'Raymond'?"

Malone could not answer the question—the cables,
again—and so he said nothing.

The two agents looked at each other once more, and
like that, Malone realized they had cut him out. When
he'd come to New York it had reassured him to be once
more in the company of men who were only what they
seemed to be, but now he realized that to them he
himself was someone to be regarded warily. He was the
man with secrets kept from *them*. He was *their* Minot.
And they had begun to hate him.

But that did not distress Malone as once it might have.
On the scale of his obsession, his fellow agents' disdain
barely registered. When he was not in the squad room at
the field office in the courthouse in Foley Square, or at
Gold's interrogation cell in the lockup in the same building, Malone haunted New York, his other futile effort,
looking for Anna.

It was the simplest thing in the world to keep her
image before him, pictures of her face from different
angles, an exact notion of how tall she was, what her
stride's rhythm did to her clothing as she moved through
crowds on sidewalks, how it felt to be beside her, how
the light struck her hair when she came toward him, that
innumerable collection of details—her physique, her scent,
the sound of her voice in all its nuances, the mark on the
back of her hand that he never noticed except when she
put her cigarette to her lips—that he'd memorized as if
knowing the days and nights were coming when he would
wander the streets of the largest city in the world, blind
to every wonder—the million identical padlocks hanging
from window grates, the fire hydrants sprouting from
curbstones, the sparks off an ironworker's torch—except

the one he did not see. Anna. It was as if, when he left
the field office to go out into those streets, he began
breathing and thinking again, certain that he would find
her but also, like a mediocre student, constantly up against
the limit of his brain's ability to take in what had happened, what was still happening.

Anna, Anna—this was his refrain—where are you?
What reason did he have really for his certainty that she
was in New York? Couldn't she, after all, have gone to
Strasbourg? But he would not think of that. As long as
Firebird was alive, he was sure she was nearby. In that
sense, Harry Gold's infuriating refusal to cooperate was
keeping the operation going, and it was keeping Malone
himself in New York, where he could look for her.

Anna, Anna, where are you? But his first question was
not about Anna. It was about her mother.

What Malone knew about Anna's mother was that,
despite the wealth left her by her deceased merchant
husband, she had maintained her ties to the self-isolating
émigré community, Russians of her generation and older
who clung together in New York, as in Paris, and before
the war, Berlin. They nurtured the ever-fading hope that
the Bolshevik occupiers of their homeland would be defeated, enabling them to return from the bitterness of
exile.

Malone corrected himself continually at first, remembering how Anna would insist that these "Russians" were
in fact also Ukrainians, Belorussians and Georgians. They
were Jews. But eventually he admitted that these distinctions among émigrés, who after all shared the *Russian*
language, were beyond him and didn't matter, even to
them, when it came to where they settled. And so throughout the month of April Malone had, nearly every night,
stalked the émigré concentrations, the shopkeepers' realm
of Brighton Beach in Brooklyn, the tidy intellectuals'
enclave on Washington Heights and the exotic West Side
neighborhood below Columbia University, where self-
proclaimed White Army veterans mingled with impover-
ished but still soigné aristocrats, Pushkin scholars who
now drove taxis and even the occasional mystical reli-
gionist affirming the Divine Right of the Tsars. They

gathered in all their neighborhoods in smoke-befouled cafés and restaurants smelling of borscht, and in cellar bookstores and newspaper shops where copies of *Novoe Russkoe Slovo,* but also *Pravda,* were sold and debated over labelless bottles of vodka. Malone heard more than one heated discussion about the deep trouble facing both the Soviet Union, because nothing was permitted, *and* America, because everything was.

One night he found himself in a small café on Amsterdam Avenue across from a hulking, unfinished cathedral. It was the fourth place he'd gone to that night, and he'd found nothing. He was sitting at a table in a remote back corner, ignoring the sour-tasting demitasse in front of him, holding out against his feelings of discouragement and weariness. The Russians at the other tables, rough-looking older men who nevertheless possessed the loud, fierce energy of students, carried on as if he weren't there.

Of course, he knew they were acutely conscious of his presence. He had made no attempt to disguise the fact that he wasn't one of them. They'd have taken any effort to do that as confirmation of their automatic suspicion that he was MGB. He'd begun his forays into the closed world of the émigrés on the hunch that they might accept him more or less for what he was. But all he really was, to them as it developed, was an outsider, and that was enough to make them treat him as though he were invisible. He was certain, of course, that their heated exchanges in his presence concerned literature or sports, not politics. But finally what did it matter? Their language was pure gibberish to him. All he could do was sit quietly, letting his eyes drift steadily around the place, as if waiting for some epiphany.

Really he had no expectation that one would come. And when it did he almost missed it. His eyes settled on a poster on the far wall behind the counter, near the ornate gleaming coffee machine. The poster showed the picture of a woman, but with her face averted, looking down in apparent sadness, grief even. Above her were three large block letters: UPA. The figure of the woman was familiar, even though the features of her face were obscure. Then he realized that he'd seen the poster in other émigré bookshops and cafés. If it hadn't registered on him more consciously, it was because the three letters, UPA, and the Russian words under the woman's picture meant nothing to him. Or almost nothing.

Malone stared at the arrangement of Cyrillic characters and realized all at once that it was familiar to him. He couldn't even identify all of the particular letters *as* letters, but he had seen those shapes before. He had seen them in that order, in those words—but where?

And then he knew. He stood up and crossed between the tables, making for the counter behind which the poster hung. The words below the woman were the words he'd seen printed on the back of Anna's icon.

By the time he drew even with the counter, where the café owner waited, having watched him cross the room, Malone knew he had to ask his question carefully. He smiled at the man, who was absently drying saucers with a towel. "I've seen that poster here and there," he said. "And I admire it. It reminds me of an icon—"

"We have no icons," the café man said sharply.

"Oh," Malone said, shaking his head to convey that he'd been misunderstood, but then he saw the opening, and adjusted. "I pay well. I'm only interested in authentic pieces. I would pay for information that led me to anyone who might be selling."

The man stared at Malone impassively.

Malone opened his hands. "I'm sorry if I offend you. I represent people who admire your Russian art, particularly icons."

When the man said nothing now Malone nodded and took his wallet out. "How much for the coffee?"

"Twenty cents."

Malone put a dollar on the counter. "But anyway, that poster. It's still striking."

The man glanced at it as he took coins from his drawer.

"What does it say there, under the woman?"

"Her name."

"What's her name?"

"Julianna Melnik."

It was the name of Anna's mother. Malone showed

nothing, but he wanted to yell with excitement: At last! At last! Calmly, he told himself, calmly. With apparent nonchalance he picked up the coins the man had spread before him. "And why is she on the poster?"

" 'Remember Julianna,' it says. She is a Ukrainian martyr. Our duty is to keep her memory alive."

"She is dead? What happened?"

But Malone had collected his change now and the man had said all that he was going to. He turned away.

Malone felt the air leave his lungs as quickly as it had filled them. He knew that once more he was at a wall. He glanced at the shrouded figure of the woman, and it struck him that her features were deliberately obscured. If she is dead, he thought, why don't you want us knowing what she looks like?

He never found Anna. He never asked his colleagues to help him, though they were aware of his nocturnal ventures and also of his obsessive searching through the field-office contact files, work that other agents assigned to file clerks. Malone knew that his colleagues took his interest in the émigrés as yet another aspect of the secret he could not entrust to them. But what could he do? What could he say?

It meant nothing to him that it was May first, the Communist feast day, when he was awakened by someone pounding on the door of his room. "Malone! Malone! Open up! It's Poole!"

Barry Poole was one of the agents on his rotation. Malone switched on the table lamp and looked at his clock, panicked for an instant that he'd somehow overslept. It was six-thirty, and as if the light had set it off, the alarm rang.

Malone slapped the alarm button, slid to the edge of his bed, drew his trousers on, then went to the door.

Poole was dressed, as always, in one of his two wide-lapelled, double-breasted suits. He had confided in Malone his secret, that every day his wife hand-pressed all the creases of the suit he left at home, not to mention ironing fresh steeples into the starched handkerchief he wore in his breast pocket. But though all Poole's creases were as sharp as usual, there was a rare agitation in him this morning. His black topcoat was slung over his left arm, the way an agent liked it, but he'd forgotten to doff his dark snap-brim on entering the rooming house.

"What's up?" Malone closed the door behind Poole, but stood where he was, in his undershirt.

"You know what day this is, don't you?"

Malone had to think: Did he mean May first? There was a CPA rally scheduled at Union Square for that morning, a protest against Gus Hall's conviction under the Smith Act. But Malone, like all the agents who worked on Soviet Espionage, knew that pinko street demonstrators, like teachers who refused to take loyalty oaths, were misguided but harmless. "May first. Red Square Day. Why?"

But the workers' holiday was not what Poole meant. "Gold's case goes to the grand jury this morning. Stevenson said he couldn't wait any longer. . . ." Stevenson was the prosecuting attorney. ". . . Maybe he was right, because Gold's lawyer must have felt the pressure. He called Davis a little while ago—"

"It's six-thirty, Poole! He called Davis this morning?"

"Yes. And Davis called me. I got over here as quick as I could. Davis said he and you and I are going to take his statement."

"What statement?"

"Gold's lawyer says he wants to make a statement. Right away. Obviously, he's trying to beat Stevenson to the pass."

"To head off the grand jury?"

"To head off the charge of treason in time of war. That's what Stevenson was going to file. Gold's lawyer wants to make a deal for a charge of conspiracy to commit espionage."

"But that's not a capital crime."

"Stevenson told him no deal, but he also called Davis and said, 'Get the statement.' Stevenson knows he needs it. So, come on, Malone. Get dressed. Wear a nice tie. Maybe Davis'll let you fly to Washington to tell J. Edgar the good news yourself." Poole grinned through his reference to Malone's status as the man from the Seat of

Government, its icy implication of a street agent's resentment.

This time they met with Gold not in the windowless white cubicle of the courthouse lockup, but in a witness's waiting room down the hall from the grand-jury chambers. It was eight o'clock, a full hour before the grand jury was to convene, and the corridors of the courthouse were still deserted. Robert Davis's thought—he was head of Soviet Espionage, New York, a fifty-year-old agent holding a rank equivalent to an ASAC and reporting not to the chief of the field office but to Webb Minot at the SOG—must have been that by conducting the interview down the hall from the Grand Jury Room, the pressure on Gold would increase as he heard the jurors assemble. The witness room had a large round table at its center, and against one wall a large office-style leather sofa. On the opposite side of the room was a smaller table holding a court stenographer's machine. Beyond that was a window. The first thing Davis did when he led Malone and Poole and the FBI stenographer into the empty room was cross to the window and drop the venetian blinds.

The stenographer took her place without a word. Davis arranged three chairs on one side of the table and two on the side nearest the door. He gestured for Malone and Poole to sit on either side of him, but he remained standing, drawing folders out of his leather satchel and stacking them neatly in front of himself, lining their edges up with the edge of the table.

Davis had had very little to say to Malone in the weeks since his assignment. He had rarely sat in on the sessions with Gold, but it was clear from his occasional question, always asked without reference to notes, that he had mastered the file. Malone sensed that Davis was arranging the bulky folders in front of himself now as a kind of nonverbal warning, a display of Gold's file, its irrefutable evidence of his guilt. Malone suspected that even Bob Davis, a veteran of Domestic Intelligence, a man who had made his name, like Minot, tracking Nazis up and down the East Coast, that even Davis did not know what *real* evidence the Bureau had against Gold—those cables

—or how useless they would be when the case came to court.

At precisely five minutes past eight the door opened.

The stenographer's keys clicked under her fingers for an instant and stopped.

Neither Malone nor Poole stood, and Davis did not sit.

The marshal pushed the door wide and stood against it. Harry Gold entered. What Malone noticed immediately was that, where before his eyes had seemed to float continually in fear, never settling in a steady gaze with which another might connect, now his expression was resolute. Malone sensed in him the steadiness of a man who, after a period of burdensome indecisiveness, had made up his mind. He went to one of the chairs on his side of the table, pulled it out and sat without being told. He blinked across at his inquisitors, and put his hands together on the table in front of him.

A moment later his lawyer entered. To Malone's surprise it was not the same nobody who had accompanied Gold before. This attorney was gray-haired, tall and confident, conservatively but carefully dressed. His cuff links flashed when he put his elegant leather briefcase on the table and offered his hand.

"Peter Mathews," he said, "from Norton, Cox and Reed." He carried himself with an implicit superiority that FBI agents sensed instantly in lawyers who had gone to better law schools and now held partnerships in firms that every agent knew he would never have been invited to join. Norton was a Wall Street law firm that even Malone had heard of, and it mystified him that such an attorney should suddenly appear with the hapless Gold.

Robert Davis shook Mathews's hand coolly, introduced Malone and Poole, then asked Mathews to be seated. Only then, with a kindly nod, did Davis acknowledge Harry Gold. "Mr. Gold," he said, "I understand from Mr. Stevenson that you have something to tell us."

Peter Mathews raised his hand a few inches off the table, a signal, Malone understood, not to Davis but to his client. Mathews's fingernails were professionally manicured, and that detail made Malone think of the icicle-

fringed signs one saw in summer on Washington theaters:
It's Cool Inside.

"My client requested this meeting on my advice, gentlemen, and since Mr. Stevenson is not present, I'd like
to make clear for your benefit the terms under which we
have come here."

Neither Malone nor Poole reacted. The stenographer
had begun typing and would continue taking down every
word. It was Davis's job to handle this bastard. Who was
he anyway? And who was paying his fee? Surely Gold
had been cut loose by his MGB control. No Soviet would
risk a financial link with him. Then who?

Davis said, "I'm not interested in terms, Mr. Mathews.
I'm interested in Mr. Gold's statement. I have no authority to deal with anything else."

"But just to be clear, we have Mr. Stevenson's assurance that if Mr. Gold answers cooperatively he will be
charged under the Atomic Energy Act, and not under
the Espionage Act."

"Mr. Mathews, it is beyond the purview of FBI responsibility to make recommendations about charges or
sentencing in individual cases. That falls within the duties
of the U.S. attorney's office, so you have properly taken
the matter up with Mr. Stevenson. However"—Davis
paused and rested his hand casually on the back of the
chair before him, leaning forward slightly like a professor
about to make a crucial point—"if I was to give Mr.
Stevenson my personal view, I'd say it would be a mistake for him to think in terms of the Atomic Energy Act
in relation to your client, since it was passed in 1946, and
the overt acts of conspiracy with which this case is concerned took place prior to that year. Therefore a prose-
cution of Mr. Gold under the Atomic Energy Act, I
should think, would violate the constitutional interdiction
of *ex post facto* laws." Davis suddenly stood up straight,
lifted the cover of the top folder on the table in front of
him and picked up a single sheet of onionskin paper that
was covered with typescript. "Our job this morning is to
find out what Mr. Gold did when he visited Santa Fe,
New Mexico, on June seventeenth of 1945. And what he
then did when on June twenty-sixth of the same year he

met in New York with a Soviet diplomat named Anatoli Yakovlev."

"First of all," Mathews said calmly, "on the matter of the Atomic Energy Act. Your point on *ex post facto* is well taken, but the relevance of that legislation to what my client is prepared this morning to admit lies in the distinction it draws between industrial uses of uranium fission and uses for national defense. As you no doubt recall, the Soviet Union in 1945 was an ally of the United States. Therefore, to have conveyed unclassified information of a merely industrial character to a representative of a friendly country can hardly be construed to have been espionage, and certainly not treasonable—"

Davis dropped the sheet of paper back into its folder and slapped it shut. "Let's go, gentlemen," he said to Malone and Poole. "This is not a court of law."

Before the two agents got fully to their feet Mathews held up both his hands. "I just wanted to set the parameters of our discussion. Feel free to address my client now."

Malone and Poole, taking their cue from Davis, settled back into their chairs.

Davis remained standing, a hand in his pocket. "Mr. Gold, did you ever make the acquaintance of one Anatoli Yakovlev?"

"Not by that name." Gold's voice, compared with the lawyer's, was thin, high-pitched and nervous. He looked up at Davis sheepishly, as if he was about to whine, as he had now for weeks, that he was innocent.

Davis took a photograph from the file folders and handed it across to him. "Did you ever make the acquaintance of this man?"

Gold looked at the photograph. "Yes."

"When?"

"In 1936, when I was a graduate student at the Drexel Institute in Philadelphia, I tutored a young Russian in English. He paid me and I gave him receipts. In 1942, this man, whom I knew as Vassili Zubilin of the Soviet Government Purchasing Commission, came to me with those receipts. He said they proved I had been working as a Soviet agent and he would expose me if I did not do as he asked. . . ."

"And what did he ask?"

"Nothing, until 1945."

"And then?"

"To convey some documents from Santa Fe to New York."

"From this man?" Davis slid a second photograph across to Gold.

Gold hesitated, glanced nervously at Mathews, then said, "Yes."

"Can you identify him?"

"It is Klaus Fuchs."

Now Davis picked up once more the densely typed pages of onionskin. "And is this, in précis form, a list of the documents you delivered from Fuchs to Yakovlev?"

Here it was, Malone thought, the admission that would seal forever the secret of the Firebird cables, the confession that would end the search for the atomic spies; this was the moment of Hoover's triumph, and Minot's; and, yes, he felt it too, Malone's. He watched the small sunken-eyed man reading the page carefully, moving his lips perceptibly. Malone, to his surprise, had stopped breathing.

Gold looked up. "Yes," he said simply.

Peter Mathews reached across and took the page from his client. "I insist on noting for the record that Mr. Gold's position is that all information exchanged through his conveyance was information of an industrial nature delivered to the Soviet Government Purchasing Commission, all of which in any case was contained in the unclassified 'Smyth Report on Atomic Energy' released publicly by the United States government in August of 1945." Mathews referred to the onionskin. "For example," he said, "this document describing membranes used to separate substances, referred to on this sheet as item four, duplicates material extensively discussed in the Smyth Report. The same applies to item six, 'An extensive discussion of the principle of implosion,' and item two, 'Details about plutonium 240,' and item seven, 'principles of multiple-point detonation.' "

" 'Detonation,' Mr. Mathews?" Davis said coolly. "Doesn't that word suggest this material's relationship to weapons development? You're going to be hard-pressed to make the case that this material is industrial, not national defense."

Mathews dropped the onionskin page; it sailed into the center of the table. "As you said, sir, this is not a courtroom. I am merely speaking for the record."

It was not a junior agent's place to speak, but Malone could not restrain himself. He leaned toward Harry Gold. "Are you saying that Klaus Fuchs provided information to the Soviet Union that they already had?"

Gold blinked eccentrically at Malone. "Klaus Fuchs was a refugee from Hitler. Hitler was his enemy, not the Soviet Union."

Malone pressed him. "Klaus Fuchs was at Los Alamos from August of 1944 to July of 1946. Isn't it true that he summarized for Anatoli Yakovlev the results of American atomic research on several key problems and essentially provided Yakovlev with the design and method of operation of the bomb?"

Gold shrugged. "I only know what Klaus Fuchs gave me. And I know that it was peripheral information or information that was already well known in the well-advanced field of plutonium research."

Malone once more felt the frustration of being up against his own intellectual limits. Gold's assertion was a rank contradiction of the basic assumption of Minot's entire operation, that Klaus Fuchs had given the Soviets crucial secret data that enabled them to build the bomb and that they had no other way of obtaining. Was it conceivable that the Fuchs documents obtained from the decoded Russian cables had made no such contribution? If so, what would that mean for this entire investigation? The likelihood, of course, was that Gold was deliberately devaluing the importance of what he had delivered to the Russians. He could hardly be expected to stipulate, with Hoover, that he had committed the Crime of the Century. But Malone had no way himself of focusing a question that might undercut the validity of Gold's assertion, which might soothe Malone's own large qualm—his reflexive, by now familiar suspicion not of the Russians but of the investigative process of which he himself was a part.

Robert Davis wasn't equipped to challenge Gold's assertion either. Instead he held fast to an interrogator's routine. "How many times did you meet Klaus Fuchs?"

"Twice."

"Once in Santa Fe . . ."

"And once in Boston, in May."

"Mr. Fuchs said that meeting was in Cambridge."

Gold shrugged. "Cambridge, Boston. To me, it is the same city. But it is not important. Fuchs is not important. The important source . . ." Gold paused for effect. And two or three seconds later the tap-tapping of the stenographer's keys ceased. Gold let the silence gather weight. He wanted to make sure they listened to him now. This was what he had come to say. He wanted them to know that this was going to be momentous. " . . . is someone else."

"What do you mean, 'someone else'?" Davis asked without missing a beat.

"On the occasion of my trip to Santa Fe, I also went to Albuquerque—"

"When was this?"

"In June, at the time of my trip to Santa Fe."

"1945?"

"Yes."

"Go on."

"To Albuquerque, where I met with a second source, at the explicit direction of Yakovlev."

Bullshit, Malone thought. If there was one principle of espionage tradecraft it was, Don't overlap. Without looking at Davis, he interjected, "The MGB would never use a single courier for two separate sources."

Gold raised his shoulders. "I made precisely the same point to Yakovlev myself. He told me a woman was to have made the second contact, but something prevented her and I would have to do it. Yakovlev gave me a torn piece of cardboard. The man I was meeting would have the other half." Gold shifted his gaze to Peter Mathews, who reached into his leather briefcase, withdrew a piece of cardboard and put it carefully on the table between them. No one of the FBI agents moved to take it, but they all stared at the thing as if they expected it to burst into flames. It was a fragment of a Jell-O box with a scissored jagged edge.

"And can you identify this second source?" Davis asked calmly, as if this was all information they already had.

But Malone knew what an explosive revelation this was. Another spy still unidentified? And perhaps still in place? Hoover would not be happy. And with his H-bomb under way, neither would Truman.

Gold did not answer Davis.

The typewriter in the corner fell silent.

Davis waited.

Finally Peter Mathews took a single sheet of graph paper out of his briefcase and put it on the table next to the fragment of the Jell-O box. "This is a copy my client made of a drawing that the second source provided him."

Davis picked it up and studied the delicate, precisely rendered lines.

Gold said, "It is a sketch of a flat-type lens mold, the key to detonating the atom bomb."

"A lens—?"

"Yes. It focuses detonation waves as a glass lens focuses light waves. The problem with the atomic bomb was always how to control the detonation. This is the answer. And there were other sketches as well."

"Which you delivered to Yakovlev?"

"Yes."

"From this man you met in Albuquerque?"

"Yes."

"Whom you had never met before?"

"That's right."

"Or since?"

"I never saw him again. I don't think he was a scientist. From the quality of the drawings I think he was a draftsman who worked, perhaps, in the technical design shop at Los Alamos."

"And you want us to believe he just gave you these drawings because of this Jell-O box?"

"He had the other half of it. And also there was the password, what Yakovlev instructed me to say."

"Which was?"

" 'Julius sent me.' "

"Meaning?"

"I don't know."

"Who was 'Julius'?"

"I don't know, but the name seemed to mean something to my source."

"Your source," Davis said dully.

"Yes."

"Whom you will identify for us only after Mr. Mathews here has satisfied himself with the U.S. attorney."

Mathews raised his perfect hands. "We have made no such representation. My client is prepared to cooperate, and we have put no conditions on his intentions to do so. As you know, this matter involves events which took place five years ago. It is not reasonable to expect him to recall details with precision."

"What about a name?"

"I don't know his name. I never did. I met his wife, however, and"—Gold glanced quickly at Mathews, who nodded—"he introduced me to her as Ruth. It was inadvertent, I think, that he used her name. Or perhaps it was not her real name."

"And you met them?"

"At their apartment."

"In Albuquerque."

"Yes."

"Do you recall the address?"

Again Gold looked at Mathews, who, this time, didn't move a muscle. His immobility, Malone understood, was quite pointed.

Davis repeated the question. "Do you recall the address?"

"No."

"But you might recall it."

Mathews leaned forward. "Perhaps a street map of Albuquerque would refresh my client's memory. We have no objection if you'd like to recess for a time to obtain one. Although . . ." He pulled a pocket watch from his vest and made a show of eyeing it.

"You're thinking of the grand jury, I take it, Mr. Mathews."

"I'm thinking of my client, sir."

*   *   *

Webb Minot flew up to New York later that morning, by which time the U.S. attorney had formally asked the grand jury to consider charges of conspiracy to commit espionage—but not treason in time of war—against Harry Gold. Gold subsequently had pinpointed on a detailed map of Albuquerque a house at 209 North High Street. He had remembered, further, that he had seen hanging in the hall closet of that apartment the Eisenhower jacket of an army staff sergeant. By the middle of the afternoon, Minot had a list of all forty-two men of that rank who had been serving at Los Alamos in the summer of 1945, and by the end of the day he was expecting a report from Washington, where his men had been systematically searching the army personnel files of the men in question.

Malone stayed at the field office, waiting for a chance to see Minot alone. It was well after nightfall when he locked his desk and cleared it. He was carrying his work trays to the vault when he saw Minot at the desk in the supervisor's cubicle in the corner of the squad room.

The parade of senior agents vying for his attention that afternoon and evening had ended. The entire field office was mobilized now to track down the leads developed from Gold's fantastic revelation. The hooks were out, or out as far as the FBI would get them that day.

The room was empty, and Malone too would have been gone, like the other agents, but he simply had to see this man whom once he'd fancied as a kind of brother, a brother to redeem him.

But once Minot had made it seem that Malone would be *his* brother too. Minot had seemed then to lift the corner on an unspeakable loss of his own, the loss of Peter. And hadn't Minot seemed for a moment to hope that Malone might soothe it? But it should have warned Malone when Minot, from the start, had called him Peter, as if to say, You can be my brother but you can't be yourself.

Now the cleared desks, neatly aligned, each with its gooseneck lamp extinguished, sat like mute witnesses as he approached Minot's corner, and the feeling was, Not brother, but opponent.

"Hi, boss," he said.

Minot had his leg hooked over a drawer. He'd been studying a folder in his lap. "Hello, Chris."

"May I?"

"Sure. Come on in."

Malone stood awkwardly in front of Minot's desk; Robert Davis's desk in fact. Davis had never returned from the courthouse that day. He'd gone to the airport instead, for a plane to Albuquerque.

Malone said, "So what do you make of it?"

Minot indicated the graph-paper drawings he'd been studying. Gold had produced six of them. "I'm told that these sketches would show a knowledgeable interpreter exactly how we built the atomic bomb."

"Do you buy what he said about the Fuchs data?"

"What, that it's of no value?" Minot shook his head dismissively. "That was just to set us up for this. The Soviets got deeper in than we thought. That's all. In Fuchs they had an inner-circle scientist. And in this guy—"

"Was there an indication in the cable traffic of a second Los Alamos source?"

"No. We wouldn't have been so quick to tell Truman the leak was plugged. He only ordered up the H-bomb, you know, because we assured him that Fuchs and 'Raymond' were the whole apparatus."

"Could the second source still be in place?"

"We'll know soon enough." Minot let his eyes fall to the telephone. When he looked up again, he asked, "What do you think?"

"I don't trust Harry Gold."

Minot shot back, "You don't trust many people, do you?" He looked at him with an overbearing fierceness for a moment, but then, shrugging, he cast it off. "The point isn't to trust him. The point is to check out what he tells us. Check it out ten ways, if we have to."

"Did you check out the Smyth Report? I never heard of it. Is that true? There was a declassified report on the A-bomb in 'forty-five?"

"Yes. It was a mistake. It came out of the army. It's one of the reasons the AEC was given control over security. They withdrew the report and classified it, but it was too late. The Soviets had had the report translated and distributed to their top scientists within a week of its publication in Washington."

"And does the Fuchs data repeat it?"

"Look, Malone, Klaus Fuchs was filing regular reports on all the most secret deliberations of the people running Los Alamos, not just theory and speculation, but details about the great engineering breakthroughs at the very end that enabled us to finally build the bomb."

"Regular reports to the Soviets?"

"That's right."

"But Gold only met him twice."

Minot stared impassively at Malone from his side of the desk.

Not desk, Malone thought, but wall. The wall again. Again he found himself thinking at two levels, wondering how it had happened that Minot had become his—what, suspect? Not brother, and not opponent either, but, yes, suspect! It was ludicrous—an inspector of the FBI, his suspect!—but that was exactly the feeling Malone had and at last he admitted it.

And simultaneously, with the larger part of his brain, Malone was trying to grasp the meaning of these endless inconsistencies. He said, "And the only intercepted cables we've been able to read date from the first week in June when the code book I found in the open safe in the embassy became operative. How do we know that Fuchs provided 'regular reports' before that?"

"We know from Fuchs, in his confession," Minot said evenly, showing no surprise that Malone knew when the Soviets had put the code book into use. If Malone was prepared to step onto Minot's turf with his questions, Minot, it seemed, was prepared to withdraw from it.

What are we to each other? Stalkers? Circlers? Animals sniffing out an enemy? Malone nodded slowly, shifting his work trays to his other arm. "I'm just trying to get it straight." He smiled with a warmth he did not feel. "I'm just a dumb gumshoe, boss."

Minot did not soften the edge of his stare.

Not that Malone expected to charm him. He made his next move carefully, yet with all the apparent casualness he could muster. "About the Smyth Report, sir. If that's going to surface in Gold's defense, we probably should have checked it out, don't you think? It would probably give me a headache to read the thing, but I'd like to give it a go."

Of course, Gold's lawyer had dragged the report into the case as pure smokescreen, a too-facile undercutting of Fuchs's data. But he had done so not, as Malone and the others first thought, to make Gold's crime less serious—a crime of the year, say, not the century—but to make his nameless second source more important, as if *he* was the one who gave the Russians the bomb. If he was, and this was exactly how it had worked that day, the U.S. attorney had no choice but to make a deal with Gold. Peter Mathews was a hell of a lawyer. And that thought gave rise to another, one that Malone wasn't ready, quite, to entertain.

The Smyth Report was the point. He forced himself to take one thing at a time. So the Smyth Report was just one of Mathews's throwaways and Malone knew it as well as Minot. Checking it against data would lead nowhere. But Malone also knew that Minot would welcome the chance to send him down a blind alley, away from what he thought of as the center of the case. And this particular alley, however blind, began at the AEC. And Malone had other reasons for going there.

"All right. Good idea. I'll tell Davis." As if the decision released some tension in Minot, he threw his arms back to stretch, and then slapped his pocket for a cigarette. He offered one to Malone, who, for the sake of the releasing ritual, took it. When they'd both lit up, Malone said casually, "This is your town, I guess, huh?"

Minot nodded. "During the war I was on Long Island. Amagansett. But I reported here."

"Before the war, I mean. After law school. Before you joined the Bureau, didn't you practice here? It's one of the things they say about you, what makes you a little different from other agents, that you started out with a firm downtown."

"It's true." Minot smiled. "Why is it that in the Bureau that seems an embarrassment?"

"It's unusual."

"When the war broke out lawyers from Wall Street joined the navy. I was a *lawyer*. It seemed to me that in the Bureau, I could serve my country with what I'd learned." Minot smiled again, ironically now. And he inhaled on his cigarette.

"What firm?"

"Norton." Minot's smile disappeared. Smoke billowed in front of his face. But he kept his eyes rigidly fixed on Malone's.

"Norton, Cox and Reed. I've heard of it."

Minot sat very still for a moment, then said, "You heard of it today."

"That's right. I did."

Minot nodded. He said quietly, using a voice that surprised Malone with its kindliness, a throwback to the intimacy of their beginning, "Is there anything else you want to know, Chris?"

"Yes, sir," he answered automatically, surprising himself as much as Minot. "Where does Anna Melnik's mother live?"

But before Minot could react, the phone on his desk rang. Dust flew. The phone seemed to leap.

But it was Malone who'd leapt.

Minot calmly put his cigarette in the ashtray and answered the phone. "Minot," he said.

And then, picking up a pencil, he began to make notes.

Malone watched in silence.

After several minutes during which the only sound was the scratching of Minot's pencil, he said, "That's it?" And then, "Tell Brigham we'll want a meeting with the director in the morning." Minot was absently underscoring a single word. The thick black line set it apart from all the other words on the page, but Malone, from his side, couldn't read it. "Make it for noon," Minot said, looking at his watch. "I'll catch the last plane tonight if I can, but if I miss it, I'll have to come down in the morning." After another exchange or two, he hung up.

"What do we have, Mr. Minot?"

Minot studied his notes, retrieved his cigarette. "We

have a man named Greenglass. David Greenglass. Formerly of 209 North High Street, Albuquerque. Formerly Staff Sergeant David Greenglass, U.S. Army Corps of Engineers. Married to Ruth."

"Jesus Christ," Malone said. "You mean Gold is telling the truth?"

"He got those sketches somewhere. The production chief at the AEC looked at them this afternoon. . . ." Minot read from his notes. "He said, 'Why, they show the atomic bomb, substantially as perfected!'"

For the first time the magnitude of what Gold had revealed hit Malone. There was a spy at Los Alamos entirely independent of Klaus Fuchs. And they'd nearly missed him. They *would* have missed him if Harry Gold hadn't served as courier for both.

"And that's not all," Minot said. "Do you remember Gold's password, what Yakovlev told him to say?"

" 'Julius sent me.' "

Minot referred to his notes again. "Greenglass has a sister Ethel. She's married to a man named Julius." Minot raised his eyes, squinting with the smoke. "Julius Rosenberg."

"You seem skeptical."

Malone had said nothing, though he knew that Minot wanted some confirmation from him that he too saw their target in the cross hairs. If Minot had to present this turn in the case to Hoover the next day he had good reason to want to think the unknown subjects were identified. But Malone wondered if there were other reasons, in Minot's mind, for buying this.

Malone said carefully, "I thought the Russians were better at this stuff. Don't you think it sounds a bit amateurish, using Gold as a courier for Fuchs *and* Greenglass? And using for a password the man's real name? Would the Bureau do that? Would Yakovlev?"

Minot snuffed his cigarette. "We don't know what 'Julius's' connection is to any of this. Maybe none. Maybe just a point of identification. I don't think we have cause for skepticism, Malone, just because Gold's story checks out."

"It seemed a little easy to me, is all I mean."

"You tell me it's too easy once we get these people in custody." Minot began gathering his papers with a rare show of anger. "You tell me it's easy once we get some convictions!" Minot stood up suddenly, his eyes flaring. He leaned across his desk at Malone. "You tell me it's easy once somebody *dies* for this!"

"Yes, sir," Malone said, and he backed out of Minot's office, frightened by what he'd seen in the man.

It was after nine o'clock when Minot left the court-house. Malone was watching for him from the doorway of a church across the street. The last plane to Washington was at ten, giving Minot plenty of time to get to the airport. He hailed a cab, and so did Malone, right behind him, and almost at once it was clear that Minot was not going to La Guardia, and Malone was not surprised.

Minot's cab took him to Gramercy Park. What's this? Malone thought. When Minot got out of his cab Malone told his driver to circle the park slowly, and he craned back to watch Minot, to see which building he went into. But almost immediately Minot hailed another cab and continued uptown, and Malone realized that his supervisor was taking measures to shake surveillance.

Malone was able to stay with Minot, unmade, through two more taxi changes and a one-stop ride on the subway that took them to Grand Central. Malone watched from across the waiting room while Minot threw back three stiff drinks in the deserted commuter bar. Then the FBI inspector and the FBI agent tailing him took a New York Central train north of the city. They got off an hour later in Tarrytown, a quaint Hudson Valley town just south of Sing Sing. Malone had to cling to the shadows on the station platform because he and Minot were two of only half a dozen passengers to disembark. Malone then followed from a distance. Minot walked through the dark village purposefully, without a glance over his shoulder, apparently satisfied by now that he wasn't being tailed.

Minot came to the gate of a large estate on the hill above the village, and he used a key to open it. At once a man and a woman came out of the adjacent gatehouse and they each embraced Minot with a warmth that seemed foreign to Malone, and he understood that they were Europeans. After a moment the couple returned to the gatehouse and Minot's figure receded as he walked up the long estate driveway.

When Malone turned to look around, to fix the location of the place in his mind, he saw the lights of the town below and stretching far beyond it the dark swath of the Hudson River. He thought of the Potomac, of Tumark. But there were the lights of boat traffic here. The Hudson had no need of a canal for navigation. The sky was clear. The night was warm, a promise of good weather to come. It was the first of May, he remembered, and it shocked him to realize that in all these weeks he had not allowed himself to notice that the winter had ended.

Once the lights in the gatehouse were extinguished, Malone crept along the fence, looking for a place to climb over it. He came to a hill well up from the road, and only from that vantage, finally, was he able to see the dark outline of the estate's looming Tudor house. But that wasn't the sight that stopped him. That wasn't the miragelike epiphany that made it impossible for him to go on that night, not even for the glimpse he was sure by then he could get of Anna. He ached to see her, but he went no farther.

On the hill behind the mansion, silhouetted against the sky, was the form of another building, above the roofline of the main house and behind it. Not a building, but a tower, a kind of steeple that was crowned unmistakably by the peculiar onion dome of a Russian chapel.

18

The Atomic Energy Building on Constitution Avenue was familiar to Malone because it was located just a block away from the State Department, where he'd worked in Protocol. But he'd never been inside the AEC, and as he approached it now he realized that, during his months in Washington, the building had registered on him subliminally as a kind of shrine to secrecy. Built of crisp white marble and set on a raised, landscaped esplanade, it embodied his idea, in fact, of a Greek temple, a site of cultic ritual and formulaic initiations, a place in which he had no business. He climbed the few short steps to the entrance, taking in the squared-off, three-story building with a fresh eye. Now that he measured it, the marble structure seemed small to him. The AEC had divisions of research, raw materials, military application, biology, medicine, reactor development and production. It had already embarked on the development of the superbomb at Los Alamos and it continued to produce atomic bombs in Oak Ridge, Tennessee. The Manhattan Engineer District had involved the war's largest massing of facilities and personnel outside the Pentagon, and it amazed Malone, now that he thought of it, that such a program could be administered from this simple temple standing barely higher than the magnolias blooming beside it.

A single uniformed guard sat at a desk inside the unimposing entrance. Malone showed him his credentials. The guard put a pencil mark on his clipboard, handed up a temporary building pass that Malone clipped to his coat and then pointed down the main corridor, citing the number of the room that Malone wanted. Malone was aware that, as he walked away from the desk, the guard picked up his phone.

Malone's heels clicked off the polished terrazzo floor; the echo filled the broad, vacant corridor. He walked with no apparent self-consciousness, a man without reluctance, or so it seemed. In fact, he channeled an overwhelming anxiety into an act of focus, concentrating, for example, on the closed doors he was passing, doors that, with only their simple numbers, should have told him nothing. But he noted that each one was secured by a locking knob as well as by a separately keyed dead-bolt lock. What secrets lay behind those doors? he wondered. What wizardry? What awesome scientific mumbo jumbo?

To Malone the atomic bomb was a set of photographs he'd first seen in the Chicago papers five years before; the mushroom cloud over Hiroshima, the *Enola Gay* landing at Tinian after the strike, the panorama of devastation in the Japanese cities. He remembered reading that the first bomb had been code-named "Fat Man" because the air force wanted spies to think that the special plane it had set aside was for Winston Churchill. He remembered reading first that forty thousand people had died in Hiroshima, but the number kept growing to eighty, then a hundred, until finally, a year later, the estimate was put at two hundred thousand dead. He remembered that Truman called it the greatest thing in history.

At the time Malone was a twenty-four-year-old stockyard worker and night student, and like all veterans home from the war before it ended, he first felt the relief of his own burden of guilt. The bomb meant that all those thousands of nameless buddies he'd left behind when he took shrapnel in Italy would not now die on the beaches of Japan. Hard as it had been to defeat the Germans after Normandy, it was going to be infinitely harder to defeat the Japanese with a like invasion. Thus news of the first atomic fireball had incited among members of Malone's generation, those still in the army and even those, like him, already out, the greatest joy of their young lives. They understood viscerally the bomb's first meaning: that, as a generation, they were going to survive.

Of course, the bomb had a second meaning too. Now that the Russians had it, there was no doubt the atom bomb would be used in war again. Having spared a single generation of Americans, it now threatened every generation of every nationality.

But to Malone it did so abstractly, and as he walked the length of the bare corridor, it was only by a rigid act of imagination that he could picture the men behind those doors going over not sales reports or balance sheets but drawings, equations and calculations. He pictured men at blackboards, doing algebra, men at microscopes and geiger counters, all manipulating figures that defined the movement from the theories of physics to actual devices for blowing up the world. Malone knew that there were scientists who deplored Truman's decision to build the superbomb because its only conceivable purpose was the extermination of whole populations, but wasn't the more telling point that whole populations had already been exterminated by Stalin? How to stop Stalin was the problem now—as before the problem had been how to avoid an invasion of Japan. And, as before, the solution was the awful weapon these geniuses were devising even now in these twice-locked rooms of theirs.

Malone wouldn't have known what to say to a tuft-haired, chalk-dust-covered physicist, but he wasn't looking for a man like that. Room 74 was the office of the chief of security, and Malone expected that he—a former CIC colonel named Gleason who'd supervised security at Los Alamos and who'd left the army to stay with the project when civilians took it over—was a man more like himself. Malone slowed as he approached the door, then knocked on it and waited.

A moment later it opened. A gray-haired woman stepped aside for him. "This way, Mr. Malone, please."

He crossed the small cabinet-lined anteroom, passed

the secretary's desk and went through the open door behind it. When Malone saw the heavyset man alone at a desk in the cluttered inner office, his thought was, Casey Stengel. It was Gleason.

Gleason stood and offered his hand across the chaotic desk top, which was littered with spilling piles of folders and manila envelopes. Malone recognized the FBI dossiers and guessed at once that most of Gleason's time was spent reviewing the endless Bureau background checks on new personnel for the geared-up H-bomb program.

"Have a seat," Gleason said, but Malone had to remove a stack of folders from the only chair. He put them on the floor, then sat.

"Thanks for making time for me."

"Not at all," Gleason said amiably, and when he smiled Malone thought, Yes, a baseball manager, a coach. "I gather from Webb Minot you came for this." Gleason reached across his desk with a thick bound volume. On its cover were only a seven-digit number and the stamped legend Top Secret.

"The Smyth Report?"

"The very same." Gleason sat back and began to fill a pipe.

Malone flipped through the pages, but without a pretense of reading what was written on them.

"I told Minot"—Gleason paused to light his pipe, sucking air through the flame, popping his cheeks, then waving out the match—"that Harry Gold is full of bull if he wants us to think Fuchs was only passing on what the Reds already had."

"That's the point he made. Nobody buys it, Mr. Gleason. But we have to be prepared to respond to his story when it goes public."

"You can't go public with that report. It's classified now."

"I don't mean 'public.' But the judge in the case will have to review it."

"Who's the judge?"

"His name is Kaufman."

"Another kike. Hell, there are kikes everywhere in this thing."

Malone stared at Gleason, saying nothing.

"You can't introduce the Fuchs material in court."

"What Gold handed over to Yakovlev? That's the essence of the case."

"It's too sensitive."

"But the Russians already have it, Mr. Gleason. Like this. . . ." Malone indicated the report in his hand. "They already have this too. I don't think you need to worry about what goes before the judge."

Gleason glared at Malone, a full colonel suddenly glaring at the buck private who'd dared admonish him. But Malone was no private now. He was an FBI agent, and as if Gleason recognized that fact in Malone's refusal to drop his eyes, there was a faint note of deference in his voice when he asked, "Are you people doing a full-field on him?"

"On Judge Kaufman?"

"Yes."

"You'd have to take that up with Mr. Minot . . ." Malone paused to deflect a scruple, then sliced at Gleason, saying, " . . . or with Mr. Hoover. I'm sure he'd be glad to hear your views on how the Bureau should proceed."

Gleason shook his head. "I'm not talking about the Bureau. I'm talking about the court. Hell, in New York you'd think they could have found an Irishman. Aren't there any Irish judges on the bench up there? A Semite judge is bound to be prejudiced, even if he's not a pinko. This guy Kaufman has already made a deal with Gold, I gather."

"Not Judge Kaufman. The prosecutor made that deal, a deal that gives us Greenglass, and his brother-in-law, Rosenberg."

"Yes, but there's my point, two more Jews."

What was this, Malone wondered? Weren't Jews at the heart of the Manhattan Project? Hadn't Jews given us the A-bomb in the first place? He reined his dislike for the man, though not before admitting to himself that he'd misjudged him. Gleason was no Casey Stengel. He was Father Coughlin.

Malone leaned forward to put the Smyth Report on

the corner of the desk. When he sat back he said evenly, "And speaking of Greenglass, we could also use material that will help us evaluate his drawings."

"Greenglass is a red herring, if you'll forgive the goddamn pun. Those sketches of his are doodles. Worthless. Useless. Don't tell a thing about the bomb. Gold is playing a shell game with you guys."

Malone sat quietly for a moment, recalling what Minot had said to him in the squad room four nights before. He said quietly, "My information is that the Greenglass drawings would show a knowledgeable interpreter pretty much what he needed to know to build the atomic bomb."

Gleason shook his head emphatically. "How could they? Greenglass is no scientist."

"He was a design draftsman, though, with access—"

"Wrong. He's a two-bit machinist." Gleason picked up a dossier from the top of a pile and flipped it open. "The man's education consists entirely of six courses he took at the Brooklyn Polytechnical Institute before the war." He dropped the folder dismissively. "And he flunked five of them. And you're telling me he could sketch the design of the bomb from memory?"

Malone remembered the obvious self-interest in Harry Gold's assertion that Fuchs was not the central Soviet spy. And here, Gleason's self-interest was equally obvious. Greenglass, an army staff sergeant, had been his responsibility at Los Alamos. Now, at all costs, Gleason had to keep the onus of the most grievous failure of national security in any nation's history on someone else. On, that is, the British. And the only way to do that was to keep the British scientist—not the American technician— at the dead center of the espionage conspiracy.

It seemed suddenly to Malone that everyone had his own secret to protect. Once more he was up against lies. Harry Gold's lie, first. And now, perhaps, Gleason's. And always, of course, Webb Minot's: Minot's lie to him.

Malone had an insane impulse to stretch out on the cool floor and think. He wanted to clean his brain and start over; he wanted to remember exactly what he'd seen and heard. Shell game, Gleason had said, and Malone realized that he was its victim, and the victim never wins.

He reviewed the moves: Minot said the Greenglass drawings were crucial, Gleason said they meant nothing. If Gleason was lying, his reason was his own self-interest. What would be Minot's? That was the question now. Malone, like the perplexed tourist touching the same shell a second time, refusing to believe he was being swindled, said, "Your people evaluated the Greenglass—"

"That's right. It's just so much scribbling. Our research chief had those drawings on his desk in Aberdeen six hours after Gold gave them over. And he told Minot himself what they were worth. And he told me."

Malone was sidetracked by Gleason's reference to Aberdeen. Aberdeen, Kansas? How was that possible? The drawings to Kansas in six hours? He felt himself dropping into an entirely new hole, and he recognized the lurching, awful feeling as the one he'd had in the black abyss of the elevator shaft in the Soviet embassy months before. Only now, instead of clinging with his hands and feet, it was with his spread-eagled brain. If there was an AEC facility in Aberdeen, he'd surely have heard of it when he was in Kansas City. But then he thought, Surely not! He was a man with a special knack for hearing nothing.

"Aberdeen," he said, and even to himself the dull repetition of the word seemed imbecilic.

"Aberdeen Proving Grounds," Gleason offered. "I'm not surprised you don't know we took it over, just last month for Super. It's in Maryland." Malone sat dumbly before Gleason, trying to think of what to ask. He had leapt at the chance to come here, but expecting what?

Ages ago he'd had the intuition—a vague, unfounded wish, he saw now—that unknown AEC documents would give him clues to take to Father Abetz so that Abetz could open up the secrets of the unbroken cipher cables. That was what had passed once for his plan. But now, suffocating in the windowless core of a stone building that was a shrine finally to his ignorance, Malone admitted what a futile fantasy that was. Even if he could magically get access to AEC files, picking all those locks in all those doors he'd passed in the long vacant corridor, how could he possibly select among them, distinguishing the documents and sorting through the calculations? Had he expected files to be arranged by date right back to the crucial weeks of 1945? Had he expected colored tabs on folders to be inscribed, "Clues for the Young Gumshoe and the Old Priest"?

The truth was he hadn't expected anything explicit because he hadn't thought his so-called plan through. And no wonder! He couldn't think anything through! He was horrified at himself, a walking arcade game bouncing from pin to pin with lights flashing, slapped periodically by Minot's flipper, making lots of noise but ringing up no true score before falling finally into the inevitable hole.

Everything had hinged on obtaining at least fragments of true plaintext, copies of transmitted documents—but before they were encoded—from which Father Abetz, comparing them with intercept material, could work backward, constructing word by word his own version of the Soviet code book. Only in that painstaking way would they have been able to read the late spring and late summer cables, the transmissions from Washington to Moscow that the Russians did not want read. But it was impossible! Imposs—!

He stopped.

And there it was—his first conscious recognition of what had been all this time both unthinkable and obvious.

There was material the Russians did not want read.

And there was material they did.

The Russians *wanted* the Firebird cables broken. They *wanted* their secret but oh-so-carefully delimited cipher system to be vulnerable for a moment. Therefore they *wanted* the FBI to have its harvest of leads. Therefore they *wanted* Klaus Fuchs, Harry Gold and David Greenglass tracked and exposed as spies. That was why Gold had been assigned, against all rules of tradecraft, to serve both Fuchs and Greenglass as courier. That was why their Soviet control, Yakovlev, hadn't bothered to en-

code the name—"Julius"—of the contact Gold and
Greenglass had in common. Yakovlev *wanted* Rosenberg
found out.

From that first visceral jolt he'd felt on finding the
referentura safe unlocked, Malone had been walking, like
a man blindfolded, into obstacles.

Now the blindfold was off and though he had yet to
focus, he saw that the cloudy obstacles were all one
obstacle, the obstacle of the truth. Operation Firebird,
under the curious direction of Webb Minot, had been
proceeding step by step down trails carefully mapped out
ahead of time in Moscow.

That recognition led immediately to another.

Father Abetz's decrypted cables had turned up Klaus
Fuchs as the atomic spy, but "Raymond," surfacing as
Harry Gold, had insisted that Fuchs wasn't alone or even
central.

But here was the AEC's Gleason insisting Greenglass
wasn't the crucial spy either.

And what Malone knew now, still instinctively, was
that they were both right. Jesus Christ, he thought, and
he could feel the blood pulsing into his face. Oh my
Christ! His puerile self-doubt had evaporated before this
certainty: The real Soviet atomic spy, the one Fuchs and
Gold and Greenglass—Minot's entire Firebird operation—
were supposed to lead away from, was someone else.
And the entire point of this elaborate Kremlin-sponsored
not shell game but scavenger hunt was—Malone saw it,
he saw it all—that the spy, now that the H-bomb was
under way, was still in place.

All of this had taken mere seconds, but the recognition
had so jolted Malone that it felt as if hours had passed
since his last exchange with Gleason.

Gleason. The security man was staring at him strangely.

Malone calmly reached forward to pick up the Smyth
Report again. Idly, he opened the cover to the title page
and read, "Atomic Energy for Military Purposes, Henry
DeWolf Smyth, Princeton University." At the bottom of
the page was a column of nonsense letters.

Malone looked up at Gleason. "This was released to the public?"

Gleason nodded. "Along with the War Department press release announcing the bomb. A lot of people were appalled, but that's because they didn't bother to read it. They didn't know enough to appreciate that it really gives away almost nothing. General Groves's idea was to go public right away with something, to forestall leaks of *real* secrets. But politicians thought *this* report was secret and as usual they overreacted, and so we pulled it back."

Malone grinned amiably. "That's why you'll let me take it, I guess, eh? If it's not really top-secret."

"You'll still have to sign the form." Gleason pushed away from his desk to touch an intercom button on the table behind him.

Malone flipped the pages, reading section and paragraph headings at random. The words and phrases—"tube alloys," "isotope separation," "uranium pile," "neutron-resistant"—were disjointed and meaningless to him. He remembered with what self-assurance Harry Gold's cultivated lawyer had referred to this document, and it only now struck him that Peter Mathews—Minot's former law partner—had been able to obtain a copy of it.

Gleason's secretary came with a clipboard and pen and, without a word from her boss, she held the release form in front of Malone for his signature. With the report still open in his lap, he signed his name, feeling anxious to get out of here. This was the last act of what had turned out to be a pointless charade. The crucial realization that he would take out of this office had nothing to do with what had brought him here, the classified but thoroughly public report.

The secretary backed away from him.

The pages of the report had flopped, and now when he looked down, it was open to its last page, and suddenly—as if all at once his perceptions had become infallible—something leapt off it, slamming him.

A few spaces below the last line of text, in the right-hand corner, was the date May 7, 1945.

"May seventh?" Malone said aloud, involuntarily.

"If that's what it says."

"But you said it was with the press release announcing the bomb. That was August."

"That's when it was released. But General Groves had had Professor Smyth preparing it throughout that previous spring."

"And the idea was to make people think you were explaining the bomb without really doing it."

Gleason nodded. "The spirit of openness and crap like that."

"So the Russians would have been anxious to get their hands on this, I guess."

Still nodding, Gleason said, "They would have been thrilled with it, until their scientists actually took it apart. It's a very careful job."

Malone looked down at the date again. May 7. As casually as he could he asked, "So who actually saw this report when it was finished? In May, I mean. Not August."

"The distribution is listed there, isn't it? Turn back to page one."

Malone did so. Below the title and Smyth's name was the column of letters that now he recognized as a list of abbreviations. At the top of the column were the letters POTUS, which Anna Melnik had once explained as president of the United States. Below that were JCS for joint chiefs of staff, SOW for—Malone's mind seemed suddenly unstoppable—secretary of war, MED for Manhattan Engineer District and then two other sets of initials that Malone, even ringing all the bells the way he was just then, could not decipher.

"IC," he said. "What's that?" He tried to keep his mind on the question and the answer, but his mind wanted to drift back to one of those obstacles he'd fallen over before. What?

"The Interim Committee . . ." Gleason was saying.

But Malone felt sweat rush into his hands as he realized what that date, May 7, meant to him; into his hands that held not the useless document he might have dropped in a wire basket on the street, but an entire volume of plaintext, of clear. These were words and letters—if they had them in May—the Russians surely would have sent to Moscow in the perfect double-safe cipher system. These were the pages Abetz wanted.

" . . . the scientific panel under Vannevar Bush set up to advise the president when it came time to use the bomb."

Malone's eye fell to the last abbreviation. "And CPC?"

"Combined Policy Committee."

"Which is . . ."

"The organ for British-American liaison."

"Fuchs!" Malone said, thinking, Back to Fuchs. The Russians got this from Fuchs.

But Gleason was shaking his head. "Smyth's work was strictly in Washington. The on-site scientists had no interest in this report as such. Fuchs was British chief at the Los Alamos Tech Area. He wouldn't have seen this report in May."

"Then who—?"

"The CPC is Washington-based, the link between our policy people and theirs. The joint secretary works out of the British embassy."

"Oh, right," Malone said, nodding slowly. Inwardly he felt a hunter's rush of adrenaline; now his quarry *had* stepped into the cross hairs of his scope. His spyglass.

Like a hunter, he held himself rigidly, but not in any way that showed. Lazily he closed the report and put it under his arm to stand. "I can never keep these initials straight. I know the CPC." He smiled easily. "That's Victor Woolf. He's been with it from the start as I recall."

"Yes. Since 'forty-four."

First things first, he told himself, and that meant the easy part.

He went directly from the AEC to an out-of-the-way building on Sixth Street off Independence Avenue, between the Botanical Gardens and the old B&O switching yards. Identified on tourist maps only as Federal Office Number Six, it was a large, unornamented building five stories high, relieved from an appearance of massiveness only by row upon row of narrow, vertical windows. The building was new since the war but it was faced with limestone, not marble, and it lacked utterly the smug grandeur of other federal edifices. This one, in fact, struck its note of anonymity so successfully that many native Washingtonians, not to mention newcomers and tourists, had no idea it was there.

This was the Identification Division of the FBI, the fingerprint service. With nearly two thousand employees of its own, including hundreds of highly trained "fingerprint technicians" and with dozens of acres of filing cabinets holding hundreds of millions of fingerprint jackets, it was by far the largest concentration of Bureau resources. Ident was the base of the FBI's power in America, the source not only of its ability to track criminals, but also of its enormous access, the growth of which had been massively stimulated in recent years by wartime registrations and by internal security investigations, to information about ordinary citizens.

But Malone was not going to Ident for fingerprints. He didn't know the building well, having toured it only during his agent training two years before, but it didn't matter. What he was after were the sealed subbasement file rooms, which were not on any tour, for that was where the Shamrock intercepts were stored.

He entered the building casually, still carrying the Smyth Report under his arm. In this building, unlike both headquarters on Tenth Street and the field office on Twelfth, the vast majority of employees were clerks and secretaries, so agents had a special, almost princely status. A quick flash of his badge, which he then pinned to his coat according to regulation in the restricted building, was all it took to get him by the guard at the entrance. It was late morning, the hour between the rigidly defined periods of coffee break and lunch, and the corridors were deserted except for the occasional messenger wheeling his file-laden basket from room to room.

Malone stopped one of the messengers, an acne-scarred youth who, in his black pants, white shirt and black tie, looked like a seminarian. Alarm showed on his face when Malone raised his finger at him—Me, sir? Did I do something wrong? And he didn't relax when Malone smiled at him easily and asked directions to the card index section. When the young man turned slightly to point the way, Malone reached quickly into the basket to slip a paper clip off a folder. He put the paper clip in his pocket without the boy seeing. He thanked him and set off for the section where were filed, among other things, the largest collection of names of the deceased in the world.

When he reached CI, he paused at the door, looked back to see if he was being observed, then turned away to head back down the corridor.

FBI file clerks, timid high school kids really, from the hollows of West Virginia and the crossroads towns of the eastern shore of Maryland, were not given to unauthorized wandering around that building, so that when, a few minutes later, Malone slipped into a back staircase at the end of a long hallway, no one saw him. He moved quickly down the stairs until, even in that closed chamber, the air changed, becoming dank and cool, when he went below ground level, past the basement to the sub-basement. He was not surprised to find the broad metal door at the bottom of the staircase securely locked.

He listened carefully. No sounds in the stairwell above him. No sounds from the other side of the basement door.

He put the Smyth Report on the floor and took the paper clip out of his pocket. He straightened it and fashioned a tiny hook on one end, then inserted it into the lock. He jiggled the wire, pushing the pins of the lock up one by one, feeling the old satisfaction. This was something, still, that he could do. When the lock gave, he opened the door, and the first thing he was aware of, apart from the darkness on the other side, was the blast of cold air.

Freezer air. He imagined his father standing behind him, but instead of clapping his shoulder his father would be screaming at him, This is the FBI you're burglarizing now!

As he bent to retrieve the Smyth Report and then

pushed the heavy door open to go through it, Malone
had to reassure himself that this was what he meant to
do. If he was caught here it was no longer at risk of a
mere disciplinary transfer. This was an act infinitely beyond
his capacity to justify it, and for that reason the one thing
that kept him from turning back was the darkness. The
fact that the narrow hallway open before him was not
illuminated meant the subbasement file rooms were not
attended.

But it also meant, when he closed the stairwell door
behind him, that he could not see. There was no point in
waiting for his eyes to adjust, for the absence of light was
complete. He groped his way along. The cinder-block
walls were cool to his touch. Once he was confident that
the corridor was clear of obstacles he groped along swiftly,
alternatively touching both walls, waiting to come upon
doorways.

Since the layout of the subbasement was completely
unknown to him he had no choice but simply to move as
efficiently through its hallways as he could. Periodically
he did find doors, but they were not locked and so he
closed them as quickly as he opened them. Record stor-
age rooms, he guessed, or the building's utilities. He was
sure that the room he wanted would be locked.

It was nearly an hour before he found it, having blindly
felt his way through the labyrinth of a dozen separate
hallways.

The door would not budge. He ran his finger over its
surface, feeling the lock, and also the raised edges of a
sign. For the first time he struck a match. When he held
it up he read, Authorization 555.

555 was John Brigham's room number at SOG. John
Brigham, assistant director for Domestic Intelligence. Minot's boss.

He waved out the match, which, when it cooled, he
put into his pocket. He put the report between his knees
now, then snapped his handkerchief out of his hip pocket
and used it to cover his left hand. Malone was acutely
aware of his own fingerprint jacket in the file upstairs,
and it heightened his sense of violation to hide the skin of
his hand now. Not violation, merely, but sacrilege.

Yet his hands remained steady. He took the doorknob firmly into his left hand, pressing the handkerchief smooth. With his right hand he applied the straightened paper clip to the lock, and despite the darkness he closed his eyes. It was what he always did when picking.

Carefully he manipulated the wire through the ridges and slots until, by its stubbornness, he identified the single pin that held more than the others. With one deft thrust he pushed it up, turning the doorknob at that exact moment. It opened.

When he was in the room he closed the door behind him, took off his coat and laid it on the floor to block the seam of the doorjamb. Then he ran his hands up and down the wall until he found the light switch.

What he saw after the initial blinding glare when he snapped on the lights was a long narrow room with a low ceiling—he could touch it—along which were arranged four rows of filing cabinets each holding six drawers. As he walked along the center aisle the first thing he noted was that the cabinets were equipped with locking rods that fit down through the handles of the drawers. They were fastened at the top of each cabinet with a small padlock and at that sight his heart sank. His hooked paper clip would not be delicate enough to slip through the working of those locks. For the first time Malone felt a wave of panic, and suddenly he was light-headed; his legs seemed unsteady beneath him.

He forced himself to concentrate on the drawer labels, but they were marked only with numbers and at first he thought the labels were in code. Intercepted cable traffic from all the Iron Curtain embassies going back years, but how were the transcripts organized? There were dozens of separate file cabinets in that room, hundreds of individual drawers. How would he ever find what he was looking for?

But then he realized what the numbers were: undifferentiated dates. The cabinet in front of him was marked 111447, and he saw it suddenly as November 14, 1947. He was quickly able to come to cabinets marked for the months of April, May and June 1945.

He opened the Smyth Report to its last page and once more read the date written in its bottom corner. May 7, 1945. He found the drawer marked 5745 and stood staring at it, at the steel rod that ran through its handle, and he resolved that the padlock holding that rod fast was simply not going to stop him.

He put the report on the adjacent cabinet and, again using his handkerchief, he lifted the padlock to look at it. Without his thin and extraordinarily sensitive needle picks, there was no way he could open that lock.

He looked down the row of file cabinets, drawer after drawer secured by rods and padlocks. He could tell at a glance that the locks were not identical, and that was what tipped him off. In that room there must have been seventy or eighty separate locks; seventy or eighty separate keys, therefore. How likely was it that the Shamrock operators kept that many keys organized elsewhere?

He looked at the filing cabinet in front of him again and saw, etched on the steel plate that held the padlock, the number 27. Then he turned back to retrace his way to the door, running his eye along the wall as he did. In the weapons rooms of field offices the keys to the locking gun racks were mounted inside simple wall cabinets—"tel-key" cabinets—and that's what he was looking for now, and that, as he neared the door, was what he saw.

Its lock was easily picked, and a moment later he'd returned to his target cabinet with key number 27. A moment after that he had the steel rod free of the drawers. In his excitement he stopped using his handkerchief, as he pulled the dated drawer open, and began fingering through the folders.

They were marked with the names of cities. "Washington-Prague," "Prague-Washington," "Budapest-Washington," "Washington-Warsaw." These folders were thin, each containing a few dozen pages at most. Soviet control over those capitals was not formal yet in '45. But in the back of the drawer was a single bulking file marked "Washington-Moscow." It held a hundred pages at least.

Malone took it out and opened it. The first page he looked at was covered with numbers, thirty or forty rows of them arranged in groups of five. In the margins were the penciled notations of an early, pro-forma and futile cryptanalysis.

He placed the file on top of the Smyth Report, then opened the next drawer, May 8. He took that day's Washington-Moscow file as well as, from another cabinet, the files dated May 9 and May 10.

He locked the cabinets and returned the padlock keys to their hooks. Then he took his handkerchief once more and wiped every surface he had touched. And only then did he gather the Smyth Report and the files into both his arms. He'd have needed a mailman's satchel to carry them. There were far too many to hide inside his clothes.

At the door he put the stack down. He turned the light out, picked up his coat and put it on, opened the door, then picked up the stack of folders and went out. He made his way through the dark labyrinth without hesitating until he came to the doorway to the stairwell. After listening for a moment he went through it.

At the ground-floor landing he put the folders on the floor in the corner behind the door. Then he went out into the corridor. The first half of the staggered lunch hour was just ending, and the hallway was crowded with clerks and secretaries returning to their desks and cubicles and typing pools. Malone stood watching them. Those who passed near pointedly looked away, though it was clear they'd taken in the gold badge pinned to his coat. He might have been an inspector, and the last thing they wanted was to be noticed.

A messenger came by pushing a nearly empty basket. Malone gestured at him. The boy came over without hesitating. "Yes, sir," he said.

"Aren't you supposed to be up at Classification?"

"No, sir. I . . ." He pressed at a cowlick on the back of his head, totally perplexed. He knew better than to contradict an agent.

"What's your name?"

"Buckley, sir."

"Go back and check with your supervisor, would you, Buckley?" Malone spoke firmly, but with a veiled kindli-

ness. "There's a special on at Classification and your unit
is covering it."

"I didn't know that, sir. No one—"

"Just go back and check, all right?" Malone put his
hand on the basket. "Leave this here for now." Malone
pushed the cart against the wall. Buckley looked down at
the handful of fingerprint jackets in the basket. What if
he lost those? But how could he disobey an agent's direct
order? He looked helplessly up at Malone, then turned
on his heel and nearly ran.

Malone watched him thread his way through the crowded
corridor, then pulled the basket back to the door.

Moments later he was pushing the cart down the corridor. Fingerprint jackets were carefully arranged on the
top of the stack of intercept files. When he came to the
intersection of two corridors, he turned down the hallway
that led away from the building entrance. He fell in with
the flow of the Ident employees, purposefully pushing his
cart along. Since he made nothing of the anomaly of an
agent's tending a messenger's basket, neither did the
others. Nor did they miss a beat when he stopped abruptly,
apparently impeded by one of the wheels. The employees
fanned around him, like a tide around a stanchion.

Malone, in fact, was carefully looking back toward the
entrance. The guard's desk was obscured by the clerks
and secretaries filing into the building after lunch. The
balmy spring weather had drawn them outside. The guard
was preoccupied with the task of visually checking for the
building passes that hung on dog-tag chains from every
clerical employee's neck. Some young men had stowed
the plastic rectangles in their shirt pockets, and though
the chains could still be seen, the guard was requiring
each of them to remove his pass from his shirt pocket, to
let it hang free and visible. The guard's picayune preoccupation, so typical of the Bureau regimen, was just what
Malone needed.

He picked up the stack of files, adjusted the load so as
not to obscure his badge—his agent's credentials, not
clerk's—then walked briskly toward the entrance.

He crossed into the foyer on its far side, with at least a
dozen employees between himself and the guard. His

eyes were rigidly ahead, though he was trying to walk both casually and purposefully at once, with an implicit air of understated superiority.

"Sir!"

He kept going, but he was aware of it when the guard stood up.

"Sir!" The guard had his right hand raised toward him.

Malone made a show of realizing that the guard was addressing him. He allowed a cloud of impatience to darken his face as he cut through the traffic to approach the guard's desk, but inwardly what he felt was a first surge of panic.

"I'm sorry, sir," the guard was saying, "but I'll have to see."

"Call the director's office," Malone snapped. He held his bundle out for the guard to eye it.

"The director?"

"Yes. Call Mr. Tolson. He'll tell you."

The guard sat down uncertainly. "Tell me what, sir?"

"These are duplicate sets of the fingerprints of every congressman and senator, which Mr. Hoover intends to autograph and present as a gift to each one. He wants them on his desk this afternoon, which is why Mr. Tolson sent me. You call him."

"That's all right, sir." The guard's eyes were wide. The very thought of calling downtown was enough to shrink his sinuses. "I'm sorry, sir." The guard was appalled at himself. "Go right ahead."

Malone turned on his heel and walked out of the building.

On the street he continued to stride efficiently away, not quite daring to hail a taxi yet, as if that act would expose him for the fraud he was. As if someone would overhear him telling the driver, not "The Justice Building," but "Catholic University, please. The residence for priests."

He could not think of—or want—anything just then except putting distance between himself and that dark labyrinth. No, not the labyrinth, but the deed.

He realized he should have felt exhilarated. He should have felt relieved. At last he was doing something. At last he was beginning to see. But all he really saw at that moment was an image of himself, lying like the others.

Instead of joy, he felt dread. Instead of exhilaration, dizziness. He told himself it was the midday sun, the glare of light after the darkness of the Ident basement, an aftershock of the unsteadiness he should have felt while moving through that maze.

But it wasn't the sun and it wasn't darkness.

What he felt was just sickness. Nausea. His own body repudiating itself. He couldn't risk a taxi.

The sheer, bare force of his will, and only that, kept him moving, kept him from leaning into the gutter in sight of the U.S. Capitol, in sight of the green streetcars on Independence Avenue, and throwing up.

19

During the weeks that followed, Malone and Poole and a dozen other SE agents under Robert Davis worked on David and Ruth Greenglass. Malone took pains to avoid any special initiative, to show no interest that might set him apart from the other agents. This was a period of anxiousness for all of them as they tried to nail down the last corner of the espionage conspiracy, but no one guessed that Malone's anticipation was cocked more toward an old priest in Washington than toward a terrified machinist in the lockup at Foley Square. He resisted the impulse to return to Tarrytown, to find Anna, to tell her what he was doing. Anna; he tried without success to keep her out of his mind. One thing at a time, he told himself. And the one thing now was to wait.

The agents worked a system of shifts covering twelve hours a day, six days a week, designed to keep the pressure on the Greenglass couple building. As with Gold, eventually the relentless interrogation paid off. By the end of May both Greenglasses had confessed to everything they were accused of, and they didn't hesitate to identify their superior, the man who had recruited them early in the war, as David's brother-in-law, Julius Rosenberg. In addition they insisted that David's sister, Ethel, was as much a part of the cabal as her husband was. The Greenglasses testified that it was Ethel who convinced them that only the Soviet Union's counterbalancing possession of the A-bomb would assure that it would never

be used. And the Soviet Union, in those days, was our
ally! The Greenglasses were idealists, in other words,
wanting only to make their small contribution to world
peace.

The Rosenbergs were arrested in New York in late
May. By then anti-Communist hysteria was at a pitch.
Legislators were requiring loyalty oaths not only of teachers but of applicants for fishing licenses. The same week
the Rosenbergs were arrested the Cincinnati Reds changed
their name to Redlegs, though one ballplayer said, "We
were Reds before they were." The blacklisted star of
"The Goldbergs" killed himself.

The Rosenbergs, however, seemed unmoved by the
storm swirling around them. But when Davis's team turned
its attention to them, they denied everything.

Malone sensed the difference at once. There was an
assertiveness in their denials that both Gold and the
Greenglasses had lacked utterly. The woman seemed especially fierce. Julius Rosenberg was a quiet-mannered,
plainly dressed man whose pinched eyes, pointed nose
and toothbrush moustache made him look like a cartoon
rodent. At one point he admitted recruiting David
Greenglass, but into a simple left-wing study group, not a
spy ring. But Ethel rebuked him. She had the fixed stare
of a prizefighter and under it her husband wilted, back-
tracking immediately.

David Greenglass went beyond even what Harry Gold
had said, citing Julius as the mastermind of the conspiracy. Apparently the Greenglasses had had no contact
with the real mastermind, the Russian diplomat, Yakovlev,
and their statements suddenly gave the government's case
an urgent new meaning. With Yakovlev gone, now safely
returned to Moscow for four years, and with Fuchs already convicted of lesser charges, but in England, the
American prosecutors had been resigned to pursuing the
relative small fry of the conspiracy.

The vehemence of David Greenglass's accusations
against his brother-in-law gave Malone the sense that he
had instinctively understood the government would
welcome—and reward—a portrayal of Rosenberg as the
central figure in the entire A-bomb espionage spy ring.

Or maybe it was not mere instinct at work. The gravity of the Greenglass accusations increased markedly the week after U.S. Attorney Stevenson submitted his charges to the grand jury. Yet another pair of active, confessed atomic spies would be spared the penalties of a capital crime, leaving who?

Would the Rosenbergs make a deal too? At whom would *they* point the finger? But then Malone understood that Stevenson and Davis—and presumably Webb Minot and J. Edgar Hoover—did not want them pointing the finger anywhere. The government had to cut the trail of espionage here, like cutting a loose thread instead of pulling it, lest the entire garment come unraveled. That was why, wasn't it, the interrogation of the Rosenbergs, unlike the others, was halted well before either subject showed any sign of giving in.

Malone, in other words, had his doubts not only about the Rosenbergs—they were liars, he was sure, and Communists, but key organizers of the most successful act of espionage in history?—but about the people who were, as they said, bringing them to justice.

But he had a host of doubts now and it had become his habit to keep them to himself. In corridors and Bureau cars and in corners of the squad room and over cone-shaped paper cups of spring water he heard his fellow agents discussing the case, but no one gave the slightest indication of sharing what by then had become his radical and acutely painful and so far unproven disbelief.

Now it was a Tuesday in late June, more than six weeks since he had delivered the Smyth Report and the dated intercepts to Father Abetz. Malone had tried to imagine the shape of the calculations required by the cryptanalyst's task, but beyond the rudiments of vowel frequency and a vague notion of statistical predictability he couldn't. Cryptanalysis, he knew, was a Platonic form of locksmithing. Both depended on improvising keys. And though he had a feel for the one, the absolute abstraction of the other defeated him. He felt his inability to reduce the problems of code breaking to terms he could grasp as a summary of all the secrets he could not plumb, and his ignorance, at

first a merely mental pain, had become quite physical. It
had begun to seem to him that the Russian code would
break sooner or later under the weight not of the priest's
genius, but of his own anxiety.

And finally whether of one or the other, it had.

Father Abetz's phone call had come at three-thirty the
night before. He'd said in a voice edged with weariness
the two sentences they had agreed upon. "This is your
father. Come home."

The priests' residence at Catholic University was a
pseudo-Gothic dormitory built of rough-hewn gray stone.
It had an air of all-purpose nostalgia, evoking the lost—
and better—worlds of kings in their castles quite as much
as of monks in their cloisters. Either way the place was
forbidding, and as he stood waiting for someone to answer the bell he remembered buildings like this at Loyola, though he had succeeded in staying clear of them. At
Loyola, after the army, he'd held himself aloof, refusing
to let down even with the Jesuit scholastics his own age.

Now Malone saw that he had refused to let down—and
wasn't this what set him apart from his fellow agents?
—with anyone. If from his earliest years, in the crucible
of his own family, he had learned always to hold something back, wasn't it exactly from the soil of that reserve
that his doubts had now sprung up like weeds, choking
first his early camaraderie with his Bureau peers, choking
then his absolute trust in his Bureau superiors, particularly Webb Minot, choking at last his cherished idea of
himself as a committed and loyal and even worthy member of the group, what he had so happily claimed years
before when he'd carved on his bedstead the letters *FBI*?

He had the touch of a locksmith's son before which,
unfortunately, everything fell open. Now what fell open
was the awful knowledge that this "touch" of his—it took
the form of his restless questioning—was just the latest
form of his inbred aloofness. He had the touch of his
father's son and he was alone.

He rang the bell again.

Aloofness from all but one.

It was only when he finally admitted that he had lost
her that Malone realized how deeply Anna had affected

him. But even with Anna the area of his reserve, though shrunken—he never used his questions to deflect her— had maintained itself. Why else would he have let her go? Why else would he have refused to return to the estate in Tarrytown to which he had trailed Minot? Why else would he have sought through all those weeks to push her finally from the margins of his consciousness? But she had refused to go. Her face illuminated by waves of golden light, like an icon's, was what he saw in the dark above him at the last moment of every day and at the first, as if he were an old Jesuit seeing the face of Mary. Her eyes, as he remembered them, made a promise that had never found its way—for all her languages— into words. And he had not known how to ask her what that promise was or how to ask her to wait while he broke its code.

The door opened.

Father Abetz stood before him, in a stained soutane, his eyes sunken into dark grottoes, his neck scrawny in an oversized Roman collar, a husk of himself. He had not impressed Malone before as robust or physically fit, but now he seemed spent, undernourished, ill even, and he was staring out at Malone the way starving war refugees stare out at their photographers. But the aura of exhaustion, of what the weeks had cost him, served to heighten the brilliance of his eyes, as if the man looking out from the wreckage of that body had left the realm in which ordinary mortals lived.

Malone had to remind himself that Father Abetz had not spent the month on Zion wrestling with an angel. If he'd been tortured, it was by the dark night not of the soul but of Firebird.

The Smyth Report, in shorthand version, made up the bulk of the deciphered material. It had indeed provided Abetz with his key, and Malone realized what a triumph of the mind this was as he turned the yellow-lined pages. He worked to follow the priest's careful handscript closely. He was determined to understand what he was reading.

After a long time Malone looked up from the page and let his eyes drift to the window at his shoulder. The

Maryland landscape passed in a blur. He felt soothed by
the rhythmic clicking of the train, as if in taking him
away from Washington, it was taking him away from
what he had to do.

The train, in fact, had solved his first problem. When
he'd left CU he hadn't known where to go and he was
impossibly burdened, like an overwrought shopper. Abetz,
having brought him to his cramped room, had made him
stand awkwardly by while he spread the material out on
his narrow bed and began to wrap it in brown paper,
cording it with compulsive neatness into five packages.
The old priest's hands shook and he seemed barely able
to rein his agitation as he described each bundle to Malone before sealing it up. Two of them were pages of
fresh, handwritten plaintext, the precious final product of
both their efforts, but of those Malone was distressed to
see that the larger stack of pages had not been translated
from Russian into English, and the pages he glimpsed
were still covered with exotic and to him meaningless
Cyrillic letters. He had completely forgotten that once
the cipher was broken and the encoded numbers were
rendered in decoded letters, they would be in Russian,
and he realized what an added stroke of luck it was that
the old scripture scholar knew the language. Or perhaps
he'd just now taught it to himself, Malone thought, to
accomplish this task. Abetz offered no explanation for
his having translated less than half of the pages, and
given his obvious physical distress—he was perspiring so
heavily that his cassock was soaked through—Malone
couldn't bring himself to ask. The man had reached a
limit, that was all.

The other bundles included his worksheets as well as a
graph-paper layout of the reconstructed cipher system, a
summary of the key, together with the original intercepts
and the Smyth Report. Everything. Once the packages
were wrapped, the priest stood back from his bed and
looked down on his work in silence.

Malone said nothing. It was like standing by a bier.

Finally Father Abetz said, *"Scripsi Scripsit."*

To his own surprise Malone's mind tossed up the meaning of that Latin phrase. He'd heard it every Holy Week

at Saint Gabriel's as a child and now he remembered the phrase as Pontius Pilate's—"What I have written I have written"—and he remembered that it referred to the words posted above Jesus's head while he hung upon the cross.

When he left he thanked the priest, but Abetz had simply closed the door as if on some horrible thing he wanted never to see again.

And then, on the sidewalk outside Caldwell Hall, loaded down with packages, Malone's problem had become, Now what? He thought of looking for the library at CU or of taking over a back pew in the half-built church a hundred yards away. He thought of going downtown to the Bureau, but how could he dare show up there until he knew what he was dealing with? A return to New York was what made sense. When he'd thought then of Union Station, it was not just for its steel luggage lockers, where he could stow all but the two packages of plaintext or where he could catch his train—he could be *alone* on a train; he could *read;* he could *think.* Union Station was where his story had begun nearly a year before. From Union Station—he had remembered this with fresh bitterness—he'd been taken to an interrogation room and handcuffed.

The train whistle interrupted him, and he was aware suddenly of his own eyes in the reflection of the window. The rural landscape that had hypnotized him had simply ceased to exist. He marveled at the tricks of the mind by which a simple adjusting of focus could change the object of his perception so radically, and then he thought that that was exactly what the pages in his lap had done. And they were only the pages in English. What would the Russian text reveal?

He picked up one of the pages. In its upper right-hand corner was the single word *Homer.* It appeared at the top of every page, a transposition of the number group that Malone recalled seeing at the top of the intercepts. "Homer" was no doubt Woolf's code name.

And that gave Malone his clue to the other reference. He turned the pages singly, slowly reviewing the text again until he found a set of paragraphs that had meant nothing to him the first time he'd read them through. Now he realized these were the pragmatic and relatively mundane reports of the agent's comings and goings. ". . . CPC pass permanent, assigned as coordinator between Sherfield and N.Y. . . . projected tour of stockpiling, Oak Ridge, early June . . ." And then he came to the sentence he was looking for, the single reference. " 'Virgil' arrived D.C. two days ago, began assignment, HQ. Request permission to make activating approach."

And there it was. Malone stared at the simple words. "Two days ago." Therefore May 5. The witches' brew had boiled down at last to one question, a question about a man named "Virgil." Malone's mind detoured into schoolboys' trivia—no, *fled* into it. Virgil was a Roman who lived eight hundred years after Homer, a Greek. They were linked in his mind because his Catholic-school knowledge of classic literature—*pagan* literature—was so superficial.

But what he knew, by God, he knew with certainty. The crucial linkage was between Woolf and Minot, and at last, like a Jesuit confessing the blasphemous thoughts he knew to be the truth, he allowed his familiar suspicion to surface, a suspicion no longer, but a conclusion. Webb Minot, the head of FBI Counterintelligence–USSR, was himself a Soviet agent. Malone had brought his legion of questions down to one—a question with which to prove this to others. He knew that Minot, immediately after the Nazi defeat at the end of April in 1945, had been transferred to Washington to take over the Soviet Espionage desk. If "Virgil" arrived at "HQ" on May 5, on what day, exactly, had Webb Minot taken up his duties at SOG? But, of course, he knew.

Malone looked out the window again, now feeling the full weight of his depression. The finality of his recognition —his admission, really—took him by surprise. There was no coming back from this, no recovery. If he had thought to establish with Abetz's cryptanalysis only the fact of the Englishman's treason, it was because he'd felt obliged to approach Minot's obliquely, by gradations.

The gradations were obliterated by the accident of that

sentence. It made Woolf's treasons seem benign. It had forced Malone to confront his own conclusions before he was ready to. As he read the sentence again—" 'Virgil' arrived D.C. two days ago, began assignment HQ. Request permission to make activating approach. 'Homer' " —he realized that even without the translations of half of the material of one measly week's transmissions between Washington and Moscow, the mysteries of Webb Minot had themselves come into the clear.

Webb Minot had refused to deal with Malone's questions about the open door of the *referentura* safe because it pointed to a helper inside the embassy.

Minot had been willing to exploit Anna, as well as Malone himself, with obscene photographs, as a way of making it appear that Vladimir Tumark was a near defector and the unnamed helper inside the embassy.

When Tumark refused to defect, intending to return to Moscow, Woolf had to kill him to make it appear he *had* been helping them. And Minot had to cover up the evidence—that flask cap—pointing to Woolf.

Malone saw, of course, that the dogged Firebird pursuit of the atomic spies beginning with Fuchs but decidedly ending with the Rosenbergs, was an elaborate ruse, long in the making, designed to protect the real atomic— and soon to be H-bomb—spy, Victor Woolf.

Every mystery about Minot came clear but one.

Why? Why would he do it? Minot was not just an FBI agent, but a privileged man, a member of the American elite. How could he, of all people, have so betrayed his country?

And where would Malone find the answer to that?

He picked up the second package from the seat beside him. He opened it, laying bare the pages of Russian text. In the upper right-hand corner of most of the pages was a word he recognized as *Moscow*. He realized only then that Abetz had translated only the traffic sent from Washington, and not even all of that. The still untranslated cables were the replies from Russia. What could they possibly tell him about the secrets of Webb Minot's conscience, of his heart?

Nothing.

But they told Malone, nevertheless, where he had to
go to ask. He needed a Russian translator, and once he'd
had one. The pages in his lap gave him his reason, at last,
to go to her, even if the real reason—the real need—was
of another order altogether.

Tarrytown had a completely different aspect in daylight.
It was late afternoon when Malone got off the commuter
train at the quaint village station along with a dozen
other men who looked more or less like him. FBI agents
were supposed to look like lawyers and brokers, although
Malone had learned over those months to notice the
slight but crucial differences between Raleigh's suits and
Brooks Brothers'. What really set Malone apart from his
companions was the pair of bundles in brown paper he
carried instead of a briefcase. That and the fact that
those other men felt free to take their suitcoats off in the
heat, hooking them over their shoulders. They were not
wearing revolvers on their hips.

Below the station, dropping over a cinder-covered hill
beyond the railroad tracks, was the Hudson River, looking muddy and uninviting. Downstream was the Tarrytown
marina, a grid of docks alongside of which sat sailboats
and sleek mahogany motorboats. A bobbing seaplane
was just nosing into its berth from the harbor proper and
Malone watched as its crew secured it. A pair of gray-
suited businessmen dismounted from the passenger cabin.
Tarrytown Air Ferry, the sign read above the wharf just
there. Malone had to rein a visceral disdain for Wall
Streeters whose time was too important to commute by
train, then he recognized his South Chicago resentment
for what it was and chastised himself. He turned and
followed the train commuters away from the station,
surprised to have found a way of feeling kinship with
them.

The village street was clogged with wood-sided station
wagons driven by attractive blond women. On the sidewalk children in short pants or sunsuits tugged at the
summer dresses of their mothers. The windows of the

stores seemed luminous with their tricked-out manne-
quins and green travel posters and crisply printed book
jackets. Bicycles were dressed in racks like rows of pri-
vates, playing cards artfully stuck in the spokes, gimp
streamers dangling from the handlebars. Even women
who fell short of the suburban ideal of prettiness had
painted their toenails red, and that seemed to Malone
like an emblem of the wish to be more, and it moved him
strangely as he climbed the hill out of the village. At one
point he looked back at the river valley and felt an
overpowering sense of the normalcy of the people who'd
made their homes there, their utter lack of secrets, the
congruence that they took for granted between the way
things seemed to be and the way they really were. He felt
sure he would never live in such a place himself.

He found the estate in the hills above Tarrytown easily, but as he approached the gate, it struck him how
different the place looked in daylight. The eerie, otherworldly air was gone. Visible beyond the gate, a quarter
of a mile up a winding driveway, was the large Tudor
house, opulent as an English manor, perhaps, but also, in
those privileged hills, ordinary, mundane even. Why had
it seemed ominous before?

As he drew closer to the gatehouse, Malone's confidence faded. Why exactly was he so sure he would find
Anna here? What if she refused to see him? What if she
called Minot? His insecurities made him feel like, of all
things, a salesman. But a salesman would have had proper
satchels for his bundles. A salesman would have had an
inkling of how to get in.

It further disoriented Malone that he saw no glimpse of
the onion-domed steeple behind the house, and for a
moment he wondered if he'd been hallucinating that night
when he beheld the tower of what he took to be a
Russian chapel. But a stand of large beech trees behind
the house would obscure such a tower from this angle in
any case. The voluptuous and exotic dome had been no
hallucination, and he knew it.

That night his impulse had been to sneak into the
estate, climbing the iron fence and stalking the house,

but his impulse was different now, both for practical
reasons—the burden of his two bundles, the bright late
afternoon light that would make his crossing of the lawns
too obvious—and because of a sudden personal reluctance. Malone simply did not want to approach Anna at
this point by stealth. It was one thing to gain entry as an
impostor to the mansions of Embassy Row, and another
to commit acts of burglary against both the Soviets and
his own Bureau. But his capacity for deceit seemed utterly exhausted now.

He understood neither what this place was to Anna
nor what it meant to Minot. The possibilities seemed
endless. But if anything was left to Malone of the man
he'd hoped to be, it was his wish to trust Anna Melnik,
despite everything.

At the estate entrance he saw wires running from the
hinges of both wings of the wrought-iron gate. He saw
the telltale ceramic disks with which the wires were attached along the length of the fence, and he realized that
the barrier was electronically monitored. What is this
place?

On the gatepost he saw the buzzer and rang it. He
heard it sound inside the gatehouse, and from the alacrity
with which the door opened he knew someone had been
watching him approach.

A large, mustachioed man appeared at the door. He
wore baggy trousers, a worn tweed coat and a cap. He
reminded Malone of the Greek blacksmith who shared
his father's locker at the stockyards. His father had hated
the man for not being Irish.

From the threshold of his door the man asked gruffly,
"What do you want?" He was the man whom Minot had
embraced that night.

"I'm here to see Miss Melnik."

"Nobody here by that name."

"I'd appreciate it if you'd just tell her Chris Malone is
here. I'm talking about Anna."

The man stared at Malone for a moment, then turned
to go back into the gatehouse. Malone saw him pick up a
telephone, and he heard him speak. He was speaking
Russian.

A moment later the guard came out and swung the gate open. As Malone went through it, the man garroted him from behind, pressing the barrel of a pistol into Malone's side. "Give me your gun, please," the man said.

Malone didn't move.

The man choked Malone efficiently, displaying an expertise. Malone gagged. "All right," he said. It had taken an expertise to know Malone was armed. When the man loosened his grip, Malone shifted his bundles to reach for his weapon, but no sooner had he taken it from his holster than the man snatched it away. He was very good.

What was he guarding? Why was the fence wired? Who were they keeping out?

The man pushed Malone ahead of him, indicating that he would follow, and without a further word they walked up the long, graceful driveway to the house.

Malone was conscious of trying to take in everything.

The nearest wing of the house was a garage. It stood in the shadow of the house proper. The shadow; opposite the river the sun had begun to slide toward the lip of the distant hills. Evening was coming. Passing the garage, he glimpsed two automobiles, a large black Packard and a smaller green Studebaker coupe.

The walkway approaching the house was lined with carefully trimmed boxwood hedges, and their distinctive aroma reminded Malone of the British embassy, the other place he'd noticed such shrubbery. He was acutely aware suddenly that he'd never been inside such a magnificent house as himself, as Christopher Malone. His experience of such places belonged not to him really, but to the phantom Peter Ward, a thin-soup version of Webb Minot's brother. Why hadn't the insult of that impersonation hit him before? The insult to his own history. But the truth was that Malone had leapt at the chance to be. one of these others, these rich, self-accepting, gifted people. There was a treason in what *he* had done and he understood that it wasn't over. The sense of being an interloper, a sneak, a liar, a salesman full of tricks, a fraud—no matter where he was—made him feel ashamed.

At the door he stepped aside for the guard, but the guard only reached forward to push the door open, and he still forced Malone to go in first.

An elaborate curving stairway graced the entrance hall, but what dominated it, on the large white wall opposite the stairs, was a large gilded triptych, an altarpiece meant to be seen across the length of a church. Up close it was too much, at least for Malone, and he had an impulse to back away, as if he'd entered a sanctuary.

He'd been backing away from sanctuaries since he was a boy. Had his rejection of religion been a product not of the revulsion against hideous pieties and meaningless credos he'd thought it was, but rather of the self-rejection that, recently, had made him want so desperately to be someone else?

Where was he?

This was not a Russian church. It was a Tudor house. Still the sacred object, however gaudy, transformed the foyer. Three votive candles flickered from a narrow shelf below it. He focused on the triple-paneled icon, and he realized the scene it portrayed was familiar to him. He recognized it—an angel, a woman with a gold halo, a dove suspended between them—as the Annunciation. His Catholic-boy brain tossed up the most familiar words there were—Hail Mary, full of grace, the Lord is with thee. . . .

The votive candles under each panel made him think of Anna. But where are you?

The guard indicated a door to the left. Malone opened it and went into a small, dark-paneled library. There was a set of leather chairs, a desk. The shelves were full of books.

The guard closed the door behind Malone, leaving him alone.

Malone stood in the middle of the room, uncertain. The leaded windows above the desk opened on the broad lawn, and beyond was the river valley and the hills into which the sun was sinking. He put the two packages on the desk and quickly moved back to the door to listen. He heard nothing. Was the guard still there or not? He softly tried the doorknob and found it locked.

He stooped to examine the door lock, an easy pick. But not yet.

Malone looked around the room, wanting to read what was written in its corners. He crossed to the wall of books. Mostly the shelves were taken up with lawbooks, bound in leather: *The Legal Code of the State of New York, Decisions of the Superior Court of the Commonwealth of Massachusetts*, a full set of the *Corpus Juris Civilis*, which, Malone remembered, was the Latin title of the Justinian Code. In the good old days the word *code* had meant an orderly list of laws, not a deliberate perversion of the language to obscure its meaning. He took one of its volumes down at random and paged through it.

The book fell open to its frontispiece. On the blank page opposite the title format was an elegantly engraved seal featuring a lighthouse with ocean waves lapping its base, and under it was the legend "ex libris Webb Barnes Minot, LLD."

The lighthouse was what struck him. Barry Poole had claimed that a lighthouse in Boston harbor was named for Minot's forebears, but Malone hadn't believed it. Half of what Minot's agents said about him seemed untrue.

So this is Minot's study, Malone thought, replacing the book. He looked around the room and saw it differently now. This was where Webb Minot had his life? It made Malone want to laugh, that he'd ever thought he knew the man. Once more, in relation to Minot, he felt the utter fool.

He crossed to the desk and noticed a cluster of small, framed photographs on its corner. The first was a photograph of Minot himself, though as a much younger man. Such vanity—a picture of himself on his own desk? —surprised Malone. He knew nothing, nothing of the real Webb Minot.

The three other photographs were of the same hand-

some woman. In one she was demurely standing by a
lake; in another, she was grinning from behind the wheel
of an open roadster. In the third she was in the playful
embrace of Webb Minot, perhaps a decade ago. Minot
was as slick-haired and natty as ever. Anna's mother—
for that was who the woman was—stared brazenly at the
camera. Minot, with an expression that was both wry and
affectionate, was looking at her.

Malone began opening the desk drawers and slapping
them closed, looking for one that was locked.

And he found it on the bottom, right.

He took a paper clip from a dish on the blotter, straightened it, hooked it and used it to push through the tiny
pins of the lock. In seconds he had the drawer open.
Expecting what, exactly?

Not, certainly, another photograph, a single, unframed
picture with yellowed edges. It was a photograph of a
group of stylish young men lounging cockily before the
camera in various postures. They were all wearing coats
and ties, a school group. And indeed above them a
homemade banner was draped across a wall of books. It
read, The Cambridge Pagans—1934.

Malone might have thought it innocuous but for its
having been in the locked drawer. He studied the photograph as if it were evidence. Eleven young men, some
dressed more foppishly than others but all smooth-skinned
and privileged-looking, nothing like the collection of rag-
amuffins Malone had gone to night school with.

Their informal pose seemed randomly arranged at first,
but in fact one young man in particular occupied the
central place, and the others had gathered around him
with an artful nonchalance. He was sitting in a Windsor
chair, exceptionally upright, a more earnest expression
on his face, as if he took this portrait more seriously than
his fellows did.

It was Victor Woolf. This was Cambridge, England.

He had his coterie in Washington. He'd have had his
coterie in Cambridge.

Malone carefully looked again at each of the other
faces in the photograph, aware of his quickened pulse.
He knew, even before he saw it, what he would find.

Webb Minot's face. Webb Minot younger still, a man in his early twenties.

Webb Minot was sitting on the arm of an overstuffed easy chair, leaning awkwardly away from the man he shared it with. He had a pipe in his mouth, a hand on the pipe.

It was the same face staring out from the framed photograph on Minot's desk. He was younger, a bit more handsome, perhaps—time had touched the man unkindly. But in both photographs Minot held himself with the same fierce reserve that had so defeated Malone. On that one quality of Minot's Christopher Malone qualified as an expert.

With a sudden visceral alarm, Malone realized that he'd been ushered into this room. Was it intended that he should unlock this secret of Minot's? A paranoid thought, yes, but a version of what had already happened.

He checked himself. There was no way Minot could have anticipated his coming here, and the Russian at the gatehouse had had no time to receive instructions. That Russian was guarding something else. Or, rather—Malone knew this by instinct—someone.

He heard the door click and immediately he dropped the photograph back into its drawer and closed it. The drawer remained unlocked.

He turned. Anna was standing in the threshold a dozen feet away. She was wearing sandals, loose white trousers and a white shirt that might have been a man's. She was deeply tanned. Her black hair was cut very short, curled above her ears, making her look boyish, making her look—the thought stunned him—like one of the angels on the triptych in the foyer behind her. She was waiting for him to speak.

"You've cut your hair," he said inanely. She was not wearing jewelry of any kind, no wedding ring, no looted gold. His eyes dropped stupidly to her fingernails, which were not painted.

"Why are you here?" she asked coldly.

Malone didn't realize what he'd been hoping for until he felt the stab of his disappointment, the blade of her rigidity. He'd wanted her to come running to him, to make it possible to put everything else aside but their embrace.

Instead of answering—what could he say: "I have a freelance translation job for you"?—he let his gaze fall off her, drifting back to the shelves in which Minot's lawbooks were displayed. Casually, he crossed toward them.

She repeated herself without softening the edge in her voice. "Why are you here, Chris?" She came into the room.

At the sound of his name—how rarely she had called him by it—he felt the gates open on a flood of emotion that knocked loose the vise he'd clamped on himself weeks before. "Because I need you," he said. The simple truth at last.

While he waited for her to respond, the layers of armor with which he'd clothed it fell away from the core of loneliness he'd been fleeing his whole life.

Anna turned away from him, facing the window and the river valley beyond.

This was why he hadn't come here before, because instinctively he'd understood that she would do this. Turn her back on him. Refuse him. Make him see that she had never loved him.

He prepared to go, stiff-arming the coming self-pity that more than anything would make him hate himself. But then he saw her shoulders move. Barely a shrug. And move again. He approached slowly, as if she would run from the room, knowing she would.

When he circled around her, coming between her and the desk, he saw that, yes, she was sobbing. He put his arms around her, full suddenly of her pain, not his own.

She didn't resist, but neither did she return his embrace, but after a moment she leaned against him and began to cry aloud.

All he could think to say was "I love you," and so he did, quietly, barely moving his lips around the three words. Those simple words, stuck in his throat, his heart, were what had been choking him all this time.

Finally she straightened, wiped her cheeks with her fingers and looked at him. "But why have you come?"

"To tell you something horrible," he said.

"What?"

"Webb Minot is working for the Russians."

She shook her head no. "It isn't true." She stepped back from him. If she was certain that he was wrong, Malone realized, it was because she had confronted this question herself. And she had answered it.

Well, he had answered it too.

"But it's why you left Washington, isn't it? You saw before I did what was happening. Didn't you know it when Minot covered up for Woolf after he killed your uncle? Minot and Woolf are together."

"I know that is how it appears. My uncle suspected Victor Woolf of being MGB, but not Mr. Minot." Anna retreated further, shaking her head. "Never Mr. Minot."

"Your uncle didn't know him."

"Neither do you. *Neither do you!*"

"You left Washington because you saw what Minot was and you couldn't stand it. You *do* know Minot," he said. He cast his eyes around the study. "He lives here. He comes here every week, doesn't he? He's been coming here for years."

"Yes."

"To see your mother."

"Yes." Anna lowered her face, as if saying something shameful. "Mr. Minot takes care of her."

"And of you?" When Anna made no response, Malone cast his glance toward the rest of the house. Was *this* the source of her obligation? He stepped toward her and said quietly, "Do you understand what he has done?"

"I know what you think, but I don't believe it."

"Fuchs, Greenglass, Gold, the Rosenbergs—they're decoys, completely phony. They didn't give the A-bomb to the Russians. Victor Woolf did. And Victor Woolf is still there, British liaison to the AEC ready to hand over the H-bomb. And Minot's whole operation—beginning with you and me—was designed to make Truman think the Russian spy ring has been eliminated, while leaving the

real spy more deeply dug in than ever. The Soviets knew
years ago that we'd go after their spies the minute they
tested their first bomb, and so they created an entire
separate but false conspiracy for us to uncover. It's brilliant. I'm sure that not even the Fuchs people know how
they were used."

"I don't believe it." She shook her head. "Victor Woolf
perhaps. Not Mr. Minot."

"They're partners, Anna. They've been partners for
years." Malone turned, opened the desk drawer and took
out the photograph. "Have you seen this?" He handed it
to her.

She stared at the picture until she saw them, Woolf
and Minot. "But they—"

Malone silenced her with a raised hand. He indicated
the two packages on the desk. "And I want you to look
at these. It's all here. These are the Soviet cables we
were not meant to read, unlike the others.

"They prove for certain that the Russian agent is in the
British embassy. It's Victor Woolf, code-named 'Homer.'
And there's a reference to his silent partner, code-named
'Virgil.' The cable describes him arriving at FBI head-
quarters, counterintelligence, from New York, on the
very day five years ago that Webb Minot did. Homer and
Virgil, Anna. Pagans."

Anna looked at the picture again. The Cambridge Pagans. When she raised her face, an expression of desperation had come over it.

"They *want* you to suspect him."

"No. What leads they gave us were planted in the
other material. Not this." He offered her one of the
packages, the transcript still in Russian. "Read this yourself. See what it tells you about 'Virgil.' "

She shook her head once, firmly.

"I need it translated."

"So you can take it to—"

"The Bureau? I can't yet. Not even a misfit like me
goes into J. Edgar Hoover's office accusing one of his
inspectors of being a Russian spy unless he has it all laid
out."

"But he isn't a Communist spy. He feels about the Communists the way I do."

"After all the lies he's told, how can you—?"

"I don't know *anything* but what I'm telling you." Her voice rose sharply, and she put her fists to her mouth. "I can't answer you except to say it is impossible!"

"All right, Anna," he said softly. "Help me understand why I'm wrong about him."

He thought at first she hadn't heard him. For a long time she did not move or speak. Then, she turned half away from him, pausing in the doorway. "Please come."

She led the way down a corridor and into a large, simply furnished living room. A glistening grand piano dominated the far end of the room. Anna walked across the room to a set of curtained French doors. When she pulled them open, the cool evening air rushed into the room.

Beyond the doors was an elaborate walled garden full of roses and orange lilies and a dozen other kinds of flowers that Malone did not recognize.

Anna led him into it. The sweet fragrance of the blossoms hung above the neatly trimmed shrubs, but Anna was not interested in the garden. A chaise longue, draped with a light blanket, was positioned near a fountain in the center, and next to it was a straight-backed iron patio chair. Anna ignored them.

She came to a stout wooden door in the far wall and when she opened it, the effect was magic. In contrast to the tidy, elegant, but unexotic walled-in garden, what Malone saw now in the center of a broad, inclining lawn were the gold-domed towers of the Russian chapel. It was a scaled-down edifice, not quite real, but at the sight of its intricately carved oaken doors and their brightly painted embellishments, its peaked windows and enameled wall designs and, especially, those classic onion-shaped domes, one larger than the other, both flashing in the twilight like mystical beacons, Malone was stunned.

A vision, frankly, was what it seemed to him.

And when his eye then fell to the figure of a woman

reclining on a lounge chair a dozen yards in front of the chapel, a dozen yards in front of him, it seemed an apparition.

Remember Julianna Melnik! He thought of the poster in the émigré café, how it had portrayed the woman without showing her face.

Anna reached back and took his hand as she drew him toward her mother, as if she sensed his unease.

The chaise, a duplicate of the one in the garden, was placed so that, even in repose, the woman's gaze would flow naturally to the towers of the chapel, and Malone realized that the structure itself, like a shrine, was the object of her contemplation.

But in fact Anna's mother seemed to be asleep. She was propped against the backrest, her hands crossed in her lap on a neatly spread blue cotton sheet that covered her to her waist. She wore a black silk caftan, closed at her throat; a black headband of matching material crowned her head. Her face was lustrous and free of wrinkles, not an aged face at all. But her hair was white, an old woman's hair, falling away from the headband to her shoulders. Malone saw Anna in her, but there was a perfection to this woman's beauty that Anna lacked. He had seen it in the photographs on the desk in Minot's study. The light played upon her hair as her upper body moved slightly to the barely perceptible rhythm of her breathing. Her repose had such dignity and the setting had such otherworldly elegance that Malone felt he was looking at the sleep of a queen.

Anna touched her softly.

At once the woman opened her eyes, and she found Anna. Her eyes were unfocused, vaguely registering what was before her, and Malone thought at first it was because she was coming so slowly out of her sleep.

Anna spoke to her gently, but in Russian. She stroked her mother's cheek with the back of her fingers. Amid the words and phrases, Malone heard her say "Christopher," and it seemed to him Anna had clothed his name with her affection. After a moment Anna looked up at him, and then so did her mother.

Her mother's expression was utterly vacant. The bright, lively eyes of the woman in the photographs on Minot's desk were gone.

Malone reached a hand toward her, but she ignored it.

Anna spoke to her again, and only then did the woman take his hand. She squeezed his fingers and did not release them, and Malone felt in that physical pressure a plea of some kind, as if there were yet another person inside this woman, wanting to reach him.

But it wasn't so. Anna's mother was barely aware that he had taken her hand. Her fierce return grip was a simple matter of reflex, not emotion. Her agitation was habitual, unconnected to what was going on around her. Anna's mother, Malone understood, was without emotion and without intelligence.

Anna leaned over to pry her mother's rigid fingers off Malone's. Her mother's eyes went to the gold domes of the chapel, and that sight alone seemed to settle her unfocused gaze.

"Only in the chapel, or here before it, does she seem at peace. I think it reminds her of Poltava." Anna began to stroke her mother's cheek again, looking down at her sadly. After a time she said, "It was Mr. Minot's thought to build this chapel for her, to make her feel at home. And it does." Anna looked up at Malone. "Mr. Minot feeds her when he is here. Mr. Minot bathes her."

Suddenly Anna reached behind the impassive woman to untie the black silk headband. When she pulled it away, she exposed a brutal red scar the size of a quarter in the center of her mother's forehead. More than a scar, it was a severe indentation, the mark left by a badly mangled frontal lobotomy. "I told you he feels the way I do about the Communists. . . ."

Malone remembered thinking that her explanations for her fierce hatred of the Soviets, even the horrors of the terror-famine, had seemed too remote, too abstract, too historic. This scar was not remote. Her mother's imbecility was not abstract. He knew that the frontal lobe of the brain was the seat of what makes human beings different from animals. Anna was still speaking. " . . . I know how

Mr. Minot feels because Stalin's police did this to my mother."

"Why?" Malone's voice was a whisper.

"She had returned to Kiev from New York, secretly. This was seven years ago. I was twenty. I didn't want her to go, and neither did Mr. Minot."

"Why did she?"

"To deliver money—more than a million dollars that she had raised among the émigrés—to the Ukrainian army, which was fighting against Hitler and Stalin both."

"Was that the UPA?"

"Yes. The Ukrainian Insurgent Army. The Red Army crushed it at the end of the war. How did you know it was called UPA?"

"I saw a poster in the émigré cafés when I was looking for you." Malone stopped to put his hands on Anna and on her mother, from the pain of whose vacancy he could not hide. He said, "The poster has a picture of her and it says Remember Julianna. You've seen it?"

Anna nodded. "She was the center of their hope. They believed because she did."

"But they think she is dead."

"Yes. The Soviets released her, at the end of the war, thinking no one rallies around an idiot. And if they knew of her condition they would not. The reason we are secret here, from our own people, is to keep my mother alive as a symbol of resistance. A martyr can be such a symbol. Our secrecy deprives the Soviets of their victory, and it spares my mother the indignity of being pitied."

"No one knows but you and Minot and—?"

"Nicola, who greeted you. And his wife. They were servants in my father's household in Poltava."

"And your stepfather? The wealthy merchant whom your mother married, the dishonest man whom you said you hated?"

"The man I hated was my uncle, Vladimir Tumark. I blamed him for what they did to my mother. I was sure that he was the one who told Stalin's police she had returned to Kiev."

"Which is why you agreed last year to help Minot force him to defect."

Anna nodded. "For his trial at Nuremberg."

"But then, in Washington, Tumark convinced you that he did not betray your mother."

"That is right. On the contrary, it was he who found her in the torture hospital in Grigoriev. It was he who convinced the Executive Committee to release her. It was what happened to my mother that turned my uncle finally against Stalin. We will never know who it was who betrayed her."

Malone's unspoken thought began, Unless—

But he did not allow himself to complete it. Instead he returned to the question she had not answered. "And so all this time, your stepfather—?"

Anna nodded. "Yes. Since I am nineteen"—in her voice was a plea, and to his surprise Malone was not indifferent to it—"my stepfather is Mr. Minot."

20

Malone didn't know where he was when he first awoke. The room was bright with sunlight. The curtain in the bay of the window beyond the bed stirred feebly in the stale air. He knew it was still early, but already the heat of late June pressed down upon the day. He groped for his watch on the table beside the bed. It was quarter to seven.

Jesus Christ, he thought, sitting up with a sudden queer feeling that he had done some heinous, evil thing and now, like a drunk or a madman, he could not remember what it was.

He remembered Anna.

Her place next to him in the bed was empty now, but the linen was twisted and the pillow was crushed as if she'd spent the night in torment.

Torment?

What Malone recalled was something else. After seeing to her mother, Anna had come out to the terrace beyond the dining room, where he was sitting with a glass of brandy, having watched the stars appear one by one, tiny miracles of illumination. She sat in the chair next to him. The silence between them was like a wall. Now Malone realized why she had always seemed inaccessible to him. How could he ever have thought he knew her, when he knew nothing of what had happened to her mother?

"She must have been a strong woman," he said.

He sensed Anna's assent but she said nothing.

"I didn't know resistance survived in the Soviet Union."

"It didn't."

"I mean for as long as it did."

"It was . . ." She paused for a word, then said, " . . . absurd."

"I think it was noble. I think your mother is noble."

Anna reached across to take his hand. "You have a very simple view of things," she said. "An American view, I think."

"What is that?"

"We are noble. We are malevolent. One or the other. It disturbs you when the two categories seem mixed, because then you don't know what to do. As with Mr. Minot. You didn't know what to do so you came here."

"What would you do?"

"If your suspicions about him proved true?"

"Yes."

Instead of answering, Anna pressed his hand. He looked in her eyes and saw the darkness in them. Darkness was her exact truth. They sat in silence for a long time. Finally Malone put his glass down.

"You said the resistance was absurd. But that's resistance, keeping the memory of your mother's courage alive."

Anna shrugged wearily. "It is not a question of politics with me anymore. Not a question of nations at all. Nations mean nothing to me now. If I wanted my uncle to go back to Russia, it was to make peace with his life there, not with the party, but with his wife and daughter. It's the only idea of loyalty left me. My loyalty is only to one person."

"I could say something similar but I'd be talking about you." This was his exact truth. "I didn't come here because of Minot."

"But you refuse to do the one thing I ask. I asked you and asked you."

"To leave Minot alone. To let my questions go."

"Yes."

Because, he said to himself, if I was right it would mean that Minot was the one who betrayed your mother. And *then* what would your hatred be? What would it make you do? He stared at her with those questions in his face. Anna did not drop her eyes. If Minot's love for her mother was simply the primordial lie, if his care for her now was simply an attempt at atonement, an act not of love, but of guilt, then she would—what?

Nobility and malevolence, she had said. He understood now what she meant about him, his American view, what he saw suddenly as naïveté, imbecility.

He put his free hand over hers, sheathing it. What he wanted was to cover her everywhere, while sheathing himself inside of her. He wanted to sleep with her. "Anna, I mean it. I'm here because of you. Can we put everything else aside tonight? I mean it. I want to let everything else go."

"I too," she said. "But I am afraid something died in me. I am feeling"—she paused, looking for a way to say it—"made of stone."

Malone shook his head, lifting her hand to his lips. "To me you are very soft."

Anna stroked his face. "With you I could feel soft again. I have been saying that to myself all this time, wishing you would come."

How that pleased Malone, and how bold it made him. "For a long time I thought I loved you because with you I was someone else. But now I realize, with you for the first time in my life, I am myself. You make me feel like I can do anything."

"Even what I ask you?"

"Yes."

Anna left her chair; he left his. They fell together to the terrace floor kissing passionately, pulling at their clothes. Malone had never felt, in combination, such relief and such a peak of lust. For once his doubt was gone, his nagging voice was stilled. His fear was swamped, like hers, in the flood of desire. No, she was not stone. Neither was he.

There it was, he thought from his place bolt upright in her bed, the thing he'd done last night, what felt so evil to him now. But why evil? All he'd done was allow himself a respite from the horror of his own perceptions.

He threw the sheet free of his legs, feeling a flash of the pressure they'd taken when Anna had clamped herself around him. The evil thing was not their lovemaking. Their lovemaking had rescued him. He remembered how, afterward, he had closed his eyes with his arms entwined in hers and how, to his surprise, he had actually prayed that he would never have to leave her.

She had left him.

He leapt from the bed and pulled on his trousers. The exotic scent of stale incense—yet another icon adorned the wall and on a stand in front of it stood a gleaming thurible—made him think of fire. He put on his shirt and shoes and hurried from the room. He followed a dark corridor past several closed doors. He crossed through the living room, past the gleaming piano. An electric fan purred by the open French doors, wafting the curtain energetically. In the garden beyond was the stout figure of a woman clipping flowers. She didn't see Malone.

Instead of smoke he caught the scent of coffee as he approached the dining room, and he recognized the aroma of the strong Viennese blend to which Anna had introduced him in Phelps Place. That familiar sensation—a sign that she was real if nothing else was—took the edge off his alarm. When he came to the closed kitchen door on the far side of the dining room, he stopped and stood motionless with his fingertips pressed against the doorframe, listening. He shut his eyes as if the darkness would sharpen his ability to hear, as if some sound was going to explain to him what was wrong.

The anxiety with which he'd awakened had not left him. For a moment, for an hour, for an entire night he had allowed himself to lay aside everything he'd come to believe about Webb Minot. He had handed himself over to Anna's diehard hope and he had done so because otherwise he could not have stayed with her.

She had her reasons—her loyalties—and he had his.

The tips of his fingers were pressed against the cool wall but it was her warm soft skin he thought of. From his fingers she'd kept no secrets.

He pushed the door open and saw only an empty kitchen.

The ceiling light burned above the room. On the counter beside the refrigerator sat the silver coffeepot, but now Malone read its aroma more acutely. The coffee had the pungent harsh odor of having been overcooked. It was hours since Anna had put it on to brew. She'd left him in bed in the middle of the night. That realization panicked Malone. At his worst moments—and he had one now—he felt enslaved to his own distress. He had come to her the night before shuddering like a sick man, and if he'd rediscovered an equilibrium in her arms, now it seemed completely false. That she had left him made her seem false. Gloom rose in him as he turned his back on the kitchen to search the house for her, because he already knew he would not find her.

He had traced the faint lines of her veins up and down the insides of her arms, across her chest, above her heart, on her breasts. He had convinced himself that he knew her.

He made his way to the front of the house, to Minot's study, and when he found it, the door was open. It was dark because the heavy curtains were drawn. Behind him, in the foyer, the three votive candles burned on the shelf beneath the triptych, throwing an unsteady shadow into the library. A cone of light from a green gooseneck lamp fell onto Minot's desk. Malone recognized at once what was spread across it—the pages of Father Abetz's handscript.

A coffee cup held one stack down, and as he approached the table he saw that other pages of the priest's material had been carelessly laid aside. Centered on the green blotter was a spiral notebook, a cup of pencils, a book with the heft of a dictionary. She had begun to translate the Russian intercepts after all.

He leaned forward to separate the shuffled pages, the Cyrillic in the old priest's tidy script and the English on sheets torn from the spiral binder, in Anna's less eccentric but equally painstaking block printing.

He picked a page up at random. " . . . Seventeen days," he read, "after launching at the naval shipyard in Quincy, Massachusetts, escort vessel number 253 joined T.F. 87 off Virginia coast . . ." He put the page down, then noticed another on the floor between the chair and the table. He picked it up and saw scrawled—not tidily printed—across the bottom of an otherwise neatly transcribed paragraph the words "You are right! You are right!"

Oh Jesus, he thought, and he felt sick. He felt guilty. Anna had wanted only to protect herself from this. To avoid this she had turned to stone. But his very arrival had forced the brutal truth on her. He had made her soft again so she would feel it.

The paragraph above her scrawl began, "Curzon concludes Truman will seek to achieve his ends by distancing himself from Churchill. . ."

Skipping down the page Malone's eye was drawn to a space break and then the words " 'Virgil' agrees. Taking up FBI assignment, field supervisor Counterintelligence—USSR, Washington. Recommend 'V.' remain inactive until position secure. Recommend exclusive contact through 'H.' since circumstances of recruitment—Cambridge 1933—(photographs, file number 10744) remain source of control. Shows signs of reluctance, regret. Political motivation secondary. Recommend sustained observation. Homer."

Now Malone felt the wash of clean air, what he felt whenever he succeeded with a lock. But this wasn't his success. It was Anna's. She'd unlocked the language. Her success and her defeat.

He stared at the words as she must have: Cambridge 1933. Minot was already a Soviet agent when, a decade later, he married Anna's mother. Webb Minot, with stunning malevolence, had alerted Stalin's police that she was coming to Kiev with money for the UPA.

And Anna could no longer deny it. "You are right!" she'd scrawled.

" 'Virgil' agrees," he read once more. Then he looked wildly around the library as she must have, trying to control the strongest emotion of her life.

His eyes went to the triptych in the hall beyond the door, an angel announcing such good news to a woman—it struck Malone as a cruel parody of what had happened here. He was no angel, and he'd brought the news of how, far from blessed, the woman he loved was cursed.

And what had she done with that news?

Mary, he remembered from his catechism, had roused herself at once to go off on her Visitation to the mother of John the Baptist, the man who was beheaded to appease the daughter of Herodias.

And Anna?

Of course, he knew.

He forced himself to stand there, refusing to bolt from the room. He forced himself to collect all those pages, neatly aligning and stacking them, then retrieving a leather satchel from a corner, filling it with all of Abetz's work and hers.

He left the bag on the table and walked from the study, through the quiet house, to the kitchen again and the door that opened on the garage. He went there simply to confirm what he'd already concluded, that one of the cars—the dark green coupe, in fact—was gone.

He was as clearheaded now as she had been. She would have known exactly where she was going and what she needed. He went to the front hall, to the closet, to get his suitcoat and his gun. It only made his intuition seem infallible when he found his holster empty. Every agent's nightmare, but for Malone the nightmare had nothing to do with Bureau strictures. His gun was gone.

Back in Minot's study he used the telephone to dial the operator and ask for FBI headquarters in Washington. He looked at his watch, and calculated. If she'd left as early as three o'clock she'd still be two to three hours away. She would be driving through Baltimore at rush hour.

The duty agent answered and suddenly Malone's heady sense of his own omniscience evaporated. The familiar intimidation returned. He nearly stuttered when he identified himself, but he managed to have the agent verify that Minot was in Washington and was expected to be at his desk that morning. But the duty agent took him completely by surprise when he gruffly informed him that this telephone contact did not constitute a proper response to "code four," since Malone was not assigned to SOG.

"Code four?" Malone had had no idea that the Bureau emergency alert status was in effect. Because of Anna? "Since when?" he asked.

"Since midnight."

At midnight she'd been in his arms. It wasn't Anna.

"What's up?" Malone asked.

Instead of answering him, the duty agent said, "Call your field office." Malone heard the sounds of the typewriter, and then the agent said, "This tickler for Minot—"

Malone wanted to interrupt him: No tickler! Forget it! But he checked himself.

"—did you want a message on it?"

Message? All he could think of was, Anna's coming! Stop her! But only he could stop Anna without hurting her. "No," he said. "No message."

At once the dial tone sounded in his ear, and as if it were a clapper snapping him into action, he hung up the phone, put his coat on and picked up the satchel. He knew exactly what to do. He looked at his watch once more. Fuck the field office, he thought, then snapped off the desk lamp. In the foyer, before leaving the house, he blew out the three votive candles. All the gold highlights— the halos—in the brilliant Annunciation disappeared.

The boats in the Tarrytown marina were rocking gently as the wake from a small work scow that had crossed the harbor lapped against the pilings of the dock. As Malone approached from the village the water settled again, and in the still air the broad river harbor took on the sheen of glass, a perfect surface for taking off.

Beside the large sign—Tarrytown Air Ferry—the seaplane was still moored and a man in khaki was straddling one of the pontoons with a gasoline hose. He looked up when Malone called him but otherwise waited impassively while Malone closed the distance between them.

Malone realized only when he sensed the crewman's surliness that the owner of the seaplane could say no to him. At the very least the owner would demand some confirmation of Malone's claims from the FBI office in New York and some guarantee that his fees would be covered. Well, Malone had no guarantees and he had no

one to vouch for him. As he pulled his credentials folder
from his pocket, what had once seemed to him the perfect symbol of his membership in the most precious company there was, he knew that for the first time in his life
he was completely on his own.

"FBI," he said sternly. "I want to see the owner."

The crewman squinted at Malone's folder. He released
the trigger of the gas pump, then looked up at Malone's
face with a new expression on his own. Relief, Malone
realized, that he was not another Wall Street high-stepper.
"I'm the owner," he said. "And I'm the fucking pilot
too."

"I need your plane. This is a government emergency. I
need you to fly me to Washington right now." Even as he
made the demand Malone knew how ridiculous it was.
How impossible.

The man in khaki did not react as if he thought Malone
ridiculous, however. He said, "Because of the war? Is
that it?"

Malone stared at him, not risking a word.

"They say it's war. Those Russians have gone and
done it. War against the United Nations."

"Gone and done what?" Malone asked cautiously, but
he was thinking, This is the reason for code four.

"It's been on the radio. You don't have to be mum
with me. It's not secret now that they invaded South
Korea last night. 'Six-pronged sweep,' they said, across
some parallel. Fucking Commies. Hell yes, I'll take you
to Washington. Gladly." The man leapt from the pon-
toon to the dock, coiling the hose with an energy he
hadn't felt so freshly, so it seemed to Malone, in years.
War? Malone remembered the nightmare of his time in
Italy, how he'd hated it. But this man was a pilot. And
pilots loved it. "And while I'm down there," he said, "I'm
joining up again."

From a phone booth in a luncheonette across Pennsylvania Avenue from the Bureau, within sight of its entrances, Malone called Minot's office. It was ten o'clock.
The Tarrytown seaplane pilot, violating every regulation,
had not even registered his flight with the National Air-

port Control Tower. He had put down on the Potomac
River between Key Bridge in Georgetown and Roosevelt
Island, then taxied to a canoe rental dock above the
Watergate, where Malone leapt ashore, satchel in hand.
Fifteen minutes later he was talking to Minot's secretary.

"This is Malone," he said. "Is he there?"

"Yes, Mr. Malone. He's in conference with Mr. Brigham, but I know he wants to speak to you."

"Thanks, I'll check back later."

"There's an order out for you—"

He hung up the phone, cutting her off, thinking, One
thing at a time, dearie. He couldn't deal with Minot until
he'd dealt with Anna. Now he knew he'd beaten her
here.

He went out onto the avenue at Tenth Street, then
walked the block to Ninth. Washington was steaming
already, and the people he passed on the sidewalk—
tourists, mostly, since government workers were in their
offices already—had shed their jackets. He wished suddenly that he were lighthearted Peter Ward again, a
version of Minot's brother, wearing basket-weave calfskin shoes and a cool linen suit, thriving in the heat,
standing on a D.C. corner as if he owned it. But no, he
was Gumshoe Malone, reeking of the stockyards, a loser
like these other people. They blotted their faces with
wilted handkerchiefs as they walked. At the corner a
perspiring newsboy was hawking the *Times-Herald*, crying
hoarsely, "War in Korea! War in Korea! Commies cross
thirty-eighth parallel! War in Korea!" Malone realized
that the boy had been shouting the alarm for hours, but
still a steady stream of passersby bought copies, to begin
reading them at once with worry-furrowed brows. Malone bought one, but instead of reading it he crossed into
the center of the avenue to the streetcar stop, where he
took up a position from which he could watch the building, the two avenue entrances as well as the drive-through
on Ninth Street. Only then did he put the satchel on the
pavement between his legs and snap the newspaper open.

POTSDAM AGREEMENT VIOLATED, he read, but he checked
himself. He could only pretend to read this newspaper.
"MacArthur Dubs Enemy Action 'Cobra Strike.'"

He forced his eyes off the page and onto the passing
traffic, onto each automobile, individually, looking for
Anna's.

Streetcar after streetcar went by. No one seemed to
notice that he remained where he was, but Malone was
painfully aware that he was standing in plain sight of J.
Edgar Hoover's corner office. Once he would have felt
certain that the omniscient director had spied him at
once, marking him for a goldbricking agent, but now he
pictured the more likely scene: Hoover bent over his
huge mahogany desk, attended by Miss Gandy and Tolson,
reviewing cables and reports, preparing to brief the president on procedures for the move to war. Inanely, Malone's memory tossed up the image of the framed copy of
Kipling's "If," and he imagined Hoover reciting the poem
to Harry Truman.

Periodically Malone's eye flew up to the ornately curved
fifth-floor window as if he expected Hoover to appear on
its pseudobalcony like the pope. The window was closed
against the heat. He saw nothing.

At quarter to eleven a green Studebaker coupe slowly
approached the FBI Building from the west on Pennsylvania Avenue. As the car pulled into the curb lane,
slowing further but not stopping, Malone adjusted his
newspaper. He watched, moving nothing but the pupils
of his eyes, until, as the car crossed through the middle
of the block, he was sure it was Anna's.

When she turned onto Ninth Street, he dropped the
newspaper, picked up the satchel and stepped into traffic
against the light. Automobiles had to halt joltingly to
keep from hitting him. Horns honked. He walked briskly
after her, prepared to run if she speeded up, but she
didn't.

Anna never saw Malone coming. She had slowed nearly
to a stop in the middle of the block that ran between the
mausoleumlike Archives and the FBI Building. As she
drew even with the drive-through, even while the car was
still moving, he opened the passenger door and jumped
in.

"Keep going," he said. Instinctively he knew which

aspect of her paranoia to appeal to and he added urgently, "The Russians have this entrance watched."

It was true, wasn't it? When he'd been driven into that entrance nearly a year before, Minot's men had made him hide. They had appealed to his paranoia, and in the months since, paranoia had become the city's motif, the nation's. Everyone suspected everyone. The scare was rampant. But now the news suggested that the scare had been not paranoid at all. The Russians had begun a war. And they had the bomb. And they had men inside the AEC and inside—Jesus Christ, it was true!—the FBI. And why shouldn't we be paranoid?

Anna had been too startled to disobey him, but in her surprise she'd popped the clutch and the car stalled.

"Get it going," he ordered. "Right now, Anna. We have to move."

She started the engine successfully and pulled back into the middle of the street, gaining speed.

Malone opened her purse, which lay on the seat between them, and he found his revolver. He took it and put it into his holster without a word.

Once she'd crossed Constitution Avenue into the grassy preserve of the Mall he told her to stop. On one side of them, half a mile away, was the Washington Monument, on the other, at an equal distance, the U.S. Capitol. He remembered how on first coming to this city those shrines had seemed to exude the moral majesty that for him had been implicit in the word *America*. Now that assumption of virtue seemed a kind of vanity, a vulgarity. But still the geography of the Mall, the pristine axis of the nation's symbolic city, suggested the nation itself and Malone, like the seaplane's pilot and all those newspaper buyers, was worried for her. America was about to be at war.

"Stop the car, I said."

As if she hadn't heard him the first time, Anna pulled over now with the efficiency of a taxi driver. Once she'd killed the engine, she opened her door to get out.

"Close it," he said.

It was the first time he'd ever spoken to her with such

authority, and whether she was aware of the difference in him or not, he was.

Anna fell back against her seat. The door clicked shut. She sat with her head against the hot upholstery, her eyes closed, too exhausted to dispute him or even to marvel that he had caught her. But he sensed that it was his having caught her—having stopped her—that gave him his authority. She seemed to take for granted his presence here ahead of her, as if he were one of those figures in her icon, an apparition if not an angel.

She was so still that a shiver ran up his back, as if she'd simply leaned back and died. But then he realized that her breasts were rising and falling under her loose white shirt, the same shirt she'd worn the night before. In her hurry—her mad fit—she'd thrown on the same clothes; her dark hair was snarled. Her face was as white as her shirt. Her mouth was stretched with tension over the locked gate of her jaw. She was breathing, perhaps, but her very life seemed to have been poured out of her like water out of a jar. Her body's question was the oldest one there is: How do we go on after *this?*

But Jesus Christ, Malone thought, even now she is so beautiful.

He touched her.

She turned and, opening her eyes, looked at him with madwoman vacancy. The vacancy of her mother.

Is anybody there? He hadn't a clue what to say to reach her. What leapt into the void of his mind was the caption of that triptych, the Annunciation—Hail Mary full of grace—but he shut it off. How he hated the piety of his youth.

Piety had nothing to do with Anna, however much she surrounded herself with icons and candles. She and her mother had survived so much, the loss of their own paradise. But the devil followed them until he struck like a snake—cobra strike!—leaving a life worse than death.

The Lord is with thee—

Anna's savior and her mother's—their angel—had been Webb Minot. Hadn't he taught Anna how to treat her mother as if she were still herself, enabling Anna still to be herself? Minot had rescued both of them. But the real devil doesn't come as a snake, aiming fangs—a doctor's scalpel—at the brain. He comes wearing wings, to stab the heart.

And Malone, how was he coming? He knew he had to explain himself and so he began with what he knew for sure. "I was worried about you."

At that she leaned toward him slowly, lowering her forehead to his shoulder.

"Are you going to be all right?"

She shook her head no.

"Because of Minot?"

"Yes," she said, a whisper.

He touched her face. "There's a war now. Did you hear?"

She raised her eyes to him, and they were clear suddenly, sharp. "What did you say?"

"The North Koreans invaded South Korea last night."

She said something, an exclamation, an expression of distress, but in Russian.

"So bringing down Minot is more important than ever," he said. "And the only way to do that is to go back to the Bureau with the truth." He paused for a moment. He knew how important it was that she exorcise her hatred—the woman with her heel on the serpent's head—but that wasn't why he then said, "I could use your help."

She nodded with decisiveness. "Yes."

They left the car where it was and walked back to the Justice Building. As they approached the FBI entrance Anna took her Bureau building pass out of her purse and put it around her neck. Malone realized it would have been ID enough to get her through the outer office, past the desks of the SE squad and Minot's secretary, giving her a shot at Minot himself. If her middle-of-the-night impulse had survived, a shot exactly.

The ground-floor corridor was crowded with tourists standing in line for the famous tour. The death mask of Dillinger had been recently replaced as the tour highlight by a display board giving a mostly fictional account of the tracking down, even to Great Britain, of the notorious Klaus Fuchs. The corridor was cool compared with the street outside, and ordinarily relief from the summer heat would have unleashed the visitors' excitement and that section of the hallway would have resounded happily with their chatter. But the tourists today were somber and reserved, shocked still by the news from Korea.

Malone recognized their anxiety as a version of what he and his fellow GIs had felt as the time of combat approached. In their faces he read the question—one American civilians had never had to ask before: Am I in danger now? And the answer was yes. This is the new ground zero, he thought. If the Russians have only one bomb they'll aim it at this city. That was what he read in their faces: We should never have left Milwaukee.

As he and Anna walked past the tourists to the elevator, it struck him forcefully that they were in danger as much because of Webb Minot as Klaus Fuchs.

The elevator took them swiftly to the fifth floor, which, by comparison with the first, seemed cloistered. Somber men moved through the corridors, both agents and messengers, but they were initiates. The very air they moved through was charged with the emergency. No one gave Malone or even Anna a second glance as they strode toward Hoover's office.

If the corridor was the cloister, the northeast corner of the fifth floor was the inner sanctum. The outer door, of frosted glass like all the others, was marked simply with the number 500, but no one opened it—certainly not Malone—without a physical sensation of how this door differed from all others. As he took his credentials folder out to have it ready, he remembered how Brigham and Minot had wiped their palms on entering Hoover's lair— the ferret's lair. He remembered surreptitiously wiping his own palm. But now his palms were dry.

A young girl sat at a lone desk inside the door, the outer-office receptionist. Four men sat in dark wooden armchairs along the right-hand wall and a glance told Malone who they were. One was John Brigham himself— his black-and-white wing tips—and the others were three of his fellow assistant directors. Brigham looked startled to see Malone, and he was about to speak, but Malone kept going. He reached back for Anna's hand and led her past the receptionist to the door behind her desk. The girl hadn't time to react.

Malone went through the door to Miss Gandy's office, the second circle. "I'm Christopher Malone," he said to the director's secretary, who was ordinarily a far more formidable gatekeeper than any of her young protégées, but Malone didn't wait for her permission either. "I have urgent business with the director," he said, and he released Anna's hand and firmly took hold of the doorknob to Hoover's office.

Miss Gandy was on her feet, flying at him like a terrier, too late.

But the knob would not turn. The door was locked.

Miss Gandy grabbed at Malone's coat. "How dare you!" she screamed. Anna tried to pull her back from Malone. Malone ignored them both to bang on Hoover's door.

Once he'd been terrified to go into that room without a necktie.

The noise brought the agents in from the outer office. Brigham pulled Anna roughly back and a second man threw his forearm around Malone's throat.

Hoover's door opened.

Webb Minot stood there staring at them all, as if they'd gone mad. "Let him go," he said to the agent holding Malone.

Malone stared at Minot without speaking.

"What in blazes is it?" a voice demanded gruffly from inside. Hoover's voice. Minot stepped aside. Hoover appeared in the doorway so suddenly and so fiercely concentrated on Malone that everyone present, including Anna, expected Malone to agree at once that nothing justified this unspeakable outrage.

But instead Malone said quietly, as if he and Hoover were alone, "I have to see you, sir. Right now."

Hoover didn't move a muscle. His eyes bore into Malone. The man whom his critics derided as an old washerwoman stood there like a granite block, waiting for Malone to finish. Malone threw a glance back toward Anna, but he waited Hoover out.

To everyone's surprise but Malone's, Hoover nodded.

"All right. Come in." He led the way back to his desk, where Clyde Tolson had stood frowning throughout the commotion. Tolson glared at Malone and the woman, and his disapproval doubled when they ignored him.

Malone pointedly studied the wall on which Hoover's mounted sailfish hung.

Webb Minot remained where he was by the open door. Malone and Anna crossed to the center of the office, stopping on the carpet seal—Fidelity, Bravery, Integrity. The other agents, including Brigham, had not dared to cross the threshold and now crowded it like boys at a stadium gate. They, and Minot too, were waiting for an indication from the director whether to go or stay.

But it was Malone who said, when Hoover had taken his chair, "Mr. Minot has an interest in what I am going to tell you, sir."

Hoover raised a finger, communicating efficiently, if mysteriously, that of the agents at the door only Minot would be party to this meeting. Minot closed the door and crossed the room, a hand in his pocket, jingling change, to stand beside Hoover's desk, opposite Tolson. The contrast between Minot and Tolson was never more marked. Tolson's studied foppishness was like a badge of his insecurity. Even the knot of his hand-painted tie, protruding above his gold-plate collar pin, looked continually fussed over. His hair, so sharply parted just off the center line of his head, looked frozen. Minot clearly hadn't given his tie a second thought since he'd put it on, but it rode between the soft white wings of his collar like a general's flag. Malone remembered how keenly he'd envied Minot's self-assurance.

Malone put his satchel on the desk. He opened it and withdrew the crucial pages, spreading them before Hoover. Then he looked at Minot. "These are the cables you didn't want us reading. They tell us all about a man named 'Virgil.' "

Minot glanced at Hoover, who raised his hand abruptly. "Hold on, Malone."

"We have a Soviet—"

"Hold on!" Hoover ordered, his hand rigid as a traffic cop's. He didn't speak for a moment, neither did he take his eyes from Malone. When he lowered his hand, finally, he swiveled toward Tolson. "Clyde, I want you to leave the room."

"Mr. Hoover—"

"Get out!"

Tolson glared once more at Malone, but now he was blushing. It was unheard of in the Bureau that Clyde Tolson should be dismissed from Hoover's office. Tolson's power depended on the impression that he was privy to everything.

But not this? Malone tried to figure it as he watched Tolson cross resentfully to the side door that led to his own office.

When Tolson was gone, Hoover reached to the squawk box on the left edge of his desk and snapped it off. Then he looked at Anna.

"You're Miss Melnik?"

"Yes, sir."

Hoover glanced again at Minot, who nodded. "She knows," he said.

And with that—Hoover deferring to Minot?—Malone felt a dose of the old insecurity, what he'd felt, first, on finding the Russian safe unlocked.

But he pushed his qualm down, refusing to let it surface, and he focused instead on what was clear and cold in front of him—the pages of Anna's translation. He fingered through them until he found the one that identified "Virgil," and he handed it to Hoover, like a courtroom exhibit. He began his recitation with the calmness of a prosecutor who has his evidence. "This cable was sent from the Soviet embassy to Moscow in May of 1945. It's a report from an agent code-named 'Homer.' Internal evidence will confirm that 'Homer' is Victor Woolf, who, as you know, was our British partner in Operation Firebird. I'm sure Firebird in fact originated with him.

"As you know, Woolf is an attaché at the British embassy for Trade and Commerce. Do you also know that he is head of the top-secret Combined Policy Committee on Atomic Energy? And has been since it was established in 1944?"

Malone paused as if he expected Hoover to respond.

Hoover held the transcript page in both his hands but he was still staring at Malone.

"Those cables, Mr. Hoover, prove that Woolf has been a source of Soviet intelligence on atomic research since before Hiroshima. My guess is he's been the main source, and he's still there, with full AEC clearances, waiting to scoop the new superbomb. I've thought from the beginning that Firebird was too easy. Klaus Fuchs, Harry Gold, the Greenglasses and now the Rosenbergs were just a row of decoys the Russians set out for you to pick off one by one so that when you assured the president that atomic research was secure, their real atomic spy could stay in place. Victor Woolf.

"The cables suggest that Woolf began to lay out the scheme even then, back in 'forty-five. The Russians knew that once they tested their bomb we would tear Los Alamos and the AEC apart looking for the man or men who gave it to them. But we didn't have to tear anything apart. They served it to us on a platter, beginning with the code book that I copied, which led, finally, to Ethel and Julius Rosenberg. I've been in on the Rosenbergs' interrogation, Mr. Hoover, and it's clear that they are just a pair of pathetic diehard lefties who were dropped in our path like doped meat.

"We would never have fallen for it except for one thing. The man in charge of Firebird, of our entire operation, is working for them. His name is 'Virgil.' " Malone faced Minot, but continued his narrative without varying his inflection.

Minot was staring away from Malone, toward Anna.

"I told him there was no way the Russians would have left that safe open and he told me he had a man inside the embassy who had done it. Vladimir Tumark. But Tumark wasn't working for Minot and when he prepared to go back to Moscow, depriving Woolf and Minot of the cover they needed for *their* connection to the embassy, they killed him. I gave Minot hard evidence that Victor Woolf was at the murder scene: the top of his whiskey flask. Minot claimed that the flask was Tumark's. But there was no alcohol in Tumark's blood; I read the lab report right here on your desk." Malone forgot that, despite looking at Minot, he was actually addressing himself to Hoover, and he said, "You murdered Tumark."

Minot brought his eyes to Malone's but otherwise made no response.

It was Hoover who broke the silence. "Have you conducted this investigation on your own?"

"Sir?" Malone blinked at him. Was this a question about procedure?

"Does anyone else know?"

"No, sir."

Now Minot did speak, but only to ask what seemed to Malone an irrelevant technical question. "How did you break the ciphers on those cables?"

Malone waited for Hoover to rebuke Minot, to demand his weapon, to arrest him. But no. Hoover was watching Malone, waiting for his answer.

"Father Abetz broke it. I guessed that Woolf had transmitted certain AEC documents and I got copies of them to Father Abetz. I guessed right. Father Abetz worked backwards to the key."

Minot glanced at Hoover. "So Abetz knows."

In the look exchanged between Hoover and Minot a dismissal of everything Malone had said was implicit. "*I* know!" he said, suddenly choking with emotion. Hoover hadn't understood him. He'd failed to lay it out right. He looked back at Anna and saw disbelief in her face too. "Impossible!" she'd screamed the night before. "Impossible!"

Minot was slipping away again, Malone could feel it. Minot had some power over Hoover. Minot had had that power over him and he'd used it every time to deflect Malone's suspicions. But these weren't mere suspicions anymore. He had hard, certain knowledge. "*I* know," he repeated and he closed the distance between himself and Minot. "I know everything! We have a war now because of you! Men are going to die now because of you! I *know* why the Russians feel free to challenge us! It's because of you! *You!* I know everything except *why*."

Malone grabbed the lapels of Minot's coat and pushed him briskly with his question. "Why?" Minot didn't resist. "You're an American, aren't you? You married

Anna's mother, didn't you? You said you *loved* her!
Then why did you give her to Stalin's police? Then why
are you protecting Woolf? *Why?*"

Minot made no response whatsoever, not even a move
to break free of Malone's grip.

It was Hoover who snapped the spell of Malone's rage.

Hoover swiveled around in his chair to the safe behind
his desk and he bent forward to twirl the combination
dial. Malone released Minot to watch Hoover. He noticed that it was not the safe he'd cracked nearly a year
before. This one lacked the door handle that he'd used
for pressure against tumblers, to get those telltale clicks.

Hoover pulled the door open, then took a key from his
watch pocket and unlocked a metal drawer to withdraw a
plain manila envelope. He turned back to his desk. Malone saw that the envelope was marked with the letter *V*,
and he remembered seeing it inside the safe he'd opened.
All that time ago.

Hoover took a photograph out of the envelope and
pushed it across the desk. "This is why."

Malone stared down at the image. At first he saw it as
a picture of himself and Anna, but those were other
photographs, what had supposedly justified Tumark's treason, not Minot's.

Malone's brain refused to register what it was seeing,
except in the dullest way. Two naked people in a sepia
cloud. The woman was kneeling before the man, her
arms at his waist.

Then Malone saw that the person kneeling wasn't a
woman, but a man. Victor Woolf, but young. And the
man whose prick he had swallowed to its stem, also
young, was Webb Minot, whose back arched with ecstasy.

21

"You knew about this?" Malone stood looking down at J. Edgar Hoover, waiting for him to explain.

But Hoover was blank, pretending he'd just handed over a racing form from Bowie, not an obscene photograph.

Malone looked at it again. Was this faked? All at once he didn't care.

He dropped the photograph on the desk in disgust, empty suddenly of the desire to know what it meant, what any of it meant.

"I guess our mistake," Minot said quietly, "was to bring in a locksmith."

Malone ignored him. He let his eyes fall on the manila envelope marked *V*. "This was in your safe a year ago."

"Yes," Hoover said. "It's been in my safe for five years, ever since Victor Woolf approached Minot with it, to blackmail him."

Malone nodded. "And that cable from May of 1945 reports the approach."

"That's right."

Now Malone did look at Minot. "You came to Mr. Hoover with it?"

"Of course."

Malone looked back down at Hoover, the legendary puritan, amazed. "And you let Minot stay on to deal with his, his . . ." What? Malone could not think of the word.

"That isn't me, Chris, in the photograph."

"Oh, come on! Jesus Christ!" Malone's face reddened with anger. "What is it, more trick photographs? Is this where you learned the technique you later used on me and Anna?"

Minot shook his head. "It's no trick. It's just not me. That's Victor Woolf with my brother."

"Your brother?"

"My twin brother."

"Your twin?"

"Yes. Peter. I told you I had a brother. I told you—"

"You told me he's dead."

"He is. He killed himself in 1940 when Victor Woolf tried to blackmail him. My brother had just signed on with OSS. He'd been a member of Woolf's circle at Cambridge."

"You told me he went to Harvard."

"As an undergraduate. Then he went to Cambridge, where he hooked up with Woolf."

"The Pagans."

"That's right. The photograph you've just seen was taken in 1933. Peter laid some of the story out for me before he killed himself. Victor Woolf was born in England and raised there, but his parents were Bolsheviks, and he returned with them to Moscow after the revolution. After five years of intensive training he went back to England in 1927 as a deep-cover agent. At Cambridge he became part of a decadent coterie, but he kept careful records and photographs for later use. My brother was only one of a number of people he compromised, and in fact that's one reason he's had such a successful career in the Foreign Office. He has, as they say, influential friends. By the time he tried to recruit Peter to work for the Soviets, Peter was ashamed of what he'd become at Cambridge and he refused Woolf the only way he could."

"But how did you become—?"

Minot leaned forward, putting his hands on Hoover's desk, as if to keep it from moving. "I was in the practice of law at that time, with a firm in New York—"

"Norton, Cox and Reed, Harry Gold's lawyer's firm."

"That's right. The war had just begun. When I joined the Bureau, my colleagues took it as an act of misguided patriotism. But I had something personal in mind. Eventually I found it possible to approach Mr. Hoover—"

"We were on a war footing," Hoover put in. "Minot wasn't the only one to come to me with a harebrained scheme, but he was one of the few I listened to because he was talking about heading off the Soviet infiltration we already expected. We knew the Reds had succeeded in riddling the British Foreign Office."

"I told Mr. Hoover I had joined the Bureau to lay a trap for the man I held responsible for my brother's death and I wanted to bait it with myself. Peter hadn't told me who the man was, but I assumed he'd used his Cambridge contacts to recruit a circle of British spies. My brother had represented their best effort to snag an American. So I thought, Why not offer them another one? It was a fairly simple matter of working into a position of such potential value to them that they'd have to notice me. Therefore, Mr. Hoover put me in charge of German counterespionage, and therefore, when the war ended, Soviet counterespionage. That's when they bit."

"But they couldn't incriminate *you*. It was your brother who—" Malone stopped. Once more his brain seemed too small for this. He said, "Even if he was your twin, Woolf wouldn't have been fooled."

"There was no question of that," Minot said. "Woolf knew that Peter was dead. But he also knew how my family would value his reputation. Woolf approached me, with that photograph and others like it, as if all he wanted was money, and I paid him, to protect my parents from the scandal. Once Woolf had my money, he had me. And that was the idea. I was compromised. He turned the screws very slowly. Trivial requests became more substantial until I couldn't say no. He snagged me by the classic pattern. I'd also developed a certain overfondness for whiskey, and then, too, my personal life—owing to the stresses of the work—had taken on a certain, shall we say, non-Bureau aspect."

"But that incriminating photograph includes Woolf too. A scandal like that would have ended his career no matter who his Foreign Office friends were. He was already on the AEC. Why would the Russians risk losing an agent in such a crucial position?"

"He had already delivered the A-bomb data. The U.S. atomic research program was shut down. The cupboard was empty at that point, nothing left to steal. Plus, the Russians knew the British would be our first suspects once we discovered they'd penetrated the Manhattan Project, and soon enough we'd be on to Woolf. So basically he was already expendable. He was already in our line of fire. What they were playing for was a way to keep him on for the next round by deflecting our attention toward Fuchs and Greenglass, who had access to a much narrower angle on our research."

"Was the Fuchs-Greenglass data important?"

"Not compared to what Woolf got."

"But because of Operation Firebird he's still getting it."

Hoover shook his head violently; this was the point for him. "He's getting what we *want* him to get. And because he is, the Russians aren't working to penetrate us elsewhere. We *control* their access. We know exactly what they have. They're going to get this stuff anyway, but now they get it on our terms, with little adjustments here and there to slow them down. We want Woolf where he is for as long as the Reds will keep him there."

"What about the British? Do they—?"

Hoover snorted contemptuously. "They wouldn't know a Red spy from a green leprechaun. The ambassador leaves Woolf alone because he knows Woolf is fucking the deputy foreign minister, another one of his Cambridge buckos. This bastard fucks a lot of people."

Hoover's use of such profanity was, as far as Malone knew, utterly uncharacteristic. It drew attention to itself, deflecting Malone for a moment from yet another recognition. Slowly he faced Minot. "A lot of people—including you?"

For the first time Minot dropped his eyes, and a hint of a blush rose in his cheeks. "It's part of the deal. It's why he's certain that he has me."

Malone's impulse was to say, This is how you avenge your brother? This is how you love your half-dead wife?

But he felt chastened by Minot's finally having shown some capacity for personal shame. He said nothing, waiting.

When Minot looked up, his eyes went to Anna.

She asked quietly, "Is there anything you won't do?"

"Yes." He answered without hesitation. "I won't give them your mother."

"You didn't betray her?"

"No," he said simply. And at last, from Webb Minot, Malone knew he'd heard the truth. Malone remembered what pains Minot had taken to shake off any surveillance when he'd gone that night to Tarrytown. Minot had created a small, exempt world for Julianna, and Malone believed him, that he would protect that world, that woman, with his own life. Here was the core of Minot. Was it love?

Anna said in an eerie monotone, "I came here to kill you."

Minot did not flinch. "I would not have blamed you."

Anna squeezed her eyes shut against her emotion to stand frozen there, as if waiting for some cauterizing thunderbolt. Malone had an impulse to go to her, to gather her with his body, to shield her from the sordid truth he'd forced on all of them. But before he could act on the impulse, Anna shook off her paralysis to cross to Minot, who gratefully folded her into his arms. She leaned against him, weeping not with the constricted, hated spasms Malone had felt shaking her body when he'd held her, but with the self-accepting, uninhibited flow of a child's sobbing against her father's chest once he has saved her yet again from her worst fear.

Hoover pushed away from his desk, and swiveled toward the window as if it embarrassed him to witness such display. He fiddled with his Dictaphone on the table behind him for a moment, then he forced himself to sit still, gazing uneasily out over Pennsylvania Avenue, and Malone realized how far outside his boundaries this entire situation had dragged the director. A woman weeping in his office? Homosexual photographs on his desk? A Russian spy whom he was protecting? An agent of his FBI who on his own initiative had built a counterespionage house of mirrors in part with a motive of personal revenge? Hoover rested his brow on both his hands, and to his credit he found it possible to wait until Minot and Anna drew apart.

But Hoover had used the time to think, and when his two agents and the woman finally adjusted themselves before him again, he swiveled back to his desk, blinking, as if to drive the memory of their emotional excess from his eyes. He pointed abruptly at the junior agent. "I should send you off to Provo, Utah, or someplace, Malone. You've intruded here. You're way off base."

"Mr. Hoover, I didn't—"

"*I'm* talking now, Malone. I can't send you to Utah. Nobody in the Bureau knows what you know now. Not even Tolson. You're on the case until it plays out. You're married to Minot."

Malone didn't look at Minot. He shook his head. "I won't work with him, sir."

Hoover's scowl brought his heavy lids forward over his eyes, transforming his visage with malice.

Minot interrupted. "Mr. Hoover, you could keep Malone in New York. He could stay on the Rosenberg case. The indictments were supposed to come down this week, but I think if war develops we should get it postponed. The war works for us. We nail the Rosenbergs for every man who dies in Korea. We say that's what their giving the Russians the bomb has led to." Now Minot looked at Malone. "You're already on the case, Chris. You would take it over. You'd run it. I'd leave you alone." He faced Hoover again. "We should have somebody on the Rosenbergs who knows what the stakes are."

"But wait a minute—" Malone took a step toward Minot. Anna backed away from both of them. "You said *Fuchs* wasn't important. How important could the Rosenbergs be? They didn't commit the 'Crime of the Century.' Victor Woolf did."

"Right. But if the Russians are going to buy what we feed them through Woolf from now on, especially during the crucial development of the H-bomb, we have to convince them that *we* bought what they fed us first. We have to convince them that *we* think Fuchs and Greenglass and Gold and the Rosenbergs are the ones who did it. And of that group everyone else made a deal, because they all got the picture quite sharply in focus. For the Russians to believe that I'm really theirs and that Victor Woolf's data is bona fide, we have to charge someone with treason in time of war."

"And the Rosenbergs won't have one of your former law partners defending them."

"No, they won't. As a matter of principle they will have left-wing lawyers who won't do them any good. The Rosenbergs will die."

Malone remembered Minot screaming those words in the squad room that night: Someone has to die.

"And you want me to run the case?"

"We want someone to run the case who understands the importance of getting the death penalty."

"Even if the two saps don't deserve it, you mean. You want somebody who won't be bothered by it when it turns out the facts don't really support such a verdict."

Minot shrugged. "They are hardly innocent."

Hoover interjected, "*They* thought they were delivering the A-bomb, even if they weren't. *That* makes them just as guilty as if they had."

"Not in my view, Mr. Hoover."

"Your view?" Hoover couldn't believe an agent of his had contradicted him.

But Malone wasn't finished. "Yes, sir, *my* view. The facts won't support the death penalty for the Rosenbergs. If you use them in this way, however Minot wants you to justify it, then you are betraying the oath you took. You are asking me to betray mine."

"You have one hell of a nerve—"

"No, sir, I don't. If I had nerve, I'd have come to you a long time ago, the minute I began to see what Minot's scheme involved." Malone faced Minot. "You've lied. You've helped murder an innocent man. You've exploited Anna. You've deceived the very men you're sworn to trust. You've corrupted everything the Bureau stands for."

Minot shrugged sadly. "Maybe preserving our innocence isn't the most important thing."

Malone shook his head angrily. "I refuse to be dismissed as some kind of Boy Scout, as if I'm talking about
protecting our virginity. I'm talking about an outrageous
violation of the oath we took! What in God's name do we
uphold, if we don't uphold justice? Justice for *all!* Isn't
that the point? For a couple of diehard Commie dopes
too!" Malone slammed his fist on Hoover's desk, swinging back to yell at the director. "Even the Rosenbergs
deserve justice! You don't put people to death as a way
of fooling the Russians, not in the Bureau's name, you
don't!"

Hoover leaned forward. His hooded eyes were cold
and unyielding. "Yes we do. In this case, if the court
agrees, that's exactly what we do."

Malone trembled inwardly but his hand was steady as
he reached into his pocket for his credentials folder. He
dropped it on Hoover's desk. "Then I resign," he said
calmly.

Hoover fell back against his chair. "You can't quit the
FBI like this."

"How do I do it, sir?" Malone did not flinch. "With a
phone call to Drew Pearson? Or perhaps to Senator
McCarthy? Or should I call up the Rosenbergs' defense
attorney and volunteer my services? If you impede my
resignation those are exactly the steps I will take. I'm out
of this obscene operation, Mr. Hoover. If you try to stop
me, then I'll get back in, but on the other side." Malone
stared at the director.

Hoover dropped his eyes to the familiar credentials
that had fallen open, plainly visible. When Malone looked
at them he saw his badge, his glum photograph below the
etched letters *FBI*. He remembered the awe with which
he'd scratched those letters into the headboard of his
bed, and a rush of that feeling choked him. He could not
breathe. The feeling was, he would never breathe again.

He took his gun from its holster and put that beside his
credentials. When he stepped back his eyes brushed the
floor and he saw the staid Bureau seal on which he stood;
he saw it for what it had been all this time—*his* icon.
He'd done everything but light candles to it.

Hoover looked up at Malone, showing him neither

anger nor disappointment; showing him—this was the point, for Malone had just ceased to exist—nothing.

Malone shook his head, once, at Hoover, a last, instinctive rejection. He glanced at Minot—also nothing—then turned to Anna.

Her eyes stunned him with their abundant welcome. A life without icons, he thought, taking her arm. But did it have to be—and wasn't this the issue from the very start?—a life alone? As he led her out of Hoover's office, air once more began to fill his lungs.

With their backs to the U.S. Capitol, which was resounding by then with outraged clamor against the "Crimson Clique," they drove up Pennsylvania Avenue past the White House. Now the workmen's scaffolding made the president's mansion look like the national gallows. Across the street in Blair House, Truman was drafting his address to the nation on the Korean Emergency.

They turned up Sixteenth Street, past the Victorian mansion that served as the Soviet embassy. Now a detachment of American marines in combat dress, with fixed bayonets, was standing guard outside the wrought-iron gate. It was hard for Malone to remember that once he too had worn fatigues, that once he had been as young as those grim leathernecks, and that once he had burglarized that building.

It shocked him to see war-ready soldiers on the sidewalks of America's first city. Would the Red-scare alarmists be proven right? First Hiss, then Fuchs . . . First China, now Korea . . .Would the A-bomb fall on these streets this year? What *had* fallen on them was an eerie, frightened silence.

At Dupont Circle, six blocks farther on, Anna and Malone exchanged a glance. This was where they'd met, under the gaze of the fountain's marble women. Malone reached across the seat for her hand and found it warm, responsive, not stone at all.

They detoured past Phelps Place. The house had revealed them to each other, but only to a point, and they felt no urge to stop.

They drove along Embassy Row, where in pretending

to be strangers they'd become themselves. Now those embassies were getting ready for war. At the British compound they slowed the car the way drivers slow down at bloody accidents.

They turned north on Wisconsin Avenue, at the National Cathedral, which anchored one end of the great axis of Massachusetts Avenue. At its opposite end was Union Station, and when Malone thought of that imitation of the great Roman baths, a pagan shrine at the very gate of Washington, he heard the voice of an old Jesuit quoting the greatest pagan of them all, Plato, that all knowledge is only remembering.

He remembered himself, young Chris Malone, arriving the year before, a different man, a man as innocent as he was alone.

He and Anna Melnik had driven to the edge of the city that had changed them both forever. At a last stoplight, the car in neutral, they faced each other. What now? A life behind her walls was as unthinkable, finally, as a life behind his.

He found it possible to smile. "What was it Minot said, that *Firebird* was a fairy tale?"

"When I was a child, it was my favorite."

"And now?"

"Now I prefer a man and a woman to a prince and a princess."

Malone stared at her. It had all come down to this. He said, "So shall we leave the enchanted realm behind?"

Anna nodded. When they kissed then, only their lips touched.

The traffic light changed to green, and they drove out of the city together.

About the Author

James Carroll was raised in Washington, D.C., where his early preparation for writing *Firebird* included working summers during college as a cryptanalyst's aide for the FBI. Now he lives in Boston, where he is writer in residence at Emerson College. He and his wife, the novelist Alexandra Marshall, have two children, Elizabeth and Patrick.

His earlier novels include *Mortal Sins, Family Trade, Prince of Peace,* and *A Supply of Heroes.*